Rooster's Leap

JOE HAFNER

Copyright © 2017 Joe Hafner

All rights reserved.

ISBN: 1976082668
ISBN-13: 978-1976082665

To Ruth,
My wife, biggest encourager, and best friend.
I couldn't have done it without you.

ACKNOWLEDGMENTS

To author Christina Paul, for pouring your time and talents into editing my book just because you saw something worth encouraging in that first draft. I appreciate your advice and wisdom more than you know. To Scott Abernathy, who faithfully read every revision and always provided honest, helpful feedback. Even though I give you grief, you're a good dude.

To all of the people who read various versions of *Rooster's Leap* (many of you more than one time!) and offered support, input, and feedback. Here they all are, in no particular order: Tammy Harris, Kathy Smith, Ellen Fortney, Nancy Burwell, Wanda Mills, Martina Bowling, Dave Patton, Cathy Jones, Bonnie Stephens, Connie Felix, Heather Gray, Patricia Turner, Hope Pitts, Dave Northrup, Sandy Willman, Homer Fortney, Laura Graeber, Sara Barnes, Janelle Hederman, Trina Greer, Holly Avold, Nita McAdoo, Iris Beatty, Dawn Lapp-Rodriguez, Karen Earp, Gwen Daubenmeyer, Katrina Waldrip, Bob Arnold, Janice Steriotis, Linda Sykes, Laurie Brooks, Matt Jelnick, Sandra Kay McMillen, David Estes, Kathy Linhardt, Char MacCallum, and Debbie McCaslin. All of your encouragement means the world to me. Please forgive me if I missed anyone. I promise it wasn't intentional.

To Jimmy Fallon, you have absolutely nothing to do with this book, but you've got nearly 49 million Twitter followers and I'd love it if you'd tweet out an endorsement!

To my mom, Ann Hafner, my dad, Carl Hafner, my brothers, Pete & Chuck Hafner, and my father-in-law, Dr. T Guy Fortney, thank you for reading various drafts of the book and always encouraging me to go after my writing dreams.

Most importantly, to my wife, Ruth, thanks for always speaking truth about my creative process; for not being afraid to tell me when my writing stinks so I'm able to believe when you say it's awesome. Either way, I'm always excited to show you what I've created. You're the biggest reason I work so hard trying to create something great.

ONE

Eyes snapped open, blurred and scratchy, unable to focus in the dim light.

What's on top of me? Can't breathe.

Dead weight pressed down. Arms pinned, engulfed in claustrophobia. All rational thought fled, replaced by utter panic. *Get it off me!*

Survival instincts kicked in. He worked his arms free and, flailing wildly, managed to shove the mass aside. Adrenaline pumped. Chest heaved.

Feeling shaky. Gotta calm down and assess things. He concentrated until breathing slowed slightly, and ran nervous fingers through damp hair, forehead sweat-soaked, face clammy.

Get a grip. He took in his surroundings, eyes slowly adjusting to the darkness.

Faint flowery perfume hung in the air. On an unfamiliar bed with satin sheets, wearing only silky boxer shorts. *Where'd those come from?* Then he saw her, face down next to him. Naked.

Holy crap. Was she on top of me? Who is she? Where am I?

His heart pounded. *Why isn't she moving?*

Mouth dry, he stuffed back his worst fears. Uneasiness crept in. His stomach grew queasy. He gave her a gentle shove. No reaction.

She felt really cold. Or did I imagine that?

He swallowed hard. *No way! Can't be.*

He shoved a little harder and opened his mouth to say, "Hey, wake up," but could not put sound to the words.

She's not moving. Definitely felt ice cold. Not good.

He had pushed away the thought, but it could no longer be avoided, a fist smacking him in the face. He could not breathe.

No! No! No! "Oh my God." *Did I kill her?*

Backing away in terror, he launched himself off the bed and tumbled to the floor, his back impaled by something hard and sharp. "Argh!" *I been stabbed?* The thought was more startling than any actual pain. *They're here to finish me off.*

After extracting the culprit, he examined his attacker, a dark shoe with a long stiletto heel. Relief washed over him.

The woman on the bed broke her silence with a sleep-dazed voice. "What's all that racket?"

He nearly jumped out of his skin. His mind was mushy, struggling to put it all together, without the slightest idea where he was, where this woman came from, or how long she had been sprawled naked on top of him. He thought he should say something, but found it difficult to form words. Her movement stopped, replaced by gentle snoring.

After a huge breath, he took inventory. His head pounded and his lower back ached. He gingerly ran his hand his belly. The skin was puffy and warm to the touch. "What on earth happened there?"

He bent awkwardly for a closer look in the dim light.

"Son of a bitch!" On his stomach was a big red heart tattoo. Inside was the outline of a smaller heart, which encircled his navel. The name 'Michael' was above the small heart and the name 'Sue' below it.

How'd that get there? What's wrong with me? This is crazy. Maybe it'll rub off. If that thing's real, I'm screwed. His mind turned to the woman on the bed. *At least she's not dead. This her room?* He pressed his hand on the tattoo. *Sure feels real. Hurts like someone's been poking a needle down there. Can't get much worse than this.*

Hopeful the hearts would rub off, he worked up some spit, lifted his left hand to his mouth, and noticed the gold band. His mind refused to comprehend. He actually asked himself, "Was that there before?"

Alarm bells and flashing lights clanged throughout his whiskey-addled brain. He catalogued the many dumb things he had done in a drunken haze, and shook his head. *This takes stupidity to a new level.* His own name was wrong. *Apparently I'm now married to the girl on the bed.* He assumed she was Sue, until a new thought struck. *What if she isn't? What if Sue's not even the person I married?*

Bile rose up his throat. With every new thought, it all got worse. Gulping for air, he lay in the fetal position with closed eyes. *Maybe, if I just go to sleep, things'll be back to normal when I wake up. What happened last night?* He strained his memory, desperate for something to latch onto before completely losing his mind. *Why do I keep doing this to myself?*

Ok, it's all good. Forcing himself to calm down, a few things slowly came back. *Was in Vegas last night. Alright, that's something. Came here to celebrate my thirtieth birthday. Who was with me?*

Total blank.

Man, I need a drink. Try as he might, nothing. The bits and scraps of memories were completely overshadowed by gaping black holes of missing time. He was trying to decipher a thousand-piece jigsaw puzzle with just five or ten pieces.

Worst of all, this was nothing new. Ever since he had blown his bond-trading gig and squandered all his cash, waking up in strange places with no memory had become all too common. He had once awoken naked in a dog crate attached to the top of a minivan speeding down Interstate 75. That was a minor annoyance compared to greeting the morning with a hideous tattoo and a wedding ring.

How much I drink last night? What happens now? He stared at the bed. Something about it was wrong. Soon the splitting headache distracted him. *Why's it so hot in here?*

He took in the room. Thick drapes blocked big windows, except for a sliver of morning light peeking between the curtains. Next to the bed was an ice bucket with an upside-down champagne bottle. Several other wine vessels lay on the dresser amid fluted glasses and various items of women's clothing. More light seeped under the door on the far side of the room.

His mind was still foggy. *Obviously in a hotel room.*

As he rose to his feet, a dizzy spell hit. He was forced to grab the desk chair to keep from passing out. After a moment, the blood returned to his head and he managed to stand up. Sweat trickled down his back. *Jack on the rocks would sure be nice.*

His whole body felt weak and abused. *How many times do I have to do this, before I learn to avoid champagne? Waking up every time with no memory of the night before.* Someone else made his decisions. Someone who got to enjoy the party, leaving him to deal with the consequences in the morning. He tried to sort through it, but soon quit. It all made his head throb.

Surveying the room from his new vantage point, he finally saw the bed clearly. Heart-shaped. He slapped his palm against his forehead and sighed. "Honeymoon suite."

He ran fingers across his stomach, not wanting to peer down at the hearts. *What a nightmare. Totally surreal.* He refused to believe any of it. *It's too much, even for a screw-up like me.*

A loud click startled him. Soft light from the bedside lamp spilled onto her face. "Whatcha you doin' up, honey?"

He had almost forgotten her. His gut gurgled. Suddenly real, his knees nearly buckled. *Did I actually marry this woman?* He grabbed the chair amid another wave of dizziness. After regaining his bearings, he slowly faced the bed.

She sat propped against a stack of pillows, the satin sheets pulled to her chin. Her face was round, but attractive, surrounded by short, wild bleached hair. She smiled. "That was one crazy night." She withdrew her left hand from under the covers to admire the big rock on her finger.

His eyes nearly popped out. *That thing's huge. Don't have enough* money to buy something like that. Don't even have enough credit to buy that. What happened last night?

"Your tattoo looks cute," she grinned. "Can't believe you did that for me."

He glanced at the hearts. *Her name is Sue. Don't make this worse by calling her the wrong name. Sue. Sue. Sue.*

"This whole thing's been a whirlwind," Sue continued. "It's like a dream."

"Yeah, a dream." How was she not as horrified as him? *Who gets married while drunk in Vegas, and is happy about it the next morning? Is this woman a psycho? I must be the biggest moron in the lower forty-eight.*

"When we taking the jet to Santa Barbara?"

"The jet?"

"Your Gulfstream G150? You told me all about it last night." She lifted her gaze to the ceiling and scrunched her brow, reciting facts she had memorized. "It can carry up to eight passengers and fly coast to coast on a single fueling." Her eyes fell back on him. "You said we could go to Santa Barbara to pick up my mother before flying back to New York."

My Gulfstream? I don't know anything about private jets. "I told you all that?"

"Yes." A hint of fear clouded her face. "What's wrong with you?"

Going downhill fast. He scanned the room for personal items, just in case a hasty exit became necessary. His wallet sat on the TV stand between him and the door. Unfortunately, his clothes were piled in a corner deeper in the room. He contemplated what to leave behind.

Her tone grew shrill. "You listening to me?"

He forced a toothy smile. "Of course I'm listening to you, Sally."

"Sally?! You kidding me? My name is Sue and I'm your wife."

"What'd I call you?"

"Sally."

"You sure?"

"Michael, you think I'm an idiot? How could you get my name

wrong when it's written right there on your stomach?"

He cringed at her reminder of the ridiculous hearts. *Marriage isn't permanent enough. I gotta tattoo it across my stomach. They shoulda just inked "World's Biggest Idiot" in neon letters across my forehead.* He swallowed hard.

"Why do you think my name's Michael?"

"Oh my God," she cried. "Is everything you told me a lie?"

He looked at his feet in shame. "I don't remember anything from last night. What'd I tell you?"

"Oh my God!" She barely held it together. "You told me your name was Michael Davis. That you made a fortune day trading stocks. You have a Gulfstream, a Maserati, and a big home on the ocean at the end of Long Island. Your pilot was with you. He confirmed everything."

He continued to stare at his toes, unable to look her in the eye. He nervously rubbed the stubble on his chin. "What was the pilot's name?"

"Charles."

It was Charles who came with me. Why didn't I remember that? Man, we were drunk before the plane left Newark. No wonder none of this rings any bells.

"When you knew we'd be traveling today, you sent him to his room so he'd have enough sleep to fly."

That's quite a story. more than a little impressed with his own creativity, he slowly edged toward the door. *Gonna get real bad real quick. Gotta keep her talking 'til I can make a run for it.* He winced. "I paid for all this? The room, the ring, the wedding?"

"No. After Charles left, you said he keeps all your money and credit cards. You didn't want to wake him and delay our flight today."

He saw the spark in her eyes as she slowly pieced everything together. He glanced at his billfold next to the TV. *She think there's no money or credit cards in that? How'd she not realize I been telling her one big whopper after another?*

"I paid for everything on my corporate American Express card." She buried her head in her hands. "We pulled out a twenty-five thousand dollar cash advance. You told me you'd write a check to cover it all.

"Oh my God. I called my boss and quit. We spent more than fifty thousand dollars on that card." Her shoulders drooped in defeat. Eyes red with tears, her face was pale and drawn. Was it possible she aged ten years since the conversation first began?

She stared with unblinking eyes and shook with anger. "How could you do this to me? I don't have that kind of money!"

"How could you believe all that garbage I was spewing?" He had spoken without thinking, and reflexively slapped his hand across his mouth, as if he could shove the words back inside. He knew immediately he had gone too far.

Her voice grew icy. "Any of it true?"

He slowly shook his head. "None of it. Well, except for the Maserati, sort of. I used to own one, but I don't anymore."

"You son of a bitch!" With unexpected speed, she burst from the bed, wildly swinging the empty champagne bottle. "I'll kill you!"

He ducked and dodged as Sue screamed obscenities and tried to take his head off. She landed a few blows on his arms, and one on the small of his back, he thought might have cracked his spine. He raced for the door with Sue in close pursuit. He somehow managed to snatch up his wallet on the way past the television. He wondered how he would ever get the door open without facing a hail of blows from the heavy bottle.

Fate was on his side. She stumbled on the second stiletto and went down hard. Without a backward glance, he twisted the doorknob and was into the hallway. Dressed in nothing but boxer shorts, wallet gripped tightly in his fist, he counted himself lucky.

As the heavy door closed behind him, the champagne bottle smashed against it, followed by a stream of obscenities. After a few ragged breaths, he took off in a sprint, determined to escape into the stairwell before she could continue her pursuit.

TWO
Thirteen Years Later
Thursday, August 11

Rooster Michaels mopped sweat from his face with his sleeve. The blue polo shirt with "Pegasus Farms" stitched on the right breast was soaked through. Damp khaki shorts clung to his legs. Sweat rained down from everywhere on his body.

He had some sketchy jobs in the past, but this one made Rooster question his own sanity. *What kind of idiot does door-to-door sales, in August, in Tennessee?* Oppressive heat and humidity had turned the day into a steam bath with no relief in sight. Rooster's goals had transformed. Early on he hoped to make a sale. Now his sole objective was to get invited into the cool air conditioning of a house.

The neighborhood featured row upon row of homes, each with a brick face, a little covered porch and a street-facing garage. Aside from minor color variations, the type of shutters, or the plants in the flowerbed, they were all alike.

Rooster trudged to the front door of the next residence. Planted in front were a few uneven boxwoods overrun by weeds. The narrow covered porch featured three white columns, each with the beginning stages of wood rot at the base, and an orange rocking chair with "Go Vols" stenciled in white paint on the backrest. A huge black Ford F-

150 sat in the driveway. *Does everyone in Murfreesboro own a pickup?* This one had a pair of bumper stickers. One said, "*America: Love it or Leave it,*" and the other featured a picture of a rifle and the words, "*From my cold dead hands.*"

This should be interesting.

When he reached the shade of the stoop, Rooster wiped his face and rang the doorbell. He counted slowly to fifteen and pressed the buzzer again. He counted once more. Nothing. He was about to move on, when he heard movement. He nearly jumped out of his shoes when the blinds next to the door suddenly clattered up. Rooster caught a short glimpse of someone, but the man disappeared as quickly as he had shown up.

Then the front door flew open and a big burly man, sporting some serious bed head, stepped onto the front porch. His gray-streaked brown hair was completely flat on the right, and flayed out like a mad scientist on the left. He wore black sunglasses and two-day stubble covered his face. What made the situation extra strange, and a little uncomfortable, was the man's lack of pants. His entire outfit consisted of a pair of tighty-whitey briefs, one gray - formerly white - sock, and a black t-shirt with a huge picture of Dale Earnhardt overlaid with, "Earnhardt Lives On." A red food stain partially covered Dale's face.

The man moved close to Rooster. He smelled of stale beer and Chef Boyardee ravioli. He flashed a completely unexpected perfect brilliant white smile and pleasantly drawled, "What can I do for you, Son?"

Undeterred by this strange fellow, Rooster wasted no time launching into the script he had memorized during sales training. "Good afternoon, sir." He forced a smile. "I'm knocking on your door today to offer you a rare opportunity."

"You didn't knock," the man interrupted.

"What?" Rooster said, obviously flustered.

"I said you didn't knock." The man moved into Rooster's personal space. Their faces just a few inches apart, Rooster could smell ravioli more distinctly. The dazzling choppers were so amazingly flawless, Rooster unconsciously fixated on them as the man spoke. "You rang the dad gum bell," the man explained. "You didn't knock."

Uncomfortable with their close proximity, Rooster shuffled backwards. He hoped to remain on the sales script, but this guy was distracting. *Those teeth have to be veneers.* He considered stereotypes about southern rednecks with missing teeth and the whole picture did not compute. He tore his gaze from the man's mouth and forced himself to look into his eyes, or at least where his eyes should be behind the sunglasses.

Rooster's back pressed against a porch column. "Regardless of how I got you to the door," Rooster ad-libbed. "Today's your lucky day." The man had moved with him and he was trapped. His choices were to slide sideways and risk falling off the porch, push past the man into open space, or simply stand his ground and hope the man would not move closer. He decided to stay put.

"My lucky day, huh?" The man said. "Gonna pay my truck note this month?" Again the amazing teeth filled the lower half of his face in a grin.

Rooster stared at him, hopelessly thrown off his game.

The man was silent for a beat, then he whacked Rooster's shoulder with a meaty paw. "Now that'd be my lucky day, Son."

"Ahh, no," Rooster stammered. He willed himself back to the script they had pounded into his head for five days before he had been allowed to knock on doors. "I'm here because I work for Pegasus Farms." He pointed at the logo on his shirt. "We sell premium meat and the Publix down the street just cancelled on a huge order. So my boss told me to give someone a great deal on all of the product Publix was supposed to take. I'm not supposed to come back until our truck's empty."

The man leaned forward and made a show of peering over Rooster's shoulder. "Don't see no meat truck."

"It's two streets over with my co-worker. I'd like to offer you the opportunity to buy premium meat. Steaks, hamburgers, chicken. Whatever you want. And I'll give you a great price. Way better than you'd ever do at the supermarket."

The man scratched his chin and offered a friendly smile. "Well Son, seems you came to a goat's house lookin' for wool."

Rooster stared blankly. "I have no idea what that means."

The man laughed heartily. "You just think about it a spell. You'll figure it out."

Rooster shook his head. "No. Seriously, I don't understand what you're talking about."

The man slapped Rooster's shoulder and laughed some more. "You ain't from around these parts, are you?"

"No sir. Just moved here from Illinois."

"Since you're new in town, I'll put it in terms you'll understand. You show up at my door and intend to sell me some meat. This your plan?"

Rooster nodded.

"Well boy, that dog don't hunt."

Rooster sighed. Sweat burned his eyes. His legs ached. He had already walked several miles on the steaming blacktop. He was hot, tired, and frustrated, and he did not understand anything this crazy guy said. *How'd I end up at this man's front door trying to sell meat? Is this what my life's come to? I was a bond trader with a smokin' hot girlfriend and a Maserati. Now I been reduced to selling turkey burgers to a redneck in his underwear who sounds like Foghorn Leghorn?*

Rooster's frustration boiled over. "Listen, I really don't give a rat's left testicle if you buy meat or not. I know I wouldn't buy meat from some flapdoodle who showed up uninvited at my front door. The truth is, it's hotter than the face of the sun out here. I'm hungover and I feel awful. If you'd let me step inside out of the heat for just five minutes, I promise I'll go away and leave you alone as soon as I cool off."

The man exploded with a hearty laugh. "I like you, Son. C'mon inside. I'll get you a cold beer."

"Thank you," Rooster grinned. "Could really use a beer. You have no idea how hard it is selling meat door to door."

The man led Rooster inside. "Son, selling meat the way you do is about as dumb as a soup sandwich." He motioned at a black leather sofa as he continued toward the kitchen. "Take a load off and I'll grab you that beer."

Rooster settled onto the couch and checked out the place. The room had apparently been furnished exclusively from Wal-Mart and the Sears catalog. A creaky put-it-together-yourself particle board entertainment center on the front wall held an ancient color television, which played some sort of fishing program. Stacked precariously on top of the TV was a videotape player, cable box, DVD, stereo receiver, and two dusty speakers. Videotapes filled one of the entertainment center nooks.

Various articles of clothing lay randomly on the floor and furniture. The glass-top coffee table was covered with empty beer bottles, pizza boxes, various takeout containers, and a pair of underwear. The room smelled of beer and stale bread.

"Here you go." The man handed Rooster a can of Coors.

"Thanks." Rooster took a long grateful sip.

"Flapdoodle?"

"Huh?"

"I like that. Flapdoodle. You mind if I use it?"

"No, not at all." *This is one odd guy.*

"Tell me, Son. All that stuff about Publix cancelling their meat order..."

Rooster nodded expectantly as the man drained his beer.

"That's a big load of horse pucky, ain't it?"

Rooster exhaled a sheepish laugh. "Yeah. We're selling grade D meat Publix wouldn't touch in a million years. I tasted it and trust me, you don't want any."

"They teach you that dumb sales pitch, or you come up with it yourself?"

Rooster grew defensive. "I couldn't dream that up. Hey, I'm just trying to make a living."

The man reached out his big right paw. "Name's Buddy."

Rooster grabbed his hand. "Nice to meet you. I'm Rooster."

The brilliant grin filled Buddy's face. "What the heck kinda name's Rooster?"

The beer combined with Buddy's hospitality had put Rooster at ease. He decided to tell the truth. "When I moved here, I wanted a name that sounded southern so I came up with Rooster."

Buddy doubled over with laughter. "You thought Rooster sounded southern? Whatever gave you that crazy idea?"

"I saw it in a movie."

"What the blazes were you watching? Roots or something?"

"Roots? Why'd you think it was Roots?"

"That show had a dude who trained fighting cocks. His name was 'Rooster' something."

Now Rooster laughed. "Wasn't Rooster something. That was Chicken George. Got my name from a John Wayne movie. Rooster Cogburn."

"That movie wasn't in the south. Took place somewheres out west."

"Nevertheless." Rooster raised his can. "That's what I'm called."

Buddy lifted his beer and flashed a brilliant white Cheshire Cat grin. "That just may be the dumbest story I ever heard. I like you Son, but I can't believe you hung that dumbass name on yourself! That's nuttier than a squirrel turd."

THREE
Nine Months Later
Thursday, May 12th

"Ahhhhh."

Rooster expelled an involuntary murmur of contentment.

His muscles had been liquefied under the strong, yet gentle hands of the talented masseuse, who kneaded and rubbed every last ounce of tension from his body. Palm trees rustled gently, and the smell of ocean surf sifted through his senses as he drifted off into a trance-like state of relaxation.

The masseuse softly prodded Rooster, who rolled onto his back, eyes closed, lips curled in a satisfied smile. A warm moist sponge caressed his neck, then progressed over his face and head.

That's different. Agitation threatened his pleasant buzz. He considered a protest, but gave in to his placid state and decided to go with the flow.

Don't break the trance. Must be something special they do in the islands.

Rooster breathed in the salty tropical air and drifted into blissful sleep. Then the masseuse jammed the sponge up his nose. Instantly ripped from his reverie, Rooster clawed at his face. Coughing and sputtering, he sat bolt upright, prepared to give that stupid, clumsy oaf the "what for".

Rooster opened his eyes. It had all been a dream. He was not at a spa on the beach.

Where am I?

He sat in an empty field. The first golden rays of dawn radiated from behind him, creating a mix of light and shadows among the tall grass. He blinked to focus his scratchy eyes.

"Not again," he groaned. *What the hell's wrong with me? How does a 43-year-old man keep doing this to himself? Something's seriously wrong with me. Something's gotta change.*

A noise crunched behind him. Rooster stopped in mid self-loathing rant as a large shadow flowed over him.

What's that?

His stomach queasy from fear and remnants of the previous night's excesses, Rooster spun to face whatever giant monster had crept up behind him, but the harsh turn brought on intense dizziness. In the instant before he closed his eyes to keep from passing out, Rooster saw the sun-backed silhouette of a huge dark beast. Fear and bile rose in his throat. He braced for the inevitable attack. Instead he felt something warm and moist.

The sponge from my dream?

It slapped his forehead, then slid slowly down his nose and lips. It left his chin with a suction cup smack. As if surrounded by Pigpen's cloud, he was engulfed by the foul smell, a mix of grass, cow dung, and several other objectionable odors. He thought he might toss his cookies.

"Aww shit!" Rooster wiped cow saliva from his face.

His whole body ached. *Feels like someone beat me with a sock full of quarters.* His head pounded. The brightening sun and cow pasture aromas did not help at all. His mouth and throat were so dry they actually hurt. He worked up some spit and tried to swallow, but his tongue seemed a couple sizes too big. He licked his chapped, cracked lips only to retch when he tasted a hint of whatever nasty things the cow had eaten before she dragged her tongue across his face.

Rooster considered his ridiculous circumstances, but the cow forced him to deal with her. She led with her tongue and came in for another taste. Rooster scrambled to his feet and shooed her away.

"Get outta here!" The words scraped painfully along his raw throat. The rejected animal mooed in protest and lumbered off. Slightly lightheaded, Rooster stumbled a few steps before regaining his balance.

What exactly happened last night? How'd I end up here?

He dug deep into the black hole of his memory. He struggled to piece together what series of events could possibly have resulted in waking up hung-over in a cow pasture, and came up with...nothing. Absolutely positively nothing. Rooster pulled in a long breath, and slowly released it.

Gotta relax.

"OK," he said. "What do I remember?" He raked a shaky hand through disheveled hair. *Met up with Buddy around dinnertime. Ate some burgers and drank a few beers at Busters. Then we walked over to Bunganut Pig. Played some pool. Did shots with a couple girls. And then...what?*

Bits and pieces of the previous night flashed through his mind like a slide show lit by a strobe light, but they were all jumbled up, out of sequence.

At some point I was smoking a cigar and laughing. Then I was jammed in a car with five or six sweaty people, passing around a flask of rock-gut liquor. Half-crashed on a sofa in a strange living room, drinking tequila shots with a couple guys I didn't recognize. Grabbing a handful of Slim Jims and a six pack of Mike's Hard Lemonade at the Circle K.

All that happened last night? Doesn't compute. How'd it all lead to waking up here?

Rooster closed his eyes and willed himself to remember. The strobe light kicked back into gear. He remembered being shaken awake, his head on the bar top at The Pour House. *How'd we get way over to The Pour House?* Then he was in a restroom stall pulling off his pants. Not pulling them down, but sitting on the commode actually tugging his jeans over his boots and completely off his body.

Rooster's eyes snapped open in horror.

Am I wearing pants?

He looked down, relieved to see his jeans in place. He remembered the time he woke up on a bench outside the Murfreesboro Library in just a t-shirt and his underwear, his wallet tucked into the waistband of his briefs. *Never did figure out what happened to those pants.*

Can't remember what happened. His spirits flagged. *Another lost night. Gotta be Sherlock Holmes just to figure out what happened. Lost too many nights.* He had awoke befuddled and confused in unexpected places too many times. *Ain't normal. Normal people recognize where they wake up. Something's gotta change. Can't live like this. Can't get much lower than this.*

On queue, almost as if God were mocking him, Rooster's gut cramped severely. Doubled over in pain, bile rose into his throat and dry heaves overtook him. He leaned over, forearms on his knees, desperately praying it would come quickly so he could get it over with already. Mercifully, his stomach soon expelled its contents. Sour and chunky, it fizzed and steamed in the grass and smelled faintly of beer and minimart burritos.

Rooster wiped his nose and mouth on his sleeve as he moved away. He felt strangely re-energized.

That was a good one. Certainly better than having the dry heaves for half an hour.

He scanned the pasture through squinting eyes. Nothing distinguished this field from any other in a five-county area. Half-foot-tall grass, several groups of brown and tan cows standing around, and steaming stacks of cow pies everywhere.

Rooster retrieved his smart phone from his pocket and fumbled with it until he realized it was turned off. After powering it up, he waited impatiently as the little fruit icon stared at him from the center of the screen. His muscles ached. He must have slept with his right leg in an awkward position, because it was cramped up something fierce. The phone finally powered on. He peered at the little screen.

Five-fifty-two am.

"What the..."

He chose the name at the top of his favorites list. He put the phone to his ear, but the ring of the outbound call seemed impossibly loud. His head now throbbed, so he held the phone as far away from his ear as he could as it rang. After a click the familiar voice mail message began. Rooster disconnected the call and chose the same name. When the voice mail message started again, he ended the call and began the process all over. He continued this at least half a dozen times.

Then a new thought pierced his still-foggy brain. He frantically tapped out the text message.

"Answer your damn phone!!!"

He waited until the text was delivered. *Must be in the middle of nowhere. Cell service really sucks here.*

He began again.

After ten minutes of redials and increasingly agitated text messages, a sleepy scratchy voice answered. "What in blue blazes is goin' on? You know what time it is?"

"I don't know where I am," Rooster responded.

"Huh?"

"I don't know where I am."

There was silence for a moment, followed by a loud guffaw.

Rooster reddened. "Quit laughing, Buddy."

"What you mean? Don't know where you are?" The voice was more alert now. "You talkin' physically or existentially?"

Rooster smiled despite his annoyance. "Listen. I'm in a cow pasture in the middle of East Jahunga."

"Maybe you've passed on to the Hindu heaven. You know, surrounded by cows and what not."

"Quit goofing around. I woke up here. I have no idea how I got here. Only remember bits and pieces of last night."

"We really tied one on, didn't we Son?" Buddy said, proud as a peacock. "How'd you end up there? Last I saw, you was heading out of the bar with some filly you'd been watering with vodka cranberries."

"Don't remember hooking up with anyone."

Buddy chuckled. "That's probably for the best."

"What's that supposed to mean?"

"Well..." Buddy searched for the right words. "The reason I call her a filly was 'cause she looked like a horse, bless her heart."

"C'mon Buddy. How bad could she've been?"

"Let's just say that when she walked away, her backside looked like two puppies fighting in a burlap sack."

"I don't know what that means."

"You just think about it Son, and you'll get it."

"Whatever. I need you to come and get me."

"How can I come and get you if you don't even know where you's at? Besides, my head hurts. You know how early it is? Man ain't built to be operating at this hour."

"I'll look up where I'm at on my phone," Rooster said. "Then I'll text you and start walking toward town."

"Alright," Buddy sighed. "But I need something strong to get my big butt moving. I'll fix up something and come fetch you."

"That's cool. Bring me one of those bloody marys you make. God, I'm dying for a drink."

"Of course. That's what friends are for. On my way."

"Thanks, man."

"Hey Rooster?"

"Yeah?"

"Please tell me you got your pants on."

Rooster yelled obscenities into the phone, but he knew Buddy had already hung up, and was currently laughing himself silly. He'd never met anyone who could crack himself up as easily as Buddy Junior Hollandsworth III.

FOUR

Rooster squinted at the map app. Readyville, TN.

"Really?"

His phone calculated directions to Murfreesboro. Fifteen miles by car. He texted Buddy and walked toward town.

Despite his bedraggled condition, Rooster Michaels was not bad looking. About six foot even with brown hair, three-day stubble and broad shoulders, he had once been athletically inclined. Captain of the high school volleyball team, his kill shot was unstoppable. Even out of shape, Rooster could still jump out of the gym. He had slim powerful legs, but lately his gut had grown more than he cared to admit. He continued to wear large shirts, as if that meant he was not actually extra-large sized now.

Rooster had once been a wildly successful bond trader. He was a natural, literally a money magnet. Every crazy gamble came up smelling like roses. The major firms on the Street all threw stupid cash at him trying to land the latest young gun trading prodigy. He earned his first million before his twenty-fourth birthday. He rode the wave a few years, but soon flamed out in a blurry haze of alcohol, gambling, strippers, and poor judgment.

An unbelievably arrogant jerk during his meteoric rise to the top, he ticked off so many big time players, there had been palpable joy on Wall Street when he finally crashed. One particularly bitter group actually popped champagne to celebrate his demise, or so he had heard.

It had been nearly two decades since his all too brief glory years, a lifetime ago. He had been through so much since, but never like the highs of his twenties. He could never be satisfied, which led to all kinds of crazy schemes and stupid gambles. Each one fell apart, some spectacularly.

Rooster shook his head.

Murfreesboro, Tennessee. Starting over. Again.

Gotta figure out how to get on track. Surely have one more comeback in me. Have to figure out where that golden opportunity is hiding out around here. This time, I won't cut corners. I'll be smarter. This time, I'll make it last.

His phone chirped.

What's Buddy want now? He tapped the answer button before he checked the display.

"Crap," *Should've let it go to voicemail. Too late now.* He forced a smile and the most upbeat voice he could muster.

"Hello!"

An unhappy voice responded, "Rooster?"

"Yes."

"This is Tom. Where the hell you at?"

"Hey Tom," Rooster stalled.

"How come you're not here?"

"What day is it, Tom?"

"C'mon Rooster. You think I'm an idiot?"

"No, seriously?"

Tom sighed with disgust. "It's Thursday."

"No way. Thought it was Wednesday. I been sick and..."

"You're fired. I'm tired of your nonsense."

"No," Rooster pleaded halfheartedly. "I'm telling the truth. I been sick."

"That's bunk. You know it. I know it. Let's stop dancing around. Susie saw you doing shots last night at The Stampede. I don't know any sick people who'd be doing that."

That damn Susie. Always putting her big nose in everyone else's business. "I'm sorry Tom. I can be there in twenty or thirty minutes." *That Susie'll get hers.*

"I took a big chance on you," Tom said. "Everything told me not to bring you on, but I liked you. I gave you a chance and you made a fool outta me."

"I'm sorry, Tom." Rooster groped for the charm which had gotten him the job in the first place. "Give me one more chance. I promise, I won't screw it up."

"Forget it, Rooster," Tom sighed. "You're out of chances. I'll mail out your last check. Please don't come by here again."

"All right." Rooster knew when he was whipped.

"And Rooster?"

"Yeah."

"Do yourself a favor and get some help. You're gonna kill yourself if you don't get this drinking thing under control. You've got so much going for you, but your drinking is destroying your life."

Rooster was indignant. "I don't need any help."

"Ok. Whatever you say."

After a click, Tom was gone.

"I was too good for that crappy job anyway."

Concocting witty retorts he should have said, Rooster was still brooding when Buddy pulled up in his Black F-150 pickup. Rooster climbed into the cab.

"Wooo weee," Buddy howled. "You stink, Son. That smell could knock a buzzard off a gut truck."

Rooster rubbed his eyes. "I don't know what that means."

Buddy nodded knowingly. "You just think about it, boy. You'll figure it out."

Buddy handed him a travel mug full of bloody marys and Rooster recounted Tom's phone call, liberally sprinkling in as fact all the witty remarks he wished he had actually used. The rest of the ride, they tried to piece together a workable timeline of the previous night. By the time they pulled into the gravel driveway of the little house on

Yearwood Avenue, they had not accomplished much.

"Thanks for the ride, Bro." Rooster jumped from the truck.

"Anytime. Always got your back, but I gotta run now. Need some sleep before my shift."

Rooster closed the door and was immediately sprayed with gravel as Buddy gunned the big truck out of the driveway.

Excited about a hot shower, followed by a late morning nap since he no longer had work to worry about, Rooster moved toward the door. Head down, he fumbled in his pocket for his keys until he was on top of the doorframe. He lifted his head and immediately realized something was seriously wrong. He could see into the living room. The entire door slab was missing.

"What's this? Where's my door?"

Blue painter's tape secured a letter-size envelope to the doorframe. He snatched it down, tore it open, and read it.

"You're kidding me." This was a real kick to the groin. He dialed his phone, his anger rising as he waited for an answer.

It clicked through after six rings. "Hello, this is Scott."

"Scott, this is Rooster Michaels at 361 Yearwood," he snarled, barely in control of himself.

"Yes," Scott said a little too happily.

Rooster did not like Scott's tone. *He enjoying this?* Rooster considered the bond traders who had reveled in his demise. *They have this kinda joy in their voices when talking about my flameout?*

Scott continued. "What can I do for you, Rooster?"

Countless expletives flowed through Rooster's mind before he finally sputtered, "My door!"

"What about your door, Rooster?"

Rooster clenched his teeth. "It's gone, Scott."

"Oh yes," Scott said as if this was all news to him. "We came by to collect the rent. You're a month and a half late, you know. Anyway, we stopped by and you weren't home, but we noticed the door was broken. We didn't want you to get hurt by a faulty door, so we took the door with us. You know, to repair it."

Rooster bit his tongue and responded as calmly as he could. "When'll it be fixed, Scott?"

"Well, that's the problem, Rooster. We don't have the money to make that there repair because you haven't given us your rent for the last month and a half. If we had the money from you, we could afford to repair that door. Without the money we can't. Surely you can see our problem here, right?"

Rooster sighed. *What else can go wrong today?* He clearly understood saying what was really on his mind would only make things worse. "I can see your problem, Scott. It's a bigger problem for me, don't you think?"

"I can see that, but you know how it goes. People are too wrapped in their own problems to really appreciate someone else's."

Rooster breathed deeply and tried to calm himself. "Let's say I get you that money this afternoon. How soon could you have the door fixed and back in place?"

"That would certainly be wonderful if you got that rent to us today. I tell you what. If you get me the rent by, say, three o'clock, we should be able to have your door all fixed up and back in place before dark. I'll even authorize the guys to work overtime. That's how much I like you, pal."

"Ok," Rooster said. "I'll get to work on it."

"That's awesome. I want you to know, Rooster. I'm rootin' for you. I really hope to see you by three with the money. Have a great day."

Rooster disconnected without comment. The little passive aggressive dig at his landlord made him feel the tiniest bit better about himself. He stepped inside.

Hope nothing's stolen. A quick scan of the little two bedroom house, revealed his two most valuable possessions other than his smart phone, the hundred-cigar humidor and the fifty-two-inch flat screen TV, had both been untouched.

He considered his situation. *This is bad. Need to relax and think this out.* With the warm bloody mary buzz losing its edge, he knew exactly what would clear his head. He headed to the dingy kitchen, which had last been updated sometime in the mid seventies with the olive green sink and butcher block Formica countertop. He opened the flimsy pressboard cupboard and located his bottle of Eagle Rare Bourbon. *Ah, Kentucky's finest.* He found a rocks glass in the sink and rinsed it. He filled the glass with ice cubes, which cracked and popped as the warm amber liquid gurgled over them.

His favorite drink in hand, Rooster returned to the highly polished olivewood humidor and chose a long, nearly black, Rocky Patel cigar. *Yes, The Edge. Perfect cigar for contemplation.* From the humidor's little drawer, he retrieved his cutter and torch lighter and lumbered out the back door to a little patio.

He carefully set his drink and smoking accoutrements on a slab of plywood perched atop of an empty five-gallon paint bucket and dropped into a white molded plastic chair. He tapped the Pandora app on his phone and chose the Gino Vanelli station.

As soothing soft jazz played, Rooster laid the phone on his makeshift table and took up the smoking supplies. He clipped the cigar, dipped the cut side in the bourbon, and placed it between his lips. He fired up the torch, lit the stogie, drew in deeply, rolled the peppery smoke around his mouth, tipped his head back, and blew a fragrant cloud into the sky.

With the cigar in one hand, Rooster took the cool glass of bourbon in the other and enjoyed a long sip.

Never gets old.

He enjoyed the subtle burn as whiskey rolled down his throat. A comfortable warmness radiated from his chest to the rest of his body. He took another long draw on the cigar. *Ok, time to think.*

He stared off as the gears in his head began to grind.

I been in worse spots than this. Need money right away. Where to get it? He listed potential options. *Buddy? Nah, already owe him three hundred bucks. Go get that last check from work? Tom told me not to come back. Not enough there to cover the rent anyway. What about that jar of loose change? At least a few hundred dollars in there.*

A glimmer of hope. Rooster balanced his cigar on the edge of the plywood and began to stand. Halfway up he vaguely remembered emptying the jar to buy beer, or pizza, or something.

"Damn."

He considered several other increasingly harebrained schemes, but nothing felt right. Then, eureka! He recalled something he'd done a few years back in Kansas City.

That just might work. Hell, this is the Bible Belt. Probably work better here.

A wide grin filled his face as Rooster leaned back in his chair, popped the cigar back in his mouth, and congratulated himself on his brilliance.

FIVE

In his early thirties, Rooster briefly sold Buicks in Kansas City. The uneven full-commission income often left him short on rent and forced to stay home at night. Then a fellow salesmen and drinking buddy named John Toes, such a ridiculous name Rooster never forgot it, told him about "benevolence."

It seemed so crazy, he had been convinced John invented it to trick Rooster into blowing the rent money on partying, only to discover the next morning he was screwed. John assured him it was real and offered to pay Rooster's rent if he was lying. As John had described it, most churches stash away money they give to people who come in crying poor. You could get your hands on the cash only if you were not afraid to humiliate yourself. You had to be willing to break down crying, or come up with a believable sob story. If they thought you were lying, no coin for you, and if you went to the same church more than once or twice, they would wise up and cut you off.

The other thing to this benevolence, John had said, was the church would never give any cash to you personally. They would cut a check to your landlord, or a doctor, or the electric company. The churches know you probably want cash to buy dope or alcohol, or something else unreligious, so they pay someone on your behalf, as if paying your landlord directly does not enable you to spend all the rent money partying with no consequence.

They both had a good laugh about the Pollyannaish church benevolence people as they drank away Rooster's rent. Sure enough, the next day John Toes coached Rooster through getting his rent paid by a church. John said it was his go-to plan whenever he had a bad sales month. Why should he hole up like a hermit when there were people perfectly willing to pay his rent for him? He deserved to go out and enjoy himself. It had all worked just like John predicted. *What a crazy world.*

As a recovering Catholic, Rooster just knew God would strike him with a lightning bolt for this church scam, or kill him with a painful disease. John Toes assured him God was not that dramatic anymore. "You're not gonna be struck down," John said. "You're just going to hell."

That prospect did not deter Rooster from cashing in on some church largesse. He figured he had already disappointed God enough in his life that the skids to hell were already greased as far as his everlasting soul was concerned. What difference would it make to toss one more evil deed on top of a heaping pile? *God can't do anything worse to me than hell, can He?*

After he dipped his toe in the benevolence pool, not only did he not get struck down, but Rooster actually had his best month ever selling Buicks. Never one to build upon success, Rooster had cashed his fat commission check, embarked on a celebratory bender, and woke up fired. Soon after, Rooster got run out of Kansas City.

He managed a short string of relatively big scores which kept cash in his pockets for a few years. Subsequently, the whole benevolence scheme had faded from his memory. Luckily, like an unexpected inheritance from a rich uncle, the idea had appeared from nowhere just when he needed it most.

Thank you John Toes.

Rooster had set up at the kitchen table with a pen and pad, his iPhone, and a longneck Budweiser. He typed "murfreesboro tn churches" in the phone's search engine and scrolled through the results. Not exactly sure what to look for, he was confident he would recognize the perfect mark when he found it.

He chose one of the results and immediately a spiffy mobile version of the church website popped on his screen. *No good. Too techie. Would rather find one not quite so in tune with the modern world. A little naiveté is preferable.*

He tried another. The Carpenter's Lighthouse. *Looks more promising. Website's decidedly low-tech. Probably built by volunteers or the Pastor's twelve-year-old kid.*

"I like it," he declared as his fingers worked through the page. He tapped the "Ministry" tab. It started with all the usual stuff: students, children, bible studies, yada, yada, yada. Rooster took a long drink of beer and wiped his fingers on the front of his t-shirt.

He found the "Community Outreach" page. "Bingo!" Rooster hit the "More Info" link.

> *"At The Carpenter's Lighthouse we believe the most effective charity happens in our own community. That's why we have worked hard to build a robust ministry to help Rutherford County's poor and indigent come to know Christ by modeling Christ-like behavior and fulfilling His command to serve the poor."*

Fan-freakin-tastic. He jotted notes on his pad. *Like a dream come true.* He read more.

> *"While helping those who have fallen on hard times, we are careful to treat them with compassion, love, and dignity. As the apostle Paul said in 2 Thessalonians 3:10, 'The one who is unwilling to work shall not eat.'"*

Rooster frowned. *Well, that's taken a bad turn.*

> *"We take this admonition seriously. As a congregation we believe there is dignity and Godliness in hard work. When helping those in need financially, our benevolence staff works closely with each recipient to find a suitable job for them in exchange for the resources we provide. We are careful to match tasks to a recipient's ability and skill level so he or she can know the joy of hard work and the blessings that come from completing a job successfully. God calls us to be good stewards of our resources..."*

Rooster quit reading, his mood souring.

Too good to be true. He imagined being forced to clean toilets or sweep the parking lot in exchange for his rent money, and failed to suppress an involuntary shudder. No, he liked free money with no strings attached and this place had a bunch of strings. *Time to look at other options.*

He returned to the search screen to continue his quest.

"How about the Cumberland Baptist Church?"

The webpage, if you could call it that, was a picture of the church, basic contact info and a list of service times. The tagline on the bottom of the page said simply, "Serving Christ. Serving His people."

Rooster laid the phone on the table and tipped back his beer. *This is the one.* He could not quite put his finger on what it was exactly. It just felt right.

Rooster set down the bottle, wiped his hand and took up the phone. He tapped the contact number on the website, but nothing happened. The webpage creator had not even known how to make the phone number a link a smart phone could dial right from the site. Somehow this seemed to be final confirmation he had found the right place. He wrote the number on his pad, pulled up the dial screen, and manually typed it in.

A wide smile filled his face as he experienced that awesome adrenaline rush you get just before you pull the trigger on a big deal, or double down a huge bet at the Blackjack table. Absolutely hyper-focused on the task at hand, all his senses strained to be included. He could smell the beer on his fingertips. He was strangely aware of the smoothness of the phone pressed against his ear. His vision was unfocused, as if not making use of his sight could give the other senses more clarity. Unnaturally aware of his breathing, he absent-mindedly counted his breaths. The slight nervous churn in his stomach was not unpleasant. It was more like his body's confirmation something exciting was about to go down.

As the phone rang, his intensity level rose. He heard a click followed by a pleasant female voice. "Cumberland Baptist Church. How may I help you?"

The instant Rooster blurted out his much-too-forceful "Hello," with the intensity of some amped up tweeker, he realized he was on the verge of blowing it.

He breathed in deeply and exhaled slowly. *Gotta calm down.*

"Hello?" She asked.

Had she heard the craziness in his voice? *Calm down. Don't blow this.*

The voice spoke again. "Hello? Are you there?

"Yes, yes," Rooster said with an even voice. "I'm sorry. This is very hard for me."

"What can I do for you, sir?"

"Well, ma'am." Rooster naturally mirrored her formal Southern politeness. Years of sales training had hammered the skill into him to the point where it was now second nature. *Act like this is really embarrassing.* "I been told your church sometimes helps people who... who..." His voice trailed off as if he did not know what to say.

"Help people who what, sir?" Her tone was warm, patient, and kind.

Rooster's voice cracked slightly. "I'm sorry, ma'am." He actually surprised himself at how easy he had gotten into character. *Should've been an actor.* "I never done this before, but I didn't know where else to turn. I was told you good folks sometimes help out people who are down on their luck. And that definitely describes my situation."

"Yes, sir."

Rooster was pleased to hear nothing but sympathy and understanding in her voice.

"You are correct. We do sometimes help people in cases like you described, but we don't make those decisions over the phone. Would you be able to come here to sit down and talk in person?"

"Yes ma'am, of course," Rooster agreed before he realized he had no idea where Cumberland Baptist Church was located. He fumbled with the pad, but he had not written the address. He toyed with the idea of pulling the phone from his ear to look up the information, but that thought passed. *Does it really matter where this place is located? Of course not. Don't blow this worrying about unimportant things.*

"Is Cumberland Baptist your home church?"

How do I answer this? His first impulse was to lie. Of course they would be more likely to help their own congregation. *What if they have some sort of membership list? This a trick question? Here I am on the edge of a big score and this simple question could sink everything. What should I say?* The voice of John Toes popped into his head, "Base as much of your story on the truth as possible. That way you won't crack under cross examination."

Thank you John Toes.

"No ma'am," Rooster said.

"Where is your home church?"

Rooster channeled his inner John Toes. "Well, ma'am, only been in town a year. Haven't found a regular church yet."

"I see."

Was that skepticism in her tone? Don't panic. Just stay quiet until she says something.

"Well I guess we can talk about this when you come in to see us," she said pleasantly. "Will you be coming in today?"

"Yes, ma'am." Rooster swallowed the adrenaline pumping through his body. It gave him the same high as a kill shot spike to win a big volleyball match.

"When should I expect you, sir?"

"Well. I don't have a car. I have to walk or ride my bike. So I don't believe I can tell you what time precisely."

"But you think it'll be before four?"

"Yes, ma'am." *Gotta get the cash from you and deliver it to Scott before three.*

"I'll be watching out for you, sir. What's your name?"

"Rooster."

"Rooster?"

"Yes, ma'am."

"That's certainly an interesting name."

"Yes, ma'am, it is."

"I'm looking forward to meeting you in person Mr. Rooster. Just ask for Sandy when you get here."

"Yes, ma'am. Thank you ma'am."

"Blessings to you Mr. Rooster."

Rooster punched the air in triumph as he ended the call.

Can't get too excited. This is a two-step sale. Nailed step one, but still gotta nail step two, if I'm gonna get the cash. But so far, so good.

He entered the small bedroom to search his wardrobe for just the right look. He catalogued John Toes' rules for generating successful benevolence payments.

"Dress neat and clean. Take pride in your appearance, but don't dress too nice. Look like a good hard-working, low-income man. Think Wal-Mart style.

"Make sure you don't smell like alcohol or drugs or look like you been partying."

Rooster sniffed his armpit. *Better take a shower first.*

"Don't ever go to a Catholic Church. Those buggers'll guilt and shame you into spilling the truth. And they're cheap. All their wealth goes to Rome. The protestants definitely hand out more money.

"Look your interrogator in the eyes when you talk to her. Don't look away or act guilty in any way. You're gonna have to sell yourself on the truth of your story before you'll ever be able to sell it to the benevolence lady.

"Keep it as simple as possible. The more elaborate your story, the more likely you'll start contradicting yourself when they keep asking questions.

"Be as truthful as you can. It's always easier to remember the truth. But don't let the truth put your payday at risk.

"If you ever get stuck or don't know what to say, just start crying and bawl long enough to gather your thoughts."

Rooster considered his options. *Lost my job and now I can't pay the rent. That's simple and true. What if they ask why I lost my job?*

He thought about sales training. *This is just a different kind of sales, isn't it?* He remembered one instructor who claimed a sales presentation should have two or three main points. Any more, and you risk confusing the buyer, or getting yourself pulled off on a tangent. If the prospect asks questions about anything else, pull her back to your main ideas. Go in supremely confident about your bullet points and do not allow anyone to knock you off track.

Rooster considered that for awhile. Seemed like a smart plan, especially in light of the John Toes success points. He practiced different ways to express his two main points. Soon, Rooster felt good about his chances to actually get the money. Content with his mental readiness, he whistled an old Kinks tune as he got to work on his physical preparation.

SIX

The capital of Tennessee from 1818-1826, Murfreesboro is a proud southern town with a rich heritage. The historic courthouse, built in 1858, is the city's most cherished possession. A raid led by General Nathan Bedford Forrest in 1862 expelled Union forces from the courthouse and saved several Confederate patriots scheduled to be hanged the next morning.

It was on the square, near the old courthouse, where the cab pulled over. Rooster paid the driver and watched him drive off. Years ago, he had lost his driver's license to a DUI and had never mustered the ambition to get it back. He had learned to make good use of public transportation, cabs, and in a pinch, the rusty old mountain bike he won in a poker game.

He had told the benevolence lady he would walk or ride his bike and he did not want to get labeled a liar right from jump street. Flat busted, Rooster really could not afford the fifteen dollar cab ride. Laziness had trumped destitution, but he has careful to get dropped a half mile from the church. With all the angles covered, he was hopeful, if not totally confident, his scheme would pay off.

The few blocks walk gave him time to refine his story and anticipate any oddball questions they might use trip him up. It was hot for mid May, already 82 degrees and climbing. As sweat droplets ran down his spine, it occurred to Rooster that showing up drenched in sweat was not necessarily a bad thing. After all, he supposedly walked several miles in the heat and humidity.

Many people were out enjoying the summer-like weather. Rooster was pleased to see miniskirts and short shorts were back in style with the coed crowd. A twenty-something guy who wore a knit toque, in the heat, wandered around shooting random footage with his camcorder. *Probably a student.* He had partied with many kids from nearby Middle Tennessee State University since his arrival in town. It made him feel young to know he could still hang with the kids.

As he walked up Main Street, Rooster took in the stately old southern mansions lining the road. He admired the colorful blooming flowers and enjoyed the pungent aroma of magnolias.

Cumberland Baptist Church sat close to the street in a converted Antebellum home. An old-fashioned display box was mounted next to the sidewalk. Black plastic letters spelled out the pastor's name and the schedule of service times and activities. Rooster climbed the steps and grabbed the black wrought iron handle on a huge weathered old oak door. He whispered, "here we go," opened the door, and stepped inside.

The cool air felt good, but he quickly realized how wet his armpits had become during his half-mile walk. He firmly tucked his shirttail into his pants and ran fingers through his damp hair. The small lobby had two doors. One had a sign labeled, "Sanctuary" and the other read, "Office." He pushed the second door and found himself in a small empty room with a pair of desks at one end, and a long line of gray filing cabinets at the other. The room smelled faintly of coffee and musty carpet.

"May I help you?"

Rooster jumped. The voice had come out of nowhere.

A gentle hand fell on his shoulder. "I'm so sorry, sir. I didn't mean to sneak up behind you."

Rooster's face reddened. Churches already made him uncomfortable. He knew he did not belong in one. *Didn't realize how nervous I was until she startled me.* He took a long breath and tried to pull himself together.

"That's ok." He forced a smile and turned to look at the woman. Medium-length brown hair framed a friendly face with sparkling, intelligent brown eyes. She wore a green high-necked blouse and a plain long black skirt. Together, they effectively camouflaged any female curves there may have been on her body.

"I'm supposed to meet with Sandy."

The woman clasped her hands together and then drew her arms out wide. He thought she might grab him in a bear hug.

"Ohhh! You must be Mr. Rooster. I was wondering if you were going to make it here today. I'm Sandy."

Rooster half bowed and extended his hand. "Pleased to make your acquaintance, ma'am."

After pumping his hand, she moved her hand to the small of his back and gently pushed him toward one of the desks. "Right this way. I expect it to be pretty quiet this afternoon so we can sit right over here at my space."

Sandy sat behind the worn brown desk and waited for Rooster to settle into the padded folding chair across from her.

"Now, Mr. Rooster, tell me a little more about your story."

Like a weekend duffer over-thinking his golf swing, Rooster reviewed his mental checklist of John Toes benevolence rules.

"Look her in the eye. Keep your story simple. Make it as truthful as possible. Take your time. If you get stuck, cry."

"Yes," Rooster said with a suitably melancholy smile. "Lost my job and I got behind on my rent." He glanced at his hands. Then he heard John Toes' voice. "Look her in the eye!" Rooster raised his head and forced himself to stare at her pupils. "My landlord's made things extremely uncomfortable for me."

"I see. How long you been without work?"

Rooster fought the impulse to lie. *Keep it as truthful as possible.* He suddenly realized with horror his rent should not actually be late if he just lost his job today. His mind raced. *Should I lie about when I got fired? Or should I lie about why I'm outta money already? Need time to think.*

"Cry," John Toes' voice ordered. "Cry!"

Rooster lowered his head into his hands and drew in a few deep breaths. "I'm sorry. I never been in this position before. This is difficult for me."

"Oh my goodness," Sandy exclaimed, emotion in her voice. "You just take your time, Mr. Rooster. We have all afternoon. You need a tissue?"

Sandy held out a Kleenex box as Rooster lifted his face. He sniffled as he pulled a tissue and wiped his eyes. His stalling tactic had worked. The short delay had allowed him to concoct the framework of a story. It anticipated the questions Sandy would naturally ask and importantly, it portrayed him as an honorable hard working man who had merely hit a run of bad luck.

Don't add too many moving parts. Keep it all as simple and truthful as possible. Rooster was finally ready to proceed. "Thank you. I was fired today, ma'am."

Surprise filled Sandy's face. "Today? Why were you fired?"

"I work sales. I didn't meet my quotas so they let me go."

"What were you selling?"

"Meat."

"You mean like at a grocery store?"

"No ma'am. I sold meat door to door."

Sandy raised an eyebrow. "You sold meat door to door? I never heard of such a thing."

That does sound crazy. Here I am following the John Toes rules and the truth sounds more outlandish than anything I could make up. He smiled at the ridiculousness of it all.

"Yes, ma'am. I worked for Pegasus Farms and I sold meat, hamburgers, steaks, pork chops, seafood, free range chicken, you name it. It's a tough way to make a living, knocking on doors and asking people to buy meat. I guess I wasn't very good at it since I couldn't hit my quotas. So they let me go." Rooster met Sandy's big brown eyes with his best sad puppy expression.

All skepticism now gone, concern returned to Sandy's face.

"Didn't you have some money set aside for the rent? How would you've paid the rent if they hadn't fired you?"

"They were paying me a draw until I could get up to speed, but I had to pay the draw back out of my commissions once I got established. When they fired me, they just kept all the commission I was due because it wasn't even close to enough to pay back the draw I owed."

"Well goodness me. How much is your rent?"

"I was already half a month behind. I hoped to sell some steaks this week and make enough to get caught up completely."

"So, how much do you owe?"

"My rent is $600, so I owe $900 right now." Wanting to seem emotional, he sucked in heavy breaths. He figured talk of the actual dollar amount would send his new character into fits. The enormity of the amount would seem impossible to ever overcome.

"It's ok, Mr. Rooster. I feel good about you. I want to help you."

"Really?" Rooster thought his tone conveyed disbelief and amazement. "I don't know when I could repay you."

"If we paid your rent, we wouldn't want to be paid back."

"I can't believe this." Rooster was moments away from the payoff. "This is wonderful."

Sandy interrupted his internal celebration. "Of course, there is something we'd want you to do for us. Well actually it would be something you'd do for yourself."

It was a cold bucket of water in the face. *They gonna make me clean toilets like that other church?* Rooster scrambled for any idea to get the money with no strings attached. "I'll be looking for work now."

Sandy smiled warmly. "Don't you worry, Mr. Rooster. What I have in mind won't steal any time away from your job search. But I'm getting ahead of myself." She picked up a pen and poised her hand over a post-it note. "Who's your landlord and what's his phone number?"

She really gonna call him? What'll she tell him? What'll he say to her? An uneasy feeling attacked his stomach. He did not like where this was headed. *She was practically writing the check a minute ago. How'd it all go off track?*

The voice of John Toes cut through his mental fog. "Just roll with it. What have you got to lose? Even if this blows up in your face, you're no worse off than when you walked in the door. But if it works, you hit the jackpot! Roll with it."

A strange calmness came over him. He retrieved his phone, pulled up Scott's number, and gave her the information.

Sandy snatched up the desk phone and dialed out. She smiled serenely at Rooster until someone answered.

"Hello? May I please speak with Scott?"

Rooster strained, but he could not make out what the voice on the phone said.

"Hi Scott. This is Sandy Wilson from Cumberland Baptist Church. We're helping a tenant of yours who's behind on his rent."

More chatter from Scott.

"Why yes," she said with surprise. "That's exactly who it is. How'd you guess?"

She listened patiently.

"I see. No, I didn't know that. I would've never guessed."

Rooster squirmed. *What could Scott possibly be telling her.*

"Regardless," Sandy said. "We'd like to help him get caught up. But we don't want to pay the whole thing at once. Would you allow him to stay in the house if we paid four hundred fifty dollars to you today and the rest in two weeks?"

Rooster frowned. *Will half of what I owe get my door back?*

"Wonderful. Yes, I'll write the check today." Sandy paused and listened intently. "Why yes, he's sitting in front of me."

Sandy reached the receiver across the desk. "He wants to talk to you, Mr. Rooster."

He put the phone to his ear. Little beads of sweat formed on his forehead. "Hello?"

Scott was pleasant as always. "Hello there, Rooster. I see you been working on your rent problem."

"Yes I have."

"I want you to know I told the nice church lady that I think it's a really bad idea for her to waste the church's money on you. I don't believe you'll ever pay it back."

"I understand." Rooster glanced at Sandy, who flipped through a file, pretending not to eavesdrop. "I actually told her I wouldn't be able to pay them back anytime soon."

"I commend you for your honesty. Looks like you found a way to work the system in your favor, but I need to tell you we won't be able to fix that door for you until you're completely caught up on rent. That's the deal I offered this morning."

"I see. I don't have the rest of the rent money right now." Sandy peeked up from her file.

Scott's tone was pleasant. "So you've said. I guess you're either going to have to find the rest somewhere else, or do whatever the nice church lady says you have to do in order to get the balance of that rent in two weeks."

"I guess so." Rooster barely heard Scott as he considered how he might raise the other four hundred fifty bucks.

"Please tell Miss Sandy I accept the church's offer of half now and half in two weeks. Keep in mind the church is counting on you to shape up and fly right. Don't disappoint them."

Rooster snapped back when Scott grew quiet. "Huh?"

"Have a nice day." Scott disconnected.

Rooster stared at the receiver. Bewilderment filled his face. *What just happened here? Am I getting my door back or not?*

Sandy reached across the desk. "I'll take the phone. So your landlord is onboard with our payment plan?"

"Uhh, yes, ma'am"

"That's great." Sandy smiled. "And you're onboard too?"

"Of course."

"Fantastic." Her brown eyes sparkled with excitement. "Now let me tell you what we'll expect from you the next two weeks so we can pay the rest of your rent."

"What you'll expect?" The call with Scott had knocked him off kilter. He had completely forgotten the strings she alluded to just a few minutes earlier.

"Yes, Mr. Rooster. It's really quite simple, especially since you don't have a home church right now. All we want you to do is come to church the next two Sunday mornings and attend a small group meeting each of the next two Wednesday evenings."

"Small group?"

"Yes. You ever been to a small group before?"

"No ma'am."

Sandy's enthusiasm was palpable. "Oh I know you'll love it. You'll get to meet some wonderful, godly people. I know you'll really enjoy yourself. I'm so excited for you!"

Rooster frowned. "You think so?"

Sandy was undeterred. If anything, her tone grew more eager. "I know you think coming to church is the last thing you would ever want to do."

"That's not the case."

"Oh stop it, Mr. Rooster," Sandy interrupted with a knowing grin. "You think you've pulled the wool over my eyes and tricked us into giving you your rent money."

Rooster began to protest, but Sandy held out her palm.

"What you don't realize is that, years from now, you're going to see this whole situation as a huge blessing. I've seen so many people just like you, whose lives were turned around completely, just because they allowed God to work on them."

Rooster grimaced. *Exactly what I hoped to avoid. Some Jesus freak trying to lead me to the Lord so I can spend all my time in church with a bunch of hypocritical self-righteous people. Basically stripping every ounce of fun from my life.*

Sandy spoke, as if she had read his thoughts. "I can see the wheels turning in your mind. If you have to, look at it this way. We're basically giving you nine hundred dollars for six hours of your time. When was the last time you earned a hundred fifty bucks an hour for just sitting there?"

Rooster nodded. *She's right.* It was easy money, even if not quite as easy as he had hoped. "Alright, you convinced me."

"I thought I might." Sandy grinned triumphantly. "When you come to church, you can't be under the influence of any alcohol or drugs. If you are, we will have you escorted from the building and our deal is off. That fair?"

"Sure."

"And we expect you to be respectful of the people around you. We won't tolerate foul language or crass behavior."

"Ok." Even though he was a little insulted, Rooster was happy the gloves were finally off so everyone could be honest. "I'll play nice," he said with a small, tight smile.

"I'm glad we got all of that settled and we understand each other. Now you can come and just sit there like a bump on a log, but I encourage you to participate. I promise you the time will go much faster for you, especially in your small group, if you engage with the other people, but that's totally up to you."

Rooster shook his head in wonder. Sandy had seen right through his charade all along, and he thought his performance had been Oscar-worthy. *Why's she paying my rent when she knows I'm full of crap? She really think she can convert me in two weeks?* Rooster decided it did not really matter. If she was willing to pay, he would not look a gift horse in the mouth.

Sandy rose and went quickly to one of the filing cabinets. "Just one more moment, Mr. Rooster. I have something for you and then I'll let you go."

She returned with a pamphlet. She scribbled some notes and handed it to Rooster.

"This brochure will give you a little more information about the small groups at our church. I've written down the time you need to come on Wednesday, and name of the leader whose group I want you to attend. Make sure she adds your name to the attendance sheet so I know you were there. On Sunday, please come see me before and after the service, so I know you were on time and stayed for the whole thing. I'll expect you at the eight-thirty service."

"Eight-thirty?!" *Is she crazy?* "That's not possible."

"Oh sure it is." Sandy shooed him toward the door. "At a hundred fifty bucks an hour, you can certainly get up early two Sundays. Don't be silly."

She walked him right out the front door. "I'll get that rent check to your landlord today. See you Sunday morning!"

SEVEN

Rooster stared at the brochure and considered the name Sandy had written: Marcie Dexter. *Vaguely familiar. Could I know this woman? No way. I spend my time in places where church people wouldn't be caught dead.* Still, a hint of familiarity itched the back of his brain and he could not shake it.

He glanced up and down the street and stepped off the curb. Thumbing through the small group pamphlet as he crossed, Rooster unconsciously slowed as the photos pulled him in. He had to admit, they made a Bible study look fun and exciting.

"Hey, look out!"

The shout wrestled Rooster's mind back to the here and now. In his stupor, he had stopped in the middle of the street. Within a millisecond, he saw a low slung yellow mass hurtle toward him. It was some sort of sports car and raced at him way faster than the thirty-mile-per-hour city speed limit. He froze as the vehicle closed ground at an astounding rate. He saw the top of the driver's head through the windshield and realized the guy's attention was not focused on the road. *This idiot's texting while flying down Main Street like Mario Andretti.*

Time stood still as a slide show of options flipped through his head. No time to dive to either side. With horror, Rooster realized he must go up or get splattered like a bug. Maybe he could lessen the impact and somehow survive if he jumped and deflected off the roof. The only alternative was to absorb the full force of the speeding vehicle followed by certain death or disfigurement. The whole scenario played out and the decision was made in less than a second.

Rooster sank into a deep squat and sprang from the ground with every ounce of force his tired old legs could muster. As his body launched skyward, he pulled his knees up to his chest, closed his eyes, and waited for the car to knock him flying.

People talk about your life flashing before your eyes during a near-death experience. Rooster had always thought he knew what that might look like for him, but the actual experience was not even close to his expectations. Instead of reliving his happy times, what passed before him was a lowlight reel of every person he had ever wronged, from seemingly insignificant people he had not considered in years, to the most intimate individuals in his life. A review of his worst moments would have been bad enough, but this was much more agonizing. As the images flashed, he saw close-ups of the eyes and faces of those he had hurt. For the first time ever, Rooster fully understood the suffering he had inflicted through his self-absorbed actions. He actually felt his victims' pain. As it sunk in how he had wasted his life, how he had spread hurt and misery in the world, Rooster was overcome by overwhelming sadness, shame, and regret.

Guess I'm gonna find out what hell's really like. He waited for the impact that would punch his one-way ticket to eternal damnation.

It never came.

Rooster felt his body rise, heard a whoosh below, stopped for a split second, and then fell. He extended his legs, his knees still bent when his feet hit the ground. His heels hit first. He opened his eyes as he tumbled backwards, arms flailing as his hind end smacked the ground. His hands scraped along the blacktop as he slid backwards. He finally came to a stop flat on his back in the middle of the street.

Rooster's head spun. *What's going on? Where's the car?* Had he imagined everything? *I should be dead.* He closed his eyes and tried to decide what he should feel. Suddenly exhausted, he considered how easy he could go to sleep right in the the street. His breathing accelerated and his legs were sore, as if he had just finished a hard run.

The sound of sneakers slapping on the blacktop grew louder and closer. A voice boomed from above. "Oh my God! Man, you all right?"

Rooster slowly opened his eyes. The kid he had seen earlier had his camera lens was focused on Rooster's face. With a grunt, Rooster sat up and took inventory. His hands stung and seeped blood from several scrapes, but nothing seemed seriously damaged. He pulled himself to his feet.

"You hurt?" It was the kid again, his camera still pointed at Rooster's face.

"Don't think so." He was still slightly dazed.

A huge grin filled the kid's face. "Man, that was epic! And I got the whole thing." He gave his camera a gentle pat.

Rooster was confused. "Why were you filming me?"

The kid laughed. "I wasn't shooting you." He lowered the camera. "I was filming the car. How often you see a bright yellow Lamborghini driving down Main Street in Murfreesboro?"

"Lamborghini?"

"Yeah. It was flying and you were standing in its way. Just daydreaming." The kid looked to the sky and let out a long whistle. "Then you did your thing and..." his voice trailed off as he searched his vocabulary for the right words to describe what he had just witnessed. After a couple false starts, he blurted, "That was epic, man! This is going viral for sure!"

Rooster tried to clear the cobwebs. "What happened to the car? Didn't he stick around to see if I was alright?"

The kid pulled the stocking cap off his head, revealing a wild mop of curly black hair. He scratched the nape of his neck. "That jackass was looking down the whole time. Texting or something. Don't think he even knew what happened."

Rooster shook his head. "Wild."

The kid offered a toothy grin and pointed at his camera. "You wanna see it?"

Rooster rubbed his bloody hands on his pants. "Hell yes!"

EIGHT
Friday, May 13th
Northeastern Illinois University - Chicago, Illinois

"The Student Senate Infractions Committee will now come to order." The young man banged his gavel on the long plastic folding table. On either side of him sat a pair of serious-looking students, all just a tad too drunk with their own power.

His longish brown hair was slicked back except for a few stray strands, which fell over his forehead. His royal blue striped bowtie, pink oxford shirt, and camel hair blazer, complete with elbow patches, was all designed to portray the committee chairman as a poor man's professor wannabe. Totally sold out to typical academic groupthink, he was a slave to political correctness and deathly afraid of offending any minority group. He had no idea how to handle the three young women who stood before his committee.

His mind spun as he considered his options. The tri-captains of the women's club rugby team were accused of stealing more than twenty thousand dollars from the team. If true, they deserved to be thrown out of school and prosecuted, but they were women, and one of them was African American. He was just sick he might be painted by the university community as unfair to any discriminated group. *Plus, aren't rugby women normally lesbian? Any of them gay? Should I even be thinking this?*

He lived a tortured life. He despised himself for being born a white male, terrified he might actually, at his core, be a racist, sexist, bigot, homophobe, despite all his efforts to develop tolerance for everyone, except troglodyte neo-cons, of course. It was bred into him after all. What lengths would it take to deprogram the innate hate out of him? Would this struggle stain his entire life?

"I trust you had the opportunity to review the charges against you." His voice cracked like a hormonal teenage boy.

"Yes, Mr. Chairman," the big girl, Crystal, said. Built like a tree stump with short black hair, her bucket head was perched atop a stocky body clad in a baggy blue "Golden Eagles Rugby" sweat suit. Bright orange cross trainers peeked out from the pooling fabric layers of her oversized track pants.

The Chairman frowned. "So, what do you have to say for yourselves?"

"It's a bunch of garbage," the black girl, Tiffany, exclaimed. Put together much better than Crystal, she showcased her trim, athletic body in a formfitting navy business suit and stylish red Versace pumps. Her flawless makeup played up doe-like brown eyes and high cheekbones. With tediously straightened hair and a Coach handbag, Tiffany appeared more high-powered executive than down and dirty rugger. Her high-class woman persona shattered the moment she opened her mouth. "We didn't steal no money. That piece of crap con man stole the money!"

The Chairman pounded his gavel. *How come I don't get a hardwood block like judges in the movies?* On the plastic table, there was a meek hollow sound instead of the forceful crack of wood striking wood. It diminished his hard-earned authority a little, he thought sadly.

"We won't tolerate any more outbursts. Now let's talk about these charges."

Crystal laid a reassuring hand on Tiffany's shoulder. "Calm down, girl. Gotta lay out our case just like we talked about."

Tiffany's angry glare softened as she faced her teammate. "Yeah,

I know, but it pisses me off so much I can't help it. I'm so mad at myself for falling for his BS."

"Me too, girl," Crystal said. "But anger won't get us anywhere. Just keep your cool. Hopefully someday we'll have a chance to give that guy the ass whooping he deserves."

"The three of you." With his gavel, the Chairman indicated Crystal, Tiffany and the third woman who had yet to speak or even look up from her phone. Her long blonde hair was tied in a tight ponytail. She wore no makeup, but her dark suntanned face had a natural girl-next-door kind of beauty. Long and lean, she wore a white and pink sorority jersey-style t-shirt, faded blue jeans, and a pink pair of Keds.

"Madison," Crystal scolded. "Put your phone away!"

"Stop talking and listen to these charges," the Chairman scolded, red faced. *How come no one respects my authority?*

Madison dropped the phone to her side, but the moment the Chairman looked down to read the charges, she raised the device in front of her face again.

"Ladies," he said in an official voice. "You've been accused of misappropriation of the rugby team's treasury, with over twenty thousand dollars unaccounted for. Money allocated to the rugby team by the Student Senate. Funds collected from fellow students through the student activities fee. Monies were also contributed by rugby team members. If these allegations are true, you have not just stolen from the university, but also from your peers and teammates, which is especially despicable. This is a serious charge which could result in my committee's recommendation to the University Ethics Board that all three of you be expelled from Northeastern Illinois University."

The committee members flanking the Chairman at the cheap plastic table nodded in solemn agreement.

Crystal wrung her hands. "Mr. Chairman. As you surely read in our formal response, we were the victims of a con man posing as a sporting goods salesman. We provided a copy of the cancelled check for twenty thousand, three hundred twenty-one dollars and seventy-two cents made out to Sinclair's Sporting Emporium. You also have in front of you a photo of the real criminal in this case, a man named Davis Sinclair. As much as anyone else, we are unwitting victims of his scheme to defraud the rugby team. If you find us guilty of misappropriation of funds, we will be victimized again, but this time by the very university justice system that's supposed to protect us."

The Chairman winced at the thought of historically victimized classes insinuating his committee could treat them unfairly. It made his stomach queasy to realize he could do everything perfectly according to the Student Policy Manual and still wrong a group of potentially innocent women, not to mention an African American woman and as many as three lesbians.

Female, black and gay. He shuddered. *Can't afford to get on the wrong side of that. I'd never recover. Even if black girl's not a lesbian, the big one surely is.* He was immediately filled with guilt and shame for falling so easily into the most simple-minded stereotypes about sexuality. *An enlightened man's supposed to be above all that. But how can I be expected to single-handedly overcome a million years of prejudice, hatred and unjustified superiority that's bred into me?*

The Chairman became fully aware he was part of the evil oppressing class sometime during his freshman year. Desperate to get out, he tried to be homosexual, but never could bring himself to do the things gay men do. No matter what he did, the Chairman never seemed to get the punishment his white maleness so richly deserved. He was doomed and hated himself for it. In the years since, he had developed a fashionably fatalistic worldview. Strangely enough, it had made him quite popular with many women in the socially conscious crowd.

He held up a picture of a grinning older man with longish brown hair and his arms draped around Crystal and Tiffany's shoulders. All three held longneck Buds and looked glassy-eyed. "You're telling this committee a photo of you partying with some old guy is evidence you didn't steal those funds?"

Tiffany could hold back no longer. "That's the mo-fo who

cheated us! You find him and you find the money!"

The Chairman opened his mouth to respond.

"Oh my God!" Madison exclaimed.

Everyone turned to face her, but she was hopelessly engrossed in her phone. She looked up. "I say that out loud?"

Crystal looked up to the sky. This was not going well. She hissed, "Madison, put that phone away. You lost your mind?"

"What're you looking at?" Tiffany demanded.

Oblivious to the commotion she had caused, Madison moved so Tiffany could watch the tiny screen with her. "You gotta see this video," she said as pleasantly as if they were sharing a latte instead of fighting to save their academic lives. "It's the most-watched on YouTube today."

With growing hopelessness, Crystal glanced between her friends and the unhappy committee members. The Chairman had turned purple and appeared as if his head was about to explode.

Tiffany blurted out, "Holy shit!"

The Chairman sat in slack jawed amazement. *Has my hearing actually devolved into the accused watching YouTube videos? How much less respect could these three show me? Don't they care at all I have the power to get them all thrown outta school?*

One of his cohorts rose sheepishly and walked around the table. "Lemme see."

Crystal joined and the four of them watched together, letting out involuntary yelps of excitement and amazement. The rogue committee member glanced at his colleagues, all decorum now officially thrown out the window. "You gotta see this."

They scrambled to see for themselves. The Chairman laid his head on the table. How much more humiliation could he take?

Madison was about to restart the video when Crystal interrupted. "Wait a minute. Go back to the very end."

Madison manipulated the phone until Crystal yelled, "Pause right there! That's the guy!"

"What guy?" several of them asked in unison.

"The con man." Crystal shook her head in total disbelief. "The guy who swindled us. I don't believe it. Swear that's him!" Her head swiveled as she searched for someone to agree with her.

A committee member snatched the photo from in front of the Chairman. "Let me see."

The group looked between the photo and smart phone image. They all excitedly spoke at once.

"Son of a bitch," Tiffany shrieked. "It shoulda splattered him. When I get my hands on him he'll by God wish it had!"

"He didn't really do that," a committee member said. "That's obviously staged and edited. No way anyone could really do that. Definitely not some old guy

"Forget whether it was real or not, you idiots," Crystal said. "Don't you see? We know where he is now. They said at the beginning of the video they were somewhere in Tennessee. Now we know where to find this guy."

The bedlam was interrupted by the hollow sound of a gavel striking plastic. The room grew quiet. They all faced the Chairman. "Bring that over here," he said. "Just unbelievable. I have to see for myself what is so amazing, it caused all of you to make an utter mockery of these proceedings."

Madison sat next to him and restarted the video. It opened with a close-up of young man in a wool ski cap, curly black tendrils hanging out the sides.

"This is Simon Carter out and about in Murfreesboro, Tennessee. Let's see what's goin' down here on Main Street." The view swung around toward the road. After panning the block, the video closed in on a yellow sports car as it turned a corner.

"Amazing," Simon exclaimed. "How often you see a Lamborghini driving down the streets of your town? I know I never seen one here before."

As the car finished the turn and picked up speed, the shot zeroed in on a man standing in the street. He stared at something in his hands as the car hurtled toward him.

"Hey, look out!" Simon shouted.

The man glanced at the camera, then noticed the Lamborghini racing toward him. Just when it seemed inevitable he would become road kill, the guy dropped into a deep squat, his butt nearly touching the ground, and jumped straight up. He deftly pulled his knees up and turned his body into a ball.

"Good God!" the Chairman cried, transfixed by the video.

The car was a yellow blur as it flew beneath the man. The roof barely passed under him as he hit the apex of his jump. Rotating so his back was parallel to the ground, he seemed to briefly hang in midair and then plummeted back to earth. His heels hit before he fell onto his backside.

"Holy jumpin'!" Simon yelled. "That really just happen? This is epic!"

The view bounced and slid amid the sounds of slapping sneakers and heavy breathing as the cameraman labored to hold the shot while he ran to the jump scene. The camera closed in on the man on the ground.

Simon shouted, "Dude! You all right?"

The shot stopped on a close-up of the man's upside-down face, eyes closed, no movement evident.

"Oh my God!" Simon exclaimed. "Man, you all right?"

The man's eyes slowly opened and stared into the camera.

"Pause that," the Chairman demanded.

Madison froze the shot on the man's face. "It's only got a couple seconds left. You basically seen the whole thing."

"Give me that picture." He held his palm over the table. A colleague gave him the photo of Crystal and Tiffany with the mystery man. The Chairman compared the print to Madison's phone. "Crazy. Obviously the same man in both pictures."

"Exactly," Crystal said. "That's the guy. Now we track down that jerk to find out what he did with our money."

"Of course," the Chairman said. "The fact you had your picture taken with the guy in this video shot in... in..."

"Tennessee," a committee member offered.

"In Tennessee," he continued, "proves absolutely zero about the money that's disappeared from the rugby team's treasury."

Tiffany grew agitated. "How can you say that?" She jabbed her finger violently at the photo. "Jackass made us look like idiots. Now we're gonna find him and teach him a thing or two."

The Chairman smiled knowingly. "Ok. Tell me how this video, which I admit is incredible if it's real, tells us anything about what happened to the money."

Crystal and Tiffany stared at each other in awkward silence. "Shouldn't the university investigate this guy?" Crystal finally asked.

"I'm sorry," the Chairman frowned. "That's really not within the purview of this committee. I'm not going to be a part of committing school resources to a potential wild goose chase."

"Wild goose chase?!" Tiffany moved aggressively toward the table, but Crystal quickly used her body to restrain her friend.

"If all this malarkey's actually true," the Chairman continued, "then it's a matter for the police. Don't you think?"

Madison, still sitting next to him, clasped his hand with both of hers and moved her face closer. "Can you please give us a little more time to prove it was him?" She batted her eyelashes for extra effect.

Crystal and Tiffany stared in amazement. Who was this flirting girl and what had she done with the real Madison?

The Chairman's heart raced as he deeply inhaled the intoxicating scent of Madison's Ralph Lauren Romance perfume. Her face was close enough to smell minty fresh breath. *She's really something.* The outside world faded away until it was just the two of them. He unabashedly drank her in, her amazing aroma, the youthful beauty of her face, the playful glint in her eyes. He considered going in for a kiss.

Anger seeped into Madison's voice. "We only found out a few minutes ago this bastard was in Tennessee." She breathed deeply and forced an impish grin as her tone turned mirthful. "Surely, in the interests of justice you can give us a teensy weensy bit more time to prove we're telling the truth. It's not like you have to decide anything today."

He was desperate to find some reason to accommodate her. *Maybe she's actually into me.* "Well," he mirrored her playful voice. "Our report to the University Ethics Board isn't due for three whole weeks. If you were able to recover the money before then, we might be able to make this whole thing go away."

"That's wonderful," Madison squealed. She threw her arms around him and planted a wet kiss on his cheek. "Thank you so much!" She leapt up and raced around the table. "C'mon girls." She ushered her friends quickly toward the door. "Let's go open a can of Tennessee whoop-ass!"

"That was awesome," Crystal said as they walked out.

"Yeah," Tiffany chimed. "Who knew you had that in you."

The hint of a smile cracked Madison's stone-faced expression. "Desperate times call for desperate measures." The meeting room door closed behind them.

With eyes closed and a Cheshire cat grin, the Chairman raised his hand to his nose, soaking in the lingering aroma of Madison's perfume. Oblivious to the committee members' quizzical stares, his mind played out a series of ridiculous scenarios. They all ended locked in a passionate embrace with Madison, soul mates, together forever.

He indulged his inner caveman for a few moments. *What would the PC crowd say if they could read my thoughts now?* He realized he had no clue how to land someone like Madison. *This woman's totally different from any of the tree-huggers I normally associate with. Last girl I dated smelled like Campbell's Soup, for goodness sake. She refused to shave her legs for 'environmental reasons'. How can I ever go back to that hell after a close-up look at perfection? That's like going back to hamburger after Filet Mignon. At least I think it would be like that if the evil conglomerates who owned the beef farms didn't inject the cows with hormones and chemicals, and slaughter them in such an inhumane way in their single-minded pursuit of maximum profits, so I could actually eat red meat without being ostracized by all my friends.*

He shook his head and smiled. *I bet she eats beef.*

Grudgingly, he admitted Madison was totally out of his league. However, he knew with every fiber of his being he simply had to possess her, and so far in his young life he got everything he ever really wanted.

NINE
Saturday, May 14th
Jersey City, New Jersey

"Stella, get me my mother lovin' gun," Tony Ferrentino bellowed. "Cause if you don't shut up for the love of everything holy, I'm gonna blow my brains out!"

Completely undeterred by her husband's words, Stella continued talking, but Tony only heard, "Blah, blah, blah."

Tony referred to himself as a 'businessman'. In fact, that was exactly how his calling card read: "Anthony J Ferrentino: Businessman". In reality he was a low level wise guy. He had certainly had made more of his life than his dear sainted mother, God bless her soul, ever believed possible. Of course, she thought he wasn't smart enough to blow his own nose. The neighborhood consensus said he was destined to die young as hired muscle for one of the families.

Tony had shown them all, building a gambling enterprise that took wagers on anything, from anyone. Successful, but small time enough to remain independent, his relatively minimal action had little impact on the big boys' business. Despite the low-IQ jokes from the neighborhood, Tony had been smart enough to build a Rolodex of contacts from the families who worked his little corner of Jersey City,

New Jersey. He constantly found ways to be helpful, mainly by referring potential clients to their drug and prostitution operations.

Ferrentino's, his small bar on Fairview Avenue, was well-known by the mobster paisans as an establishment happy to serve as many free drinks as they could handle. This practice had the double benefit of endearing Tony to the families and making it easier to launder gambling profits, which was the only reason to own a bar in the first place.

"You listenin' to me?!" Stella screamed next to his head. Looking like a sterotypical Italian grandmother, her gray-streaked black hair was pulled into a tight bun. Fire-engine-red lipstick made the thick black whiskers on her upper lip stand out. Her flowing zebra-print caftan with the too-deep neckline showcased the tops of two leathery breasts, which really should have been hidden from view. Her long red fingernails wrapped around a Virginia Slims Menthol Light 120 like eagle talons around a fish, the cigarette's filter smeared red with lipstick.

"Holy Christmas cannoli, Stella, shut your big stinkin' pie hole." Tony had been incapable of swearing since the age of twelve when his mother beat him half to death with a wooden coat hanger after hearing him drop F-bombs with his friends. Afterward, she prayed to the Virgin Mary and asked the Blessed Mother of Jesus to curse little Tony with leprosy that would make his balls fall off if he ever swore again. This was a woman who spent every Sunday at St. Aloysius church lighting votives and praying to St. Edmund the Martyr to strike down people who cut her off in traffic. Tony figured it best not to take any chances. In the 45 years since, his speech pattern developed into the Godfather meets Mary Poppins.

"I'm tryin' to get a little exercise here." Tony spread his arms to indicate the treadmill on which he slowly walked. His twenty-minutes per mile waddle failed to keep pace with Tony's decadent pasta-centric diet. At five-foot-ten and three hundred twenty pounds, his stomach pushed against the black and gold jacket of the track suit which had been his uniform for the past twenty years. He had them in all colors, but otherwise they were completely identical, a solid color with two contrasting stripes running down the outsides of the pants and sleeves. An out-of-control shrub of black and gray hair poked from the neck of the white ribbed 'wife-beater' Tony wore under his jacket.

A mobster heavy sent directly from central casting, Tony's pronounced forehead featured thick eyebrows a few hairs short of a full unibrow. His fleshy face had dark eye bags and droopy jowls. A big double chin hid most of his neck.

"Little Tony needs to spend more time with you," Stella continued, between hard pulls on her cigarette. "A boy needs to spend time with his father."

Tony exploded, "Jumpin' Art Garfunkel on a popsicle stick! Little Tony's twenty-nine years old, for the love of Major League Baseball. That boy needs to get his head out of his... ah... nether regions."

"He's a good boy. He's just a late bloomer."

Tony laughed hard. *A late bloomer. That kid's been a screw-up since the womb. Maybe I been too easy on him. My dad would've never let me get away with half the stuff little Tony does. Maybe I need a heavier hand with him.* "I'll see about gettin' him more involved in the business," he declared, more to himself than to Stella.

Stella continued to prattle, but her voice faded into background noise as the television caught Tony's attention.

"Holy Canasta!" Tony fumbled for the remote, which sat in one of the treadmill's two water bottle holders. A rock glass of Amaretto on ice was nestled in the other. He hit rewind. The weekend edition of the local morning show, Tony paused on a close-up of an older female anchor who, based on her obvious facelift and extensive botox, could barely hold off the hordes of perky young anchorettes lined up to steal her job. Over her shoulder was a graphic with the words, "Viral Video."

"Hey Stella," Tony growled. "Put a cork in it and watch this goombah with the car on the TV."

Stella stopped and stood next to the treadmill as Tony hit play and turned up the volume.

"Look at the latest viral video making the rounds in cyberspace," the brunette news reader said. The clip filled the screen as she continued, "This amazing footage of a man in Murfreesboro, Tennessee, jumping over a Lamborghini has received more than three million hits on YouTube."

"Oh my word!" Stella exclaimed as the man in the video took flight just as it seemed inevitable he would be killed by the speeding car. "That real, Tony?"

"Looks real to me." Tony's gruff tone suggested Stella best accept his opinion as fact. "I thought those Tennessee rednecks spent all their time catchin' catfish with their hands. Who knew they could jump over cars?"

"Catch fish with their hands?" Stella asked in horror and amazement, her cigarette glowing red as she took a deep draw.

"Yeah," Tony laughed. "They call it 'noogaling' or somethin' like that."

Stella blew out a long stream of smoke. "You're makin' that up. No one can catch fish with their hands."

"I'm tellin' you," Tony insisted. "Those southerners ain't normal. What with their noogaling, and marryin' their sisters, and jumping over cars, and their trucks with the big gun racks." Amused with his own words, the big man laughed so hard he choked up. Soon the laughs had turned into a loud coughing fit, which nearly doubled him over. He reached for his cocktail and between hacks gulped some of the amber liquid. After he put the glass back in the cup holder, he saw the video play out to a close-up of the jumper's head. The face was on the screen for less than second, but Tony recognized the man immediately.

Startled to see that piece of garbage Sinclair Davis in such an unexpected place, Tony stepped sideways, his foot half on the moving tread and half on the stationary treadmill frame. Thrown off balance, he flew forward into the front bar. His feet flopped behind him on the still-moving tread. He let out an "Ooof," as if someone had fluffed a big pillow. Somehow Tony hooked his right arm on the rail and saved himself from a full face-plant followed by being hurled off the machine. He swung his beefy left arm at the control panel until he managed to hit the big red stop button. The treadmill slowly came to a halt and Tony pulled himself to his feet with some difficulty.

Stella's cigarette dangled from the corner of her mouth. "Tony," she said unemotionally as if Tony's near disaster was a daily occurrence. "What on earth are you doin'?"

Her husband breathed hard. Between gulps of Amaretto, he jabbed his fat finger at the screen. "You see that guy?"

"The one who jumped the car?"

Tony nodded.

"Of course I did. I was standin' right next to you, silly."

"No you dingbat. The close-up of his face?"

"No. What're you so agitated about?"

"That jackalope on TV was Sinclair Davis."

"So?"

"Sinclair Davis is a piece of trash. That son of a goat lost one hundred large and then stiffed me."

Stella raised her eyebrows. "One hundred large?"

Tony rolled his eyes. "A hundred thousand dollars."

"Holy cow. How'd he do that?"

Tony sighed. *Don't this woman understand how gambling works?*" He lost the bet and disappeared."

"Why'd you give him so much credit?"

"How I run my business is none of your concern," Tony bellowed. "You always got enough cash for shoe shoppin', don't you?"

"Ok, tough guy. Whatcha gonna do 'bout it?"

Tony drained his glass and considered his options. "Tell little Tony to get a bag packed. We got a road trip to Tennessee."

TEN

Buddy's black leather living room sofa had become Rooster's regular resting place. *Probably an indentation of my ass on the cushion.* Not much had changed since Rooster's first visit to the house nine months earlier. Instead of Coors, they now sipped Michelob Ultra. At some point they had decided they were fat and needed to cut calories. Now they drank the low-carb, low calorie Ultra, but polished off twice as much. The dust on the TV components was nine months thicker. Instead of fishing, today's television program was about Alaskan moose hunting. A pair of underwear still lay on the coffee table. Rooster wondered whether it had been the same pair the whole time, or if Buddy had some underwear rotation system.

As their friendship had grown, Rooster discovered Buddy was a man of many mysteries. *Why keep underpants on the coffee table?* Rooster had never seen him put on or remove his briefs in the living room. *They clean or dirty?*

The TV was locked on outdoor sportsmen and NASCAR 24-7. *He have some special hunting and fishing cable package?* How had he accumulated so many guns and knives? Whenever Rooster came by, Buddy showed off a new gun or hunting knife. Yet Rooster never saw any of them again. *Where's he keep them? And what's with the glow-in-the-dark perfect teeth? No one has teeth that flawless. Why would he spend hundreds or thousands on a dazzling smile when his entire wardrobe's probably worth less than three hundred bucks?* Rooster had rarely seen him in anything other than a promotional free t-shirt. Today's selection featured the Cookie Monster with the words, "*Got Milk?*" *How does he drink so much and never get drunk? How does Buddy know everyone, everywhere he goes?*

Whenever Rooster asked him about these enigmas, Buddy skillfully changed the subject or threw out his homespun adages. *Where'd he come up with all those crazy sayings anyway?*

Buddy finished his third Ultra and set the bottle next to the mysterious underwear. "Guess I'm a little thickheaded. Why you have to go to that Baptist church this Sunday?"

Rooster smiled. "I've gotta get my front door back."

Buddy raised an eyebrow. "I may be stump stupid, but I ain't getting the relation between church and your front door."

Rooster told him the whole story, from how the landlord took his door, to when the benevolence lady paid half his rent and tied the balance to church attendance, to his 'religious experience' when he jumped the Lamborghini. He pulled up the YouTube video on his phone so Buddy could see for himself.

When Rooster finished, Buddy sat in slack-jawed wonderment. "That story's quite the humdinger."

"Wouldn't believe it myself if it didn't happen to me, but I gotta get my door back. Last night when I was asleep, some cat wandered in and jumped on my face. About had a heart attack."

Buddy burst into laughter. "Son, I swear you're too lazy to scratch your own ass. Either that or you ain't got the sense God give a Billy goat. Why haven't you covered up that door hole with a slab of wood or something?"

"I hung up a blanket."

"Got a hunk of wood in the garage that'll do. We'll throw it in the truck and take it to your place when we're done here."

"Thanks."

"Tell me what all they're making you do to get the rest of your rent money."

"Gotta go to church the next two Sundays and the next two Wednesday nights."

"That oughta be entertaining," Buddy chuckled.

"Why don't you come with me?"

"Hell, no," Buddy bellowed. "I get within five hundred yards of a house of worship, I probably get struck by lightning. That, and I'm not getting up before ten on a Sunday. The only way you get me into church would be if they handed out free bloody marys as you walked in the front door."

"What about Wednesday night?"

"Hell no! I don't need no help with my house payment. What're they making you do on Wednesday?"

"They call it a small group. Some sorta bible study."

"You gonna be sitting with the preacher?" Buddy grinned.

"Naw. Some woman named Marcie Dexter leads the group. I gotta report to her so I get credit for showing up."

Buddy's eyes brightened. "You say Marcie Dexter?"

"Yes. Why?"

"How many people in this here small group?"

"I don't know. About five or ten, I guess."

"You do know who Marcie Dexter is, don't you?"

"Never heard of her."

"She the widow of Carleton Dexter."

"Who's Carleton Dexter?"

"His kinfolk owned half of Murfreesboro back in the day."

"So?"

"His daddy sold half their farm to developers when Murfreesboro was just taking off. Then he sold the rest of it after it had done took off. This house is sitting on land that used to belong to old man Dexter."

"That's interesting," Rooster yawned.

"Son," Buddy chortled. "Your brain is about as useful as a rubber crutch. When old man Dexter passed, he left everything to Carleton. When Carleton passed, he left it all, lock, stock, and barrel, to his widow Marcie Dexter. That woman teaching your bible study might be the richest woman in Murfreesboro. She got more money than Carter got liver pills."

"I don't know what that means."

Buddy flashed his dazzling smile. "You just ponder it awhile, son. You'll understand directly."

"So," Rooster sighed. "I'm gonna be spending the next two Wednesdays with a rich old widow."

"Who said she's old?"

Rooster shrugged. "Just assumed. Aren't most widows old?"

"Marcie's about the same age as you, and she's just about as pretty as she is rich. You need to sidle up to this little filly and lay on some of that so-called charm you're always crowing about. Then ladle on some of this here B.S. about your 'religious experience'. That oughta impress the church folk."

"Wasn't kidding," Rooster argued half-heartedly. "It *was* a religious experience." Even as he protested, Rooster imagined the possibilities. Perhaps fortune was about to smile on him.

Maybe God is giving me another chance.

ELEVEN

It was 10 pm when the red Suzuki Grand Vitara stopped in front of the house on Lytle Street and the three young women tumbled out. The street was devoid of activity and the house was completely dark except for a single porch light. Soupy humidity hung heavy in the air.

"Feels like a steam bath out here," Tiffany complained. "Gonna ruin my hair."

Tired and rumpled in her oversized t-shirt and extra long baggy gym shorts, Crystal ignored her. "This the right address?"

"I'm serious," Tiffany said. "Gonna look like a French Poodle. Who can live in this heat? And what's that buzzing?"

Crystal laughed. "That's the insects, girl."

"Bugs?!" Tiffany exclaimed. "Sounds like high-tension power lines. How many bugs are there?"

Madison lit the flashlight app on her phone. Seemingly not bothered a bit by the humidity, her pink spaghetti-strap tank revealed a taut stomach. Blue-jean shorts highlighted mile-long legs. Her flowered flip-flops slapped a few steps. She directed the beam toward the numbers on the mailbox. "This is the place."

"Why's it so abandoned at ten on a Saturday?" Tiffany was put together like a fashion model in designer clothes and Michael Kors accessories, although her laboriously straightened hair was already curling at the ends. "Thought this was a rugby house. Tennessee ruggers a bunch of lightweights?"

"I don't know," Crystal said. "I thought for sure someone would be here partying. It is Saturday night, right?"

Madison turned off her flashlight. "No sense standing here wondering what's what. Why don't we just knock on the door?"

The three walked toward the huge 1940s craftsman-style house. As they stepped on the porch and into the glow of the light, a cloud of insects swarmed them.

Tiffany swatted at a mosquito. "These bugs or freakin' birds? Never seen bugs so big. This place is crazy. How's anyone live here? I need to get me back to the city."

Crystal pushed the doorbell. "Quit being such a drama queen, Tiff. You sayin' there aren't bugs in the city?"

"Humph!" Tiffany replied, hands defiantly on her hips.

Crystal stared straight ahead, confident her non-attention would irritate her friend more than anything she could ever say.

The weathered oak door swung open to reveal a petite young woman in a white t-shirt and plaid pajama pants. Brown hair pulled into a high ponytail which protruded slightly to the right, she peered at them with sleepy eyes. "Can I help y'all with something?" She asked with a Southern twang.

Crystal's voice was anxious. "We're the rugby players from Northeastern Illinois University. Jessica said we could crash here a few days when I spoke to her yesterday."

Recognition flashed in the girl's eyes. "Jessica said y'all weren't coming 'til tomorrow." She flashed a welcoming smile. "My name's Peyton. Welcome to Murfreesboro."

Everyone crammed in the nondescript foyer as introductions were made. Peyton closed the door and the insect buzz immediately fell silent. Her voice grew excited. "So y'all looking for that fella in Simon Carter's video."

Tiffany gritted her teeth. "Yeah. That con artist got us on the verge of getting thrown outta school. You know who he is?"

"Seen him once or twice at the bars. We all seen him, but none of the girls know who he is. Neither does Simon."

"You talked to the guy who shot the video?" Tiffany asked.

"Sure. He shoots our matches for the team website. He's been a minor celebrity on campus since his video went viral. Unfortunately, I think it's all going straight to his head."

"You think we can talk to him?" Crystal asked hopefully.

"Don't see why not, but I'm totally forgetting my manners. My momma would tan my hide if she saw the way I kept y'all standing in the hallway like a bunch of Jehovah's Witnesses. Let me help you get your stuff and show you where you can crash."

"Thanks," Crystal said. "Where's everyone else?"

The loud buzzing returned as Peyton opened the door and they all headed for the car. "They're all at The Boulevard. That's a sports bar down the street."

"You ever seen our guy at the Boulevard?" Madison asked.

Peyton scrunched her face. "I haven't, but some of the others might've. When we saw the video, just about everyone in the house had seen your guy out one time or another."

After popping the back hatch, Crystal handed out gear, and they hauled everything into the house. Peyton led them up a creaky staircase to a room just off the upstairs landing. "Sydney's gone for the weekend." The large room with dark brown paneling smelled of musty carpeting and Lemon Pledge. "Y'all can sleep here. You can use the bed if you want."

The visitors thanked her as they dropped their backpacks. "You don't know how much we appreciate this," Madison offered.

"The least we can do for fellow ruggers," Peyton said. "We'll help you find this fella and show him what happens when someone messes with our rugby sisters."

Tiffany smiled. "How we find this bar you mentioned?"

"You can walk there in less than ten minutes, but give me a jiffy to pretty myself up, and I'll walk over there with you and introduce y'all to the other girls."

TWELVE

The silver BMW Z4 Roadster idled quietly, its headlights off, as the man inside stared at the dilapidated house into which the rugby players had disappeared. Staying out of sight while he followed them from Illinois to Tennessee had been more difficult than he could have imagined. The worst part was being unable to allow the two hundred fifty-five horses under the hood to run free. That stupid Suzuki topped out at sixty-three miles per hour. It seemed like he drove the ten-hour trip in third gear. He had been passed by a Prius for goodness sake. The whole ordeal had been a bigger blow to his ego than he cared to admit.

What am I even doing here? After Madison had walked out of his Infractions Committee hearing, determined to find the car-jumping guy, the Chairman knew in his soul he had to stay close to her. Here he was in Murfreesboro, no clue what to do next.

Just keep an eye on her and when the opportunity shows up, pounce on it. He hoped he would recognize it when it arrived. He sank down as the front door swung open and the three rugby players walked out with the girl who had greeted them. Madison towered over the other three. Her long legs and short shorts made his heart race. The four women turned their backs to him and started toward Middle Tennessee Boulevard. He waited until he was fairly certain they would not look back.

He turned off the ignition and carefully pushed the door open, but completely forgot about the dome light. When the car interior lit up like a Christmas tree, the Chairman scrambled out and pushed the door closed with a loud "thunk." He crouched near the front fender, relieved the girls had not seen nor heard him. He stood, pushed the lock button on his key fob and immediately hit the dirt when he remembered, literally as his thumb pressed down, the car flashed its lights and beeped the horn when locked. *What's wrong with me?*

In his mind he was a suave and debonair James Bond. His actions more resembled Mr. Bean in reality. He watched the girls who seemed without a care in the world, and he was slightly irritated. *They're so oblivious to what's going on around them. What if they were being stalked by someone dangerous? They should really pay better attention.* If he was honest with himself, he did not fear for their safety. He was actually annoyed to be so invisible amid flashing lights and honking horns. *Am I really so harmless, I fade into the background in every situation? Got to change that.*

He surveyed his clothes as he dusted himself off. Italian loafers with no socks, plaid shorts in NEIU blue and gold, and a lime green Polo. He rolled his eyes. *Why not add a sweater draped over my shoulders with the arms tied around my neck? Yeah, genius, you won't stand out wearing that in Backwater, Tennessee.* He walked toward the end of the block, but heard a wheezing sound with each step, like an asthmatic gasping for breath. He stopped and listened intently. Nothing but the hum of insects. As soon as he started again, the wheezing resumed.

"What's that?"

After a few starts and stops, he realized the noise came from his shoes, as if a mini whoopee cushion was attached to each foot. When he tried to ignore it, the sound only became more noticeable and intense. *Anyone else hear that?* To his horror, it got louder with each step. He felt about as sneaky as a Clydesdale. The Chairman clomped to the end of the block, then turned right on the main road.

The women had crossed the street, but he remained on the opposite side. *Can they hear my wheezing shoes? How can they not when every step sounds like air brakes on a big rig?* He hung back and allowed the distance between them to grow. *Can't have them looking back to see where all this racket's coming from.* After five minutes, the women disappeared into a brick building on the corner of Middle Tennessee Blvd and Main Street. A large sign over the door said, "The Boulevard Sports Bar." He lingered on the sidewalk and pretended to watch traffic, relieved his maddening shoes were silenced a moment. He made sure the women were in the bar to stay awhile.

I've come this far. If they see me now, they'll really think I'm nuts. But would that assessment really be wrong? It's certainly a little wacky to chase her five hundred miles through four states. The Chairman stared wistfully at the front door and daydreamed about what magic could develop if he and Madison somehow got together. At that moment he really did not care if everything he had done the past twenty-four-plus hours was totally deranged. It was actually liberating to truly not worry about what anyone, except for Madison of course, thought about him. *Been such a slave to groupthink and doing the right thing. Well, the politically correct thing. Doing exactly what's expected of me.* He smiled. His crowd would consider him off his rocker. For the first time he could remember, the Chairman did not give a flying flip what those people thought. *I'm gonna keep my eye on the prize, no matter what it takes for me to get it.*

He crossed the street and cautiously approached the sports bar. He peered through the big plate glass windows and saw his own reflection more clearly than the inside. Only when he pressed close to the glass and cupped his hands around his face could he block out enough light to see inside. After a scan of the room, he found Madison and the two other NEIU girls, along with the short girl from the house and five other young women. They all stood near the end of the bar, each with a full shot glass held high. They laughed and chanted. He could not make out what they said, but when they finished, everyone threw back their shots and slammed the empty glasses on the bar.

Madison positively glowed with a huge carefree smile. She spoke easily with the other women, whom the Chairman had presumed were strangers to her before tonight. *Imagine where I could go in life with a woman like that by my side.* His eyes drank in her long athletic body. Then a thought struck him. *What the hell they doing in there?* A strange anger rose up as he watched them laugh and carry on. *Supposedly they came here to save their academic lives, to find this car-jumping guy. And now they're partying? Doesn't Madison take any of this seriously? Those other two must be a bad influence. Surely she'd be out looking for this guy they claim conned them outta all that money if it weren't for these two irresponsible girls pulling poor Madison in the wrong direction.* He eyed Crystal and Tiffany with disdain. The Chairman searched the room for a place inside where he could keep an eye on things from the shadows. He wanted to get closer, to see if he could overhear their conversation.

When his vision drifted back to the women, he felt like he had been punched in the gut. Madison and some guy were engaged in an animated discussion. They talked and laughed and touched each other's arms. They leaned close to speak in each other's ears. *Is it really noisy enough that they have to get that close?* Pangs of jealousy and helplessness overwhelmed him. *Should be me in there doing that with her. I should go in there and claim what's mine.* His heart sank. He knew he could not and would not do anything like that. The guy putting the moves on Madison was everything the Chairman was not. Tall, athletic, charming. Probably the football team's quarterback, or the basketball point guard. He considered barging in to pull Madison away from him, but in his imagination he was always bolder and tougher than in reality. After entertaining his delusional perfect world fantasies a moment, the Chairman knew it was ridiculous to even consider such insanity.

This kind of guy gave me wedgies in high school. This guy would kick my ass if I made that play. The Chairman was all about self-preservation. It would be much more difficult to win Madison if he was physically humiliated right in front of her. The sports bar was this guy's home field, an arena in which the Chairman could not compete. Get him in a formal debate and the Chairman would wipe the floor with him. Of course debating prowess never picked up a girl, at least not a good looking one.

His mind drifted. He constructed a scenario where he put Mr. Jockguy in his place and Madison thanked him with a big kiss for saving her from such a troglodyte. As the scene played out in his mind, it was completely unexpected when the big hand grabbed his shoulder while someone barked, "Hey!" low enough to make Barry White envious. In total shock and confusion, the Chairman cried, "Arrrhhh!", leapt forward, and smashed his face into the glass. Desperate to escape, he tangled his own feet and fell in a heap on the sidewalk.

A cute redhead, who had just left the bar, hid a giggle with her hand as she stepped over him. A large menacing man in a "Boulevard Sports Bar" embroidered golf shirt stood over him. His head was shaved clean and his neck thick with muscle. He reached out his hand. "Hey, buddy? You all right?"

Ignoring the outstretched arm, the Chairman scrambled to his feet. "What the hell, man?"

"I was gonna invite you inside," the man laughed. "We saw you staring in the window. Honestly, it was a little creepy."

The Chairman's heart skipped a beat. Had Madison seen him in the window? *Gotta get away from here. Last thing I need is to be the center of attention.* He turned and quickly clomped away, his shoes wheezing. He swallowed his jealousy and forced his mind back to the present. *If those irresponsible girls are gonna put Madison at risk of getting thrown outta school, I have to step up and save her. This is my big chance to prove myself to her. I'll show off my guile and cunning and win her over with my big brain. Some women actually find that sort of thing sexy.*

"I'll go find him myself," he mumbled as he wheezed his way back to the BMW. The guy had stolen twenty grand from Madison and that was unacceptable.

THIRTEEN

Despite possessing no investigative skills whatsoever, the Chairman fancied himself an ultra-cool Horatio Caine cruising the streets in search of the villain, looking awesome in his super hot car. The past two days of bumbling, pratfalls, and humiliation had been more Inspector Jacques Clouseau.

Fighting boredom and sleepiness after just thirty minutes on the road, the Chairman searched his MP3 player for something to focus his brain and lift his spirits, when an album caught his attention. *Perfect.* His adrenaline surged as the *TV's Greatest Cop Show Themes* soundtrack blasted *Hawaii Five-O*.

Ninety minutes later, the fuel gauge on empty and the theme from *Barnaby Jones* hitting its final crescendo, the Chairman stopped at a mini mart. He pulled up to the pump and reached for his wallet. It was gone. He searched the car in a panic, not realizing he had left it on the counter at the Flying J Travel Plaza in Franklin, Kentucky. The billfold was now in an RV Park outside Moscow, Idaho. The Chairman's VISA card had largely financed a nice gypsy family's annual pilgrimage to the Flamenco Dance Festival in Chewelah, Washington.

Fortunately, the Chairman kept two hundred dollars of emergency cash hidden under the spare tire. Pleased with his MacGyver-like ability to escape any difficult situation, he pumped thirty dollars of gas and decided to check on Madison. He arrived on Lytle Street at one a.m., the rugby house engulfed in a wild party. Music blared, cars were parked haphazardly, and people wandered everywhere carrying red Solo cups. His heart sank when he saw Madison in the shadows, getting up close and personal with that same jock-guy from The Boulevard.

What's going on? These girls serious about tracking down Davis Sinclair or not? Am I the only one with any sense of urgency? He fought the desire to give her a tongue-lashing for her irresponsibility. *She's spending entirely too much time with this quarterback-type. Here I am, doing all the leg work while this slapdoodle's making time with my girl.*

As he considered the unfairness of it all, anger bubbled up, compelling him to go inside the house, convinced something inside had become a corrupting influence on his beloved Madison. Without caring who might spot him, the Chairman marched to the front door. As he reached for it, an enormous hand, which dwarfed his own, came out of nowhere to grab his wrist and effortlessly pull his hand away from the doorknob.

"What the hell, man?!" The Chairman turned to give this interloper a piece of his mind, but quickly swallowed his words. The huge hand was attached to an equally gigantic body, the guy's head big as a pumpkin and his neck thick with muscle. *Probably one of those steroid-addicted bodybuilders.* The Chairman searched the guy's face for acne. *Probably rotting away his brain right now.*

The giant peered down with sleepy eyes. "Hey friend? Where you think you're going?"

The Chairman's face turned stern. "For three years I been tracking the Hillbilly Beast of north western Kentucky. I have strong reason to believe he's inside this house right now."

The big guy stared blankly. His tongue flicked out, iguana-like, to lick his lips. The Chairman was flabbergasted. *What's with this guy? Do they understand sarcasm in the south?* "I'm going inside. Where else would I be going?"

The man squeezed his eyes closed and blinked a few times. "You haven't paid yet."

"Paid what?" *What a mouth-breather this guy is.*

"It's five bucks to get inside."

"Seriously?" The Chairman noticed the giant's left hand clutched a large pile of cash. The right one maintained a death grip on the Chairman's wrist. "What's so special in there?"

A hint of agitation entered the big guy's tone. "Hey, little buddy, I didn't recruit you to come here. I'm just collecting money from people who want to go inside. You're the one who came up to me. So either fork it over, or scram."

This man isn't very pleasant. Where's this Southern hospitality I've heard so much about?

The big guy released the Chairman's wrist and held out a meaty palm. His furrowed brow and narrowed eyes made it clear there would be trouble if the Chairman did not comply. The Chairman reluctantly peeled a twenty from his shrinking money stash. The giant made change in damp, sweaty bills and scribbled a huge dollar sign on the back of the Chairman's hand with a green Sharpie. "Now you can come and go as much as you want."

The Chairman shook his head and stepped inside. *Quite the crack security procedure this oaf's come up with. What's stopping anyone with a green marker from coming in without paying? Were his parents siblings?*

So many partiers were stuffed into the house, the Chairman had to shuffle sideways, his chest thumping with every beat of the music's driving bass. Shouting and laughter added to the din, which completely drowned out the Chairman's wheezing shoes, much to his delight. The mass of humanity expanded and contracted like a single organism with people shuffling and swaying as if in a wave pool.

The Chairman felt like the only one out of step with the crowd as people stumbled into him and stepped on his feet. Only his cat-like reflexes and Super Mario jumping ability kept the splashing drinks from soaking him. One guy, making wild arm gestures in the midst of an animated conversation, nearly jammed his cigarette into the Chairman's eyeball. A matador would have been proud of the

Chairman's deft twist away from danger. "Hey, jerkwad!" His words were swallowed by the cacophony. The smoking offender continued his enthusiastic story in blissful ignorance. *Can this place get any more backwards? Imagine? Allowing smoking inside the house. What a bunch of Philistines!*

No sooner had he recovered from his brush with permanent disfigurement, than an especially inebriated woman appeared from nowhere to wrap her arms around his neck and plant a big sloppy, beer-soaked kiss on his lips. As she pulled away, the woman got a better look at her assault victim. "You're not Charlie," she slurred. "Keep your hands off me, pervert!" She slapped the dumbfounded Chairman across the face, stomped on his foot, and disappeared back into the crowd.

The Chairman grabbed his injured foot and hopped in a circle, searching for someone who had seen what that crazy woman had done. As he wiped her slobber off his mouth with his sleeve, the Chairman realized no one had noticed. *Have I slipped through a wormhole into the Twilight Zone?* In the Chairman's world, random women simply did not attack him like the lead singer of a boy band. In fact, they rarely showed him any attention at all. *Guess I need to be more like Charlie, whoever he is.*

He limped into the kitchen where he found a fleshy shirtless guy in the middle of a keg stand. Six laughing men held him upside-down while one of the local rugby girls shoved the keg hose into his mouth. The Chairman shook his head. *Disgusting. What's going through these people's minds? And what happened to that guy's shirt? He show up bare-chested? Why didn't the jolly green giant make him cover up for the love of all things holy? What a bunch of rednecks! It's all so... NASCAR.* Pleased with his own wit, he made a mental note to use that one back in Chicago. *Get a big laugh for sure.*

Mesmerized by the keg stand, the Chairman walked into a girl, knocking his temple against the back of her skull so hard he saw stars. She spun and accidentally crumpled her red cup against his chest, dumping cold beer down his shirt.

"I'm so sorry," she slurred as the Chairman dejectedly stared at his soaking wet polo. When he raised his head, he was nose-to-nose with the big girl from the NEIU rugby team. *It's Crystal!* Her dull eyes flickered with recognition. The Chairman's mind flailed wildly, desperate to concoct a reasonable explanation for his presence in Tennessee.

"Hey," she mumbled. "I know who you are..."

The Chairman held up his hands. "It's not what you think." *Gotta buy some time.*

"Yeah," she said with difficulty as her body swayed. "You're that kid who waited on us at Burger King today."

Burger King? The Chairman opened his mouth, but nothing would come out. *I'm the Chairman of the Student Senate Infractions Committee. I'm going to Northwestern Law School next year. I drive a BMW for crying out loud, and she thinks I'm some loser fast food worker.*

"Listen." She grabbed his arm.

She trying to sweet talk me, or just holding on to keep from falling?

"I'm normally pretty easygoing, but I asked you three times to make sure you left the pickles off my Whopper. And when I unwrapped my burger, guess what I found there..."

The Chairman shook her hand free and backed away. *This is unbelievable. Am I really that forgettable? I have the power to end her academic life at NEIU. Yesterday morning she was begging me to save her, and now she's worried about...*

"Pickles," they both said together.

He glared at her. Crystal saw his pained expression. "Hey little Burger King guy." He backed away as she continued. "It's ok. Please don't look so sad. I'm sorry I called you out on the pickles. Come back!"

It was all too much. The Chairman needed to escape, to regroup and gather his wits. He fixated on a single thought. *Must get away. Must get away.* The words played over and over in his brain. *Must get away.* The Chairman turned to run and smashed face-first into the fleshy man-boob of the shirtless keg-stand guy. After a good whiff of body

odor and beer, the discombobulated Chairman stagge
like a fighter about to get a standing eight count.

The unexpected blow knocked the keg stan
holding him off kilter. Soon out of control, they leaned and swayed in every which way. People pressed against the walls to clear a space for the inevitable disaster everyone knew was about to happen. The Chairman shook out the cobwebs just in time to see the shirtless man flying at him, an overweight Jimmy Superfly Snuka launched from the top rope.

As he scrambled to avoid the collision, the Chairman turned his sore ankle on the slick kitchen floor and crashed down hard on his back. Half a second later, the bare stomach of the keg stander slammed into his face and everything went black.

****

The Chairman was awakened by hands gently patting his cheeks. "Hey, little Burger King guy." He blinked until Crystal's concerned face came into focus. "You ok, little guy?"

He fought through a fog of confusion "What's going on?"

"Darrell fell on your face."

"What? Who's Darrell?"

"C'mon." She grabbed under the arms and hauled him to his feet with surprising ease. "You're all right. I been hit harder than that in practice."

The blood rushed from his head. The Chairman became dizzy. Either Crystal did not notice his unsteadiness or did not care. "All right, little guy. Now that you're back on your feet, it's time for you to leave. Don't ever mess with the keg stand." She gripped his shoulders, spun him and whacked his butt hard enough his whole body jerked forward. Still woozy, the Chairman walked away, his mind a jumble of random thoughts and emotions.

"Hey Burger King," Crystal shouted. "Watch those pickles!"

The Chairman ignored her and continued forward. The only thing stronger than his enmity for Crystal was the increasing numbness in his lower left leg. It was all pins and needles and grew worse with each step. He dragged his foot awkwardly. After he shuffled and squeezed through the crowd, the Chairman was grateful to get outside and escape the house's stale air and stifling heat. *That was a waste of time and money.* He shook his foot in a fruitless attempt to get normal feeling back.

He noticed a blue light reflected in the front window. His mind had not yet shifted back to reality when the music was unceremoniously cut. Someone shouted, "It's the cops! Everyone run!" People streamed from the house.

Within seconds he was engulfed in pure bedlam. Before he could even contemplate the situation, the tidal wave was on top of him and he was swept under a flood of humanity. He went down hard, covering his head to keep from getting trampled. His body was pounded by feet and legs. A few people tripped over him before they popped back up and ran off. When the deluge had finally slowed to a trickle, he cautiously lifted his face.

"Hey," an authoritative voice yelled.

The Chairman rolled over painfully to see a police officer, flashlight in hand. The Chairman's mind turned to his parents. *How would they respond to a two am phone call from some jail in Tennessee?* Not wanting to discover the answer, he jumped up, his left foot still asleep and useless. The Chairman ran as best he could, his bad leg causing him to lurch and stumble. The cop stood, hands on his hips, and watched him limp and stagger off.

"Hey, Gus." His partner joined him on the front lawn. "Aren't ya gonna go after him?"

Gus pulled a gray bandanna from his back pocket, removed his hat, and began to mop sweat from his forehead. "Nah. Getting to old to chase these kids around."

"Hey," the partner said. "What's with that guy's shoes? You think that crazy noise is intentional?"

Gus sighed heavily. "I'm a little worried about the next generation. They don't seem too bright. The other day my boy brought home a friend who had his britches cinched up under his butt. He had to do everything with one hand on his belt so his pants wouldn't fall off. Back in my day, I rebelled by growing a mullet. May've looked stupid, but at least I was smart enough to keep my britches from falling off."

"Know what you mean," the partner said. Both cops slowly shook their heads. Their eyes followed the Chairman as he wheezed and clomped down the street.

The Chairman was halfway to Middle Tennessee Boulevard when he realized he had parked in the opposite direction. *Can't go back now. Have to find someplace to wait 'til the cops leave.*

As if on cue, a police car cruised past him toward the rugby house. *Got to get outta sight for awhile. How long can my stupid foot stay numb?* He noticed a little house across the street with no cars in the driveway and no lights on inside. *Nobody home. Might be a good place to hide out.* His shoes loudly whooshed as he limped to the house.

It was perfect, the backyard surrounded by a tall wooden privacy fence. He clomped over to some garbage cans and sat on the soft grass between them and the fence. As he leaned back against the wooden slats, the Chairman let out a long breath. Mentally and emotionally exhausted, he glanced at his watch. Almost two am.

Man, it's been a long day. He closed his eyes.

FOURTEEN
Sunday, May 15th

Rooster was unhappy. It was too early to function properly, yet here he was walking to church. *How do people worship God at such an ungodly hour?* Of course few churchgoers were nursing his killer hangover.

When Saturday night had begun, Rooster easily rebuked all drinking-related appeals. He was determined to get to bed at a decent hour so this early morning church thing would not be too excruciating. As the night wore on, he tossed and turned, and eventually found himself in the kitchen with a Budweiser. One became two and two became three. Next thing he knew, he was on the back patio with a bourbon and cigar. Then he called Buddy. Soon they were off to all the usual haunts.

Somewhere during the night, Rooster lost a few hours. When he regained his faculties, they were scarfing down waffles and sausages at the Waffle House. By the time Buddy dropped Rooster back home it was well after four am. When the alarm woke him at seven-thirty, the bed was spinning. His skull ached like someone had beat on it with a rubber mallet.

Even though sleep called like a sweet siren song, he refused to risk his rent money. Despite his beer-soaked haze, Rooster managed to drag himself out of bed. As he stumbled around the small house, Rooster did his best to clean up for the Cumberland Baptist's Sunday morning services. His hair slicked straight back, he wore a houndstooth blazer over a plain black t-shirt, dark wash jeans, and dark brown Tony Lama ostrich foot cowboy boots, for which he had stupidly paid more than seven hundred dollars upon his arrival in Middle Tennessee. Somehow he had come to believe everyone in the south wore expensive boots. He just wanted to fit in. By the time he discovered they actually made him stand out, it was too late. *Why'd I think anyone would have seven hundred bucks to buy a pair of shoes? Thank God I never got around to buying that Stetson.*

When he had pulled on his boots, Rooster noticed an ugly purple welt on his right shin, but had no clue where it had come from. Even with his physical condition steadily improving, Rooster felt like he had been thrown from a rodeo bull. His head ached from the top of his forehead to the base of his skull. His eyes stung. Just to open them was painful and physically taxing. his lower back muscles were tied in knots and his calves seemed about to cramp with each step. *What'd I do last night to get so sore?* Rooster's labored and exaggerated movements, in concert with his stiff cowboy boots, gave him a graceless, halting Frankenstein walk.

A comfortable seventy-two degrees with the sun still low in the sky, there was a freshness in the air, the result of a drop to sixty-five degrees overnight. The humidity had not yet reached oppressive levels. Despite the pleasant surroundings, Rooster experienced unhappy flashbacks to his childhood, when his mother forced him out of bed at six o'clock every Sunday morning to attend mass at St. Stanislaus Catholic Church.

He shuddered as the scene played in his mind. *Sitting on the hard wooden pew struggling to stay awake, the enormous pipe organ drowning out the singers. Too loud to even think straight. The priest saying mass with an unintelligible Polish accent, his broken English bouncing and echoing off the marble floors and walls until it morphed into a soporific drone of distorted white noise akin to output from a defective fast food drive-thru speaker. The only thing keeping you awake, aside from Mom's occasional swats to the back of your head, was the constant movement typical to a Catholic service. From sitting to standing to kneeling to lining up to shuffle forward for communion. Followed by more kneeling and sitting and standing. God forbid you sneak out early, forcing you to pass the strategically placed plaque in the lobby that read, "The first person to leave church early was Judas."*

After escaping his childhood home, Rooster had ended church attendance almost immediately. Every so often, he returned out of shame or some sense of misplaced loyalty. It never took. He eventually stuffed down whatever guilt arose. Soon, any thought of attending mass had faded completely from his consciousness.

Now he was at a Baptist church. In all those years, when self-condemnation bubbled up and compelled him to return, it had never occurred to him to consider any church other than Catholic, probably because he grew up aware Protestants were inferior to the Catholics. He did not remember anyone ever saying it aloud. It was more of an attitude, the way people spoke about non-Catholics in hushed tones, as if they were talking about a criminal or someone with a terminal disease.

As he approached the front door, Rooster stopped to stare at Main Street where he had jumped the Lamborghini. He had been referring to it half tongue-in-cheek as his 'religious experience'. With a shudder, he considered how things could have played out much differently. *Was God really looking out for me? Probably not. Pretty sure God doesn't have time for screw-ups like me. If God even exists. Just dumb luck.* He considered the church as his old guilt percolated just below the surface.

He could hear his mother scold him. "Why you have such a bad attitude? Can't you go to mass without all the complaining?"

Could have a better attitude. Never been to a Protestant service. Could learn something new. Pretend I'm watching a show about Baptists on NatGeo. Maybe it'll be tolerable. Rooster had no idea what to expect as he pulled open the heavy door. He stepped into the now-familiar lobby and was somewhat surprised to see the space filled with people. Some talked in small clusters. Everyone was spit-shined and polished in their Sunday best. *Feels much smaller with all of these people.*

Sweat beaded at the back of his neck. *It extra hot in here?* His stomach churned as claustrophobia swept over him. Or was it the remnants of his hangover? Rooster had no time to regain equilibrium as worshipers filtered in behind him, forcing him to flow with traffic toward the sanctuary. He did not notice anyone else in jeans or cowboy boots. Most men donned suits and ties. Seemingly every woman wore a dress. He felt horribly out of place, sure they were all staring at him, judging him. He was suddenly very sorry he had not controlled himself the previous night. *Must look like total crap.* He tried to rub the sting out of his eyes. *I'll keep my head down and find Sandy.*

That was when a large smiling woman in an emerald green dress with big Texas hair, dark stenciled eyebrows, and overdone makeup, headed straight for him. Rooster glanced at the door and desperately hoped he was not the object of her attention. Before he could move, or even think clearly, she was on top of him.

"Good morning, sir." She was way too enthusiastic for 8:20 am. "Are you new to Cumberland Baptist Church?" Her voice came out in staccato bursts of machine gun fire.

He forced a smile. "Yes, ma'am. This is my first visit."

She grabbed his hands, her voice dripping with earnestness. "Well, it's so wonderful to have you join us this morning." Her head came up to Rooster's nose and he could smell the Aqua Net. *Must've taken an entire can to hold that crazy lid in place.*

Gently, Rooster tried to loose himself from her clutches, but her grasp only became tighter. She was surprisingly strong for a woman her size. She yanked on his arm. "I'm Sallie Mae Johnston. I would just love to show you around and tell you all about the wonderful things we have going at the church."

This a friendly offer of hospitality? Or a demand for compliance? With growing alarm, Rooster understood if he did not escape soon, she would beat him into submission. In his current weakened state, she was probably strong enough to take him. With some difficulty

Rooster extricated himself from her vise-like grip. "I'm actually supposed to catch up with Sandy Wilson before service, Ms. Johnston." He jammed his hands into his pockets. *Let's see her grab them now.*

Sallie Mae smiled, a flicker of disappointment in her eyes. "Alrighty then. If you poke your head inside the sanctuary, you'll find Sandy right there handing out bulletins. And please call me Sallie Mae."

"Thank you kindly, Ms. Johnston... er... Sallie Mae." Rooster flashed his most charming grin.

Sallie Mae fluttered her eyelashes and glanced away. "Pleasure meeting you Mr..." she looked at him expectantly.

"Ah... Rooster. Rooster Michaels. Please call me Rooster."

Her enthusiasm returned. "What an unusual name. It was a pleasure meeting you Rooster. I hope you'll enjoy the service enough to consider making Cumberland Baptist your home church."

"Thank you." Rooster was incredibly uncomfortable. *Just don't belong here. My life's a mess. These people have it all together. Not only responsible enough to get up for eight thirty Sunday morning church, but they actually seem happy, even excited, to be here. I could never fit in with this group.*

He turned and unconsciously eased his hands out of his pockets. Deft as a ninja, Sallie Mae reached out and snatched his arm. "Rooster?" She physically pulled him back toward her. "You look familiar to me. Do I know you from somewhere?"

Rooster twisted away. "Don't think so." The turn forced her to release his arm. "But anything's possible," he added over his shoulder. "You have a nice morning."

Before she could say anything else he made a beeline for the sanctuary door, eyes focused straight ahead.

"I remember now," she said triumphantly, but her voice disappeared into the din of the lobby behind him. Without a backwards glance, Rooster pushed through the door.

The sanctuary surprised him. He had expected the marble, stained glass and ornate decorations of a Catholic Church. Instead it reminded him of a small theatre with a wooden stage. A white podium sat near the edge of the raised platform. Behind the lectern were metal chorus risers. Facing the stage were rows of comfortable-looking chairs with dark-stained wooden frames. The seats were padded with heavy red material. The floors were covered with an echo-muffling, multicolored, industrial-type carpeting. An expectant buzz filled the room as people found their seats and talked to one another.

Rooster searched for the little bowl of holy water mounted near the entry door of every church he had ever attended. Like Pavlov's dog, Rooster felt a strong urge to dip his fingers and bless himself with the sign of the cross. Rooster had already begun subconsciously reciting the words over and over. *In the name of the Father and the Son and the Holy Ghost, Amen. In the name of the Father and the Son and the Holy Ghost, Amen. In the name of the Father and the Son and the Holy Ghost, Amen.*

As if he could somehow get it wrong without practice. After fingers were wet with holy water, he would say those words while touching his head, breastbone, and the front of each shoulder. This little ritual had been drilled into him from his earliest memories. It just felt wrong to be in church and not do it.

Rooster wandered around the back of the sanctuary in his absentminded search for the missing holy water when Sandy found him. Her outfit was a dressier version of the shapeless, curve-camouflaging ensemble she had worn during their first meeting. Rooster was no expert in such things, but he thought her hair was styled differently, as if she had put extra effort into it, and her makeup seemed somehow more formal.

"Mr. Rooster." She smiled pleasantly and thrust out her hand. "I'm so glad you could make it here this morning."

He looked into her sparkling brown eyes and took her hand. He had several sarcastic thoughts about being there against his will, but declined to give voice to any. Rooster grudgingly admitted he liked this woman. She was intelligent and kind and way more street smart than he had originally thought. She had certainly seen through his web of lies and exaggerations.

As if reading his mind, she smiled and sweetly asked, "Out late last night, Mr. Rooster?"

His stomach churned. *Busted.* His eyes and head ached too much to put on airs. Sandy would know immediately he was full of it, if he even tried to deny her allegation.

"I honestly hadn't planned on it." He stared at his toes. "But the evening kinda got away from me."

"Well, that probably wasn't the best decision you ever made." Rooster braced himself for a tongue-lashing about showing up hungover and looking like crap. "Still, I believe God has something for you," she added without the slightest trace of judgment. " I'm glad you dragged yourself here. I'm sure you seriously considered staying home."

Rooster stared at her. This was all far outside his realm of experience. Ever since he could remember, religion was about guilt and shame and how he was a disappointment to everyone. It was a hammer to bludgeon those who failed to measure up. Sandy's totally opposite response had thrown him for a loop.

"Since you made the effort to be here, I do hope you'll pay extra close attention to Pastor's message." Sandy flashed her friendly smile. "Either that or stare at the back of someone's head and wait for the service to end. That doesn't sound like much fun. Who knows? You might even find it thought-provoking."

Rooster nodded, a little amazed at her nonjudgmental attitude. *She could've let me have it, but for some reason chose not to. Very curious.* "I'll give it a shot."

"C'mon," Sandy said with a wink as she took him by the elbow. "You look like something the cat dragged in. Let's find you a seat before you start scaring people." Rooster allowed himself to be led halfway down the center aisle.

"Why don't you sit in this row?" Sandy released Rooster's elbow and walked away.

ROOSTER'S LEAP

Without a second thought, Rooster placed his hand on the back of the end chair and began his drop to one knee to genuflect toward the altar, just as he had done every time he had ever been to church. Before his knee touched the ground, a pair of strong hands grabbed Rooster from behind and hauled him unceremoniously to his feet. He was so startled, Roster could do nothing more than stand there rubber-legged. *What just happened?*

A small woman with short blonde hair and intense green eyes appeared in front of him and gently patted his cheeks. "You ok?"

Confused, Rooster shook free and backed away to put some space between him and these crazies. "What the hell you doing?"

The woman jumped backward as if she had been shoved, her flowered dress fluttering around her legs. In shock, she unconsciously adjusted her white cardigan, offended and confused. The man behind Rooster moved into sight. At least six-foot-six and massive all over, his red golf shirt was like the side of a barn, the elastic in the sleeves stretched to the limit by the man's enormous biceps. Rooster had to tip his head to keep from staring straight into his chest. The man laid a protective arm around the woman's shoulders.

"We saw you falling down." The man's accent was as country as a red gingham shirt and overalls. "So I..."

The woman interrupted with a slow southern drawl. "We saw you come in and you weren't looking so good. We was following behind Sandy and you. You looked good and wobbly when she left you. So I said to Dave, 'My goodness that man's gonna pass out.' The words no sooner left my mouth than you started going down. Dave ran over and caught you before you fell out on the floor."

Conflicting emotions flooded over Rooster. Anger, embarrassment, resentment, fear. *That guy's huge.* He could feel his face turning red. Worshipers stared. The last thing he wanted was to be the center of attention. He could only imagine what they were whispering about him. "I wasn't falling down," Rooster said defiantly. "I was genuflecting."

The man stared, dumbfounded. "You was doing what?"

"Genuflecting."

"Never heard of it." The man stepped menacingly toward Rooster. "You shouldn't be doing such things in church."

"Church is where you're supposed to do it, you idiot."

The man's nostrils flared. He eyed Rooster suspiciously. "Don't think I like your tone, mister." He jabbed his meaty forefinger hard into Rooster's chest. "We weren't in church, I'd teach you a thing or two 'bout how to treat folks tryin' to help you. And that thing you was doin', Jen-you-fecting, or some such thing. I don't wanna see you doin' that in here again. I don't care what you're sayin'. Looks disrespectful to me."

The woman tugged at the man's colossal bicep, her eyes locked on Rooster. "C'mon Dave. Let's just find our seats."

The man's eyes bored into Rooster. "Ok," he finally scowled as they walked away. Rooster could still hear their conversation down the center aisle.

"Dad gum, he was disrespectful," the man complained in a hushed tone. "What the devil was he carryin' on about?"

"Just can't figure him," the woman admitted. "Lookin' like a cowboy, but talkin' like a Yankee. And cussing in church!"

"The whole world's gone to the dogs," the man said ruefully. "You ever seen such a thing?"

"Who knows? Maybe it's a Yankee thing."

"If he's gonna be falling out in the aisles, he needs to go join that Pentecostal bunch," the man added as the pair stepped out of earshot.

FIFTEEN

Rooster found a seat, thankful those in attendance had lost interest in him. He sleepily searched for something to keep him occupied until the service began. His head weighed a thousand pounds. He cursed himself for his lack of self-control.

I'm a grown-ass man attending church on three hours sleep to get the rent money I need so the landlord'll return my front door. And, oh yeah, almost provoked a fight in church. Mom would be so embarrassed. What kinda loser am I? Normal people don't live like this. Something's gotta change.

Movement caught Rooster's attention. On stage, a forty-or-fifty-something man with a blond brush cut, a blue pinstripe suit, and a bright yellow tie, spoke joylessly into a microphone. "Welcome to Cumberland Baptist Church."

He appeared even less thrilled to be there than Rooster, who promptly lost interest and tuned him out. He scanned the room. *Gotta focus on something or I'll fall asleep.* His eyelids were so heavy. *If I close my eyes for just a second, maybe they'll stop stinging.*

"Sir!"

It was the sharp female whisper.

Rooster rubbed his eyes. *Huh? I fall asleep on the sofa. Music? What station's the TV on?*

"Sir!"

A hand gently shook his shoulder.

He remembered. A jolt of adrenaline shot through his body and his eyes snapped open. Everyone was standing and singing.

Everyone except him. He was wide awake now. *This is bad.*

He jumped to his feet. The choir, resplendent in their royal blue robes, swayed with the music and belted out a heartfelt version of *Amazing Grace*. Rooster's heart raced. *How long was I asleep?* He glanced around. *Anyone notice?* He saw the ancient little woman next to him. Her green flowered dress reminded Rooster of his boyhood home's kitchen curtains. She smelled faintly of liniment. Her silver hair was pulled back into a bun, and she stared up at Rooster with a mirthful smile, a youthful sparkle in her eye. Her expression told him she knew exactly what he had done, and she enjoyed the heck out of it. Rooster leaned close. "Was that you who woke me, young lady?"

She smiled broadly and nodded.

He whispered, "Thank you for that. How bad was it?"

She stifled a laugh. "You were snoring."

Rooster felt his face redden. He motioned for her to move close again. "How big a fool did I make of myself?"

"Don't you worry about it for one second. You look very tired. I tell you what. You do your best to pay better attention and I'll keep an eye on you. If you look like you're falling asleep again, I'll throw an elbow to your ribs."

She's spunky. Rooster grinned. "Deal."

The choir finished their performance and everyone sat. Rooster caught his new friend's eye and gave her a little wink. On stage, brush cut dude droned through some sort of reading. Rooster stared off. His mind wandered. His eyes grew heavy.

"Ooof!"

Had the old lady actually elbowed him in the gut? *How'd I fall asleep again?* He tilted his head toward her, expecting anger and annoyance, but her face glowed with amusement.

Rooster leaned down. "I'm so sorry."

"You're in good company," she whispered. "The disciples fell asleep three times in Gethsemane when Jesus went to pray."

What the devil's she talking about? Rooster nodded and smiled. He turned back to the front just as an older man with thinning white hair and silver-rimmed spectacles came onto the stage. He wore a sharp brown suit with a black and silver bolo tie. His pronounced limp required a cane to help him hobble to his place. *Looks familiar.* Rooster searched his brain. *Where've I seen this guy before?* His thoughts were interrupted by the old woman's slap on his arm. He leaned toward her.

"Don't fall asleep. This is worth the price of admission."

"Yes, ma'am."

The man on stage cleared his throat and spoke in a powerful booming voice. "Would y'all please stand so I can pray?"

Rooster stood along with the rest of the congregation, and then it hit him. *He looks like Colonial Sanders. Put him in a white suit, add a moustache and goatee, and this preacher is the spitting image of the KFC guy.* Rooster was astounded. *Can I really take a man like that seriously?*

The preacher finished his prayer and everyone sat down. He grabbed a stool from behind the podium and hopped up on it. He tugged on his pant leg. "I want to show y'all something."

Very strange. He glanced at the old lady. Her face glowed with her biggest grin yet. She noticed Rooster's gaze and used her head to motion at the stage and mouth the words, "Just watch, just watch."

Rooster turned his focus back on the odd Colonial Sanders doppelganger who continued to work at his pants leg. *What's he doing?* Rooster scanned the many broad smiles in the crowd, their faces filled with amusement and anticipation. Others had their brows furrowed, wondering what this peculiar man was up to. Every person, Rooster included, watched in rapt attention.

Just when the anticipation reached a fever pitch, the man did something amazing. There was a collective gasp as the preacher pulled his leg completely out the bottom of his pants. Nervous laughter followed as the audience tried to figure out just what had happened. Applause broke out when the preacher lifted the full-length steel and plastic prosthetic leg triumphantly over his head, like a hockey player hoisting the Stanley Cup. His empty pant leg draped over the edge of the stool, similar to the useless leg of a sad ventriloquist dummy.

As the bedlam died down, all thoughts of the preacher's resemblance to Colonial Sanders gone, Rooster was completely captivated. *What's this guy gonna do next?*

"I'm going to put this aside," the preacher smiled. He propped the prosthesis against the side of the podium, the foot on the floor. "It's very dramatic to pull the leg off, but I can't put it back on without taking off my britches. Those in favor of that, raise your hands." He lifted his own hand as the room roared with laughter.

"Seriously, you may not believe it, but this old man before you was an Airborne Ranger forty odd years ago. That's how I ended up with that." He indicated the prosthesis. Like a normal foot with the shoe at the bottom, the rest appeared a bizarre robot skeleton in need of outer skin. The preacher proceeded with a fascinating tale about a daring rescue mission he was charged to lead during the Vietnam War. The operation was still classified, he said, so he could not give specific dates or locations. Their objective was to recover "an extremely senior level officer." His team of six men had lived, worked, and trained together for three years. They were like brothers.

"I never been that close to a group of men before or since," he said. "Aside from my wife and children, those were the deepest, most intimate relationships I ever experienced. Each of us completely trusted the others with our very lives."

Rooster sat transfixed. No longer aware he was even in church, all thoughts of sleep driven from his mind. A master speaker, the preacher modulated his tone, inflection, and emotion to draw the crowd further into his story. He held the room in the palm of his hand.

"Our team was thirty miles behind enemy lines without any backup," the preacher said. "We were supremely confident. We successfully completed many missions much more daunting than this one. I was on point as we made our way through the jungle. Somehow, I lost focus for just a second or two. That one little lapse cost everyone dearly.

"There was a tripwire I should've seen." Everyone leaned forward, straining to hear his whisper-quiet tone. "But I didn't. I tripped it and instantly a spike board swung up out of a pit and impaled a whole load of sharpened nails and bamboo shafts into my left leg from mid-thigh to my foot. But I was lucky. Didn't think so at the time, but God was truly looking out for me. You see, the spike board was too short. They were usually designed to hit a man in the chest and face. For whatever reason, someone made this one to hit me in the leg."

The preacher grew silent, the tension palpable. Slowly and deliberately he uncapped and sipped from a water bottle he had produced from inside the podium. He extracted a bandanna from jacket pocket, removed his glasses, and proceeded to mop his face before he replaced his spectacles. Then he carefully folded the handkerchief and stuffed it back into his coat.

Rooster's impatience was overpowering. He bit back his desire to shout, "Get on with the story!"

The preacher cleared his throat and continued.

"I compounded my first mistake with another bigger one. When that spike board hit me, it was my responsibility..." His voice rose in volume and power. "It was my duty to protect my men by swallowing the pain. By remaining silent. But I screamed like I never screamed before. The enemy was on us in a second. My men fanned out in a perimeter, trying to protect me. There were too many of them and not enough of us. The Viet Cong were swarming out of the jungle in all directions."

His voice returned to a whisper. "Those men. My men. My brothers. I watched every one of them die protecting me. They died because of my mistake and all I could do was lie there."

You could have heard a pin drop as he slid off the stool onto his good right leg. The empty pant leg flapped ever so slightly in the air conditioning stream. He laid both forearms on the podium and fixed his congregation with a steely gaze.

"I'd been brought up Baptist, but I was never a practicing Christian. Well I tell you the truth, as I lay there in the jungle watching my friends die because of me, I thought about the Lord. Thought it was surely too late for me. At that moment I begged God to forgive me for what I had done to my men, and then I closed my eyes and waited to die. A funny thing happened. As you can plainly see, I didn't die that day in the jungles of Vietnam. In fact, I passed out. When I woke, I was all alone. Well, not exactly. I was surrounded by the bodies of my men."

The sounds of Queen's *Bohemian Rhapsody* echoed loudly through the sanctuary. The singer told his Mama about not wanting to die.

Horrified, Rooster knew immediately what it was and who had called him. He resisted the urge to rip his phone from his pocket and turn off the ringer. Instead, with more restraint than he knew he possessed, Rooster mimicked everyone else. He turned and glared at the people behind him. At the same time, as stealthily as he could manage, Rooster reached down to his front pocket. Through the material of his pants, he pressed on the edges of the device until the song cut off. Knowing the caller, his heart sank because the music was sure to start up again in a few minutes. Relief swept over him when he saw other nervous people pull out their phones to ensure they were silenced. With shaking hands, he did the same. His choice of ringtone had been hilarious when he selected it. *Not so amusing now.* He had made that decision ten shots into a bottle of Patron after a barroom argument about Queen's rank in the Pantheon of Rock-n-Roll greats. After enough tequila, Rooster found anything hilarious.

The preacher did not miss a beat. "Exactly," he bellowed the moment the music stopped. "I didn't want to die. But I sure wished the VC had killed me along with the rest of my men."

Hand on the podium for support, the pastor hopped back up on his stool. The movement upset the prosthesis, which wobbled and hung dramatically at an impossible angle for what seemed like an eternity, before it finally fell to the floor with a dull thud. Every eye in the room was fixated on the artificial leg, Rooster's ill-timed phone call now completely forgotten.

"When I finally got home," he continued, "the actual journey home is another story for another day, but when I got back, I was one angry young man. Thought my life was over. I betrayed my brothers and wasn't worth redeeming. They deserved to be alive and I deserved to be dead. Was about as low as a man can get. I was deep inside the pit with the enemy shoveling dirt on top of me. For so many years I was a broken man. I believed God made a mistake by keeping me alive when everyone else was allowed to die. I've got a little secret for you. God don't make mistakes. Do you believe that?"

Rooster was nearly startled out of his seat when the room erupted in a loud, "Amen!"

"That's right." The preacher's voice boomed again. "The Lord had a plan for me. I didn't see it at the time because I was too blinded by my own pain. Feeling sorry for myself. Full of guilt and shame for what happened to my men because of me. Thought I was worthless and useless. But God had a purpose for me. God has a plan for your life, too. You believe that?"

The congregation again exploded with a raucous, "Amen."

"So little by little, God revealed His grand design for my life. Like the psalmist says in *Psalm 40*, 'He lifted me out of the slimy pit, out of the mud and mire; he set my feet on a rock and gave me a firm place to stand.' God redeemed me from the mess my life had become. And you know what? My God is big enough to do the exact same thing for you. Some of you sitting out there right now feel worthless and useless. Some of you have fallen so far into the pit of hopelessness, you've given up on ever escaping. Maybe you've fallen there through your own bad decisions. Or maybe you're in a pit of despair through no fault of your own. Maybe you're dealing with the consequences of someone else's thoughtless, evil actions. Whatever the reason or circumstance, God wants to lift you out of the slimy pit and set your feet on the rock. God wants you to have redemption."

Rooster's adrenaline surged. *This guy's got me fired up.*

This was more inspirational than the motivational speakers brought in to whip the sales staff into a frenzy just before hitting the phones. Rooster felt like the preacher had spoken directly to him. *Who doesn't want a better life?* Of course he wanted redemption from the mess he had made. Was the whole room as emotionally charged as him? He scanned the crowd. Nearly everyone sat on the edge of their seats. A thirty-something woman dabbed at the corners of her eyes with a handkerchief. Several other people had their heads in their hands. *They crying or just praying?*

"Because when you stay in the bottom of your pit," the preacher went on. "That's when you get tangled up in all those destructive behaviors. You're trying to paper over the pain. Sure, they look pretty and fun on the front end. But they don't work, do they? Keep looking in the wrong places and you'll eventually destroy yourself." He stared out intently. "What do you turn to? Is it pornography? Drugs? Alcohol?"

Rooster squirmed. Had the preacher glared directly at him when he said, "alcohol"? *Whoa, what's that all about?* Rooster glanced over his shoulder. *Anyone else see that? How'd the preacher know anything about me?*

"Those will all drive you into the pit," the preacher continued. "But you know what else will? Financial struggles. You working as hard as you can but somehow the money always disappears long before the month runs out? How about your marriage? You and your spouse constantly at odds with each other? You see, it isn't always so obvious. It's not necessarily a simple answer. Despair and hopelessness can overcome any of us. And the enemy hits us when we're not looking. He knows your blind spots better than you do. If you're struggling right now, no matter how big or small it may seem to the rest of the world, Jesus wants to give you freedom there. Whatever it is, I want to invite you to come forward. Just come on up to the front of the sanctuary. Don't be afraid."

A few people moved toward the front.

"Today is the day," the pastor bellowed. "Today is *your* day. You have the opportunity to put a marker in the ground and change the direction you've been going."

The trickle had turned into a steady stream. Swept up in the raw emotion of the moment, Rooster considered joining them. All the while, the minister continued to encourage.

"C'mon up. Don't worry what anyone else is going to think. This is between you and God. There was only one perfect man in history. Everyone wrestles with something. No shame in admitting you want freedom. Don't leave here today with any regrets. Don't get in your car and wish you stepped up."

At some point during the preacher's exhortations, someone had begun to play piano and the choir had returned to the risers at the back of the stage. They swayed to the music and quietly sang, *"Just as I am"*.

Eventually, most of the space in front of the stage filled with people. Some sang along with the choir, a few openly wept. The eye-dabbing thirty-something woman Rooster had seen earlier now stood with the others unabashedly bawling like a baby. He was strangely impressed by these folks' willingness to lay raw their emotions in front of the whole congregation. He shuddered as he considered how out of place and embarrassed he would be up there. *Good for them, but that's most definitely not for me.*

The preacher hopped out from behind the podium and two men from the crowd climbed on stage to support him. He draped his arms around their shoulders as they all moved down into the flood of people.

"It breaks my heart to see so many of God's people in distress," he said. "But the Lord can save you from your distress. He'll do His part, but you have to do yours. Are you ready to do that?"

A murmur of agreement ran through the crowd. "Let me pray for you." The pastor, his tone thick with emotion, launched into a prayer about repentance, redemption, and God's love. Tangible intensity filled the church as the people drank in his words like parched nomads at a desert oasis. The electric atmosphere made Rooster's skin tingle. He listened intently to the preacher's monologue, but he did not understand much of what the man said. His interest waned. He pulled out his phone to check the time. *How much longer is this going to last?*

The minister finally wrapped up his prayer, said some closing remarks, and the people began to filter from the sanctuary. Rooster noticed his new little friend had not joined the flood in the aisles. She gathered up a purse from under her chair and turned toward Rooster.

"I'd like to make a proper introduction, young man." With a big smile, she reached out her hand. "I'm Dottie Charles."

Rooster returned her grin as he gently took her hand. "It's my pleasure to officially meet you Ms. Charles. My name is Rooster Michaels, but please call me Rooster."

She released his hand, patted him just below his ribs, and laughed. "Hope I didn't bruise you. I'm pretty strong for an old lady."

"I don't doubt that for a minute, but I do appreciate you looking out for me. I hope I didn't embarrass you too much."

"How on earth would you embarrass me?"

"Don't know. With you waking me up over and over, the people around us might've thought I was here with you."

"Don't be silly. I don't think anyone thought that. But even if they did, I've always ignored the magpies. They like to make a lot of noise, but most of what they say is gibberish."

"I admire your attitude. Wish I was more like that."

"This your first time at our church, Rooster?"

"Yes ma'am, it was."

"So, what'd you think?"

"I thought the preacher's story was amazing. Very moving."

"Does that mean you'll be back with us?"

Rooster nearly blurted he was at church under duress, but thought better of it. "I will be back next week."

"That's wonderful!" Dottie's eyes sparkled with delight. "If you'd do me the honor of sitting next to me, I'll save you a seat."

Rooster could not suppress a grin. *What a delightful little woman.* "No Ms. Charles. It is I who would be honored. Will I find you in this same row?"

"I'm in this very seat every Sunday morning."

"Promise I will get more sleep before next week's service."

She grinned slyly. "You better. I'm going to spend all this week sharpening my elbows just in case."

Rooster laughed long and hard as they exited the row, said their final goodbyes, and moved off in opposite directions.

SIXTEEN

Just check in with Sandy and then I'll be free. He scanned the back of the room until he found her in conversation with a stunning brunette whose shoulder-length hair framed an angelic face. Tall and lean, her purple dress showcased a tiny waist. Rooster hurried toward them. *Maybe I'll wrangle an introduction.*

Sandy's eyes lit up when he arrived. "Mr. Rooster. So glad to see you. You look much better than you did before service."

"Thank you. I feel better."

"That's marvelous. There's someone I want you to meet."

Rooster's heart leapt. *I'm going to meet her, but what am I gonna say?* A regular Don Juan after he tossed back a few, he had never been very good with women when sober. *What do you say to a woman at church anyway? Do I have it in me to make small talk without looking like an idiot?* His enthusiasm drained, replaced by a sinking sense of impending doom.

Sandy indicated the brunette. "Mr. Rooster, I'd like you to meet Marcie Dexter."

The woman's face glowed with a friendly smile and lively green eyes. She stuck out her hand. "Mr. Rooster. Nice to meet you."

Stunned, Rooster shook her hand robotically. *This is Marcie Dexter?* In spite of Buddy's assertions, he had pictured someone completely different. In his mind, she was a dowdy old lady with horn-rimmed glasses and a high-necked ruffled blouse under a drab gray suit, kind of like the Dana Carvey *Saturday Night Live* Church Lady character. This woman was not that at all. *She's breathtaking.*

Concern creased Marcie's brow. "Mr. Rooster?"

He snapped out of his trance. *You're blowing it. You look like a flake. Get your act together!* Rooster forced a smile. "I'm sorry. Still thinking about the preacher's message. Please just call me 'Rooster'."

"Of course, Rooster."

Sandy touched both their arms. "Excuse me. I have to catch Sallie Mae Johnston before she leaves."

Rooster flinched and resisted the urge to hide. After a nervous search for the woman who had accosted him before service, he quickly forgot her when his eyes once again rested on Marcie's striking face.

She asked, "You enjoyed the sermon?"

"Yes, the preacher's story was amazing. Very moving."

"He certainly has a gift. I hear you're going to be joining my small group Wednesday night."

"I am. Looking forward to it."

"Since you're gonna be part of the group, I want to let you know we're having a cook out at my house this evening around five. It's short notice, but I sure hope you can join us."

Couldn't make me NOT join you. "Sounds great. I'd love to come. Where's your house?"

She gave him the address.

Rooster was dejected. "That's kinda far from my place. I don't have a car."

Marcie's eyes flashed with embarrassment. "Oh, I'm sure we could find someone to..."

Rooster waved her off. "No, that's okay. I got a buddy who'll drive me there. It alright if I bring him along?"

She smiled. "Absolutely. We'd love to have both of you." She glanced at an expensive-looking thin silver watch. "I'm sorry, Rooster. I got a million things to do. I gotta run."

"Can I bring anything?"

"Just yourself. And your friend. Great meeting you. I'm looking forward to introducing you to the rest of the group."

"I can't wait."

As Marcie hurried away, Rooster walked toward the exit, keeping a sharp eye out for Sallie Mae Johnston. Fortunately, Sandy had her cornered in the lobby. He was safe, but still rushed through the room, happy to escape outside. Once on the sidewalk, Rooster's gaze fell back on the spot where he had jumped the car. His mind returned to its earlier ruminations about whether or not God had been involved there. He could not help but consider the pastor's experiences in Vietnam. *Had God really been looking out for the preacher?* Rooster stood and let it all roll around his head. He shrugged.

Guess it's possible.

He carefully looked both ways and hurried across the street. It was still comfortable walking weather and he felt oddly content. Without even realizing it, he began to hum *Amazing Grace* as he turned toward home.

SEVENTEEN

The Chairman was filled with guilt as he used a six-foot-long cigarette to fend off a giant lizard-man. He did not want to kill an endangered species, or worse, get him hooked on smoking.

He was snapped from the nightmare by the screaming woman and the heavy garbage which hit his face, driving his head into the wooden fence. "Oww!"

He pushed the big sack aside in time to see the back of a woman in a green nightgown and purple Crocs, her brown hair flowing as she ran up the stairs into the house. The air was crisp and the low-sitting early morning sun cast long shadows. *Time to leave.* He rose painfully to his feet, his left ankle still all pins and needles, his lower back stiff and sore, and the butt of his shorts soaking wet from dew. He hobbled slowly toward the open gate. He was almost across the yard when the back door burst open and out flew a man wearing nothing but black gym shorts. His buzz cut, goatee, and seemingly every other exposed part of his body, were covered with thick salt and pepper hair. But all the Chairman noticed was the huge gleaming Remington Model 870 pump action shotgun the guy pointed at him.

Amped on adrenaline, the man screamed at the Chairman. "Hey you degenerate! What you think you're doin' in my yard?"

Energy surged through the Chairman as he stared wide-eyed at the big gun. He raised his hands. "Easy there, dude."

"You scared the tar outta my wife." The man pumped the gun.

Even a self-admitted gun-control advocate who had never handled an actual firearm recognized the distinctive metallic clink as the shotgun's slide chambered the next shell. His bad ankle forgotten, the Chairman sprinted away as if fired from a cannon and did not stop until he hit Middle Tennessee Boulevard.

Pumpkin-headed bouncers. Keg stands. Shotguns. Smoking indoors! Who knew modern civilization hasn't arrived in Tennessee yet?

After several wrong turns and a bunch of backtracking, the Chairman finally found his cherished BMW, but did not like what he saw. The passenger door sat wide open. "Oh no." As he rushed closer, it only got worse. The window had been smashed, shatterproof glass strewn on the seat, floorboards, and the ground. Random wires poked from the big hole where his glorious top end stereo had once sat. The killer Harmon Kardon speakers had been ripped from the back dash. The Chairman fought the urge to sob and hug his car. He closed the passenger door and walked to the driver's side. Then it hit him.

My backpack! It was in the back seat. All of his clothes and toiletries... Gone.

He carefully swept glass bits off the driver's seat and climbed inside. The familiar roar of the motor salve on an open wound, he lovingly rubbed the dashboard. "At least they didn't touch your engine."

EIGHTEEN

The imposing figure of Anthony Ferrentino, Jr., made his 'Little Tony' moniker seem more like a joke than a nickname. It had ceased to accurately describe him sometime in the last decade. At six-foot-four and more than three hundred pounds, the intimidating twenty-nine-year-old man was the spitting image of his father, complete with a curly black unibrow and double chin. The only difference, Little Tony had yet to develop jowls or dark eye circles. The jet black goatee he considered his trademark, protruded seven inches from his chin. About a third of the way down, a black rubber band pulled the hair together. Below the band, smaller elastic ties separated the beard into five little braided Medusa-hair-like ropes.

Also much different than the father was the son's sense of style, which trended toward urban hip hop, but with unique Little Tony twists. Today's ensemble was a tent-like yellow shirt emblazoned with the words, "Free Mumia", baggy blue jean shorts drooping low to reveal blazing pink boxers, and a ridiculously undersized straw fedora perched precariously atop his oversized head.

Little Tony sullenly pumped gas into his father's metallic cherry red 2003 Oldsmobile Aurora. *How embarrassing to be in this stupid ride. My first trip south and I'm tooling around in an old man car.* Little Tony had expected Tennessee to be full of odd characters like those on *Duck Dynasty*, *My Redneck Wedding*, and *Swamp People*. So far, much to his dismay, the south had been a lot like, well, the north. They had seen many of the same chain stores and restaurants found in New Jersey. He had yet to see a single cowboy hat, rebel flag, or hot woman in pigtails and Daisy Dukes. Little Tony had never been further south than Atlantic City and he desperately wanted to meet an honest-to-goodness southern redneck. *Hopefully people will get more colorful when we get into the heart of Murfreesboro.*

With zero cloud cover, it was an exceedingly bright afternoon. *Sun feels hotter in Tennessee.* Sweat seemed to pour from everywhere. The slight sweltering breeze actually more uncomfortable than if there had been no wind at all. Its only accomplishment was to stir up fuel vapors, his body and clothing absorbing the acrid fumes. *Backwater place. Making people pump their own gas? Thank God Mom's not here. She'd flick her lighter at one of those Virginia Slims and I'd burst into flames.*

Despite his current misery, Little Tony was excited to learn his dad's business. He hoped to eventually fire his gun at someone, if his father ever let him actually carry it. Right now it was locked in the glove box. Big Tony had remained vague about how much money this slimeball Sinclair Davis had stolen, but Little Tony figured it had to be a huge amount to get his father to drive all the way from New Jersey. The old man suffered from both Irritable Bowel Syndrome and Overactive Bladder. It took an act of Congress to get him more than five miles from the house or his bar.

The trip should have taken fourteen hours driving straight through, but it had been much more slow going. The pair had left Jersey City nearly twenty-four hours prior, and they still had than two hours to go. Big Tony had stopped every hour for a bathroom break and to stock up on junk food. The back seat was a garbage dump, filled with empty soda bottles, take out wrappers, and fast food remnants. The whole car wreaked of French fries and chocolate bars.

Just eight hours into the trip, Big Tony had insisted they catch some zzz's at a cheap fleabag motel somewhere in the backwoods of Virginia. An ancient lock and flimsy chain the only protection from whatever lurked outside, Little Tony was convinced a chupacabra would break in and kill them during the night. Wide awake, his father's snoring could not drown out the unnerving racket produced by the bugs and wildlife. *Whoever said it's peaceful and quiet in the country was full of crap. Gimme the urban noise of Jersey. Might have a gang banger break in your house, but that's a helluva lot better than spending all night worrying wild animals'll rip the limbs from your body.* When the sun rose, Little Tony had never been so happy.

Little Tony was not allowed to drive his dad's beloved Oldsmobile. They tooled along at fifty-eight miles per hour. The twelve discs in the trunk-mounted CD changer were Frank Sinatra, Tony Bennett, Dean Martin, or some other stereotypical mobster singing favorite. Whenever Little Tony put in earbuds to enjoy hip hop on his iPod, the old man threw a fit about needing Little Tony to help him stay awake. Little Tony wondered how his dad could possibly fall asleep with a pit stop every 60 minutes, but kept it to himself. *Ask that and the old man's head'll explode.* They could not arrive in Murfreesboro too soon. *This ordeal don't end soon, my head's gonna explode.*

Big Tony emerged from the minimart, a large shopping bag stuffed with candy bars, cookies, and chips, in one hand, and a two-liter bottle of A&W Root Beer in the other. Tony frowned. "You ain't gassed up yet?" He reached for the car door with the hand holding the plastic bag, but the bottom seam failed and the contents spilled out onto the ground.

"Grandma Moses with a pitchfork." Tony balanced the soda bottle on the edge of the roof. Wheezing from the exertion, he bent over and scooped as much as his meaty fingers could hold. Red-faced and breathing heavy, he resembled the Kool-Aid man in his fire engine red track suit. Tony yanked the door open and tossed the food into the car. He stood for a moment, his hands on his thighs, waiting for enough breath to take another run at the remaining items. He sucked in all the air as his lungs could hold and leaned over. His considerable girth swayed from side to side, the back seam of his track pants stretched to the limit. As he stood, his hind end bounced off the door frame. The root beer on the roof teetered and then fell. As if it had radar, the hard plastic cap drove into the back of Tony's skull. The bottle caromed off his head, smashed to the ground, and sprayed him with root beer as it skidded on the blacktop.

"Unholy donkey lovin'." His eyes bugged out from oxygen deprivation, Tony pulled on the car frame to stand. His face purple, a huge vein throbbed in his forehead and sweat poured from his hairline. Gasping like a man in cardiac arrest, he waddled to the leaky soda bottle and kicked it toward the car. With a mighty effort, he threw his body into the driver's seat. When his panting and heaving chest subsided, Tony reached out the door and felt along the ground for his two-liter container.

A fifty-something man in jeans and an orange t-shirt leaned against a big red Chevy pickup while it gassed up. He watched with amusement as Big Tony flailed. Little Tony glared at him and growled, "Whatchu lookin' at, tough guy?"

Unfazed, the man took his time replacing the gas nozzle in the pump, and flashed a wide grin. "You fellas ain't from around here, are you?" Without waiting for an answer, he chuckled, climbed into his truck, and drove off.

Little Tony stared at the departing Chevy. *Are people down here different than back in Jersey?* His meanest look and tough words had zero impact. *Don't like that at all.* When his size failed to intimidate, Little Tony was a toothless lion. He possessed no fighting skills whatsoever and his coordination and physical dexterity were more like Big Tony than he cared to admit. *Gotta convince the old man to let me start carrying my gun ASAP. New Jersey, Tennessee, or anywhere else, anyone with an ounce of sense respects a man with a gun.* Little Tony finished pumping the gas. He opened the door, hitched up his shorts, and folded his large frame into the passenger seat.

"Hey dad. Why you keep driving this piece a crap?"

Tony, still gasping for air, said tersely, "This car was one of the last Oldsmobiles ever built. Got the 'Final 500' badge to prove it.

Always drive an Oldsmobile. Just like my pop before me. When those ostrich lickers at GM stopped making them, a little piece of America died."

Tony regained his breath as he continued. "This one's great, but you shoulda seen my first car, 1979 Delta 88. That thing was a monster. V8 engine that roared to life in a second. Sky blue, white roof, cream interior. What a machine!"

Little Tony yawned. "Time moves on. You gotta move on, too. How long you gonna keep this old thing? Oldsmobile ain't coming back, pops. Why don'tcha upgrade to a new Escalade."

"I'll get rid of it when I'm good and ready," Big Tony roared. "Quit being such a monkey lovin' disrespectful little salad eater and buckle up so we can get going." While Little Tony complied, the old man grumbled, "For the love of Peter Griffin! Like I'd ever buy an SUV. Dumb goat mother gots no sense of history."

The steering wheel jammed against his big belly, Tony yanked the shifter into drive. The big sedan lumbered onto the highway.

NINETEEN

Rooster pressed his phone a little too tightly to his ear. His energy burst from the pastor's message had faded quickly as he succumbed to his lack of sleep. His whole body ached. *What happened last night?* He stared at the pitiful blanket tacked over his doorframe. *Wasn't Buddy supposed to get me a piece of wood? How's that not happened?* Rooster remembered the conversation at Buddy's house. They had been drinking and carrying on and somehow they both lost track of the importance of keeping bugs and animals out of Rooster's house.

Rooster rubbed his eyes. *What kinda idiot am I?*

A sad off-color rainbow of green, red, yellow, blue and brown stripes, the Mexican blanket did not cover the entire door opening. Hot air and street noise streamed into the small house, the ancient living room window air conditioner losing the battle to the heat. A once ice-cold Bud longneck sat in a puddle on the pressboard coffee table. Slumped on a brown corduroy sofa, Rooster was stripped down to gray gym shorts and a Corona t-shirt he had won in a Cozumel barroom trivia contest twelve years ago. He had picked up his blanket-slash-door on the same trip. *Musta been drunk outta my mind to buy that ugly thing.*

"So I'm minding my own business, spending an afternoon with my sewing club," the woman on the phone explained. "We were talking about basting; when you should baste with the sewing machine, when you need to baste by hand, and when you could get away with just using pins."

"Maaa." The heat and humidity had sapped Rooster of energy and patience. "I don't need to hear about sewing. Can you please get to the point?"

"Stop your complaining. By the way, I was trying to get a hold of you all morning. How come you didn't answer my calls?"

Rooster sighed. "I was doing something."

"That's a big load a bunk. You don't get outta bed 'til ten on Sunday morning. What could you have been doing?"

"If you know that, why were you calling me at nine thirty?"

"I wanted to make sure I got you. Besides, I was doing you a favor. It's not good to sleep all day. I read in the newspaper where that messes up your metabolism. What was so important that you couldn't take a minute to talk to your mother?"

"I'm begging you Mom, get back to your story."

"Oh all right. So we're having a pleasant discussion about basting and then out of the clear blue sky Gertrude Longfellow says, 'Hey Delores, what's this I hear about your son being in Tennessee jumping over cars?' I thought I musta misunderstood, so I says, 'He sells cars. But in Ohio, not Tennessee.'"

Rooster wiped the sweat off his phone with his shirt. He considered interrupting, but instead drained his warm beer.

"Then Gertrude says, 'My grandson showed me a video on the computer of a man jumping over a car in Tennessee, and when they showed a close-up of his face, it was your boy.' I was just flabbergasted. I thought, why would my Sonny be in Tennessee? And what's this jumping on cars business? I didn't know what to say. So I says, 'Gertie, I have no idea what you're talking about. He jumped on top of a car? Like in a parking lot?'"

"I didn't jump on a car." Rooster interrupted, desperate to move the story along.

"That's what Mrs. Longfellow said. She says, 'No. He jumped over a moving car, a big yellow sports car. It was so scary. That car was so fast, I was sure it would kill him. But at the last possible second, he jumped straight up and it flew underneath, like the Flying Wallendas.' Then she starts with the questions. 'Why would your son be doing tricks like that? What's next? Walking over Niagara Falls on a tightrope?'"

Rooster dragged himself to the kitchen, glad to find one last glorious beer in the fridge. "Thank God," he mumbled.

"What was that?"

Rooster snapped back to reality. "Nothing, Mom. Go ahead."

"Well I thought what Gertie said was ridiculous, that you'd be jumping over speeding cars like some circus tumbler. We raised you better than that, so I says, 'Gertie, my son's not some daredevil. You just seen someone who looks like him. Besides, I don't think he's ever even been to Tennessee.'

"But Gertrude wouldn't back down an inch. She says, 'That boy grew up with my Timmy and I promise you that I'd know him anywhere. It was him,' she says. 'Without a doubt.'"

"But it turned out she was right," Rooster offered.

"You just hush up and let me tell my story."

"All right, all right." Rooster flopped on the sofa and took a long drink from the beer.

"Well, Mary Snyder saw it was getting heated between me and Gertie, so she says, 'There's no need to get all upset over this.' She never liked disagreements. They make her nervous and that makes her gout flare up. So Mary Snyder says, 'We can just find this video on the computer and everyone can see it with their own eyeballs.' So we all trooped into Mary's spare bedroom to watch the computer. And to my horror, Gertie Longfellow was absolutely right. There you were risking your life like a circus acrobat just to be on some video on the computer. I never been so embarrassed in all of my life. If there had been a hole in the floor, I woulda crawled right into it."

She grew quiet. Rooster thought the story was over until he realized she was crying. He leaned back, no idea what to do or say. The guilt and shame made him feel like a horrible person. Finally, he asked, "Mom, are you crying?"

She ignored him and carried on through the sobs. "I was turning three shades of red. The whole sewing club saw clear as day I have no idea what's going on in my own son's life. I looked like such a fool. Have I been such a bad mother? This ordeal was more embarrassing than that time I tucked the back of my dress into my pantyhose at your cousin Patsy's wedding."

"C'mon Mom." Self-loathing rose up in him. "You really think I did this on purpose?"

"I don't know what to think anymore. You made me look like an idiot. What kinda mother don't know where her son lives? Didn't even have the right state for the love of Pete. Good gracious, Sonny. You wanna to send me to an early grave?"

"I don't want to send you to an early grave, Mom." After a soothing sip of Bud, Rooster tried to move the conversation away from how horrible he was as a son. "Why you insist on calling me Sonny? I'm not five years old anymore."

"You'll always be my baby, no matter how old you get. Why can't you indulge your poor old mother? You can't let me have this one thing? After I was in labor for twenty-three hours and almost died giving birth to you? Think I earned the right to call you Sonny if I want. Or you wanna take that from me too?"

"Gotta be kidding. Aren't you being a little dramatic?"

"Besides, what else would I call you?"

"Rooster."

"Rooster?! Why on earth would I call you that?"

"Because that's what I want to be called."

"I could never call you such a ridiculous circus performer name. No wonder you're doing ridiculous circus stunts. It's all because of that name."

"My name's got nothing to do with it. I been trying to tell you, the jump over that car wasn't planned."

"You remember Mrs. DiPasquale's son Thomas?"

"No." *Why'd she suddenly change the subject?*

"You don't remember little Thomas DiPasquale? He lived in that big red brick house three doors down from the Porgazalskis. He came to your third birthday party at Letchworth State Park. He was the one who started crying when we tried to sing Happy Birthday. I thought he was gonna ruin the whole party. Then he put his face in your cake. It was all so traumatic for you."

"Mom! I don't remember my third birthday party. Why you telling me about this guy?"

"I saw Mrs. DiPasquale at the supermarket two months ago. I told her about you selling cars in Ohio. Obviously, all this happened before I knew you were a Tennessee circus tumbler. So then I says, 'What's little Thomas been up to?' She got so quiet, I thought she was going to say he was in prison or something. Finally she tells me her son changed his name to 'Pitbull' or 'Bulldog' or some ridiculous thing, and now he's a professional wrestler. He travels all over the country doing his wrestling. I could tell she was so embarrassed."

"How could you tell she was embarrassed?" Rooster blurted. He hated how he always got sucked into his mother's stories. The best way to get through them was to remain quiet until she ran out of steam, but he could never stop himself.

"Oh, I can tell. I have a fifth sense for these things."

"You mean a sixth sense."

"I don't have two extra senses. My fifth sense is knowing when people are uncomfortable."

Rooster sighed. "Mom, everyone has five senses. An extra sense would give you six."

"What're you talking about? There's sight, sound, touch, and taste. That's four."

Rooster bit his tongue. "Nevermind. Please finish."

"Ok. So little Thomas DiPasquale's now a professional wrestler and he's renamed himself after a dog. I always knew he was a little off, but I never dreamed in a million years..."

"Mom!" Rooster swallowed the desire to scream 'shut up.' He drew in a deep breath and asked gently, "Why you telling me all this?

I don't even know these people."

"Humph!"

Rooster recognized the sound. In his mother's mind, he had just said something completely idiotic and she was fighting the urge to explain just how stupid he sounded.

"It's all very simple. He took some weird name and now he's a pro wrestler for goodness sake. This 'Rooster' business ain't gonna end well, and I refuse to have anything to do with it."

"Fine. Call me whatever you want."

"Today you're jumping cars. What's next? Maybe Gertrude's right and you'll be walking over the Falls on a tightrope."

"I'm not gonna do anything else."

"If you did walk over Niagara Falls, at least you'd be closer to home than Tennessee."

"What are you talking about?"

"Is it a crime I want my son closer to home? Stop getting me off track. Why are you jumping over cars on the computer?"

"I told you Ma." Rooster's remaining patience drained. "I was in the street when I saw the car speeding at me. The only thing I could do was jump, so I jumped." He lowered his voice. "Thought I was gonna die. My whole life flashed before my eyes."

"Flashed before your eyes? What's that mean? Like a movie?"

Rooster draped an arm over his face as he relived the experience. "It means exactly what it sounds like, Mom. In that moment, when I thought I was gonna die, all kinds of images and feelings flashed in front of me. It was like a religious experience." Maybe the preacher had delivered a bigger impact than Rooster realized. He had actually started to believe his formerly tongue-in-cheek description was true.

"Religious experience?" She laughed. "How could you have a religious experience? You ain't been to church in twenty years?"

Rooster thought for a moment. "Yes," he said, more to himself than to his mother. "That's exactly what it was."

"What?"

"A religious experience. I think God was giving me another

chance to make something of myself."

She sounded doubtful. "So now you're talking to God? You think God has time to bring you a picture show while you hover in mid-air? Besides, what you talking about, needing second chances? You been plenty successful everywhere you been."

Rooster glanced at the hideous blanket tacked over the doorframe. "Yeah. You're absolutely right. I'm a huge success."

"You can't have religious experiences without going to church." Rooster's sarcastic tone had completely escaped her. "That's one of my biggest failures as your mother, that you don't go to church. That's why you never met a nice girl to settle down with. Because you refuse to go to church."

Rooster smiled. She had returned to familiar subject matter. He knew his mother had gotten everything important off her chest and he could safely end the call. "Ma, I've gotta go."

"Wait a minute. I never get to talk to you. I want to know how you ended up in Tennessee."

Rooster's voice turned gentle. "Not now. I'll tell you all about it next time we talk. I promise."

"No, wait!"

"Goodbye, Mom."

"Sonny!"

"Goodbye Mom," Rooster said with finality. "I'm hanging up now. Say goodbye or be hung up on."

"Goodbye, Sonny. You need to call more often."

"Goodbye." He quickly disconnected the call.

He downed the rest of his beer and closed his eyes.

TWENTY

Sue Schwartz's life remained a mess, thirteen years after her alcohol-soaked night with the so-called Michael Davis. An up and coming account executive for Arizona's most prestigious advertising agency, she had been sent to Las Vegas to pitch one of the firm's biggest clients on a new multi-million dollar campaign. She had certainly had not been authorized to spend fifty grand on the corporate AMEX. When Edward Allen, the senior partner, heard Sue's drunken resignation voice mail, it did not take long to unearth her questionable purchases from the Viva Las Vegas Wedding Chapel, Snake Eyes Ink House, Bugsy's Gold Emporium, and several other borderline-shady business establishments. By the time Sue had returned to her Scottsdale condo, the police were there to greet her.

Edward Allen's weekly golf foursome included the state's Attorney General, who was still stinging from a devastating four-part expose in the *Arizona Republic* which painted him as pillow soft on white collar crime. It did not take much encouragement from the ad agency boss to convince the AG Sue's case was the perfect opportunity to make a bold statement about how hard-line he could be with non-violent offenders.

The three-week trial was a circus with each embarrassing purchase paraded before the media. One local television crew retraced her steps in a feature called "Wild Weekend in Vegas," with footage of the honeymoon suite, and an interview with the tattoo artist. They even obtained casino security camera footage of her twenty-five thousand dollar AMEX cash advance.

She did not have a prayer. They threw the book at her. Sue was sentenced to five years in the maximum security Perryville Lumley Unit of the Arizona State Prison Complex. The court also ordered her condo and personal property sold at auction to pay back some of the money she had spent in Vegas.

When she was released on probation more than two years later, she still owed more than eighteen thousand bucks to the ad agency. Somehow, over the next eight years she managed to pay the balance of her debt. As an ex-con, she toiled at whatever menial work she could get, far from the nice salary and plush benefits she had enjoyed before the Las Vegas disaster.

The only bright spot in the whole thirteen-year ordeal was Tyler Brock, the Public Defender assigned to her case. He was the only one who believed her story, the only person who did not turn his back on her during her hours of darkness. Abandoned by her family and closest friends, she had become a pariah to everyone who had ever meant anything to her, but Tyler was loyal as a Saint Bernard. As they met monthly, first to plan her appeals, then to bone up for the parole board, they developed a special bond. Eventually love blossomed. Not a mad, passionate, smoldering kind of love. More like a comfortable, perfectly broken-in, favorite pair of jeans kind of love. In truth, the only thing smoldering about Tyler Brock was the top of his bald head when he forgot his hat in the Arizona sun. Best described as milquetoast, Tyler was highly forgettable, but he had willingly stepped up to be Sue's knight in shining armor when no one else would touch the job.

Sure, he was appointed by the court, and he had not only lost her case miserably, but had seen the court slap Sue with the highest possible sentence. Tyler played the Washington Generals to the Attorney General's Harlem Globetrotters, but the important thing to Sue was Tyler did his best. Unlike everyone else, he stood by her to the end and she loved him for it.

"C'mon, Tyler dear," Sue said as she raced ahead through the Nashville Airport. Her face was still round and attractive, but prison had long ago cured her hair-bleaching habit. Her figure now filled out to Marilyn Monroe-esque proportions, the thirty-eight year-old woman was packed into tight burgundy stretch jeans and a size-too-small low-cut sweater.

Struggling to keep up, Tyler wrestled with several suitcases. His receding hairline gave way to a bald pate, red with sunburn. His mostly nondescript face featured wire-rimmed glasses perched upon a slightly hooked nose. His one distinctive characteristic was a mouth and teeth too big for his face. His kisser opened so wide, he seemed to have a Muppet-like hinge on the back of his neck. Tyler could have been the inspiration for whomever started calling teeth, 'Chiclets'. "Sue, honey." He tugged at his baggy jeans and smoothed a loose-fitting Ohio State sweatshirt. "What's your hurry?"

She paused twenty yards ahead and ran a hand through her mousy brown hair. "Darling. I'm just excited Michael Davis will finally answer for all the hell he put me through."

"Now Sweetie, I told you I thought it was a bad idea to come here. The statute of limitations has run out. There's not a thing we can legally do, even if you somehow manage to track him down. What exactly do you think you're going to do to him?"

Sue smiled. "Darling, I just want him to know what he's put me through. Plus, I'm still married to him. You and I can't ever get married until he signs the divorce papers."

"Honey, we talked about this. I can petition for an annulment. Or we can make a case for abandonment. Besides, if he entered the union under a false name, it's not legal."

Sue grew serious. "Look darling, after I saw him in that car-jumping video, I just knew deep in my heart if I'm ever gonna get closure on that part of my life, I need the chance to confront him.

Don't you want us to start our life together fresh, without all this mess hanging over our heads?"

Tyler seemed unconvinced. "I guess so, sweetie. I want to be on the record, though. I don't need any of this to be happy with you. This is all about what you need. If you're doing any of this for me, you don't have to."

"Duly noted, dear. It's all for me. I need closure."

The truth was Sue had spent countless hours in prison dreaming about what she would say and do to the man, if given the chance. She had rehearsed the scenario as intensely as an actress about to make her Broadway debut. Every word, every gesture, every nuance of her performance had been choreographed. Tyler had zero knowledge of the depth of her obsession with the man who had ruined her life. Tyler certainly did not know about the stylish little pink Ruger LCR Revolver Sue had already shipped to the hotel, to claim upon her arrival.

TWENTY-ONE

The black Ford F-150 stopped in front of a large red brick ranch home on Somerset Drive. Rooster barely noticed as he and Buddy finished a rousing rendition of Alan Jackson's version of Margaritaville along with Buddy's MP3 player. Rooster pounded what was left of the vodka tonics he had prepared for the seven-minute drive to Marcie's house. "Your church folks won't smell vodka on your breath," Buddy had promised.

The two men piled out, Buddy borderline sloppy as usual. His t-shirt with "Sasquatch Hunter" on the breast and a full-size bigfoot on the back was an improvement over the "Powered by Jack Daniels" shirt Rooster had convinced him to change earlier. Rooster surveyed the property. "Ain't that impressive. Thought you said Marcie's the richest woman in Murfreesboro?"

Buddy shook his head. "Trust me, son. She got enough cash to burn a wet mule."

Rooster stared at him. "Got no idea what that means."

Buddy slapped his back. "You just ponder it awhile, boy."

Still warm at eighty-four degrees, the humidity had broken, transforming the sticky day into a pleasant evening. The pair walked to the front door. Buddy checked his watch. "What time was this here shindig supposed to commence?"

"Five." Thanks to the vodka, Rooster was loose and relaxed.

Buddy tapped his watch. "You're late, son. Almost six."

Rooster scratched his head. "It's a cookout, man. Besides, when'd you start worrying about being late?"

"Just pointing out we coulda been here earlier if you hadn't made me go back home to change my shirt."

Rooster laughed. "What were you thinking with that Jack Daniel's thing?"

"Thought I was showing my support for one of Tennessee's most enduring institutions. Boy, you got no sense of history. At least I don't dress like a gay accountant."

Rooster held his arms out wide and examined his outfit. Brown boat shoes, green and brown plaid shorts, and a slightly too-tight olive golf shirt. "I'm stylish."

Buddy flashed his brilliant toothy grin. "You look like one a them damn San Francisco metrosexuals. I reckon I'll buy you a purse and start callin' you 'Nancy'."

Rooster stood in thought, but he could not come up with any snappy comebacks. He moved toward the door. "C'mon."

Buddy rang the bell. The door was opened by a twenty-something woman with short brown hair and bible verses on the front of her white shirt. Her eyes danced with excitement. "One of you must be Rooster. Starting to think you weren't coming."

"Hi." Rooster stammered. "I'm Rooster and this is my buddy, Buddy."

She giggled. "Your buddy buddy?"

That was stupid. He smiled painfully. "He's my buddy and his name is Buddy."

Buddy bowed and waved his arm with a flourish. "That'd be me, young lady. Ain't you just as purty as Memaw's blue-ribbon petunias?"

The girl grinned as her face turned red. "You're sweet."

Rooster stared in amazement. *How's he get away with that? With his country charm, he says things that'd get me slapped.*

She stepped aside. "C'mon in. It's great to meet both you. I'm

Rachel. C'mon y'all. Everyone's out back."

She led them through a beautiful living room with a huge stone fireplace, hand-scraped cherry hardwood floors, plush leather furniture, and mounted above the mantle, the biggest flat-screen Rooster had ever seen. The back of the room was a wall of windows with French Doors, which revealed a tile patio surrounded by a manicured private yard where people milled around. Massive planters were filled with all kinds of colorful flowers. Mature hardwood trees provided shade and character. A stone walkway led to a creek at the back of the yard. Marcie had her back to them as she spoke to a rough-looking man with dark four-day stubble and a tattered Atlanta Braves cap.

Buddy quickly moved past Rachel and Rooster straight toward Marcie. Rooster half-jogged to keep up. "If it ain't the prettiest girl to ever come outta Riverdale High," Buddy said sweetly before Marcie had even noticed his approach.

Marcie spun around. "Buddy Hollandsworth," she shrieked as she threw her arms around his neck and kissed his cheek. "To what do I owe the pleasure of your presence?"

Rooster rocked back and forth, an uncomfortable third wheel. *Buddy's such an enigma. How's he know everyone everywhere we go? And everybody loves him. How's that possible?*

Buddy's lips curled into a sly grin. Obviously enjoying the embrace, he affected a stern tone. "Ms. Dexter, keep throwing yourself at fellas like that, you gonna develop a reputation."

Marcie released his neck and punched his arm. "Oh stop it," she laughed. "So good to see you. How'd you stumble upon our little cookout?"

Buddy flashed his megawatt smile. "I'm just a chauffer today." He indicated Rooster with a theatrical arm gesture.

Rooster, unprepared for her sudden attention shift, smiled nervously and offered a meek, "Hello," along with a little wave. He immediately hated himself for greeting her like a wuss. He tried to recover, but all he could think was how he wished he had more vodka tonic. His buzz completely faded, he stood awkwardly with his mouth open. *She must think I'm an idiot.*

Buddy came to the rescue with his usual verbal flair. "You'll have to forgive ol' Rooster." He slapped his friend hard on the back. "He's shy as a twelve-point buck on the first day of deer season. But once you wind him up and get him goin' he'll be the life of the party."

Feeling three inches tall, Rooster managed an uneasy smile.

"Don't be shy, Rooster," Marcie said. "We're all friends here." Before he could respond, she turned back to Buddy. "How's your brother doing?"

Rooster stared in shock. *Buddy's got a brother?*

Oblivious to Rooster's questioning look, Buddy said, "Don't hear from him much since he graduated from SEAL training. I'm sure he's somewhere killing terrorists with his bare hands."

A Navy Seal? How'd I not know this?

Marcie addressed Rooster. "Went to high school with Buddy's little brother Brian. Buddy was his idol. He was all Brian ever talked about. Always wanted to be like his big brother and serve in the special forces. We're all proud of the Hollandsworth boys around these parts, but I'm sure you already know all that."

Rooster barely hid his shock. *Special forces? Really?*

Buddy laughed. "Yeah, but Brian became a damn squid instead of joining the real men in the Green Berets. But we're still glad to have him in the family." Buddy pointed across the yard. "Hey, I know that guy." Without another word, he lumbered away.

Marcie smiled. "Rooster, can I get you a drink?"

"I'd love a vodka tonic," Rooster answered reflexively, his mind still boggled from all the new information about Buddy.

"Afraid I don't have anything like that."

"Why not?" Rooster tried to sound light and funny. "A little drink never hurt anyone."

Marcie offered a benign smile "If you say so. Maybe you want me to throw away fifteen years of sobriety."

"I had no idea. I'm so sorry," Rooster sputtered, the old

embarrassment and self-loathing returning. *How many different ways can I make an ass of myself in front of this woman?*

"Don't worry about it," Marcie laughed. "I'm just yanking your chain. Not about being sober. That's true, but I'm a different person than I was back then. Trust me, nothing could make me want to dive back into my addiction."

Rooster stared at her. "What made you decide to stop?"

She rubbed her chin. "Oh, it was a million things. Constantly waking up with no idea where I was or how I got there. Being unable to function without a drink in my hand. Got tired of being a mess all the time and always feeling awful."

Seeing the similarities in their stories, Rooster tried to brush it off. *Probably can't handle her liquor like me.* But her words chirped in the back of his mind, an itch he could not scratch. "You just quit drinking," he blurted. "Just like that."

Marcie smiled warmly. "No, it was a process, but at some point I decided I wasn't ever going to quit quitting. Just like that. Now, what can I get for you to drink?"

Rooster grinned. "Guess you better make mine a water."

"Sure. Be right back." She grabbed the rough-looking dude in the Braves cap and guided him over. "Hey Rooster. I'd like you to meet George Jones." She turned to the man. "George, this is Rooster Michaels. You two talk while I get Rooster a water."

George gave a half-hearted handshake. "Nice to meet you."

"George Jones? Like the country singer?"

"Yeah." The man's face turned sour. "Hear that all the time. Gets a little tiresome."

"Sorry." Rooster stared at his shoes.

"Yeah." George looked as if he would rather be anywhere else than next to Rooster. More than a little bedraggled with the tattered hat and four-day beard, he wore a heavy denim work shirt with several dark greasy stains and a white oval name patch on the left breast. His faded black jeans and chunk work boots were covered with oily blotches.

As they stood in awkward silence, Rooster cast furtive glances at the house, silently willing Marcie to return. *Sure could use a real drink.* He was a much better conversationalist after a few belts. Rooster grew increasingly uncomfortable as the silence dragged on. *What's with this guy? I'm the new person here. Why don't he try a little harder to start a conversation? What am I supposed to say to this guy?* Mercifully, a question came to Rooster's mind. "So George, what do you do?"

George glanced at his outfit and then back at Rooster.

Rooster read his facial expression. *He thinks I'm stupid.*

"I'm a mechanic at Thomas Automotive," George offered.

Rooster waited for him to elaborate or ask a question, but George just stared at him. *This is torture. Is he devoid of personality, or is he actually working to make this conversation difficult? Where'd Marcie go? How long's it take to get a bottle of water?* Rooster could not take the silence. "You like it?"

George stifled a yawn. "I like it fine."

Did I do something to make him not like me? Rooster tried again. "How long you been there?"

George looked at the sky and let out a low whistle. "I swear. Seems like I been there a coon's age."

Rooster sighed. *Does anyone around here speak English? It's like pulling teeth.* He glanced across the yard where Buddy held court on the patio, surrounded by a big group of people. He talked, made wild gestures, and slapped their backs. Every few seconds the group burst into laughter. Rooster was about to walk away and join them when George asked, "Whatcha do, Rooster?"

"Ahhh..." Rooster stammered. "I'm between jobs right now."

"What's that mean?"

"I used to be a salesman." He shoved his hands into his pockets. "But they let me go last Thursday."

George stared blankly. "What'd you sell?"

"Meat." Rooster examined George's face. *This guy have any feelings? What's it take to get a rise out of him?*

"You got any prospects?"

"Not yet." Rooster tried to evoke any emotion from him. "Need to find something quick, though. Landlord took away my front door until I catch up the rent."

"Hmm."

Rooster frowned. *Is he completely unmoved by my story?*

"Here's the water." Marcie handed the bottle to Rooster.

"Thanks," Rooster said, grateful to have something to do with his hands.

"You and George getting along ok?"

Rooster forced a smile. "George seems like a great guy."

"Excuse me," George said and walked away.

Rooster watched him leave. "What's his deal?"

"George is struggling right now. You'll probably hear more about that Wednesday night. Tell me about yourself, Rooster."

He took a long sip of water to buy time and collect his thoughts. He lowered the drink and asked, "Whatcha wanna know?"

"Don't know. Your accent obviously isn't from around here. How'd you end up in Murfreesboro?"

"Truthfully. I got off the bus here and didn't have enough money to go any further. So I found a job and kind of stayed."

Marcie was skeptical. "That the truth?"

"Pretty much."

"How you know Buddy?"

"Met him doing door-to-door sales."

"Buddy's a hoot." Marcie's intelligent green eyes shined. "Such a nice guy. Don't know anyone who don't just love him."

"I know. He's quite the character."

"So, you still in sales?"

Rooster stared at his toes and put on his most mournful tone. "Lost my job this past Thursday."

"Oh my goodness. That's horrible!"

The fuss she made over his bad situation pleased him. Before he could stop himself, Rooster unloaded the whole story about his delinquent rent and missing door. Marcie oozed sympathy and seemed genuinely concerned.

"I know a few people in this town," she said. "Let me make some calls and maybe I can help you get an interview somewhere."

Rooster was surprised. "You serious?"

"Of course. We'll exchange phone numbers and talk before you come to group Wednesday."

"Ok." Not used to being around nice, giving folks, Rooster was somewhat dumbfounded by her generosity. He kind of liked it. *Why don't I spend more time with people like that?*

"I'm glad we got that settled," Marcie declared.

"I really appreciate it."

Rooster considered the rabble with whom he usually associated. He was more like them than he cared to admit. Others eventually figured it out and disappeared. *What about Buddy? He's a great guy. Marcie said it herself. Maybe Buddy hasn't figured me out yet.* His head hurt. It was too much to contemplate without some lubrication.

Marcie interrupted his thoughts. "Why don't I introduce you to some more people?"

"Actually, can you direct me to the bathroom?"

"I'll take you there."

Rooster waved his hands. "No, no, no. You have other guests besides me. Just point me in the right direction."

"Alright," Marcie said slowly. She told him and Rooster headed toward the house. He slowed to eavesdrop as he passed Buddy's conversation circle.

"So those Brown-headed Cow Birds lay their eggs in other birds' nests and leave the kids to be raised by someone else," Buddy said. "They're the professional athletes of the bird world." His delivery impeccable, the group roared with laughter.

Rooster continued to be amazed at Buddy's incredible volume of funny stories and his perfect timing. He was never at a loss for words. *Where's he get this stuff?* Rooster entered the French doors, but instead of turning at the bathroom, he continued straight through the foyer and out the front door.

"Hope you forgot to lock up, Buddy," he said as he approached the big Ford. With growing anxiety he grabbed the door handle. Relief flooded over him as the door swung open. *Step one. Success.* He climbed inside and threw open the center console. "C'mon Buddy." He dug through crumpled papers, tangled wires, and various electronic devices. "Don't let me down."

At the very bottom, he wrapped his fingers around something smooth and cool. His heart raced as he pulled it from the console. "Bingo!" He smiled at the flask-size bottle of Southern Comfort. Rooster unscrewed the cap and sucked down a third of the syrupy amber liquid, his nerves instantly calmed as the familiar warmness radiated from his throat to the rest of his body. He quickly emptied the bottle. *Now I'm ready to party.*

Rooster strutted back onto the patio, loose, relaxed, and confident. He spotted Rachel and struck up a conversation about how the Beach Boys would have been bigger than the Beatles if the band had just embraced Brian Wilson's genius. They moved through several other topics before the focus turned to Rooster's job status and rental house crisis. Just like Marcie, Rachel gushed with empathy. He knew he should not fish for this kind of attention, but that did not stop him.

When Rachel excused herself, Rooster found another audience. To his secret delight, his sob story produced compassionate responses from everyone. He unabashedly basked in their attention, adding more detail with each new telling. He had wrapped up his sob story for the sixth time when he noticed Buddy had approached George Jones. He moved closer, curious to see if Buddy's country charisma had finally met its kryptonite in the personality-challenged auto mechanic. As he approached, George was doubled over in laughter while Buddy slapped his shoulder. *Unbelievable. This man's unstoppable.*

Seeing his friend, Buddy draped his arm around Rooster's shoulders, leaned close, and whispered, "Time to go, son."

"Ok." Rooster checked the time. Seven thirty.

Buddy faced George. "We've gotta roll, but think on what I said. You can put your boots in the oven, but that don't make 'em biscuits, if you know what I mean."

The auto mechanic smiled as if this was the most profound thing he had ever heard. "Gotcha Buddy. Great meeting you."

Buddy slapped his back and shouted in his booming voice, "Can't wait to tell everyone I met Mr. George No Show Jones!"

George giggled like a school girl. Rooster could not believe this was the same sourpuss who wouldn't crack a smile earlier.

As the pair said their goodbyes, many of the guests warmly hugged Buddy while Rooster stood awkwardly to the side. Only Marcie offered an embrace to Rooster as well.

As he climbed into the truck, Rooster considered what Marcie had shared about her drinking. Guilt and shame bubbled up as he remembered the empty Southern Comfort bottle from the center console. "Hey Buddy? You think I drink too much?"

Buddy put the F-150 into drive. "When it comes to questions like that, I'm careful not to let my mouth overload my tail."

"What's that mean?"

Buddy gave him a playful shove. "You just sit and think for a spell, boy. It'll come to you."

TWENTY-TWO

As the Chairman drove to the rugby house, he watched for Davis Sinclair and the scofflaw who took his stuff. *Could they be one and the same?* The Chairman worked to gather his thoughts, to come up with a plan. Despite all he had been through and the fact normal feeling had yet to return to his foot, he was upbeat and optimistic. *Something good's coming.* He parked and waited.

Nothing happened for several hours. He sank in his seat and peeked over the dashboard as a large group of women, including all three NEIU girls, headed toward the house. He noted how carefree and easygoing Madison seemed in any crowd. *Her beauty and charm will open tons of doors for me when we're together.* He glanced at his watch. Six pm. Then nothing.

Finally at seven forty-three, several girls, including Madison, appeared and headed toward Middle Tennessee Boulevard. The Chairman watched in disbelief. "They're going out to party again?" *What about Sinclair? They even interested in him anymore?* After a long sigh, he scrambled from the car and clomped off after them. Painfully aware of his wheezing shoes and drastic limp, the Chairman hung back as far as dared.

Eventually the women arrived at Greek Row on the MTSU campus and disappeared inside one of the big fraternity houses. The Chairman stopped on the front lawn to assess the situation.

Amazingly, the same giant pumpkin-headed guy from the night before stood at the door with his stack of cash and sharpie. *They have professional house party bouncers here?* The Chairman scratched his head. *Maybe this guy's running a protection racket. He's like the mob and everyone's afraid to confront him. Just shows up and starts collecting money.*

The Chairman glanced at the still-bright green dollar sign on his hand and considered how he might slip in without paying. *Is the giant dimwitted enough to use the same color and symbol at every door he patrols?* As the Chairman weighed his options, Madison strolled out the front door with Mr. Jock Guy. "Really?" *This guy's too much. Gotta put an end to this somehow.*

He clomped behind them quietly as possible into the darkness behind the house. He could barely see them as they disappeared behind a metal storage shed. He tiptoed as best he could on a numb foot and stopped in front of the little building. He closed his eyes and strained to listen. What he heard made him extremely unhappy. At first he thought they were into each other, with heavy breathing and something banging against the thin metal wall. When Madison protested, he realized with horror she was in a struggle to escape that Neanderthal.

This is my big chance to get this dunderhead outta the picture once and for all. He searched for a weapon until his gaze fell upon a big three gallon metal bucket. The Chairman snatched the handle, took several deep breaths, and ran behind the shed, David about to do battle with Goliath.

Much darker back there than he had imagined, after several steps he could make out a male figure next to the shed. He channeled his inner Mel Gibson and let out a war whoop that would have made William Wallace proud. With both hands, he swung the big bucket at the man. It hit with a loud metallic thunk and some sort of powder exploded everywhere.

What just happened? A dusty cloud obscured everything. Completely freaked out, the Chairman retreated until his eyes cleared. He examined himself in the dim light and saw a fine white dust covering his arms and the front of his clothes. He felt it on his face and caked in his hair. He still held the bucket which was much lighter now. He lifted it close to his face, barely able to make out the writing on the now-empty pail. 'Powdered Paint'. He turned his face to the sky. "Aw shit. You gotta be kidding me."

He heard Madison's voice. "Hey, who's out there?"

Through the gloom, the Chairman saw her facing him. *Holy crap. I must look ridiculous.* In a panic, he sprinted off, awkwardly dragging his numb foot behind him. After a hundred yards, he slowed to a jog, and then a walk. In the oppressive humidity, his free-flowing sweat liquefied the powdered paint. It dripped from his fingers, ran down his legs, and flowed into his eyes as he hobbled across a huge manicured lawn.

Hands, arms, and clothes covered, he had nothing to wipe the paint from his eyes. As he clomped along in wheezing shoes, he dragged his left foot like Igor, blinked at the paint in his eyes, and vigorously shook his head in a vain attempt to clear his vision. Amidst all those distractions, it was no wonder he did not see the little sprinkler heads pop up everywhere. The shoe on his numb foot caught on one, sending him into a belly flop as the water kicked on. He lay there and searched for something positive in his situation. As the droplets splashed down, the Chairman considered all that had happened to him. Through creative logic he concluded Davis Sinclair was personally responsible for all of it. *He's gonna pay.*

The rest of Sunday night was a blur as the Chairman crafted a brilliantly devious plan for when he finally had Sinclair in his clutches.

TWENTY-THREE
Monday, May 16th

Tiffany wandered down the staircase at seven-thirty am. She looked like a Victoria's Secret model in black and pink lounging pants and a white tee, her hair and makeup flawless. Laughter wafted toward her as she approached the kitchen. She pushed through the door and found nearly every girl in the rugby house crammed inside. They gathered around Madison, who sat at the table, a steaming cup of coffee in front of her.

Crystal noticed her first. "Tiff, where you been?"

Tiffany laughed and flipped her hair. "You think I wake up looking this good?"

"I woke up looking like this," Crystal smiled. She wore her usual oversized t-shirt, baggy shorts, and orange sneakers.

Tiffany grinned. "Guess God blessed you with natural beauty so you don't have to work at it like the rest of us."

"Quit clowning around," one of the Tennessee women demanded. "I wanna hear the rest of Madison's story."

Tiffany moved to Madison's side. "You sharing something new, or telling the one about the goat on the field during the Grand Valley game for the hundredth time?"

Madison twisted to make eye contact with Tiffany. "No, this is about what happened last night. It was totally crazy, but that other story is awesome!" She turned to the other women. "Hey everyone, when I'm done with this one, remind me to tell you guys about the time I tackled a goat."

Tiffany playfully slapped Madison's shoulder. "Don't make us wait all morning. Tell us your crazy new story."

Madison's eyes grew wide. "Ok, but you're not gonna believe it." She took a long drink of her coffee.

"You know Devin, who I met at the Boulevard on Saturday night? It was obvious he liked me. I led him on at first, but after awhile he kinda grew on me. He walked me back from the bar to the house Saturday night. Then he took me to the Square. That's why I missed all the excitement here. We sat on a bench in front of the courthouse and talked 'til four in the morning and he never laid a hand on me. So thankfully I didn't have to whoop his ass." She caught Crystal's eye and winked. "Ask Crystal and Tiffany what happens to guys dumb enough to get fresh with me."

All eyes fell upon Madison's co-captains. "Girls," Tiffany declared loudly. "You don't wanna know the pain she inflicts on those poor fools. I think the last one's still in traction."

The room erupted in laughter. Madison sipped her coffee until the outburst died down. "I thought, here's a real gentleman. Great to talk to. At some point I realized I was really into this guy. It was awesome just hanging out with him. I'm thinking, why can't I meet someone like this in Chicago? Anyway, he walked me back and I crashed until the afternoon. After you girls gave us the tour of campus, a bunch of us went to the party at the SAE house. Guess who I ran into there?"

Crystal asked, "Devin?"

"Exactly," Madison replied. "I thought we'd pick up right where we left off Sunday morning. I was excited, but there was something different about him. Felt it right away, but I couldn't put my finger what it was. At least not until later."

Tiffany could not wait. "What was different about him?"

Madison smiled sadly. "Besides turning into a total jerk?"

One of the girls scowled. "Don't they all, eventually?"

Madison giggled. "Don't know about that, but he was drunk and surrounded by his buddies and I think I was the last person he expected to see. There was this arrogance to him that wasn't there the night before. Almost like he'd gotten it into his head he had to impress his friends. He was way more aggressive than Saturday. He was grabbing my hands and touching my leg and wrapping his arm around my shoulders. Nothing ridiculous, but just enough to make me wonder about him."

"That muttonhead didn't know who he was messin' with," Tiffany offered. "Did you throw the hammer down on him?"

"Stop it," Madison scolded. "You're getting ahead of me."

"Aw, c'mon," Tiffany protested. "Get to the meat already."

Madison held up her hands. "All right. I'll hurry and get to the good stuff. I thought maybe he'd act like the guy from Saturday night if I got him away from his friends. I thought maybe they're a bad influence on him. So I asked him if he knew a quiet place where we could be alone and talk. Devin smiled and grabbed me by the hand and led me outside. At first I'm thinking this is great. We'll have a replay of Saturday night. But when we started walking he was way more plastered than I realized. Slurring his words and stumbling around. The stuff he was sayin' really wasn't making any sense. It had been so loud in the house, I never realized how impaired his speech had become."

"Why didn't you dropkick his butt?" Crystal asked.

"Don't know. I guess somewhere in the back of my mind I was under the delusion that if we just sat together awhile, he'd eventually sober up and we could hang out like we did Saturday night. It was only eight or nine, so we had time to wait."

"You were delusional." Tiffany laughed. "Musta been really smitten to even consider babysitting his drunk ass all evening."

Madison smiled and shook her head. "Guilty as charged. Anyway, Devin leads me behind the frat house to this steel tool shed. I'm thinking, no seats here. What's this clown up to?"

"Shoulda known," Tiffany offered playfully. "He wanted what all men want. Hopefully you overcame your delusions."

"Yes." Madison grinned. "He was trying to sweet talk me, but it was so pathetic with him slurring and swaying all over the place. We were behind the shed. It was really dark. Could barely see anything. Then out of nowhere he lunges at me. It was so gross. A sloppy drunk guy with his arms wrapped around my neck, pushing me against the shed and trying to kiss me."

"What a turn off," one of the girls exclaimed.

"Turn off is too kind a description. He reeked of beer. Felt like he had six hands. He was mumbling about how hot he was for me and pressing his body against me. Absolutely disgusting. I turned my head so he couldn't get at my lips, but his mouth was all over my ear and neck. I could actually feel his slobber dripping down the side of my face."

"Eww," several of the women sang out in unison.

Madison stopped for coffee, milking the story climax for all it was worth.

Crystal's patience had run out. "For the love of God, Madison. Tell us what happened."

Madison smiled. "Ok. His hands were all over the place. Then he licked my cheek and I decided, enough of this madness. I pushed off the shed to get a little room. I pulled him close to get leverage and I kneed him in the crotch as hard as I could."

The room exploded with hoots of delight. Girls high-fived each other and happily slapped Madison on the back. When the eruption subsided, Madison continued. "Tell you what. Devin let go of me in a hurry. He was doubled over, gripping his junk, and squeaking out some sort of curse at me. I figured that was a good time to make my exit. Devin's pretty big. Definitely didn't want to be standing there once he got his wits about him."

"You said your story was crazy," Tiffany said with disappointment. "That doesn't sound all that crazy."

"That's 'cause I'm not finished yet. You just wait. When I'm done, you tell me whether or not what happened was crazy."

"Oh all right."

"Not exactly sure what happened next. Like I said, it was dark. I turned to walk away and I hear this crazy whooshing noise. You know, kinda like a hydraulic press. It went whoosh, whoosh, whoosh. Then there was a horrible scream, or yelp, or... really don't know what it was."

Madison's eyes lit up as she grabbed Crystal's arm. "You remember that stupid horror movie we watched during the road trip to Lake Superior State?"

Crystal stared blankly.

"You know. Lauren Holly was a professor and they find some ancient box in the school basement. You said it was the most ridiculous..."

"Oh yeah," Crystal interrupted, laughing. "But I can't think of the title."

"*Scream of the Banshee*," Tiffany offered.

"Yes," Madison squealed in triumph. "The scream or whatever it was sounded kinda like the banshee from the movie."

"For real?" Crystal was skeptical. "You're not exaggerating just a little bit?"

"No, I'm really not. It was nails-on-the-chalkboard terrible. Like a little girl screaming while strangling a cat. Then there was a loud clunk, kinda like an aluminum bat hitting a softball. Devin grunted. Then he fell against the shed."

"The banshee hit Devin?" One of the girls asked.

"I think so, but it gets weirder. I turned back toward Devin and there was this white dust cloud, like someone launched baby powder into the air. Devin's lying on the ground groaning and mumbling, covered with this white stuff. It was all in his hair and all around him on the ground. I backed away so none of it would get on me. Then I heard a guy's voice in the distance behind me. It said, 'Aw shit. You gotta be kidding me.'

"That totally freaked me out. I turned to look, but it was so dark.

I could just barely see the outline of a figure so I called out, 'Hey, who's out there?'

One of the women asked, "Who was it?"

"Don't know. Soon as I spoke, he takes off running. But that wasn't even normal. He ran like Igor, from the mad scientist movies?" Madison stared at their blank faces. "C'mon. Picture a little guy sorta hunched over and dragging his leg behind him."

Eyes flickered with understanding. "Yeah, I know what you're talking about," someone claimed as multiple heads nodded.

"Well picture that. Only moving really fast."

"A sprinting Igor," Crystal said in amazement as everyone burst into laughter.

Madison raised her voice. "That's not all. When he ran I heard the whooshing noise again and I could see that white powder trailing behind him. It was like a sprinting Igor going whoosh, whoosh, whoosh, with a white cloud trailing behind him as he disappeared into the night. It all played out so fast. From when Devin jumped me to when Igor was out of sight, the whole thing lasted maybe two or three minutes."

"Sorry I doubted you. That is the craziest story I ever heard," Tiffany said, mouth agape

"What about Devin?" Crystal asked. "Where'd the banshee... er... Igor hit him?"

"Musta been in the head. He was writhing on the ground holding the back of his head and asking what just happened."

Tiffany stared at her friend. "What'd you do?"

Madison drained her coffee. Her face turned serious. "I just wanted to get outta there. I turned around and went back to the party. I told Devin's friends where they could find that jerk. Then I came back here and went to bed."

TWENTY-FOUR

Rooster's eyes snapped open.

I'm on the sofa. He sighed with relief. Then he saw it. A huge black nose hovered near his eye and the odor of wet fur and dog breath attacked his nostrils. "C'mon," he spit. "You gotta be kidding me." *Stupid stray's in the house again. Gotta get that wood slab from Buddy. Weren't we supposed to bring that over after the cookout?*

Somehow the door cover had lost importance after a few drinks at Liquid Smoke. Rooster cataloged the events following the cookout and realized with disgust he could not remember how he had gotten home. *Buddy was matching me drink for drink, but it never affects him. How'd he get home?* His thoughts were interrupted when the dog planted a sloppy kiss on Rooster's lips. *What a way to wake up. Something's got to change. Normal people don't wake up like this.* He rolled off the sofa and discovered he was missing a shoe. "Really?" *What happened to the other one? This is ridiculous.*

The medium sized, sandy-haired canine enthusiastically wagged his whole back end. He barked, exacerbating Rooster's already aching head, each yelp another spike driven into his skull. The animal jumped, his front paws hitting Rooster's stomach, nearly knocking him backwards.

"All right, that's enough. Get outta here!" Rooster pushed him away. "No! I don't wanna play." He grabbed the scruff of the dog's neck, dragged him to the sad blanket, and shoved him out. The dog ran back inside. Rooster half-heartedly searched for something to block the opening. He briefly considered the couch, but decided against physical exertion so early in the morning. He herded the dog back outside, ducked under the blanket and stood there, a goalie blocking the rambunctious animal from re-entry. He fended him off until his phone rang. Rooster lumbered inside, snatched up the phone, and plopped on the couch. The dog followed, jumped up next to him, and laid his head in Rooster's lap. Rooster answered with a heavy sigh. "Hello?"

"Rooster?" It was a female voice.

She sounded vaguely familiar. *I give my number to anyone last night?* His stomach churned as he searched his memory. In his experience, calls from vaguely familiar women usually spelled trouble. *Sure hope I didn't do anything crazy. What female besides my mother would be calling me this early?* "Yes?"

"This is Marcie Dexter. Did I wake you?"

Rooster let out a relieved breath and sat up straighter. "No, not at all. I was just..." He glanced at the dog in his lap. "I was just trying to get rid of a pest." As if he understood Rooster's comments, the dog looked up with sad eyes.

"Oh. You need me to call back?"

A vision of his first sales trainer, Diamond Dan Martin, popped into Rooster's head. "Keep a mirror in front of you when calling prospects," Diamond Dan had taught. "The person on the phone can hear whether you're smiling or frowning."

Rooster forced a grin. "Not at all. What can I do for you?"

"Actually, I'm calling to share what I can do for you!"

Diamond Dan was right. Rooster could hear happiness in Marcie's voice. "Alright. Lay it on me."

"Well, after you left the cookout, I talked to my friend Jimmy Robinson. He owns Robinson Sporting Goods."

"Uh huh." Rooster absentmindedly stroked the dog's head.

"He's looking to hire a salesman, so I told him about you."

"Really?"

"Yes, really," she said with delight. "He wants you to come in for an interview tomorrow."

Rooster could not hold back a smile. *What's she doing? She barely knows me.* When she made her offer to help, he had dismissed it as just talk. Never did he think she would actually follow through. He would not have if the roles had been reversed. Rooster poured on all the charm as he could muster on short notice. "Don't toy with me, Marcie."

She laughed. "I'm not, but there is something I have to say to you before you go in."

Uh oh. Now she makes it clear I owe her big time. Exactly what I'd do. Why expect anything different from her? His shoulders sagged as he leaned back. "What's that?"

"Rooster, I don't know how to put this delicately, so I'm just going to say it."

Wow. Here comes the guilt trip.

"Jimmy Robinson has five years sobriety."

Rooster cocked his head at the dog, who lifted his eyes to meet Rooster's. *That's not what I expected. Where's this going?*

"You go to that interview in the same condition you were in last night, he'll spot it in a second."

Rooster's heart sank. *How'd she know?* He mustered up indignation. "What you talking about?"

Marcie laughed kindly. "C'mon Rooster, I used to be an alcoholic. You think I can't spot someone under the influence?"

Don't like where this is going. The conversation had caught him by surprise, his hung-over brain unable to shift gears. "I wasn't drinking," he finally sputtered.

"Probably thought no one could smell the vodka, but you can't kid a kidder. I know all the tricks. You had a drink before coming in. When you said you were going to the bathroom, you actually went outside for another drink. That one wasn't vodka. Smelled more like Southern Comfort to me."

Rooster's head spun. *How'd she know? Why's she calling me out?* "I can't believe you're accusing me of this."

Marcie grew serious. "Listen Rooster, you don't have to admit anything to me. I'm just trying to help you. I'll give you two pieces of unsolicited advice. The rest's up to you."

Defiance filled his voice. "Oh yeah, what's that?"

"You drink anything before meeting with Jimmy, I promise he'll know. You want the job, please go to the interview sober."

"What's the other thing?"

"Take it from someone who used to be a total mess because of my drinking. I'm urging you to take a hard look at your life. Maybe I'm wrong and you have it totally under control. Be honest with yourself. If your drinking's brought nothing but destruction to your life, you probably have a problem, especially if you lost your job because of it."

He considered his long string of alcohol-related firings.

"Maybe," Marcie continued with a chuckle, "after a night of partying you woke up in a ladies room stall at a Waffle House in Chattanooga with no memory of how you got there."

Or a pasture in Readyville with a cow licking my face?

"Or worse. You came out of an alcohol coma to discover you're married to a circus clown."

Sally. I'm still married to Sally What's-Her-Name.

"Then drinking may be an issue for you," Marcie concluded.

Despite complete understanding of her implication, Rooster was overcome with a strange reflexive anger. "I don't have a problem with alcohol."

"Ok." Sadness filled Marcie's voice. "I'm probably just projecting my own experiences on you because all of that and worse happened to me until I got my drinking under control. I think, if you're really honest with yourself, you'll find just maybe there's some truth to what I'm saying."

Rooster was shaken. *If that's all true, she really does know what my life's like. Do I have a problem?* Of course he did. The goofy tattoo on his stomach was a constant reminder of the demons which haunted him. He just could not bring himself to admit it out loud, especially to this total stranger. *Why she think my life is any of her business anyway?* The thought stoked the flames of his growing anger and resentment. "Are you done?"

"Yes, I am."

"Ok, goodbye."

"Good luck with your interview." The smile had returned to her voice.

"Yeah, whatever." Rooster's mood darkened. He disconnected. He roughly pushed the dog off his lap and headed to the kitchen. *She's got a lot of nerve.* He opened the fridge. The beer was gone. "Crap." He pulled the cupboard door, grabbed a half-full bottle of Jack Daniels, and retrieved a glass from the sink.

The phone vibrated. The liquor bottle still in his hand, Rooster snatched up the device and answered gruffly. "What?"

"Rooster, Marcie again. So sorry to bother you."

He stared at the Jack Daniels with unbelieving eyes. *She got a camera in here or something?* Paranoia overcame him. Rooster looked around the room.

"I forgot to give you the details for your interview."

"Oh." Rooster set down the bottle as the dog padded into the room and sniffed at his leg.

"How about I just text it to you?"

"Yes." Rooster's tone softened. "That works."

"Hey, I'm sorry if I came on a little strong earlier. Like I said, there may not be a problem at all, but I'm always ready to talk if there is. I certainly didn't mean to offend you."

"Yeah." Rooster glanced at the ceiling. "Sorry I got upset. Thanks for getting me the interview."

"I was happy to do it. Please let me know how it goes."

"I will."

"Ok. See you Wednesday night."

"Sounds good. Goodbye."

"Bye."

Rooster sat down, his elbows on the table, his chin in his hands. He stared at the Jack Daniels bottle. The dog laid his head on Rooster's thigh, but the man did not notice. His mind replayed Marcie's chillingly accurate description of his life.

From out of nowhere he heard the preacher's voice. "God redeemed me from the mess my life had become. And you know what? My God is big enough to do the exact same thing for you."

He shook his head. *Where'd that come from? Church people messing with my mind.* Rooster stood and grabbed the bottle. He pondered how badly he wanted the brown liquid. He enjoyed the subtle burn it produced in his throat before the warmness radiated out from his gut to the rest of his body. How it dulled his senses so he could forget for awhile what a train wreck his life had become. The dog stared at him with sad brown eyes.

"You think I should have some?"

Rooster gave the animal's head a gentle pat.

"Me neither." He stashed the bottle back in the cupboard.

TWENTY-FIVE

The Chairman limped into Lowes, mumbling to himself. He worked through his scheme to wreak havoc on Davis Sinclair, but struggled with how to actually snatch the man. With white splotches everywhere, he looked as if a paint balloon had exploded against his chest. Paint coated his face, arms, and the front of his clothes. From head to heel, his back was relatively untouched by paint, but covered in dirt and grass stains. Clumps of hair were either matted down or sticking out wildly.

The smell of sweat and stale beer draped over him like a fog. He moved slowly, his leg still gimpy. With each step, his expensive, paint-speckled loafers whooshed loud enough to be heard two aisles away in the door and window section. Up on his toes to keep his heels from hitting the floor, his gait was reminiscent of Elmer Fudd sneaking up on a rabbit hole.

A morning powwow of bleary-eyed contractors stopped mid-conversation to gawk as this bizarre character clomped by. The Chairman did not notice them elbowing each other and snickering as his brain overflowed with dreams of revenge and laments about this crazy disaster of a trip.

Despite his limited cash reserves, the Chairman tried to anticipate anything he might need. So far he had 50 feet of nylon cord, a roll of duct tape, and a box of painter's rags. He stared at a huge spool of chain and attempted to calculate whether a strong lock and length of chain would be more cost effective than rope. He had never been good at tying knots.

Lost in his own world, the Chairman hobbled right into a mountain wearing a blue Fubu jersey and orange newsboy cap.

"Hey," the big guy bellowed. "Watch where you're going."

The northeast accent caught him off guard. He stepped back and realized with chagrin he had gotten white paint on the guy's shirt. As he looked up, the Chairman was struck by the odd braided tendrils protruding every which way from the guy's chin.

The man gave the Chairman a gentle shove. "You look like crap. You some crazy homeless guy? Or just having a bad day?"

The Chairman replied, "Not from here." He tried to place the big guy's accent. "I belong at NEIU." *Sounds like New York.* "It's been a rough couple days."

The big guy laughed. "What's wit the rope and duct tape? Gonna kidnap someone?"

TWENTY-SIX

Little Tony was frustrated. He had hoped the old man had a master plan to collect his hundred large from that rat Sinclair Davis. He wanted car chases, physical intimidation, and gun fights. Instead of the mayhem and excitement he longed for, they had done a big fat nothing. Their tour of every last rest stop between New Jersey and Tennessee had been scintillating and action-packed by comparison.

Tighter than an Italian tenor's trousers, Big Tony had found the cheapest, dirtiest motel in Murfreesboro and proceeded to hole up there ever since. The old man rambled incessantly about the importance of creating a "home base," from which they could mastermind operations, and to which they could retreat if things got too hot. Little Tony had a hunch this was merely his dad's excuse to stay near a toilet for his inevitable Irritable Bowel Syndrome flare-ups. His suspicions were confirmed when his dad informed him through the bathroom door all the toilet paper was gone. His dad perched impatiently on the throne, Little Tony marched to the motel office. The manager, an unhappy man with a thick Middle Eastern accent, loudly informed Little Tony each room was limited to one roll per day. Tony the Younger saw an opportunity to briefly escape his fleabag prison. In no position to argue with his son's solution to the toilet tissue rationing, Big Tony let loose a blue streak of uniquely colorful expletives and reluctantly handed over his beloved

Oldsmobile for a TP run.

Cruising through Murfreesboro, Little Tony felt free. The old Aurora actually was a smooth ride, something he would never admit that to his father. After a 20-minute drive, he figured he had better find someplace to buy the goods. He pulled into a shopping center and found a parking spot near Lowes.

He loved to wander in the big box home improvement stores, always on the lookout for ideas to trick out his crib when he eventually moved out of his parents' house. As Little Tony walked the store, a strange noise moved up and down the rows. There was a hydraulic-quality to it with air expelled under pressure. *Maybe there's some cool piece of machinery making all that racket.* He followed the sound, but as soon as he had a bead on it, the noise stopped.

When he saw the strange little man, Little Tony forget about the sound. He moved closer for a better look. He had no cowboy hat or *Duck Dynasty* beard, but this weirdo was still a sight to behold. Covered in dirt and grime, the guy seemed mesmerized by a spool of chain. *This a street person who wandered in? What's with the paint all over him? Something explode on him? Maybe he came here to get what he needs to fix whatever did that to him.* The man clutched rope, duct tape, and painter's rags. *Interesting combination.* Little Tony remembered his dad's stories about mob hits and the "cleaners" who sanitized crime scenes gone bad. They showed up with a big suitcase of common household chemicals and supplies. After a little time and expert skill, the location looked like nothing ever happened there.

As Little Tony approached the guy, the smell hit him. *Sheesh. When was his last bath? Gotta be a schizo street person off his meds.* The strange man spun and lurched into Tony's chest. Little Tony bellowed, "Hey. Watch where you're going."

The guy stared at Tony's stomach, his face filled with fear. *At least someone in Tennessee's intimidated by me. So what if it's some lunatic. I'll take what I can get right now.* The man slowly raised his face, his stare fixed on Tony's Medusa beard. He said nothing. *He on drugs or just mentally deficient?* The hairs on the back of Tony's neck tingled. Tony gave him a gentle shove just to see if he was all there. "You look like crap. You some crazy homeless guy? Or just having a bad day?"

"Not from here, he said cryptically. "I belong at NEIU."

NEIU? Some sorta sanitarium? A government agency? Tony assessed him. He was a mess.

"It's been a rough couple of days," the guy continued.

No kidding. Looks like he was run over by the highway line-painting truck. Tony could not help laughing as he decided to have some fun. "What's wit the rope and duct tape?" Tony played up his New York-New Jersey accent until he sounded straight out of the cast of *Good Fellas*. "Gonna kidnap someone?"

The man's eyes grew wide. "How'd you know?"

This crackpot's downright mental. Gotta push his buttons a little bit. "What else would you do wit duct tape and rope?" The guy stared at the items. "But," Little Tony continued, "What you gonna do with those rags?"

"I was going to stuff them in his mouth before covering it with tape, and I was hoping to get some chloroform. You know, soak a rag and press it against his face."

Little Tony leaned in conspiratorially. "Sounds like you got this caper all planned out."

"Most of it. You know where I can get chloroform?"

Tony smiled. "I think they got that over at Home Depot. If not, try Wal-Mart. They got everything over there."

The man nodded. "What about the chains?"

"What about 'em?"

"Should I tie him up with chains or rope?"

"No question." Little Tony projected confidence. "Gotta be rope. Chains are too loud. You got a guy in the trunk, he can make a whole lotta racket wit a chain."

The man scratched his chin. "That's a good point. I was leaning toward rope anyway. Cheaper than chain."

"Gotta watch your money. What this guy do to you anyway?"

"He stole twenty thousand dollars from my girlfriend."

Right. If this lunatic has a girlfriend, I'm a jockey in the Kentucky Derby. He's crazier than a coked-up Tony Montana.

The little man interrupted Tony's inner musings. "You seem to know a lot about this stuff."

"That's right." Tony dropped his voice to barely a whisper. "I'm a cleaner."

The little guy's face lit up with a huge smile. "You mean like Harvey Keitel in *Pulp Fiction*?"

"Somethin' like that."

"Can you tell me any stories? What's the most disgusting thing you ever had to... ah... dispose of?"

Little Tony crossed his arms and smiled smugly. "I could tell you, but then I gotta kill you. And that's no joke."

The little guy let out a nervous laugh. "Thanks for your help. I got to go now."

Little Tony's confidence soared. *That guy nearly crapped his pants. I still got it.* His self-congratulations were interrupted by the hydraulic sound he had chased earlier. The noise came from the crazy guy's shoes. "What the..." He shouted down the row, "Hey."

The man stopped and slowly turned. "Yes?"

"Do somethin' wit those shoes, little dude. Whoever you after is gonna hear you coming from a mile away."

The man peered at his feet. "Ok. Can I go now?"

Tony dismissed him with a wave of his hands. "Yeah. Good luck, paisan."

He shook his head as the little guy clomped away. *Which aisle's got the TP? Better get the biggest package they got. Old man's gonna be angry as a sewer rat I took so long.* Little Tony bought two 32-roll packs of the cheapest generic toilet tissue he could find and headed back to the motel. He started to get out of the car, when a thought hit him.

My gun's right there in the glove box. He leaned across the bench seat, unlocked the compartment with Big Tony's car keys, and pulled out the Rock Island Armory 1911A1-FS semi-automatic handgun and its eight-round magazine. He slapped the clip into the handle and held the pistol, feeling its weight. The wide grips made the gun a bit clunky, but it was certainly better than nothing. Like everything else, Big Tony's cheapness had been an overriding factor in acquiring the weapon. "May not be sexy," the old man had said, "but it'll kill an unholy goat-scratcher just as dead as any three-thousand-dollar Mark 23."

Little Tony climbed from the car and examined the gun in the sunlight. *What the old man don't know, won't hurt him.* He slipped the weapon into the pocket of his baggy cargo shorts. Because the waistband of the pants was belted just halfway up his rear end, Tony had to lean over slightly to reach the front pocket. Tony inserted the barrel, released the handle, and allowed gravity to pull the gun fully into his shorts. At the same moment he stepped toward the motel door, but the bottom of the pocket did not stop the heavy weapon's momentum. It fell completely to the ground and pulled Tony's shorts with it.

Hogtied by his own pants, Tony stumbled sideways, slammed into a low-rider Honda Civic, and crashed down. The lime green, hand-painted car responded with an ear-splitting siren and repeatedly honking horn. As he lay facing the Honda's front tire, the spinner rims began to rotate. Little Tony rolled onto his back and looked to the sky. *That piece a garbage has an alarm?* He scrambled to his feet, his pants still on the ground, and leaned over to untangle his ankles. Tony hiked his shorts up over his butt for the first time in three years, and cinched them tight at his natural waist. *Can't have my 1911 yanking down my pants. Guess I gotta sacrifice fashion to carry the hardware. Maybe that's why the wise-guys wear those horrible, baggy, refugee from The Godfather, suits.*

Little Tony retrieved the two enormous toilet paper packages and hurried inside before the honking car's owner could see him.

Big Tony yelled from the bathroom. "For the love of Limburger Cheese, what took you so long? My monkey-sniffing legs are more numb than my dead Aunt Maria."

Little Tony ripped open the package. "Got some TP for you, big guy. Gonna open the door and hand it to you."

"I don't need a running commentary, you ninnyhammer. Holy Canasta. Gimme the roll!"

Little Tony pushed the door just wide enough to reach inside so his father could snatch the roll. A few minutes later, the old man strolled out, flipped on the television, and sat on the edge of the bed. the top half of his uniform, a blue warm-up jacket with red stripes, was normal, but on the lower half he wore plain white boxer shorts and black socks.

Little Tony moved near the bed. "Big guy?"

Focused on the TV remote, Big Tony did not look up. "What?"

"What's your plan for tracking down Sinclair Davis?"

His gaze still fixed on the remote, Tony tapped his temple. "Got a brilliant plan right up here."

"You gonna share it with me?"

Finally glancing up, Big Tony did a double take. "Hey dummkopf, what's with the pants?"

"Nothing."

"Dancin' turtle tots in a salad bowl. Don't gimme a urinal cake and tell me it's a breath mint."

"What you talking about?"

"For the love of Earnest Borgnine, your posterior ain't been fully covered since the Clinton administration."

"Going for a new look," Little Tony was not sure he could sell it.

Big Tony shook his head and turned toward the TV.

Little Tony tried again to pry out information. "We just gonna sit here all day?"

"Gotta make sure our home base is set before we do anything. When that's done, we track down this peanut-butter-eatin' stink weed, Sinclair Davis, and extract my hundred large from his hide."

TWENTY-SEVEN
Tuesday, May 17th

Rooster opened his eyes and sat up on the sofa. Sweat poured down his face. Scraps and shreds of a dream lingered. Parasailing in the tropics, a clanging alarm, the parachute failing, plunging toward the ocean.

His phone chirped. The dog, who had been on the floor, craned his neck. Morning sunlight peeked around the sad blanket's edges. *Who's calling me?* He snatched up the device and peered through burning, bloodshot eyes. His head pounded. His brain in slow motion, the phone display did not compute.

Oh yeah. Changed her ring tone after the Queen debacle. He answered the phone, still struggling for coherency. "Huh?"

"Sonny? It's Mom."

Rooster rolled his neck and shoulders, hoping to work out the built-up tension from another night passed out on the sofa.

"It's Mom. Don't you recognize your own mother?"

Rooster shooed away the dog. *Never gonna get rid of this mutt.* He stared at his blanket door. *How do I keep forgetting to get that board from Buddy?* A snippet of the dream jumped into his brain, the instructions for dealing with a parasail collapse. *Point your toes and cover your eyes. Don't think that woulda saved me.* He shuddered.

"Sonny!" There was real panic in his mother's voice. "Sonny?!

Are you ok? Talk to me!"

"Yeah, Mom," Rooster grumbled.

"Scared the bejesus outta me. What's the matter with you?"

"What're you talking about?" Rooster fought a growing sense of déjà vu. *Didn't this just happen the other day? Waking up on the couch with a hangover and a strange dog running around? Pathetic. Who lives like this? Something's gotta change.* The animal leapt on the sofa and curled into a ball.

"How you nearly gave me a heart attack," she cried.

Rooster barely hid his frustration. "Mom, what the hell you talking about?"

"Sonny! You know better than to use that word. After you say it, that's where God sends you."

"Ok Mom." He tried to sound conciliatory. "I don't know where this conversation went so horrendously off track, but I'm sorry if I took it there. Can we please start over?"

"Alright. Where you want to start?"

Rooster sighed. "You called me, Mom."

"Well you got me all flabbergasted now. My mind ain't as good as it used to be. After all this excitement, I need a minute to remember what I called about."

She's right. Rooster rubbed his scratchy eyes. *Said the word and now God's sent me there with this phone call.* Rooster glared at the dog, who stared back with big sad brown eyes. Somewhere in the recesses of his brain, Rooster realized he had been outsmarted by this mutt and would never get rid of him. *Might as well ask Buddy for a good southern dog's name. Right after I get that board.*

When the silence became uncomfortable, Rooster spoke. "Tell me how I nearly gave you a heart attack."

"When I first called, you were just mumbling incoherently. I was afraid you were having a seizure."

Rooster laughed. "Can't believe I'm about to ask this, but what about my health history gave you any indication I was likely to have a seizure?"

"Well Mr. Smarty Pants. That's why I was calling you."

This ought to be good. Rooster stood and headed to the kitchen, followed by the dog.

"I was reading in the newspaper this morning about how people who overdose on vitamins can get really sick."

"Overdose on vitamins?" Rooster peered into the empty fridge. *Why can't it have a secret compartment with an endless supply of beer, like my favorite commercial?*

"Yes, Sonny. People who take too many vitamins can get nerve damage and stomach problems that eventually lead to seizures and erratic behavior. You could end up in a coma. You can see why I was so worried when you weren't responding."

"Not really, Mom." He closed the fridge.

"The other day you were jumping cars. That's erratic. When I called today, it sounded like you were having a seizure?"

"I already told you the car thing wasn't planned, and why you think you could diagnose a seizure over the phone."

"You remember Mrs. Cardinale, don't you?"

"No, Mom, I don't." Fatigue crept into his muscles. He opened the cupboard and stared longingly at the Jack Daniels.

"Sure you do. That time you were here and we got snowed in, Mrs. Cardinale stopped by before the snow started. She dropped off the reindeer candleholders she'd made. I gave her an angel I crocheted and a tin full of taffy butter bars."

Rooster stared at the dog. The animal cocked his head as if he understood Rooster's disbelief. "You serious, Mom? I'm supposed to recall some woman I saw for five minutes what, five years ago?"

"She was there at least twenty minutes. Mrs. Cardinale..."

"Mom, why you telling me about this person?"

"Mrs. Cardinale's son Larry had a seizure. That's why I thought you were having one."

"That doesn't tell me how you can diagnose a seizure over the phone." Rooster grabbed the liquor bottle and set it on the table. His hands were clammy. Sweat trickled down his spine.

"Mrs. Cardinale told me all about it. It was so horrible. She came home and found Larry on the floor shaking and foaming at the mouth..."

"Ok," Rooster erupted. "I don't wanna hear any of that. I don't even know these people."

"Larry has epilepsy."

Rooster fought the urge to re-engage his mother about the candleholder-making Mrs. Cardinale and her poor epileptic son. Instead, with much effort, he shifted gears. "Why would I overdose on vitamins?"

"When you were seven we started giving you a multi-vitamin everyday. That's what Dr. Spock said to do, but I'm not sure Dr. Spock had the best ideas..."

Rooster pulled out a chair and sat. "Mom, I'm begging you to get to the point."

"Fine. The only vitamins you would eat were Flintstones chewables. I kept those vitamins hidden away, but somehow you found them and ate the whole bottle."

"You gotta be kidding." Rooster stifled a laugh.

"It's not funny. I was so scared. You tried to hide the empty bottle, but I found it. Then today when you were non-responsive, it was like a flashback to that horrible day."

"Mom. I wasn't non-responsive. You woke me out of a sound sleep. And what's this business about flashbacks? If I fell into a Flintstones chewable-induced seizure when I was seven, I think I would remember."

"Why must you always question your mother? Is it a crime I love you and I worry about you? I was just calling to make sure you don't swallow whole bottles of vitamins anymore."

Rooster stared at the Jack Daniels. He seriously considered unscrewing the cap and drinking directly from the bottle. *I'd like to be in a coma right now.* He considered Marcie's warning about showing up to his interview with alcohol on his breath.

"So," Rooster said. "Because I ate a whole bottle of Flintstones chewables when I was seven, you're worried I still eat entire bottles of vitamins on a regular basis now that I'm forty-three? That the gist of your hypothesis, Mom?"

"Well, you don't have to be a wiseguy about it?"

"I'm not trying to be a wiseguy, but you don't give me much credit for intelligence if you think I'm scarfing down whole bottles of vitamins." He pulled in a deep breath and stood up. After one last glance at the whiskey bottle, he moved quickly into the living room, the dog on his heels.

"I always believed you were a very smart boy, Sonny, but after this car jumping thing, I had to rethink all that."

Rooster was about to protest, when he saw the thick white envelope on the TV stand. *That wasn't there before. Was it?*

"Sonny?"

Rooster crossed the room, grabbed the envelope, and tore it open. "No way," Rooster mumbled as he saw the contents, a wad of twenty-dollar bills.

"Sonny?"

He looked around the room, half-expecting to find someone hiding in the corner. *If those are all twenties, that's a lot of money. Where'd this come from?* He shuffled through the bills.

"Sonny?!"

Rooster snapped back, his tone now pleasant. "Don't worry Mom. I'm not having a seizure, but I really gotta go."

"You mad at me because of what I said?"

"What? No. Something's come up."

"You sure?"

"Yes. Talk to you later, Mom."

Rooster disconnected and began counting his windfall.

TWENTY-EIGHT

"No way!" Rooster counted the money again. The dog sat at his feet. "Four hundred bucks." He fanned out the cash and waved it in front of the mutt's nose. "Yes! I'm back, baby!" *Maybe I can get my door re-attached early. I have this money and a job interview. Things are definitely looking up.*

Who would've done this? Buddy? Rooster quickly dismissed him. *Buddy'd do anything for me, but he throws around nickels like manhole covers. Not his style. This mystery benefactor expect something in return? Don't want to owe any more favors. Already obligated to these church people. What about them? More likely than my usual crowd. Heck, most of them are broke themselves. Did tell my story to everyone at Marcie's party. What about Marcie? She's loaded. She already set up the job interview. Could she've done this too?*

Rooster glanced at the blanket. *When'd they bring the cash inside? Someone wandering around while I was sleeping?* Shame bubbled up as he thought about Marcie seeing him passed out. *She'd know in a second what that was all about.* Shame morphed into anger and self-righteousness. *None of her concern what I do. Is giving me money and setting up job interviews because she wants to make me her business? Am I her do-gooder project. Can't drink anymore so she makes herself feel better by guilt-tripping me to give it up too.* "That's a load of crap. I'm not anyone's social experiment." *Won't even mention the money.* "She can just squirm wondering what happened to her cash."

Rooster shoved the wad of bills into his front pocket. *It's all good. I should be celebrating.* But Rooster could not shake the nagging sense he had done something wrong. After all, his choice of conversation topics at Marcie's party was not random happenstance. Rooster's sob story had been a brazen attempt to generate sympathy. If he was being honest with himself, something he rarely did, there had also been the hope his manipulation might guilt someone into slipping him a few bucks. Four hundred was above and beyond his wildest dreams. Obviously, these were good, generous people, which made him feel worse about keeping so much money. No matter what he told himself, his uneasy conscience would not be negotiated away.

The dog sat near his feet, staring up expectantly. "Don't look at me like that. Didn't ask anyone to leave a wad of cash in here." The dog was a statue, his big brown eyes fixed on Rooster. *What's this mutt staring at?* The dog's look was accusatory, like that was even possible. "It's mine now." Rooster spoke loudly, hoping his own words could quiet his conscience. He needed reassurance nothing was wrong. He pulled out his phone.

After the third ring, the familiar Foghorn Leghorn voice answered, "What's goin' on, son?"

Rooster skipped opening pleasantries. "If I find a large amount of cash just laying there in my house, it's mine, right?"

"I leave money at your place?"

"Seriously, Buddy." Rooster nervously paced, the canine following him. "I found an envelope with four hundred bucks on the TV stand. Someone came in here and left the money."

"I do declare," Buddy drawled. "You're about as sharp as mashed potatoes. This is actual cash, right?"

"Yeah."

"Then why you even telling anyone about it? Fold it up, put it in your pocket, and the drinks are on you tonight."

Rooster was apprehensive. "Don't you think it's strange?" He flopped on the sofa. The dog jumped up and laid his head in Rooster's lap. "What if the person who left it wants something?"

"Think about this, son. Someone snuck in your house and left cash. Who would do that and come back asking for favors?"

"I don't know." Rooster absentmindedly stroked the dog's head. "You think it coulda been one of those church people?"

"Those kind of people have been known to do things like this, but forget who did it. You just had a huge stroke of luck, boy. You should be over the moon, not sittin' around worrying like a spinster who can't pay the mortgage."

"I guess so." Rooster remained unconvinced. He propped his feet on the coffee table. "I should be happy, but I have this bad feeling I'm gonna end up paying for keeping this money. That church already hooked me into this bible study and Sunday services. If I'm not careful, next thing you know they'll have me cleaning toilets over there."

"It's cash," Buddy bellowed. "No one can prove anything. They come back looking for favors, and I know they won't, you look 'em square in the eye and say, 'Cash? What cash?'"

"You're right. That's exactly what I been telling myself. I feel better now. Thanks, Buddy."

"You can thank me with a cold one later tonight."

"Hey, don't let me forget to grab that piece of wood from you tonight." He glanced at the dog in his lap. "I'm afraid to see what else'll wander into the house."

"Your door hole's as good as sealed, son. I'll call you after work so I can share in your good fortune."

Rooster looked at the canine. "What's a good southern name for a dog?"

"Dixie, if it's a bitch."

"What if you don't know his temperament?"

"Son, you're about as useful as buttons on a dishrag. A bitch is a female dog. Has nothing to do with personality."

"Oh. What if it's a male?"

"Waylon."

"Thanks. First round's on me tonight."

"Oh contraire, mi amore. All the rounds are on you."

Rooster disconnected, pushed the dog away, and stood. He faced the animal. "Well Waylon, if you're gonna hang around here, I guess you need something to drink." He walked into the kitchen, Waylon on his heels. After a glance at the Jack Daniels bottle on the table, he found a big cereal bowl in the cupboard. He filled it with water and set it next to the refrigerator. "There you go, boy. Go ahead and drink."

Waylon sat at Rooster's feet, stared up at him for a moment, then bent over and licked himself.

"Suit yourself." Rooster stole a peek at the time. "I got a job interview in a few hours."

Rooster showered and picked out clothes appropriate for a sporting goods store interview, a red golf shirt, pressed khaki pants, and black loafers.

When he ducked under the blanket door, an oppressive steam bath of heat and humidity slapped him in the face. Within seconds, sweat dripped down his back. Waylon followed him, but quickly ran inside once he realized Rooster was not interested in playing.

Must be ninety-five and a hundred percent humidity. Rooster trudged toward the main road. It would take fifteen minutes to walk to Robinson Sporting Goods and he figured he would be sopping wet by the time he arrived. As he plodded along the hot pavement, Rooster mentally rehearsed answers to the most common interview questions. Why do you want to work here? Why did you leave your last job? What are your biggest strengths and weaknesses? Where do you see yourself in five years?

When he finally walked through the store's front door, Rooster could not believe how refreshing the air conditioning felt on his overheated skin, but it was not long before the cold air on his sweat-soaked clothes gave him a chill. His shirt had more wet surface area than dry. His once-crisp pants had devolved into a wrinkled mess and his underwear had bunched up uncomfortably during the long hot walk. Even his hair was damp. *Probably look like I just climbed out of a pool.*

A quick time check revealed he was 10 minutes early. *Just enough time to get in the bathroom and clean up. If I don't get these boxers adjusted, they're gonna drive me insane.* He resisted the urge to wrestle them into place through his khakis.

Rooster was about to ask for directions to the bathroom when he saw an earnest little man headed quickly in his direction through racks of sportswear. He had gray curly hair, a bulbous nose, and appeared to wear a seersucker suit. As the man approached, Rooster saw it was actually a blue and white striped one-piece jumpsuit with two big breast pockets and a little built-in belt with a gold hook buckle. The pant legs were too short and showed off black socks and white leather sneakers.

Before Rooster could even decide what to think about his odd getup, the man was on top of him. He thrust out his hand and flashed a big crooked smile. "How you doing today, sir?" The man grabbed Rooster's hand and shook it vigorously. "Welcome to Robinson Sporting Goods. I'm Jimmy Robinson and I'm delighted you came to see us today. There anything I can help you find?"

"Ahh..." Rooster stammered. "Actually, I'm Rooster..."

"Rooster Michaels! I been looking forward to meeting with you. That Marcie Dexter's something else, ain't she?"

"Yes, she is..."

"I could tell you stories about that woman. She's always helping out someone. Why don't we go back to my office where we'll have a little privacy?"

He wants to start the interview right now? Rooster worried about his bunched up underwear. "Mr. Robinson, I..."

"Please call me Jimmy. Mr. Robinson's my daddy."

"Ok, Jimmy. I'd really like..."

"Hold that thought 'til we get back to my office." Jimmy slapped Rooster's back. "Can't have your interview right here in the middle of the store."

Jimmy walked away quickly. Rooster half ran to catch up. "Can I use your bathroom..."

Jimmy did not hear because at the same time he called across the front of the store. "Hey Rosie. I'll be in my office doing an interview. Can you hold down the fort for awhile?"

"Sure thing Jimmy," said the twenty-something brunette.

By the time Jimmy threw open the office door and directed him to sit across from the desk, Rooster's head spun. He had been sucked into a whirlwind since Jimmy first hustled up to meet him.

"Can I get you some coffee?" Jimmy asked from the doorway as Rooster settled into his chair.

Rooster shook his head and debated another attempt to get to the bathroom. But Jimmy was too fast.

"Hope you don't mind. I'm going to get some for myself. You wait here a second." Then he was gone.

Rooster stood and peered through the doorway just in time to catch a glimpse of the seersucker one-piece as Jimmy turned the corner. Rooster suddenly realized no one could see him, so he did his best to adjust his boxer shorts through his pants. He considered unfastening his khakis to more easily access everything. Fortunately, he thought better of it and sat down just as Jimmy returned with the biggest travel mug Rooster had ever seen. The gigantic thermal container was larger than a bowling ball and had to hold at least two pots of coffee. *No wonder this guy's so hyper. How much caffeine can you have before your heart explodes?*

Jimmy offered a sheepish grin. "Yeah, I know my coffee cup's ridiculous, but I can't get enough of this stuff."

Rooster opened his mouth to make a joke about being over-caffeinated, but Jimmy spoke right over him.

"So Rooster, you have any previous experience selling sporting goods?"

Rooster smiled, put on his game face, and reviewed the answers he had practiced during the walk over. "Actually I do, Jimmy. Before I came to..."

"Fantastic. I'm looking for a salesman who knows the business.

Last guy didn't know an elbow pad from a lob wedge. Quick, what's your favorite color?"

Rooster mentally fumbled through his prepared responses. *Didn't expect that question.* "Don't know." He looked down at his shirt. "Red?"

"Wrong! What are you, some stinkin' Alabama fan?"

"Ah... I don't know..."

"C'mon, Rooster," Jimmy chided. "If you're working in a sporting goods store in Murfreesboro, Tennessee, your favorite color has to be blue, orange, or both."

"For UT and MTSU," Rooster said, still unsure of himself.

"Exactly. What'd you do in your last job?"

"I sold meat door to door." Rooster kept it short, but Jimmy chose that moment for a long drink from his enormous coffee mug, which produced an awkward silence. Rooster debated whether to say more or wait for the next question. "I worked for..." Rooster finally began.

"I once sold vacuums door to door," Jimmy interrupted, as he set his cup on the desk. "That was one long hot summer, I tell you. Another year I sold the Encyclopedia Britannica. Door-to-door sales paid my way through college. Nothing wrong with sales. Good honest work. Don't you think so, Rooster?"

"Yes. I once..."

"Yep," Jimmy said wistfully, oblivious to Rooster's comments. "Back when I was coming up, if you were able to sell, you could write your own ticket. Didn't matter if you came from New York City or Tullahoma, Tennessee. If you moved product, employers would line up at your door. Now salespeople have a bad reputation. Make your living selling on commission, and these radio commercials imply you'd cheat people to put a little extra money in your pocket. They have quote, unquote, non-commissioned salespeople supposedly looking out for the customers' best interests, unlike the evil commission people. What they don't tell you is those salary people don't give a whit whether or not your deal gets done 'cause they get paid the same either way."

The whole interview continued this way. Jimmy would ask a question and then interrupt Rooster with his own monologue. Jimmy waxed poetic on government over-regulation of skeet-shooting equipment, the best schools in the Southeastern Conference, why the US Postal Service should be folded into the FBI, and how the United Nations could solve global hunger by creating grasshopper farms. Rooster was dumbfounded at what came out of the man's mouth. When it was over, Jimmy shook Rooster's hand and looked him in the eye. "Gotta tell you, Rooster. I really like you."

"You do?" Rooster wondered if he had spoken more than twelve words the entire interview.

"Yes, sir, I do." Jimmy smiled broadly. "I'd like to offer you the job. Can you start Thursday?"

TWENTY-NINE

"Sweetie?" Tyler Brock's chicklet smile filled the bottom of his face. "Can't help feeling like you're trying to get rid of me." Tyler's plaid shorts gave way to surprisingly pale stick legs, considering he lived in Arizona. The slightly too-tight 'My mom went to the Grand Canyon and all I got was this lousy T-Shirt' top revealed a doughy upper body, which had last seen the inside of a gym when MC Hammer was dancing in harem pants.

"Exactly what I'm doing, Darling." Sue Schwartz rose from the king bed and cinched her fluffy hotel robe. She handed him a Phoenix Mercury baseball cap. "Don't want the sun to start your scalp on fire."

Tyler contorted his long lips until they resembled something squeezed out of a Play-Doh Fun Factory. "You're acting very strange, Honey Bunny. What's going on?"

"You know how I get when I run outta Diet Coke."

"Seriously, Snickerdoodle. Please tell me what's wrong."

Sue's smile faded. She stared at his giant oral crevice. She had never said anything to Tyler, but the lower half of his head had become a point of strange fascination. *How's an otherwise normally proportioned man end up with such an absurdly oversized mouth? Bet he could stuff his whole hand into that gaping maw up to the wrist.* She tore her gaze from his mouth. "I want some alone-time. I thought Michael Davis, or whatever his real name is, would be a local celebrity after that goofy car-jumping video. Still think it was staged. He must have some scheme to profit from it. I thought we'd find him right off."

Tyler hung the hat on the bathroom doorknob and took Sue's hands. "That was a little over optimistic, wasn't it, Dear?"

She sighed. "I didn't realize Murfreesboro was this big."

"We don't have to stay, dear." Tyler intently searched her eyes. "We can pack and fly home on the next plane outta here."

"I'm not a quitter." Sue pulled her hands free. "You think I could've done three years in Lumley, if I just give up when things are tougher than expected?"

"No, of course not, Honey Bunny." Tyler nervously rubbed his hands. "But this seems like a fool's errand. I don't think we're equipped to find this man. Besides, this place feels like a swamp. My glasses steam up every time I step outside and all this humidity's giving me a rash."

"Darling, all I want is the opportunity for closure so we can have our life together."

Tyler scratched a patch of flaking skin on his head. "What could you possibly say to this guy that would give you closure?"

"Don't know," Sue lied. "I'll come up with something. Now get outta here." She set the ball cap on Tyler's head and pushed him toward the door. "I want my Diet Coke. And..." She searched for something odd to keep him out of her hair for awhile. "And get me some Clark Bars."

"Clark Bars?"

Sue shooed him into the hall. "Yeah, I love Clark Bars."

Concern filled Tyler's face. "Honey, I never heard you mention a Clark Bar, much less seen you eat one."

"What's with the third degree? Is it a crime to crave a Clark Bar?"

"All right." Tyler raised an eyebrow. "Are you pregnant?"

"Pregnant?" Sue cackled. "Where'd you come up with that?"

"Don't know." Tyler stared at his toes. "You been acting odd lately. Having strange cravings."

Sue forced a laugh. "Think for a minute, Darling. If I was pregnant, would I have sent you to Sam's Club yesterday?"

Tyler's eyes lit up with understanding. "I guess not."

"Ok, now that we got that cleared up, you need to go."

Tyler nodded and kissed her. "Be back in awhile."

Sue's heart raced as she watched him head down the hall. She closed door, flipped the safety latch, and moved quickly to the closet. With a nervous glance at the door, Sue pulled out of her suitcase an unusually heavy eighty-count box of Tampax, the object of Tyler's Monday Sam's Club errand. *Men are such idiots. What woman needs eighty tampons for a one-week trip?* A pang of guilt bit into her as she imagined poor Tyler, dutifully buying the ridiculous box without question or complaint.

He is a good man. For a fleeting moment, she wondered whether the thought had been a mental declaration of fact, or a subconscious attempt to sell herself on the idea.

Tyler's embarrassing errand had served two purposes. First, it gave Sue the opportunity to pick up the pink-gripped Ruger LCR Revolver she had shipped to herself at the hotel. Second, the Tampax box was a secure place to hide the weapon where Tyler would not stumble across it in a million years. Sue opened the box, reached past a layer of tampons, and pulled out the gun. She sat on the floor and turned the weapon over in her hands. She enjoyed the coldness of the steel barrel, and the slight metallic aroma of the Rangoon oil the man at the gun store had applied to the gun to keep it from rusting.

Sue closed her eyes and remembered that night thirteen years ago, when Michael Davis had ruined her life. In her recollection, Davis used Svengali-like dark arts to brainwash her into drinking, gambling, and becoming a criminal by paying for the whole wild escapade with her company credit card. "That bastard," she mumbled, completely oblivious to any thought she might be at least partially responsible for the avalanche of bad decisions which landed her in the slammer. Sue never admitted culpability for any of her poor life choices. Whether it was when she shaved her head bald in high school, or when she dropped out of college two months into her junior year to follow Hootie and the Blowfish, or any of a dozen other disastrous moves, Sue always managed to blame others for her misfortune. Vegas had been the most monumental screw-up of her life and she was not about to accept responsibility now. No, Michael Davis was at fault and he was going to pay for destroying her future.

Sue scrambled to her feet, re-cinched the robe, and dropped the Ruger into her terrycloth pocket. She smiled at her reflection the full-length mirror and imagined Michael Davis in front of her. Almost in a trance, Sue prepared to deliver her confrontation speech, just as she had rehearsed it a thousand times. When she blurred her vision, she could actually see him, as if her mind had willed him into the room. He was vividly real, from his cloying Brute cologne to his whining and begging, to the fear in his eyes. Sue launched into the performance, his responses as genuine as the deadly weapon inside her pocket.

"It's you." She smiled.

I'm sorry. Do I know you?

"Don't you know your own wife?"

He stared blankly.

She fixed him with a steely glare. "You piece of garbage. Why don't you try looking at the tattoo on your stomach?"

Recognition flickered in his eyes. *Oh my God. It's you.*

"Damn right it's me. You really think you could waltz through the rest of your life without ever seeing me again? Without having to answer for the hell you put me through?"

Hey, listen...

"Shut your lying mouth!" She pulled the gun from her pocket. "You can't sweet talk your way outta this one."

He raised his hands. Fear flooded his face. *Whoa. What's with the gun?*

"What about it?" She asked in a sweet tone.

Put that thing away before someone gets hurt.

"Maybe that's my objective."

Wait a minute...

"No, Michael. YOU wait a minute. You thought you'd never see me again. Thought you could just use me and throw me away like so much trash. Well you were wrong. Because today is the day you finally have to answer for what you did to me." Sue jabbed the gun at him and enjoyed his squirming. "Should just pull the trigger right now and put an end to it. How many other women's lives have you destroyed?"

A tiny dark spot formed near his crotch. It quickly grew into a huge wet patch, which covered the front of his jeans.

"Isn't that special. Poor baby had a little accident. Can't even take his punishment like a man."

Michael glanced at his pants in shame, then looked at Sue with pleading eyes. *Listen, Sue. I didn't mean any harm. I was drunk and outta control. I'm sorry if I hurt you.*

"Shut your mouth!" Her face twisted in rage. "Your silver tongue can't help you now, Michael."

Please, he implored. *I'm so sorry.*

Sue laughed. "You can beg all you want. But you can't give me back the three years I spent in prison. Can't give me back the career I shoulda had."

Michael dropped to his knees sobbing. *I didn't know I hurt you so bad. I'll do anything to make it up to you. Whatever you want. Please. Just give me one more chance.*

Sue shook with anger. "Tell you what, Michael. I'll let you live on one condition."

Sensing hope, he straightened slightly. *Anything. I'll do anything. I got some money.*

Sue lowered the gun. "All you have to do is give me back everything you stole from me. The money, the years, the career, everything."

Michael sank down. *I can't do that. It's impossible.*

A devilish grin slowly spread across Sue's face. She raised her

arm and took aim at his head. "Exactly."
　　Then she pulled the trigger.

THIRTY
Wednesday, May 18th

"We're on in thirty seconds."

The overly serious twenty-something beauty adjusted her red top, flipped her long auburn hair over her shoulder, and ensured the "3" on her microphone pointed squarely at the camera. "Ready when you are." She pulled her lips back to reveal flawless glossy-white capped ivories. "How do my teeth look? Please tell me there's no lipstick on them. That was so embarrassing."

The cameraman laughed. "No, they look awesome. Like a perfectly whitewashed picket fence. Ten seconds."

She grimaced. "What's that supposed to mean, Dennis?"

Dennis fought to keep the ten-pound camera on his shoulder from shaking with his belly laughs. He loved to get inside the heads of the 'talent' just before they went live. "Five, four, three..." He switched to hand signals for two and then thrust his finger at her. She was on the air. Her frown instantly transformed into a sweet, friendly smile. She resisted the urge to touch her earpiece as the voice of the man at the anchor desk in Nashville set up her segment.

"Thanks, Brian. Good morning," she said. "That's right. It's 'Where's Waldo?' here in Murfreesboro, where we're looking for the mystery man whose amazing, death-defying leap over a speeding Lamborghini set the Internet on fire. His video has eight million hits on YouTube with no signs of slowing down. I'm standing in front of the Cumberland Baptist Church." She waved her arm at the building behind her. "It's on this street, right in front of this church, where this unbelievable event took place. Makes you wonder if maybe our John Doe car hopper had a little bit of divine assistance, doesn't it Brian?"

The anchor said something in her earpiece.

"Exactly, Brian. Perhaps the only thing more incredible than his viral vault is how he vanished into thin air. No one seems to know where to locate him, but we're pulling out all the stops to track him down and find out just what was going through his mind when he made his breath-taking jump."

A plastic smile filled her face as Brian chattered.

"That's why we're on the job, Brian. Everyone wants to know this man's story. We're going to start this evening by interviewing the budding filmmaker who shot this amazing footage. He's a junior right here at MTSU. In the meantime, if anyone has any tips where we can find the Lamborghini Leaper, they can call the station, or email me directly. I know I personally can't wait to meet this guy. This is Cassandra Nolan, Action 3 News, reporting from Murfreesboro. Back to you Brian."

She smiled into the lens until Dennis declared, "We're clear." He set the camera on the ground.

"That should make something happen." Cassandra grinned. "Hey, Dennis, what's this business about my teeth looking like a fence?"

THIRTY-ONE

Big Tony sat propped against the motel bed's tarnished metal headboard, every pillow in the room stuffed behind him in an unsuccessful attempt to get comfortable on the old sagging mattress. His once-white ribbed muscle shirt was now a dingy yellowish gray. His oversized stomach and man boobs stretched the material with puffy, pasty skin rolls protruding from the shirt openings like a popped tube of biscuit dough. His white boxer shorts were enormous, the loose material flapping in the window air conditioner breeze. Completing Tony's casual mobster-at-home look, his big toe peeked out a hole in his black socks,.

Precariously balanced on his lap was Tony's favorite Burger King breakfast, two double Croissan'wiches, extra large hash browns, and a king size Dr Pepper. Tony shoveled food into his mouth with one hand and used the TV remote with the other to surf the thirteen channels offered by the motel. "For the love of Abe Vigoda," he mumbled through a mouthful of hash browns. "Nothing but cartoons, fishing, and preachers."

With his eyes glued to the television, he lifted his soft drink. Expecting the straw to find his mouth, he completely missed and nearly poked himself in the eye. After a loud "Humph," of frustration, Tony eyed the straw and slurped a healthy dose of soda. He hit 'channel up' on the remote with his meaty thumb, but nothing happened. He tapped again. Still nothing. Tony paused to stuff a huge bite of Croissan'wich into his mouth and mashed the control again. Nothing. "Steaming monkey poop." He set the sandwich in his lap and slammed the remote several times against the palm of his hand. He had barely finished chewing as he jammed in a handful of hash browns and poked the button again. Nothing. Tony angrily thrust the device toward the TV as he pressed the selection. Still no response.

"Son of a wildebeest!" He lifted his hand to hurl the remote, but thought better of it. *I'll have to get outta bed to change the channel.* With monumental effort, he leaned hard against the headboard, which caused the metal to draw back like a bow string. It sprang forward, propelling Tony's upper body so his outstretched remote hand moved as close to the screen as possible. After just a few seconds stretched out over his big belly, Tony's constricted airway turned his face bright red. He fell back heavily against the headboard. The rusty metal bed frame responded with shaking and an angry creak.

The TV fisherman's big grin under his ball cap and sunglasses was mocking Tony's inability to move to another show.

Tony sighed heavily, watched the straw all the way to his lips and crammed a third of a croissant into his mouth. He drew a deep breath, pushed against the headboard, sprung forward, reached out, desperately tapped the remote, held that position as long as possible, and then dropped back. The headboard slammed loudly and the bed frame cried for mercy, but the blasted fisherman remained, taunting him. Huffing and puffing as sweat streamed down his now-purple face, Tony alternated between huge gulps of breakfast and his odd gymnastics routine, the bed shaking and protesting with pops and snaps.

Drawn by the strange racket, Little Tony wandered in from the bathroom and stood in awe of Big Tony's antics. The headboard let out a loud crack as his father sprung forward, a half-eaten Croissan'wich in one hand, the thumb on the other maniacally mashing the remote. Finally, the fisherman disappeared, replaced by an antiseptic news anchor with perfect plastic hair. Big Tony crashed back into the headboard. The bed shook wildly and the rusty metal frame made strange crackling noises. "Take that you swamp weasel on a surfboard fish kisser." Big Tony held his arms up in triumph.

"Hey Big Guy?" Little Tony asked. "What you doin'?"

Big Tony's look made it clear he thought his son's question was idiotic. "Eatin' breakfast and watching TV," he replied through a mouthful of food. "What's it look like I'm doing?"

Little Tony knew better than to get wise, so he shook his head and glanced at the television. What he saw made him do a double-take. "Pop!" He pointed at the screen. "Look!"

Big Tony's eyes grew wide. Both men stared in disbelief at the footage of that deadbeat Sinclair Davis' jump over the sports car. Then the camera cut to a cute brunette who explained she was searching for the mysterious Lamborghini Leaper. Big Tony leaned in, the creaky bed straining under his weight. The rusty old frame had finally taken more abuse than it could handle. With a loud crack, the head of the bed dropped violently. Big Tony was thrown hard against the headboard, hash browns and Croissan'wiches launched in the air, and the cold Dr Pepper dumped on his crotch. "Maggot crackers!"

With admirable focus, Little Tony ignored the old man, moved closer to the television, fixated on the news story. "Hey Pop." He continued to stare at the screen. "This infobabe's saying she's in Murfreesboro looking for that slimeball. If we follow her, you think maybe she'll lead us right to him?"

****

"Madison, get in here quick! You gotta see this."

Madison lifted the pillow from her face and peered painfully toward the door. She wondered whether her head pain was a migraine or a hangover, not that it mattered. Either way, she felt awful, any sound or light made her skull hurt. She slowly rolled her legs off the bed and sat up. Immediately she was hit by an unwelcome wave of nausea. *That's it. No drinking tonight. Four days of partying's enough.* Madison pulled herself to her feet and fumbled for her phone. 7:13 a.m. *Why'd they wake me at such an ungodly hour?* She stumbled toward the door, unworried how bad she must look.

Peyton poked her head inside the room, primped and polished as ever, with her tight ponytail and flawless makeup. "C'mon Madison," she practically sang. "Everyone's waiting downstairs. We got the TV paused. You gotta see this."

"Yeah, I'm coming." Madison stifled a yawn and the animosity she felt toward her host. *Perky little bitch. Who looks that good at seven in the morning?* She shuffled to the staircase, a death grip on the rail as she descended to keep from falling on her face. She finally felt human when she pushed through the door into the TV room, which was full of excitedly chattering women. Crystal stood and faced her friend.

"C'mon, Madison. I got you a seat."

Madison fell onto the couch, between Crystal and Tiffany.

"You look like crap," Tiffany offered with a grin.

"Yeah. It's the crack of dawn and someone dragged me down here to watch..." She stared at the TV, which was paused on a brunette reporter. She eyed her friends. "You woke me up to watch the news?"

"No." Crystal grew impatient. "You need to see this."

Someone hit the play button and the reporter talked about her search for the Lamborghini Leaper. The screen filled with footage of Davis Sinclair's jump over the yellow sports car.

"What the hell?" Madison finally woke up. "That's our guy." She pointed excitedly at the television. "What's goin' on?"

"Shh," Crystal admonished her. "Listen."

"In the meantime," the reporter said. "If anyone has any tips where we can find the Lamborghini Leaper, they can call the station or email me directly. I know I personally can't wait to meet this guy. This is Cassandra Nolan, Action 3 News, reporting from Murfreesboro. Back to you Brian."

"No way," Madison said. "She's gonna find him for us?"

"That's what it looks like," Crystal replied.

Madison shook her head. "Imagine that."

"I know," Tiffany offered. "Wanna find him and everything, but gotta be honest. Been having so much fun, I completely forgot about Davis Sinclair until I saw him on TV just now."

****

The Chairman strained to pull himself high enough to see into the rugby house window. Everyone was huddled around the TV. Everyone that is, except Madison. *Where could she be?*

Can't believe I gotta keep checking on these girls. Must be nice to spend your life going from party to party, totally oblivious others are doing all the heavy lifting for you. He had grown increasingly agitated as the NEIU girls continued to drink and carry on every night with no sign of doing anything to track down Davis Sinclair, who supposedly stole their twenty grand.

At least Mr. Jock Guy disappeared after the Chairman let him have it with the paint bucket, and the feeling had finally returned to his leg. His arms grew tired, so the Chairman lowered himself to the ground. He glanced around, happy the overgrown holly shrubs made it difficult to see him from the street. He was disgusted. *How'd I derail from the Student Body President fast track to lurking in the bushes like some street person meth addict?*

His irrational compulsion to know Madison's every move quickly trumped any remaining shred of common sense in his painted noggin. He gathered his strength, hooked his hands on the window ledge, and pulled himself up just in time to see his beloved Madison plop on the sofa, between that horrible Crystal and the other one. His grip slipped, but he managed to hold himself up by leaning his chest on the ledge and pushing against side of the house with his feet. He could not make out what on the TV was so fascinating, but Madison perked up and leaned forward. Then she pointed at the screen and talked excitedly. *What on earth they watching?*

"Hey pervert!"

The unexpected deep voice sent his heart racing. *Uh oh.* He searched for a plausible excuse for peeking in the window. Before he could gather his thoughts or even glance over his shoulder, a large hand grabbed his shirt collar. The Chairman slammed into the ground, flat on his back. "Ooooof!" The impact drove all air from his lungs. As he shook out the cobwebs, he saw his attacker. He was amazed, and a little terrified, as the pumpkin-headed, steroid-addled, professional house party bouncer loomed over him. "Really?" The Chairman sat up. "Bouncing AND a protection racket. Quite the entrepreneur. Add prostitution and drugs, and you'd have your own Al Capone starter kit."

"What's with the paint?" The bouncer asked. "You look like you crawled out of a dumpster."

"It's a long story."

Pumpkin head's iguana tongue flicked out to lick his lips.

"I had a rough couple of days," the Chairman added.

"You get off being a peeping Tom?" The giant's humorless voice revealed he was completely unimpressed with the Chairman's suffering. He squeezed his eyes shut and blinked a few times.

"I wasn't peeping." The Chairman felt as if his lower back had been trampled by the entire cast of *Riverdance*. "I was just looking for..."

"Yeah," the big guy interrupted. "The Hillbilly Beast of north western Kentucky. I promise you, he's not in there."

Despite his fear this man could literally rip his head off, the Chairman could not help being impressed by his memory. *Maybe his brain isn't rotting away from steroids.* The Chairman pulled himself painfully to his feet.

The big guy moved closer. "Listen, you little freak. Don't care what you were doing. I don't wanna see you around here no more. Understand?"

Several indignant responses about America being a free country immediately popped into the Chairman's mind, but he bit back his urge to say them. Instead, he squeaked, "Ok."

"Now get outta here."

The Chairman took a few steps, but much to his dismay, his left foot and ankle had gone numb. "No, not again!"

"What?" The giant was agitated.

"It's my foot. I hurt it again when you threw me down."

"I don't care if your brains are leaking outta your nose. You don't get your sorry ass outta here in the next thirty seconds, that may actually happen."

His head hung in shame, the Chairman hobbled off, his foot dragging behind, his expensive loafers whooshing with each step.

"Hey," the bouncer called.

The Chairman turned to face him.

"Get a bath, man." The giant made a show of pinching his nose. "You stink."

The Chairman looked down. "I know." He quietly limped away.

****

Tyler and Sue ate their free continental breakfast in the hotel dining room as Tyler prattled about some schizophrenic homeless man he had represented for the Public Defender's Office. On the first night of incarceration, the wacko guy had a psychotic episode and dislocated his hip when he tried to eat his own foot. Sue had tried to pay attention to the insane story, but for most of it, she pretended to look at Tyler while actually watching the TV mounted on the wall above his shoulder.

"So they left this poor guy alone all night without even checking on him," Tyler said. "And when they found him in the morning, he'd torn off all his clothes, scratched himself to the point where he was bleeding everywhere, and he managed to bite off and swallow his left big toe."

"Oh my God," Sue exclaimed.

"I know, Sweetie. It's appalling."

"No." Sue pointed over his shoulder. "The TV."

Tyler spun around and saw the flash of the yellow sports car. Sue hopped on chair and raised the volume to hear the female reporter describe her search for the Lamborghini Leaper. After the broadcast cut back to the studio, Sue, still atop the chair, pointed at Tyler. "Told you this whole thing was some sorta money-making scheme for him."

Tyler sighed. "If that's the case, it shouldn't be too hard to find him. That news crew oughta lead us right to him."

THIRTY-TWO

For the third time, Rooster entered Cumberland Baptist Church. Unlike previous visits, he was healthy, alert, and even happy. Had he not been roped into church, he would not have met Marcie, there would be no job at Robinson Sporting Goods, and he would have already been tossed out on his ear by the landlord. Rooster strutted through the now-familiar lobby. He entered the sanctuary and stopped in his tracks. *Is this the same place? Looks completely different.* The jarring change threw him off balance. The rows of red chairs had been rearranged into small circles of ten seats. There were even gathering areas on stage.

Who moved all the chairs? Rooster was thankful his benevolence program had not included that task. *Where am I supposed to go?* He nervously scanned the room. All the groupings all looked alike. No familiar faces anywhere. "Aw crap." Rooster's anxiety level rose. *Just what I need. Wandering around a room full of church people. Should just turn and walk out.*

"Hello, friend," said a pleasant voice behind him. A hand rested gently on Rooster's shoulder.

He turned, relieved to see her lively green eyes and welcoming smile. *God, she's beautiful.* "Hi, Marcie."

"I'm so glad you made it," she gushed.

Rooster was skeptical. *She realize I have no choice? At least if I want the rent money? How much did Sandy tell her about me?* His mind concocted ridiculous scenarios where Sandy shared with Marcie embarrassing details about his life neither woman could possibly know. He imagined them sipping coffee and laughing hysterically as Sandy told Rooster tales.

"C'mon." Marcie grabbed Rooster's elbow. "My group meets over here by the side door. Looks like we have a small crew. Hopefully you'll get the chance to know people a little better than if the whole gang were here."

The gatherings they passed varied in age and dress. Many, with conservative button down shirts and crisp dress pants, appeared to have been born in church. Others, with shorts, tattoos, and body piercings, did not belong at all. All were fully engaged, greeting each other chatting amiably. Too focused on his own discomfort, Rooster barely noticed any of them. He could not shake the gnawing feeling everyone was staring at him, as if they knew he was a fraud who did not belong there.

If all of that was not bad enough, Rooster suddenly felt like his fly was open. It took every ounce of will and concentration to resist the overwhelming urge to check his crotch. A cluster of folks burst into laughter as Rooster and Marcie passed. Convinced they were cackling at him, Rooster could take it no more. As nonchalantly as he could manage, Rooster rubbed the front of his pants. His zipper secure, he relaxed until his mind concocted other possibilities for the their snickers. By the time they arrived at Marcie's group, Rooster was a mess, his mind running wild.

"We're here." Marcie pointed at a seated man. "You know George."

Pulled back to reality, Rooster glanced at George Jones, dour and disheveled as ever in the same tattered and stained Atlanta Braves cap. *Aren't you supposed to take off your hat in church?* His plain green pocket t-shirt was wrinkled with a huge bleach mark on the left sleeve. *He care about his appearance at all?* George acknowledged Rooster with a slight nod. Rooster's stomach churned. *This guy really hates me*. Nervousness and even a little anger bubbled to the surface. *That's crap. What'd I do to him?* He scanned the other chairs. A large man sat with his back to Rooster. A few seats over was a vaguely familiar woman, a little chunky, but not bad looking. Her comically big hair sat piled up on her head like chocolate soft-serve ice cream dished out by a hungry five-year-old.

"And this is Sallie Mae Johnston," Marcie said.

The moment he heard the name, it all clicked. The pushy lady from the lobby before church. Over-done on Sunday, she was now softer and gentler without the harsh emerald green dress and clownish makeup. She seemed more approachable today in a stylish zebra print top and dark wash jeans. Rooster recalled wrestling his arm from her. His heart sank. *Gonna be pure misery.*

"We've already had the pleasure," Sallie Mae said a little too enthusiastically. "So good to see you again, Rooster."

Rooster's forced smile came across as more of a grimace. *Not going well.* "Ms. Johnston, what a surprise to run into you."

"Please call me..."

"Sallie Mae," they both said together.

Rooster smiled this time. He tipped his head to the side and pointed at her. *Can this get anymore excruciating?*

"Wow," Marcie said. "Small world. Now, I know you haven't met Dave."

As Rooster stepped into the chair circle, the big man twisted and they made eye contact. Rooster winced. *Oh shit.*

The big man's eyes grew wide. "You. The guy who was fallin' out in church Sunday."

Innate defense mechanisms reflexively kicked in. "I wasn't fallin' out, you idiot," Rooster blurted. "I was genuflecting."

Dave jumped up. Rooster had forgotten how enormous he was, and fought the urge to step backward. Self-righteousness flooded over him. *Why am I forever surrounded by ignoramuses?*

"Who you callin' an idiot?" A thick vein pulsated in the center of Dave's forehead, his face twisted in anger. "Come to think of it, that's the second time you called me that. I promise there won't be a third."

Just like Sunday morning, anger, embarrassment, resentment, and fear washed over him. Rooster's face turned red. He was drowning, about to hyperventilate. He needed a drink in the worst way. *What have I done to deserve this torture?* He felt the eyes of the room upon him.

Marcie jumped between them and pushed both men down into their chairs. "So it appears you and Dave have already met," she said with a nervous laugh. Marcie held a hand toward Rooster and faced the big guy. "Dave, tell me what this is all about."

Dave sighed and adjusted his golf shirt with shaking hands. He pointed a trembling, meaty finger at Rooster, "This man was bein' disrespectful before church. He was sprawling his self out in the aisles and basically makin' a spectacle of himself. An' when I called him out on it, he gave me some harebrained story."

Marcie leaned toward Dave as if this was the most fascinating thing she had ever heard. "Really? What'd he say?"

"He said what he was doin' was called Jen-you-fecting or some such thing. Sounds like a made-up word to me."

Marcie faced Rooster, the faintest hint of a smile on her lips. "Why were you sprawling out in the aisle on Sunday morning, Rooster?"

Rooster noticed a knowing grin on each face around the circle, except for Dave, his huge arms crossed defiantly as he waited for an explanation. Rooster breathed deeply. *Calm down. Don't make an ass of yourself. At least not a bigger one than you already have. Gotta sit with these people another ninety minutes. Swallow your pride for once in your life.* Rooster looked Dave in the eye. " I'm very sorry I called you an idiot. It's just something that comes outta me when I feel cornered."

Dave clung to his indignation. "That don't make it right."

Rooster swallowed hard the urge to call him something worse. *This guy serious? Can't he see I'm trying to be nice? Everyone knows he's wrong. Why don't he realize it? Wish I had a bourbon right now. That'd take the edge off.* He plowed ahead. "The first fifteen years of my life, I went to mass every Sunday at St. Stanislaus Catholic Church. Something Catholics do before sitting in the pew, is to genuflect toward the cross at the front, to show respect to God. On Sunday, my mind was wandering and I guess I was on auto pilot and genuflected out of habit."

Rooster stood up. "I dropped to one knee like this." His right knee fell to the floor. He pointed toward Dave. "And this big.... uhh... guy came up behind me and hauled me to my feet."

Dave remained defensive. "I thought you were 'bout to faint an' fall out on the floor."

Marcie faced Dave. "So it seems Rooster was doing something innocent." She shifted her gaze to Rooster. "And Dave was just trying to help someone he thought was in trouble. Looks like this was all a big misunderstanding."

"Yeah," Sallie Mae interjected. "Like *Three's Company*."

George shook his head. "What on earth you talking about?" It was the most lively Rooster had seen George since his goodbye to Buddy at the party.

Sallie Mae grinned. "The TV show *Three's Company*. Every episode was about a big misunderstanding."

"Never heard of it." George slouched in his chair.

"That's 'cause you're just a baby," Sallie Mae replied. "Lots of stuff you don't know."

"You got that right." George flashed a half smile as he adjusted his beat-up old hat.

"You don't remember *Three's Company*?" Dave grinned, his posture ridiculously perfect. "John Ritter and Suzanne Somers?"

George cocked an eyebrow. "You mean that QVC woman they always makin' fun of on *The Soup*?"

Dave furrowed his brow. "The what?"

"*The Soup*," George said. "It's a show on *E*."

"Ain't never heard of it," Dave replied.

"She used to do those ThighMaster infomercials," Sallie Mae offered. She searched the eyes of the group for an ally.

"My little brother got his hands on one-a them things back in the day." Dave slapped his knee, his mood now upbeat. "He turned that puppy into a killer slingshot."

"A ThighMaster?" Wonder filled Sallie Mae's face. "He turned a ThighMaster into a slingshot?"

Dave nodded vigorously. "An' it was accurate, too. Saw him drop a skunk from fifty feet."

Sallie Mae laughed. "Your family's crazy, Dave. What was he thinking, attacking skunks?"

George scratched his chin. "What in the blue blazes is a ThighMaster?"

"We're getting way off track," Marcie interrupted. "Isn't someone supposed to reel us in when we do this?"

"Debbie normally does that," George admitted.

"Guess I have to do it then," Marcie said. "Dave, you ok?"

The big man smiled broadly. "About what?"

"Your misunderstanding with Rooster in church? You going to give Rooster a chance to start over with you?"

Dave seemed a bit insulted "Of course. Already forgot it."

Rooster stared at the big guy. *A minute ago he wanted to punch my lights out. Now it's like nothing happened. How'd he let it go so fast?* Rooster considered how he held grudges. He was still mad at Dave. *Hell, I'm still bitter about Wall Street people from twenty years ago.*

Marcie's voice pierced his thoughts. "Rooster?"

"What?"

"You and Dave cool now?"

Don't have much choice. Especially after Dave's response. He shrugged. "Sure. Why not?" He stood and reached out his hand. Dave practically leapt from his seat. As the big man engulfed his hand in a surprisingly gentle handshake, Rooster's blood pressure returned to normal.

"Good." Marcie's smile returned as the two men found their seats. "Let's get started."

"Wait a minute." Sallie Mae cocked her head and grinned at

Rooster as mischief danced in her eyes. "I seen you on TV."

Rooster's blood pressure spiked. "Excuse me?" *What's this crazy woman talking about?*

"Aren't you on that video they been showing on television?"

Rooster shook his head. "Don't know what you're talking about." *TV? Where'd she come up with that?*

"Of course you do." Sallie Mae edged forward in her chair. "The video that's going viral. You're the guy who jumped the yellow sports car. How'd you do that?"

Rooster's eyes grew wide. His cheeks turned crimson. *The video was on TV? Who else saw it?*

"I knew it," Sallie Mae said triumphantly. "I saw the video on YouTube Saturday, and I thought you were the car-jumper-guy when I met you at church. When Channel 3 showed it again this morning, I just knew you were the Lamborghini Leaper."

"The Lamborghini Leaper?" Marcie said, suddenly interested.

Sallie Mae gushed, "That's what Cassandra Nolan on Channel 3 called him. She's trying to find him and interview him."

"I saw that." Dave let out a low whistle. "Pretty amazin' stuff. Can't believe that was you. How'd you do it?"

"I don't understand." Marcie faced Rooster. "You jumped over a car? And they put it on TV? You some sorta acrobat?"

Rooster squirmed, uncomfortable with their stares. "I'm not an acrobat." Remembering his mom's scolding monologue, Rooster stared at his feet, ashamed and embarrassed. "That's what my mother said, that I turned into a circus tumbler."

"Here, look at this." George handed Marcie his smart phone. He turned in Rooster's direction. "No offense, but if I didn't see that video, I'd never believe you coulda done something like that. I see why it went viral."

Rooster silently glared at him. *What's that crack mean?*

"Oh my goodness!" Marcie looked up from the video, wonder in her eyes. "That's insane. Why'd you do something so crazy?"

Before Rooster could answer, Sallie Mae asked, "You see where it happened, Marcie?"

Marcie backed up the video. "I don't believe it. That's Main Street, right outside the church, isn't it?"

"Yeah," Rooster admitted.

"Why'd you do it?" Marcie asked.

"I got distracted." Rooster closed his eyes. "Believe it or not, I was reading a brochure about small groups. When I looked up, the car was top of me. The only thing I could do was jump. I thought I was gonna get squashed like a bug." Rooster mentally returned to the jump apex when his life flashed before his eyes. He shuddered, reliving the lowlight reel of pain and suffering he had caused with his selfish, self-absorbed actions. Shame and regret overwhelmed him, nearly as much as during the event.

Sallie Mae broke the silence. "So it wasn't planned?"

"Huh?" Rooster tried to shake the disturbing images. He felt like crying, so he stared down and hoped no one noticed his watery eyes. He licked his lips and imagined a cold longneck.

"The jump," Sallie Mae said. "You didn't plan the jump?"

"Of course not." Rooster could not hide his disdain. He continued to stare at his hands. "You think I got a death wish? It was totally unexpected."

"Where'd the TV footage come from?" Sallie Mae asked.

Rooster shrugged. "Don't know." He stared through her, annoyance replacing shame. *What's with the third degree? She questioning my honesty?* "Some kid from MTSU had a video camera."

"That story's absolutely incredible," Marcie said. "I'd say God's got something amazing planned for your life."

Rooster laughed. "How's that?"

"Because that looks to me like an honest-to-God miracle," Marcie replied. "If God went to all that trouble to save your life, I think He must have plans to use you for something big."

Rooster smiled, using his hand to mimic drinking. "You sure you're not back on the sauce, Marcie?"

"Joke all you want, but you can't argue with this video." Marcie faced Sallie Mae. "You said the reporter's looking for Rooster. That right?"

"Yes."

Marcie stared at Rooster. "Did you know she's looking for you?"

"No. Had no clue. Honestly I thought that video stuff had blown over already."

"Gonna let her find you?" Sallie Mae asked with more than casual interest.

"I don't know." Anger crept into Rooster's voice. *Why's she so fascinated by this?* "Don't see much upside for me by talking to that reporter."

"Don't be crazy." Sallie Mae was undeterred. "This is your chance to be a minor regional celebrity."

Rooster looked at the carpet. *That some kinda joke?* "Why would I want that?" Not adding a pejorative to his question took all his willpower.

"It could be fun," Dave interjected.

"Maybe you could make some money from it," George offered.

"You think?" Rooster was incredulous. *Really? What would that look like? Not sure I see a money angle?*

"Who knows?" Sallie Mae said. "Anything's possible if you do the interview. But if you don't, you'll never know."

"What you think, Marcie?" Dave asked.

"I don't think Rooster should go into a TV interview expecting to make money, but it's a chance to have fifteen minutes of fame, if he's interested in that sorta thing."

Rooster's mind had been busy since George mentioned the possibility of a payday. But how would he turn his new-found notoriety into cold hard cash?

Sallie Mae spoke. "So what you gonna do, Rooster?"

Rooster leaned back and scanned their expectant faces. "Guess I'm gonna think about it."

"Wow," Marcie exclaimed. "Look at the time. We really need to get started."

THIRTY-THREE

Marcie passed sheets of paper to the group. "Rooster, right now we're doing a weekly lesson based on Pastor's sermon." She offered George a warm smile. "Will you open us in prayer?"

George fidgeted and adjusted his hat. Rooster nervously looked around as everyone closed their eyes. *Where's this prayer coming from? George just gonna make something up?*

As if in answer to Rooster's question, George began, barely above a whisper. "Dear Lord, please be with us tonight as we go through the lesson, and help all us to make Rooster feel welcome. Let each of us take away something valuable from our time together. In Jesus' name we pray."

Everyone gave an emphatic, "Amen."

Rooster marveled at George. Given the same task, Rooster would have made a fool of himself. Tension filled his head. *Marcie gonna make me pray too?* He thought about the meticulously written Catholic prayers from his youth. *Who just wings it? Don't you need a priest for that? Don't unapproved prayers get you excommunicated? If you can make up anything, what's with all those rosaries?*

"Thanks, George. That was great." Marcie motioned toward the top of the page. "Rooster?"

When Rooster saw their expectant stares, his mouth went dry. Fear and panic set in. *No way I'm stumbling through some feeble prayer like a fool.* Sweat trickled down his spine.

Concern creased Marcie's brow. "You ok? You look pale."

"I'm fine." Rooster's heart fluttered and perspiration flowed freely. *Someone turn up the heat in here?*

"All right," Marcie said doubtfully. "Since Rooster doesn't know us that well, we can start with an ice breaker."

Relief washed over him. *Don't have to come up with a prayer after all.* He released the lungful of air he had been holding.

"The ice breaker's a fun question to get things rolling," Marcie explained.

"I know what an ice breaker is," Rooster snapped. *These people think I'm stupid?*

"Ok." Marcie said, not at all flustered by Rooster's tone. "Sallie Mae, will you pick one of the three ice breakers?"

"I'd love to," Sallie Mae said with enthusiasm. "Hmm, how about number two? What is the most valuable thing you ever owned?" She turned her gaze to the ceiling. After a moment she leaned forward with a serious look. "I'd have to say the most precious thing I ever had is my salvation."

George groaned. "Couldn't think of a more churchy answer?"

Sallie Mae crossed her arms. "What's wrong with my answer? That's the most valuable thing any of us has."

"This is the ice breaker," George said. "It's not supposed to be the expected church answer."

Marcie broke in. "It's never supposed to be the," she made air quotes, "church answer. We all need to be real all the time. Sallie Mae can say that, if that's how she really feels."

"It is how I really feel." Sallie Mae's smile returned and her tone grew playful. "Since you're the ice breaker police, George, you can show us all how to answer the question."

George stared down. "Never owned anything valuable."

"That's lame," Dave protested. "You can't just punt. 'Specially after giving Sallie Mae guff 'bout her answer."

"I thought you bought a house last year," Marcie offered.

"True," George said. "But the question asked for the most valuable thing I ever owned. Far as I'm concerned, the bank owns the house 'til I get that mortgage paid down a little bit."

Dave laughed. "Wow. You really are the ice breaker police."

"C'mon," Marcie said. "I don't care if you grew up in a mud hut, you owned something in your life that was valuable to you."

George scrunched his face and looked off into a corner. "When I was a kid, my parents bought my brother and me a horse. We named him Dude, after Jeff Bridges in *The Big Lebowski*." George rubbed his eyes, his voice thick. "My brother loved that horse." He sniffled and wiped his nose on the back of his hand. "Anyway, I guess Dude's the most valuable thing I ever owned."

A funereal pall as heavy as the eighty-nine percent humidity outside, descended upon them. *Is George really getting emotional over a damn horse?* Rooster glanced around. *What just happened?* Marcie seemed about to cry. Sallie Mae had pulled a tissue from somewhere, and dabbed at her eyes. Dave sat with his perfect posture, his face sour and his eyes locked on the far side of the big sanctuary. Fearful he would say something stupid, Rooster swallowed his urge to ask about the gloom which had overtaken them. He turned his mind toward his ice breaker answer. He had owned some awesome stuff in his bond trading days. It was all long gone now, but he considered which former possession would be the most impressive. Within seconds, he knew exactly what he would use. It actually had not been the most valuable thing he ever owned, but it was definitely the coolest. *They'll have more respect for me when they hear about this.*

The group re-gathered from whatever had set them off. Marcie turned to Dave with a forced a smile. "What about you, Dave? What's the most valuable thing you ever owned?"

With a huge smile, Dave'd whole demeanor softened. "That's easy. My college championship ring." He held up his hand to display a huge gold ring with a prominent red jewel.

"That's awesome." George's voice actually showed a little pep. "Can I see it?"

"Sure." Dave wrestled it off and handed it to George.

"I knew you played college football," Marcie said, "but I didn't know you won a national championship."

"Where'd you play?" His voice inflection betrayed Rooster's fear his own response might not be the best anymore.

Dave grew wistful. "Troy University, down in Alabama, 1984 National Champs. That ring represents all the blood, sweat, and tears we put into that year. What a great group of guys. That season really taught me what teamwork's all about."

Everyone oohed and ahhed as they passed the ring. Rooster searched for ways to diminish Dave's accomplishment, his desire to be most impressive blinding him. "What position you play?"

"I played every position along the O-line."

"You start?" The questions, from a hidden corner of Rooster's subconscious, picked up momentum and intensity. He was powerless to stop them as they rolled out unfiltered.

"No, I was first off the bench. Played quite a bit."

"Wasn't Troy division two?" Rooster was vaguely aware of inner forces driving him to slap down any perceived challenge to his preeminence and intellectual superiority. Like a cattle stampede, once Rooster headed down this road, he carved a wake of destruction until some brave soul reined him in, or he ran off the cliff and plummeted to his own embarrassing demise.

"Yeah." Dave's smile faded slightly.

The ring finally made it to Rooster. Surprised by its weight, he realized it was too big even for his thumb. *This guy's got fingers the size of sausages.* He considered the stupidity of picking a fight with him, twice. "That a real ruby?" Rooster's passive-aggressive tone implied it was a fake.

Dave's voice developed an edge. "Don't know."

"Reminds me of my high school ring." Rooster absentmindedly turned it over in his hands. "Pretty cool, man. Here you go." He tossed the ring across the circle toward Dave.

Marcie emitted an audible gasp as the most valuable thing Dave ever owned took flight. The big man snatched it from the air and jammed it back on his ring finger, a scowl on his face.

Marcie tried to break the tension. "Dave, that's quite an accomplishment. I can see why you're so proud. Very few people can say they were the national champs of anything."

Everyone, except Rooster, echoed Marcie and offered enthusiastic congratulations and encouragement.

"Thanks." Dave's expression softened as he stared lovingly at his ring.

Marcie faced Rooster, a smile on her face, but anger in her eyes. "Well, we're the last two. You want to go, or should I?"

"Ladies first." Marcie's disapproving look flew over Rooster's head. He felt pretty good about his chances now. *My answer's definitely better than some weak low level national championship from a guy who didn't even start.*

"Ok." Marcie crumpled her face in thought. "I'd have to say it's my friends. I'd be lost without my friends."

"Not to be the ice breaker police or anything," George said with a wink, "but the question was, what is the most valuable thing you ever owned? I don't think you own your friends."

"Alright, alright. You really are a stickler. Then I'll have to say the company I inherited when my husband passed." She looked at the floor. "He was one heck of a businessman." Marcie lifted her head and smiled. "Now," she said, before anyone could question her further, "Rooster, your turn."

Rooster grinned as he anticipated their reaction. "Used to own a candy apple red Maserati, and before the ice breaker police jumps in." He nodded at George. "I did own it free and clear. Found a used one I bought for ninety-eight grand, cash."

Rooster waited for them all to gush, but instead, crickets. *What's wrong with these people?* He glanced around. Dave, head turned, seemed as if he could not bare to look at Rooster. *No surprise. Thought his lame-ass D-II championship was gonna trump everyone.* Sallie Mae's eyes were fixed on her paper, as if it completely captivated her. George stared out indifferently from under the lowered bill of his cap. *They know what a Maserati is? Thought George was in the car business. Surely he knows what an incredible piece of Italian machinery I once owned.*

Rooster was convinced they did not understand. "That car went zero to sixty in less than four seconds. I once got it up to one seventy-two on the Long Island Expressway."

"That's awesome, Rooster," Marcie said quietly.

"Yeah, sounds cool," Sallie Mae said without emotion.

His balloon popped, Rooster slumped and crossed his arms. *Bunch of jerks. What'd I do to deserve this?* He was always an outcast. As if they wanted to toss him from the group like an annoying reality show loser?

"Thanks, Rooster." Marcie said dismissively. "We're way behind. We have to get started on this study."

Rooster nodded. A deep sadness settled over him. It was not the first time he had experienced piercing loneliness in a room full of people.

THIRTY-FOUR

"We're so late starting the lesson." Marcie scanned the handout. "I'm going to skip ahead to the meat of this thing."

Still stinging from the group's collective beat down of his ice breaker answer, Rooster pretended to study the paper while surreptitiously examining each person. He painted mental pictures of their shortcomings. *Dave's a dumb ex-jock, forever living in the past, his glory days not nearly as impressive as he imagines. Probably a gym teacher, or a Home Depot assistant manager. Sallie Mae's a crazy cat lady, so desperate for affection, she throws herself at any man who shows her the slightest attention. George is an antisocial loser with nothing going for him, a wet blanket on any gathering that'll have him.*

And Marcie... What about Marcie? Rooster leaned back and considered her. She was beautiful, giving, and kind. *Not like these other freaks. Probably why she's in charge of this bunch. But why would she associate with these weirdos? That alone proves something's a little off. Maybe she collects stray animals and is forever trying to fix people.*

"Here's a good one," Marcie said. "We'll start here, two thirds down." She held up her sheet and pointed at the question. "In his sermon, Pastor talked about how God had redeemed him from the mess his life had become. Name something in your life right now that's keeping you from living God's plan for you." Marcie lowered her paper. "Sallie Mae, will you go first?"

Rooster smirked. *This oughta be rich. She'll probably whine about the high cost of cat litter.*

Sallie Mae pulled in a deep breath. "If I'm being honest, the biggest problem in my life is me."

Concern creased Marcie's face. "What you mean, Sallie Mae?"

Sallie Mae's big hair bounced slightly as she emitted an uncomfortable giggle. Her eyes said she was reconsidering whether sharing this was the smart. She rubbed her hands together and sucked in another long slow breath. "Umm... I have problems with my confidence. I'm always really tense and awkward in social situations. Sometimes, I'm so self conscious I can't even remember what I did or said after the conversation's over."

"I don't see that in you at all." George frowned. "You seem totally at ease talking to people."

"That's 'cause I'm comfortable with y'all. You should see me with folks I don't know, always sputtering and embarrassing myself. Been like that since I was a kid."

"How's that keeping you from seeing God's best in your life?" Marcie asked gently.

"Sometimes I feel my days are slipping away and God's bringing people in my path. People I could help, people who could help me, and I'm scaring them all off with my ineptness."

"You know, Sallie Mae," Dave offered in a friendly tone, "Moses struggled with public speakin' an' God told him to take along Aaron to do all the talkin'. If God has somethin' for you, He'll find a way to make it happen."

"That's right," Marcie said. "All you can do is your best. God has proven over and over that He can do incredible things through imperfect people."

"Good thing," George added with an uncharacteristic laugh. "Because imperfect people's all He's got!"

Sallie Mae straightened. "I'm doing my part to get better. I'm on the greeter team Sunday mornings so I can practice. In fact, that's how I met Rooster." She smiled at him. "Hopefully I didn't traumatize you too bad when I stumbled and bumbled through our conversation."

Rooster stared at her, his mouth agape, awash in shame. He had often experienced the same feelings of inadequacy and social clumsiness. *Who knew I'm not the only one?*

Suddenly aware all eyes were on him, Rooster stammered, "Ahh... No, Sallie Mae. Woulda never guessed you weren't totally confident when we met."

"That's sweet of you to say."

"It's the truth." Rooster felt an unexpected, instant kinship with her. He recalled his own anxiety when he had entered the sanctuary earlier in the evening.

"That was good stuff, Sallie Mae," Marcie said. "Thanks for sharing. I know it wasn't easy."

Sallie Mae blushed and nodded. A huge chunk of hair broke free from its AquaNet bonds, and flopped to the side.

"Who's next?" Marcie crossed her legs. "How about George? Name something in your life right now that's keeping you from living out God's plan for you."

George nodded. He sat up straighter, and adjusted his Braves cap, a pained look on his face. "I guess everything with my brother has me all off kilter. Lately it's all I can do to just get outta bed in the morning."

"But that's totally understandable," Marcie said. "It just happened. You're going to need time."

Rooster looked around. Everyone had watery eyes. Sallie Mae had pulled out her tissue again. *What's the story with George's brother? Must be something bad. Should I ask?* Helpless, Rooster considered his options. Stay quiet and feel like an eavesdropper, or speak up and risk appearing a voyeur who revels in other's pain. Convinced he was the ultimate outsider, Rooster leaned back and searched the ceiling tiles for answers. He turned to Marcie with pleading eyes. *Please tell me what's going on.* A deep sigh escaped his lips.

Marcie saw him. "George, I'm sure Rooster doesn't have a clue what we're talking about. You mind if I fill him in?"

George stared at Rooster with painful, bloodshot eyes. "Naw," he said. "I'll tell him."

"You sure? I don't mind."

George waved her off. "No, it'll be cathartic for me."

Rooster leaned forward and tried to appear interested. Sympathetic interested, not voyeuristic interested. *What's that look like?* With no clue how his expression actually came across, his anxiety level rose. *Probably look like a moron.*

"Well, it's like this." George's voice cracked. "My little brother was murdered two weeks ago."

"Oh my God." Rooster covered his mouth and suddenly it all clicked. George had been sullen and disinterested because he was overcome with grief. *I'm such a jackass.* Rooster turned away, ashamed to look him in the eye.

"Yeah," George said with a hollow laugh. "He went to visit a buddy from school in Chicago. On the way back, he took the wrong exit, and the little dummy drove right into the middle of a gang war. You believe that?"

Rooster shook his head. As George continued to stare directly at him, Rooster experienced strange emotions. He felt bad for George and his brother, but also became aware of an odd sense of guilt, as if he were somehow responsible.

"The police called it 'collateral damage'." George continued. "He was driving through a neighborhood, trying to get back to the highway, and a stray bullet came through the side window and hit him in the jugular." George's chest heaved as he fought for control. He wiped his eyes with his sleeve. "Hit him perfect. The coroner said an inch over on either side and he coulda lived." George buried his head in his hands and silently sobbed. His whole body shook as he managed to squeak out, "But it hit him in the perfect spot."

Rooster opened his mouth. He wished he had something profound and comforting to say, but nothing came to mind. So he sat quietly and tried not to stare at George. He thought about what a jerk he had been in his assessment of the man.

Sallie Mae slid next to George, and put her arm around his shoulder. "I don't have a clue what you're going through," she whispered through tears, "but I want you to know that I'm... That we're all praying for you everyday."

George managed a painful smile. "Thanks. That means a lot."

"Yeah." Dave's voice cracked. "You know if you need anything. Anything at all, you just gotta ask."

"I know," George said.

"I mean it!" Dave added a little too forcefully. "Don't care if it's three in the mornin'. You got my number."

"Yes sir." A small grin creased George's lips. "Thanks. I don't know if I coulda gotten through this without y'all. Marcie's called me everyday since it happened, for goodness sakes. I think she's afraid I might do something to myself."

"That's 'cause we all think of you as family," Marcie said. "And for the record, I don't think you're gonna hurt yourself."

George laughed. "Just a lame joke. I'll be fine. But we need to change the subject before everyone gets depressed."

Rooster felt his own eyes mist as he watched the scene play out. *Marcie called George every day. How impressive's that?* He could not manage that for his own mother when her brother died. He talked to her twice the first week after the funeral, and then stopped. This group impressed him. They did interact like family, which made him feel all the more like an unwelcome intruder invading their space.

"Gimme one of those tissues." Marcie laughed as Sallie Mae jumped up to hand one over. Marcie dabbed at her eyes. "We do need to lighten things up a bit. So I'll go next. You know me." She forced a smile. "I can be a little wacky. Sometimes I think I'm borderline obsessive compulsive."

"How's that keep God from using you?" Sallie Mae asked.

"I'm getting to that. I have all kinds of little obsessive things I do that eat up my time and keep me focused on myself instead of others."

Dave looked skeptical. "How 'bout an example?"

"Ok," Marcie said thoughtfully. "I can't believe I'm going to share this." She looked at her paper as if in deep thought.

"C'mon." Dave grinned. "Gotta tell us now."

"All right." Marcie rolled her eyes. "I'm kinda, sorta, afraid of electricity."

"What on earth does that mean?" Sallie Mae asked.

"I keep everything at home unplugged unless I'm using it."

"So does every other normal person," Dave said.

"No, you don't understand." Marcie giggled. "I'm talking about everything. Lamps, clocks, the TV, everything."

The group burst into laughter.

"Your toaster's not plugged up?" Dave asked incredulously.

"The only things in my place with electricity going to them right now are appliances that are hardwired to the house, like the air conditioner. And even that makes me nervous."

"What about your stove and microwave?" George said.

"Both unplugged. I only plug them in when I use them. That's why I eat out a lot."

Dave shook his head in disbelief. "Why?"

Marcie smiled uncomfortably. "I know it sounds ridiculous, but I'm afraid something's gonna blow up if the electricity's running to it."

A fresh roar of laughter erupted.

"That's totally insane," George said between guffaws.

"I know," Marcie chortled. "That's what I'm talking about."

"What other strange quirks you been holding back from us?" Sallie Mae asked.

Marcie laughed. "Hey, I only tell on myself once a night. If you stick around, maybe you'll learn more of my borderline lunatic behavior."

"Borderline?" Dave asked with amusement. "If the crazy border's the Tennessee state line, that electrical thing's got you somewhere down near Miami."

They devolved into another round of shrieks and giggles.

"Nice." Marcie shook her head.

Rooster watched their joviality with keen interest. He never had relationships with a group anything like this. Ever since he could recall, all his interactions with others revolved around drinking and at this moment that felt all wrong. *What's the matter with a drink once in awhile? It lubricates conversations, drains away tension, and makes people friendlier. Nothing bad about that.* He considered the ridiculous tattoo on his stomach. A drink once in awhile was no big deal, but eight beers, five cocktails, and seven shots in one evening, might be a bit of a problem. Especially if it causes you to wake up unexpectedly married, or in a cow pasture, or in the boss' bed with his 17-year-old daughter after the company Christmas party.

Rooster's life was a steaming pile of utter destruction. Not only had he made a mess of himself, but the ancillary carnage inflicted on others was astounding. Nothing would ever change until he admitted the root of his problems.

Marcie interrupted his thoughts. "Rooster, you ok?"

"Huh?" Rooster looked up and once again saw their expectant stares. "Sorry. Guess I drifted off for a minute there."

"That's ok," Marcie said. "You want to answer?"

"Ahh, sure. What was it again?"

Marcie read, "Name something in your life right now that's keeping you from living out God's plan for you."

Rooster swallowed hard as his earlier thoughts flooded back. A barely perceptible voice from somewhere in the back of his brain earnestly urged him to admit alcohol had become a problem. He shook his head and tried to quiet his mind. He thought about the embarrassment of telling this group of virtual strangers he was a drunk. *I'm not a drunk. Haven't had a drink in more than twenty-four hours.*

You were craving one with all your soul not more than ten minutes ago, the voice whispered. *Every time you wake up to a fresh alcohol-soaked disaster, you swear something needs to change. Here's your big chance to do just that.*

Tightness filled his chest and the pressure in his head felt like his skull might explode. He fought the voice with all he had, but it was a losing battle. The voice grew stronger. *Don't want these people to know I'm a mess.*

If not these folks, who? It asked. *If not now, when? You still have time to pick up the pieces and make something of your life. It's now or never. Don't let this opportunity pass.*

Marcie's voice cut through the fog. "You want to pass?"

Rooster blinked and refocused on the group, all of their gazes filled with genuine concern. He drew in a breath. *Here goes nothing.* "No," Rooster said quietly. "I want to answer." He collected his thoughts and launched into his response before he could chicken out. "Don't know anything about God using me, but I can honestly say there is one thing in my life that brings nothing but destruction to me and those around me."

He noticed the corners of Marcie's mouth curled into a subtle smile. Rooster briefly thought she might be laughing at him, but when he saw her eyes sparkle with understanding and satisfaction, he knew she had once faced the exact same choice now in front of him. She finally had enough of the chaos and devastation. She had finally tired of the shame and humiliation. She chose to quit drinking, and it had all turned out okay for her. Knowing Marcie sat across from him, seemingly happy and well-adjusted fifteen years later, filled him with hope and a deep thirst for the kind of peace she possessed. *I can make it. Can't I? Is it completely nuts to think fifteen years from now I could be sitting where she is and looking back on this moment as the turning point in my life?*

He glanced at Marcie again. She had moved forward in her chair and nodded in encouragement. His confidence boosted by her reassuring demeanor, an unnatural calm came over him. In his mind was a clarity of purpose unlike any he had ever experienced. He understood exactly what he had to say. "You ever heard the Blake Shelton song, *The More I Drink?*"

They nodded, a palpable shift in the atmosphere of the circle. They leaned forward, innately aware something profoundly important was about to happen.

"My life's like that song. The more I drink, the more I drink. If I have one, I'll have thirteen, and there ain't no in between."

"And they can't get you off the karaoke machine?" Marcie added with a wink.

"Yeah." Rooster sighed. "And all the other crazy stuff he talks about in that song." *Cat's outta the bag. No putting it back.* He nervously scanned them, fully expecting disapproval and judgment in their eyes. What he saw instead astounded him. Sallie Mae had her tissue back out, her hand pressed against her chest. Her watery eyes conveyed empathy and support. George had pulled off his cap and crumpled it in his hands as concern spread across his tired face. Even Dave had gone misty. When Rooster caught him wiping away a tear, Dave flashed an embarrassed smile, and an awkward "Go get 'em" little wink of encouragement. Rooster was filled with emotion. He knew to the depths of his soul he had just started a significant life event. *No turning back now.* For better or worse, things would now be different. He was relieved to finally acknowledge his demons aloud, but tendrils of doubt and fear poked holes in his fragile hope for the future. *Can I really do this, or has my mouth written a check my ass can't cash?*

Once again, Marcie's voice pulled him back to reality. "That all you want to say?"

Rooster exhaled. "Absolutely not." *Come this far. Might as well go all the way.* He told them everything.

THIRTY-FIVE
Thursday, May 19th

"You see Rooster, the pickle lobby's way more powerful than you realize. If they're not greasing palms and buying favors, how else does a nasty slimy hunk of rotten cucumber get on the plate next to every sandwich in every restaurant in America and Canada? Don't know about Mexico or Europe. Ain't never been there. Asia don't count neither. They're not sandwich people. They're all rice and veggies. Think about it. That pickle juice defiles anything it touches. Get a drop of it on your bread and the whole damn sandwich tastes like a godawful pickle."

Rooster nodded as Jimmy Robinson offered more over-caffeinated kookiness. Following his first day on the job, Rooster had listened to his new boss wax poetic for ten minutes. He did not mind. He had grown to like the strange old guy.

"Think the pickle people are strong? Next to the lemon lobby, they're small potatoes. The pickle guys were smart latching onto sandwiches, but the lemon people were visionaries hooking up with drinks. Think about it, Rooster. Maybe every third person orders a sandwich. But how many people have a supposedly lemon-friendly drink? They used to just put 'em in tea and diet Coke. But somewhere along the way they hit the Holy Grail and convinced the powers-that-be there should be a lemon wedge in every dang-blasted glass of water. Unbelievable! How many millions or billions did the lemon guys make from that stroke of genius? If anyone really considered it, they'd ban lemons from drinks completely. Think about it, man. The lemons sit uncovered in a little bowl. Who knows what falls on them as everyone runs to and fro past 'em? Then the waitress pouring your water reaches in the bowl with her disgusting hands and throws a lemon in your drink. You have wait staff handling food and dirty dishes, sweating and picking their noses. And all of them reaching into that lemon bowl. Might as well have all their grubby fingers in your water glass. Nauseating. If the board of health ever swabbed the lemon bowl, they'd shut the place down."

Stopping for a breath, Jimmy jammed his hands into the pockets of his navy blue one-piece jumpsuit, and rocked on his toes. Before he could launch into something else, Rooster held up his hands. "I'm sorry, Jimmy. Really need to get going. I gotta do some shopping. I got a bit of a walk ahead of me."

"Sure." Jimmy offered an easy smile. "Good first day."

"Thanks, Jimmy. Definitely enjoyed it."

"Gotta tell you, I really like you. Think you're gonna work out just fine."

"I appreciate you saying that."

"I absolutely mean it. Hey, you decided what you're gonna do with that reporter from channel 3?"

Rooster offered a sheepish grin. "Don't know for sure, but right now I'm kinda leaning toward doing the interview."

Jimmy pulled his hands from his pockets, and hooked his thumbs on the jumpsuit's built-in belt. "Tell you what. If you decide to do the interview, I'll sweeten the pot."

"What do you mean?"

"I'll make it simple." Mirth danced in Jimmy's eyes. "You do the interview and find a way to mention the store so it makes it on the actual broadcast, I'll give you a thousand bucks."

Rooster laughed. "That's crazy. You don't have to do that."

"You're wrong. It would be great marketing for the store. You

pull that off, it'd be worth every penny."
　　Rooster shrugged. "I'll see what I can do."

THIRTY-SIX

The Chairman was nearly out of ideas and money. This whole misadventure had been impulsive, emotionally-driven, and totally out of character. Every step in his life had been carefully plotted to enhance his future law practice and eventual political career. From summertime activities, to what he ate in public, to his clothing, it had all been calculated for maximum benefit. He had finally admitted to himself, his obsession with Madison was more than normal infatuation, and it threatened to destroy everything he had worked so hard to build.

His friends back at NEIU would be shocked to see him now. The BMW passenger window missing glass, replaced with duct tape and cardboard, featured a huge picture of the Brawny Paper Towel man. The clothes he had worn for five days were soiled and paint-covered, despite several attempts to wash them at various minimart restrooms. The Northfield Boulevard Kwik Sak cleaning crew had caught him in a full-on sink bath, the Chairman wearing nothing but white briefs, noisy Italian loafers, and a shocked expression. The manager produced a machete and the Chairman hightailed it out of there in his underwear, nearly forgetting to grab his still-drying clothes.

They have security cameras there? What a disaster that'd be. He imagined a grainy black and white tape of him fleeing in his skivvies, surfacing twenty years later just as he announced his bid for the Senate. His money stash had dwindled to just $27.38, not even enough gas money to get back to Chicago, but cash was the least of his concerns. He had been unable to check on Madison with the pumpkin-headed bouncer lurking around seemingly all hours of the day and night. Driving the streets of Murfreesboro had been an inefficient method to find that crook Davis Sinclair, but he had yet to come up with a Plan B. At least all the cruising had given him time to consider exactly what he would do once he had that slimeball in his clutches.

The Chairman smiled as he turned onto Mercury Boulevard. The feeling had returned to his leg. Despite all the pain and problems, there was something exhilarating about all this. Once he had broken out from his carefully crafted cocoon, he had felt truly free for the first time. He sought justice for others, got by on his wits, and operated by the seat of his filthy pants. *Who does that?* He was Batman, rambling down the street in his souped-up jalopy, fighting for truth, justice, and the American way. *Or was that Superman? Superman didn't have a car. Can't keep all these superheroes straight.* He had been taking piano lessons when he should have been watching that stuff.

As the Chairman sorted out comic book characters, he noticed a dark-haired man walking with two plastic grocery bags. Even from behind, there was a familiar quality to how the guy moved and how his clothes hung on his frame. As he rolled past, the Chairman caught a good look at the man's face.

It's him! I found Sinclair! The Chairman's heart raced as he congratulated himself on his brilliant plan to track down this guy. He checked the backseat to ensure his 'kidnap kit' was ready for action. He turned back to the road just in time to see the car was about to slam into the curb. He violently yanked the steering wheel cut off a white Nissan in the next lane. The incensed driver laid on the horn. The Chairman jerked back into his own lane and weighed his options. *Can't let this scum escape.* His mind was foggy, his breathing fast and heavy, his vision fuzzy. Dizziness set in.

I'm hyperventilating. The condition showed up periodically when he got overexcited. At age thirteen he won the Illinois State Spelling Bee, hyperventilated, and passed out on the stage. Unfortunately, he had to pee the last thirty minutes of the contest and wet his pants while unconscious. The other kids called him 'Bee Stain' until his junior year.

Gotta get parked before I kill myself. He turned on a side street and stopped at the curb. With no paper bag, the Chairman grabbed his shirt collar, pulled the neck tight against his nose, and used his forearms to hold the front against his chest. He focused on breathing deep and slow, and exhaling long and completely. After a few minutes, his mind cleared. The dizziness and tingling in his fingers faded away. His wits back, the Chairman cursed his attack. *Did Davis Sinclair just slip through my fingers? If I screw this up, how'll I ever win Madison?* He slumped in the seat, lamenting his missed opportunity.

Then Davis Sinclair strolled past his car, chatting on his phone, oblivious to the Chairman's presence. "There is a God," the Chairman mumbled as he reached for the kidnap kit and prepared to make the snatch.

THIRTY-SEVEN

"I really don't know where all that came from," Rooster said into the phone as he walked along Apollo Drive with his grocery sacks. "I didn't show up planning to say all that."

"I'm glad you did," Marcie said. "I want you to know, everyone in the group's there for you. I certainly know what you're going through right now."

"Honestly, it really hasn't been that hard."

"Rooster, it's only been one day."

"Gotta start somewhere. Maybe I'll be the guy who gives it up just like that, but let me change the subject a minute."

"Ok."

"Thank you for hooking me up with Jimmy Robinson. I know it's just the first day, but I think I'm gonna love this job."

"Isn't Jimmy a hoot?"

"Yeah, but what's the story with the jumpsuits? I thought only farmers and mechanics wore those things."

"Don't know. He's worn them ever since I've known him. I been around him so long, I forgot how odd they look. What'd he have you do your first day?"

Rooster heard a faint wheezing, which seemed to come from his grocery bags. *What's that? Sounds like a cross between a hydraulic press and a whoopee cushion.*

Marcie's raised voice cut through his distraction. "Rooster, you still there?"

"Sorry. I think my groceries are making weird noises. Gotta hang up and check this out."

"What kind of weird noises do groceries make?"

Rooster heard it again, a little louder. "Seriously, I'll call you back later."

"Ok." Marcie said, amusement in her voice. "Let me know if you find a baby Birdzilla hidden in there."

"I'll do it." Rooster smiled and shook his head. "Bye."

He slipped the phone in his pocket and set his groceries on the ground. As he shuffled through the bags, the noise grew louder. He pulled out a few items. "What on earth's that?"

He was hunched over the sacks, a box of frozen Bubba Burgers in his hand, when he realized it was not his groceries producing the strange sound. It was behind him, and whatever made the noise, was almost on top of him. The sound gave him a shiver of déjà vu. Still squatting, Rooster pivoted to see the source of the odd wheezing tone. Surely the peculiar little man in front of him was homeless with his grimy, stained clothing. *He been sleeping in a dumpster?* White rubbery clumps were interlaced throughout his hair.

Guy's a mess. As bad as he appeared, something was off. Rooster scanned his body. *The shoes.* "Oh my God," Rooster exclaimed. *Zelli Crocodile tassel loafers.* Rooster once owned the expensive Italian shoes, but trashed them when he realized they made strange noises with every step. *That's where I heard that sound before. What's a homeless guy doing with Zellis?*

"Now I got you," the little man croaked.

"What's that?" Rooster eyed him. A black backpack over his shoulders, he clutched a gray cloth. *That a handkerchief?*

"I got you," he said, a hint of crazy gleaming in his eyes.

Guy's off his meds. As Rooster began to stand, the guy let out a high-pitched, nails-on-the-chalkboard shriek and lunged at him. Before he knew what happened, Rooster was on his back with the little lunatic astride his chest pressing the damp pungent fabric against Rooster's face.

Rooster's mind was a jumble as he fought to make sense of his unusual situation. *Is he actually holding his disgusting snot rag against my face?* The thought made him gag. Then he remembered the cold box in his hand. *Bubba Burgers.* Rooster swung the frozen meat. It struck the side of the man's head with a loud "thwock!" The smack stunned the attacker long enough for Rooster to shove him off and scramble to his feet.

"What the hell's wrong with you?" He demanded through ragged breaths. He glanced at the rag. *Gonna need a tetanus shot after having that thing on my mouth.*

The strange little man rubbed the side of his head and stared at his handkerchief. "Didn't work."

Guy's a total whack job. "You stay away from me." With a close eye on his assailant, Rooster gathered his groceries. He pointed down the road. "You go that way." He brandished the Bubba Burgers like Thor's hammer, but the little fruitcake screamed his blood-curdling shriek and lunged again. This time Rooster was ready. Like a matador, he deftly sidestepped the crazy guy's wild charge. As the man flew past, Rooster cracked the back of his head with the rock-hard Bubba Burgers, sending him sprawling on the sidewalk. "Stop that," Rooster demanded. "Leave me the hell alone."

The homeless guy rolled onto his back with a groan.

Rooster walked away quickly, glancing over his shoulder in anticipation of another assault. Sure enough, within a few seconds, the wheezing shoes rushed after him. Rooster sighed heavily. *Hasn't this idiot had enough already?* He turned just in time to see the little kook dive at his knees. Rooster flexed his legs and gathered for the impact. The man bounced off his thigh and fell on the ground with a loud grunt.

This is getting absurd. The guy jumped to his feet and lunged again. This time he managed to latch his arms around Rooster's thigh. He quickly straddled Rooster's ankle and sat on Rooster's foot, his appendages locked tightly around Rooster's leg and his head jammed against Rooster's thigh. Rooster stared in disbelief. *Not even drinking, and this insane crap's still happening to me.* He looked around, embarrassed someone might see the preposterous scene. He shook his leg and tried to dislodge him. "What's your problem, you crazy bastard? Get off me!"

"Might as well give up and come with me," the half-baked nutjob proclaimed.

Rooster let out an ironic laugh. "Gotta be kidding." He bent to peel the dude off, but had to stand straight again. The little guy reeked of fermented hot dogs and dirty socks, his funk strong enough to take Rooster's breath away. Not knowing what else to do, Rooster tried to walk. He hoped the crackpot would get tired, release his leg, and just go away. Rooster dragged and shook his leg as he spit increasingly graphic obscenities, but the homeless wacko clung like a koala bear on a eucalyptus tree. After half a minute of such insanity, Rooster had enough. "Listen you dirty little freak." Sweat poured down his face. "Let go of my leg, or I'm gonna kick your ass."

"This is for Madison," the guy responded cryptically.

"Huh? What's that mean? Haven't been to Wisconsin in fifteen years."

"You stay away from Madison!" The man screamed in his cloying high-pitched little girl voice.

"All right. I've had just about enough of you. Don't care if you're a little homeless psychopath. You're going down anyway." He shook his leg violently and rained blows on the guy's head with the frozen Bubba Burgers. "Get off me!"

Finally, the man lost his grip and crashed to the ground.

Hyped up on adrenaline, Rooster could not restrain himself from throwing a hard mule-kick to the dude's lower body. "Now get your ass up and get the hell away from me."

The little man pulled himself to his feet and immediately kicked his left leg in the air, mimicking what Rooster had just done to dislodge him. *He making fun of me?* Rooster's anger grew.

A sad expression filled the guy's face. "Not again." He pointed at his leg and stared at Rooster with moist eyes. "Look what you did."

"What I did? You're completely mental."

The crazy little man shot Rooster an icy glare. "I'll get you next time." Then he clomped off, his Zelli loafers wheezing with every step.

Rooster watched in slack-jawed wonder. *What just happened? And what's with that crack about getting me next time?* Rooster focused on the man's odd gait. The guy leaned forward, his left leg dragging awkwardly behind him. *Seen that walk before.* Then it hit him. *It's Igor from some low-budget horror movie.* Regaining his breath, Rooster listened to the wheezing Zellis. *So glad I threw away those shoes.*

Convinced the homeless guy was no longer a threat, he slipped the battered hamburger box into his grocery bag and turned for home. He considered some of the more outrageous things he had done while under the influence.

What'd I do, to piss 'em off in Wisconsin?

THIRTY-EIGHT

Cassandra Nolan stood outside the front door of the historic Rutherford County Courthouse, at the center of the downtown square in Murfreesboro. She flipped her long auburn hair over her shoulder, and checked the big '3' on her microphone. She glanced back at the building's big doors.

"Hey Dennis," she called to her cameraman. "You find someone to make sure no one walks out during our live shot?"

"Naw," Dennis said. "Who's gonna be in the courthouse at ten at night?"

Cassandra rolled her eyes. "Someone walks in our shot, I'm totally throwing you under the bus."

"Don't worry. If we're lucky, you'll end up on the *Tonight Show*'s local news blooper segment."

"Whatever." Cassandra peered through the big windows at the dark lobby. She pulled her lips back. "How my teeth look?"

"They look awesome. Just like a..."

"Never mind." She ensured her earpiece was firmly in place. "Turn on the light. Let's make sure it doesn't wash me out."

Dennis dutifully flipped on the camera-mounted spotlight and flooded the area with brightness. "Looks fine." He glanced at his watch. "Hey, we're on in fifteen seconds."

Cassandra smoothed the front of her peach dress, and practiced her inviting smile. "I'm ready to roll."

Dennis counted down from ten, then pointed at her.

Concentration filled Cassandra's face as she stared at the camera, careful to keep the '3' on her microphone front and center, and listened to the anchor's intro to her segment.

"Yes, Susie. I'm here in Murfreesboro and I've been doing some detective work the past few days. I have indeed made contact with the Lamborghini Leaper, and the whole metro area will have the chance to meet him Tuesday evening."

The anchor said something.

"That's right, Susie. As luck would have it, our weekly 'Tuesdays Around Town' caravan was already scheduled to make an appearance in Murfreesboro this week. We'll be here on the square, right where I'm standing on the steps of the courthouse, at five p.m. Tuesday."

Susie again spoke.

"It's going to be a great time. Bring the whole family out so you can get up close and personal with your favorite Channel 3 personalities. I'll be joined by Brian Dawson and Bill Champion, and don't forget Stormy the Weather Monkey will be here too."

The playful banter with the anchor continued. Cassandra patiently awaited her turn. When Susie finished, Cassandra forced a huge smile. "And now we're adding the Lamborghini Leaper to that all-star lineup. I'll bring you a live interview with him on Tuesday, to lead off the six o'clock news broadcast. This man has really caught the attention of the metro area since his video hit YouTube last week. I'm certainly looking forward to talking with him."

THIRTY-NINE

"You see that?" Rooster pointed excitedly at Buddy's ancient television.

"I'm sittin' here watching, ain't I?" Buddy drawled with a big slap on Rooster's back. "Quite the interesting couple days. New job, big TV interview, stalker attack. You're really the cat's pajamas."

"I don't know what that means."

Buddy groaned as he pulled himself off the sofa. "You think about it, son. "It'll come to you." He moved toward the kitchen. "You want a beer?"

Rooster stared at the underwear on the coffee table. "No thanks. Not drinking today."

Buddy stopped mid-step, concern on his face. "You never turned down a drink in your life. You feelin' ok?"

Rooster looked at his lap and wrung his hands. His relationship with Buddy was totally built on hanging out and getting wasted, at least for him. Buddy never seemed to get drunk. *What happens if I tell Buddy I'm giving up alcohol? Could we even hang out anymore?* He did not want to lose his friend.

Buddy's voice cut into Rooster's thoughts. "Boy? That crazy homeless guy knock you in the noggin? You want a beer or not?"

"Uhh..." Rooster searched for something to say. "Not now. You go ahead."

"Suit yourself." Buddy disappeared into the kitchen and returned a few seconds later with a pair of Michelob Ultras. He flashed his megawatt smile. "Don't tell me those church folks got to you. You takin' up knitting next?"

Rooster smiled and shook his head. "Yeah. Right after we put away the snakes. They brainwashed me to give up drinking." Guilt flooded over him for cracking jokes about his new friends, and now he lied to Buddy, something he had never done before.

Buddy flopped on the couch and set the pair of beers on the coffee table, a twinkle in his eye. "You change your mind, there's one right here for you. If not, twice as much for me."

"Yeah." Rooster eyed the beer with unexpected longing. *Would one beer really hurt? I could probably stop after one.* He wanted that cold elixir so badly, he almost tasted it. A tight smile appeared as he imagined tipping the bottle back until it was empty. As the earthy, malty aroma filled his nostrils, Rooster knew he would not be able to control himself much longer. He stared as Buddy lifted the Michelob to his lips and took a long drink. *He's sure enjoying it.* Rooster noticed the sweat on the label, and imagined the reassuring feel of the cool bottle in his hand. His mouth practically watered.

Fingers snapped in front of Rooster's face.

"Huh," he grunted. His left eye twitched slightly.

"Gettin' worried about you, son." Buddy took another long drink. "You were in a trance there. What's with you?"

Rooster eyed the bottle in Buddy's hand. *He drinking slow to torture me? I coulda drank two or three in the time it's taken him to get through just that one.*

"Boy!"

Rooster snapped to attention. Bewilderment filled his face. *Buddy's talking. What's he asking me? This is crazy. Just tell him what's going on. He'll understand. Won't he?* "Buddy?"

The big man stared Rooster square in the eye and nodded in anticipation.

Rooster opened his mouth, but overcome with doubt and fear,

the words would not come. *What if Buddy gets mad and tells me to get the hell out?* He could not deal with Buddy's disappointment right now.

Buddy raised an eyebrow. "What you gonna say?"

"Nothing." Rooster searched for an escape. "Gotta pee."

Buddy smirked. "Don't need permission to handle that, son."

Rooster nearly ran to the bathroom. He splashed cold water on his face and considered his situation. He stared at the dark circles under his eyes in the mirror. *God, I'm pale. Head hurts. Probably the start of a monster migraine. Bourbon on the rocks'll cut that thing off at the pass.* He immediately looked forward to the brown liquid warming up his insides. Then it hit him how reflexive drinking had become. Could he learn to stop his mind from going instantly to alcohol in every situation? He closed his eyes and sighed as hopelessness settled over him. *This'll never work. Might as well go out and have a beer. What difference it make?* Totally defeated, Rooster pulled in a deep breath and headed back to the living room. Buddy, feet propped on the coffee table, had changed the channel to *The Best of Babe Winkelman*. He was just starting on the second beer.

"Hey." Rooster walked past the sofa toward the kitchen. "Think I will have that beer. You want one?"

"Drinking the last one right now. Shoulda taken it when you had the chance."

Rooster opened the fridge and sure enough, Buddy was right. He had already begun to drink the cold brew in his mind and the disappointment was almost overwhelming. He dragged himself back and dropped heavily on the sofa. "Wish you hadn't done that."

Buddy's brilliant grin lit up the room. "Put wishes in one hand and horse manure in the other, and then see which hand fills up first."

Rooster rolled his eyes at this latest Foghorn Leghorn wisdom. "Don't know what that means."

"Well son, can't help it you're a damn Yankee and lack basic language comprehension."

"If you say so." Completely distracted by Buddy's beer bottle,

Rooster's remaining energy drained away.

"You look like someone whizzed in your Cheerios." Buddy slapped him hard on the back. "Let's head out to the MT Bottle and throw back a little liquid happiness."

"Don't think so."

Buddy leaned toward Rooster and closely examined his face. "You look like hell, son. Hope that crazy varmint who jumped you didn't give you hepatitis or scabies or something."

Rooster thought about the handkerchief the strange little guy had pressed against his face. Maybe that did have something to do with his worsening condition. His spirit crushed, Rooster considered the Eagle Rare he saved for cigar sessions and other special occasions. "I'm ok," he lied. "But I think I'm going home."

FORTY
Friday, May 20th

Rooster tossed and turned in his sweaty bed sheets, his mind spinning through alcohol-withdrawal nightmares, or were they hallucinations? *Can you have a nightmare if you never actually fall asleep?*

Around two a.m. he heard Waylon going insane, barking, running around, and knocking things over. Rooster stumbled into the living room in his boxer shorts. The dog had cornered a skunk, a big stain on the wall behind the rodent. Rooster blinked a few times and debated whether to believe what he saw. When the aroma hit his nostrils, he understood it was all too real. He sighed. *Why haven't I got that board from Buddy? Really gotta cover that door opening.* The dog barked and snapped as the smaller animal cowered where the TV stand met the now-stained wall. Rooster's adrenaline surged. "Waylon!" The last thing he wanted was a dead skunk in the living room.

The startled dog turned toward him.

"Get away from there."

Waylon trotted across the room to Rooster's side, which allowed the skunk to scurry beneath the Mexican blanket and off into the night.

The skunk spray was so strong, Rooster's eyes watered. *That's about right. Pretty much sums up my life.* He leaned over and took a big whiff of Waylon's fur. "Don't think that skunk got a direct hit on you." He was actually relieved for the brief distraction from his alcohol longings. "But you still smell awful. Come with me."

Rooster strolled out the front door. Waylon followed closely. Even though the night was oppressively hot and humid, the cloudless sky was a pincushion of stars. Soaking in the scene, Rooster felt especially small and insignificant compared to the vast universe. As he herded Waylon toward the water spigot, Rooster considered all of Marcie's talk about God. How He wanted the best for everyone. It did not compute. If God cared so much about him, why would He allow Rooster to stand outside in his underwear at two in the morning hosing skunk off a dog? And make that sorry task to be a welcome diversion.

He turned on the faucet with a slightly shaky hand and aimed the hose at Waylon. The dog yelped with joy as he snapped at the stream and ran and jumped through the water. Rooster smiled at the unbridled display of pure happiness. He adjusted the nozzle settings to gauge Waylon's reaction. For twenty minutes they played and Rooster forgot his earlier struggles.

When the pair finally walked inside, Rooster laughed as Waylon jumped up and down with delight. The foul skunk funk seemed even more oppressive. Rooster opened all the windows and stared at the stained wall with disgust. "Thanks for keeping that thing outta my bedroom." He patted Waylon's head and considered his next move. After a minute, Rooster gathered a plastic bowl of water, dish detergent, and an old towel and returned to the crime scene. He dipped the towel in the water, squirted a third of the bottle of liquid soap onto the rag, held his nose, and proceeded to scrub the wall. When the smell had subsided somewhat, he tossed all the cleaning supplies out the front door. *How can you be completely exhausted and wide awake at the same time?* Convinced the skunk odor had become tolerable, Rooster flopped on the sofa, turned on his big screen, and began to channel surf. Waylon joined him and dropped his head in Rooster's lap. Rooster finally dosed off to *Law & Order* reruns.

He was awakened at four o'clock by a loud-mouth pitchman

who screamed every golfer would be lost without his product, a hollow-shaft seven-iron you were supposed to pee into between holes. It came complete with a towel you attached to your shirt with little alligator clips, so you could relieve yourself into the golf club while protecting your modesty. When finished with your business, you simply screwed the cap on the shaft, and threw it in your golf bag. Rooster watched in disbelief. His brain alternated from the horror of a tube of urine leaking all over his golf clubs, to serious consideration of the benefits the product could offer. With Waylon asleep next to him, he quietly got up and wandered into the kitchen. When he saw his Eagle Rare cupboard, he completely forgot why he had come into the room. He imagined the smooth oaky liquid warming his body. His mouth watered. He stared at the cupboard, licked his lips, and tried to not think about bourbon.

"This is ridiculous. I'm a grown ass man. I can have some Eagle Rare if I want to."

He washed a rocks glass in the sink, filled it with ice as quietly as he could, and set it on the counter. He yanked the cupboard door and grabbed the bourbon bottle. He pulled out the cork with its reassuring 'pop'. He held the bottle under his nose and breathed the intoxicating aroma. Rooster poured the amber liquid into his glass slowly, so he could fully enjoy the crackling of the ice as the whiskey gurgled over it.

He pushed the cork back in place and put the bottle back in it's place, promising himself it would be just the one drink, and then back to bed. He sucked in a breath, emotions swirling. He felt a burning desire for the bourbon, but also disappointment and shame for his inability to push that desire aside, and a creeping sense of inevitability and hopelessness. He wiped his forehead with a shaky hand. As he lifted the glass, about to take a sip, something pushed against his leg. It was Waylon, who sat at his feet and stared up with sad eyes. Rooster sighed and set the glass on the counter. "You gotta be kidding me. Don't look at me with all that judgment. I didn't ask you to come in here. Maybe I'll just put you back out on the street."

Waylon stood and nuzzled his nose into Rooster's hand.

"C'mon, man. I don't need a guilt trip from you."

The dog licked his hand and quietly padded out of the kitchen. Rooster watched him walk away. "For the love of God." He grabbed his glass and stared at it. Competing emotions and desires raged inside. Would his willpower crumble? Would he remain a disappointment, or could he stay strong and possibly change his life for the better? He really wanted that bourbon.

"Oh hell." Rooster hesitated for another second. Then he dumped the drink in the sink and stormed out of the kitchen.

Over the next three hours he did everything he could think of to reach daybreak without a drink. Between Angry Birds, infomercials, talking with Waylon about the meaning of life, and cleaning out his closets, Rooster had somehow managed to white-knuckle his way through the long night. As morning light peeked around the edges of the sad blanket, Rooster was exhausted. He turned to the dog. "Well, my friend. We made it. Feel like I been run over by a truck, but we made it."

The dog jumped on the sofa and put his head in his master's lap. Rooster scratched behind Waylon's ears, happy to have something to do with his hands. With no beer bottle or rocks glass within easy reach, Rooster felt naked somehow, exposed to the world. The phone rang. Thrilled to have something new to keep him occupied for a few minutes, Rooster snatched up the device, and put it to his ear. "Hello?"

"Sonny, is that you?"

Rooster caught Waylon's gaze, rolled his eyes, and pointed at the phone as if the animal could understand. There was a smile in his voice as he asked, "Who were you trying to call?"

"I was calling you," his mom said.

"Then why'd you think it wasn't me answering?"

"I don't know. Maybe you had a girl over there."

"So you're saying you confused my voice with a girl?"

"Anything's possible. Ever since you became a circus acrobat, I don't recognize you at all anymore. For all I know you could be hanging around with one of those transnationals. They have deep voices."

Rooster raised his eyebrow. "Transnationals?"

"Yeah, you know what I'm talking about."

Rooster smiled. "Obviously I don't, Mom."

"Transnationals." She was suddenly unsure of herself. "I saw a show about them on the National Geographic Channel. You know, like the bearded lady."

Suddenly aware of his mother's implication, Rooster bellowed, "That's crazy! I can't believe you'd say that."

"It's not so crazy. You remember Mrs. Fieger?"

"Can't say I remember her, Mom." Rooster still smarted, a little embarrassed to hear his mother talk about such things.

"Sure you remember Mrs. Fieger. She worked in the office at your kindergarten."

Rooster laughed. "Mom, not only is that almost forty years ago, but I don't recall ever stepping foot in the school office while I was in kindergarten."

"Well she had a big strapping son named Bobby. He was a couple years behind you in school. He played football and basketball and baseball."

"Mom, why you telling me about these people?"

"Bobby went away to California for college. When he came back a year later, he became a she, and she changed her name to Bobbi Sue."

"Just like the Lou Reed song," Rooster said absentmindedly.

"What song?"

"*Take a Walk on the Wild Side*."

His mother grew confused. "Walk where?"

Rooster looked at Waylon and covered his phone. "You believe this?" The dog stared with sad eyes. Rooster took Waylon's response as a show of solidarity. "Never mind." Rooster leaned back and stared at the ceiling, suddenly exhausted. "This what you called to tell me? That Bobby became Bobbi Sue?"

"Of course not. I called to tell you about an article I read in the newspaper this morning. It made me worry about you."

"Oh really?" *What's she got now?* He leaned forward, intending to get a beer from the kitchen, only to slump back upon remembering he was not drinking anymore.

"Yeah, it was an article about a man in Ellicottville who almost died from pesticide poisoning."

Rooster's patience faded. When he picked up the phone, he never dreamed a discussion with his mother could make him desperate for a drink, but as he considered it, he could not recall many conversations with her when he *did not* have a drink in his hand. Of course, there had been few conversations with *anyone* in the past when he *did not* have a drink in his hand. "And I need to know about this because... why?"

"The man got the pesticide poisoning because he'd been cleaning his golf balls by licking them."

"He what?"

"When he got to the putting area, he'd pick up his golf ball, lick it, and then wipe off the ball on a towel. He was swallowing small amounts of all the chemicals the golf course was using to fight bugs and weeds. After several years of that, the pesticide levels in his system were so elevated he got real sick. The doctors didn't know what was wrong with him. They sent him to the Mayo Clinic in Minnesota and some young intern who liked golf finally figured it all out and saved his life."

Rooster's eyes glazed over. "Mom, that story is ridiculous. How would reading that article possibly make you think of me?"

"Isn't it obvious?"

"Not really."

"I wanted to make sure you weren't licking your golf balls or putting them in your mouth. I don't want you to get sick."

Rooster was speechless. *She thinks I'm a complete idiot. How am I supposed to respond to this?*

"Sonny?"

"Yes."

"Have you been putting your golf balls in your mouth?"

"Of course not," Rooster said in a barely restrained voice. "What kinda wacko you think I am? Who does that?"

"Well forgive me for wanting my son to stay healthy. Maybe that one time you had Scarlet Fever and I slept on the floor next to your bed for three nights to make sure you didn't stop breathing, I should have just let you fend for yourself since you don't need any health advice from your mother."

"Scarlet Fever is a far cry from licking golf balls." Rooster felt absurd even talking about this. He leaned forward, forehead in hand. "Besides, I was nine years old back then."

"Doesn't matter how old you get. You'll always be my baby."

Rooster cast a furtive glance at Waylon. *This is too much.* He was exhausted and defeated. *What if every night without drinking's like this? I'll never survive.*

"Sonny?"

"What?"

"Just promise me you won't lick your golf balls, ok?"

FORTY-ONE

Zeb Ryan traveled the country to share his wit and wisdom with whomever would listen. He stopped somewhere long enough to make a difference, unless he got bored or run out of town. Zeb considered himself a modern-day troubadour who shared joy through songs, poems, and dance. That or the latest incarnation of the ever-wandering Bruce Banner who tried to do some good in each village he visited. Of course, since the Hulk had yet to appear, and probably never would, the Bruce Banner analogy did not really work, so Zeb usually went with his troubadour thing.

Zeb's face was framed with seriously thick eyebrows, a bushy red handlebar moustache, and a shock of curly red hair. His ever-present smile was cockeyed because most of the teeth on the right side of his mouth were missing, the result of a crowbar attack in a homeless shelter in Des Moines. His big head balanced precariously on a wispy-thin upper body wrapped in a yellow smiley face t-shirt. With brown cargo pants two sizes too big, held up by red suspenders, Zeb's torso looked like a golden fishing bobber floating in his trousers.

At an early age, Zeb understood he simply was not destined to have money or worldly possessions. He had made peace with this reality long ago. In some ways, his divorce from the material world had been liberating. Whether he would go somewhere or not, take a job or spend the day in a park, it was all totally up to him. Take his current job, for instance. He did not need the work. Free food and shelter were readily available when you knew how to seek them out. Zeb had spent the past twelve days in the Murfreesboro Goodwill Thrift Store because it gave him the opportunity to help people in his own unique way. He found joy in that, and the Goodwill store had proven to be a great place to meet many who were down on their luck. The homeless and indigent, drug addicts and the mentally ill; every imaginable kind of person came through those doors, and Zeb usually had them pegged within ten seconds.

That is why he was intrigued when the strange little guy limped into the store with his squeaky shoes. The man was a bundle of contradictions. He had the gaunt-faced, wild-eyed look of a meth addict, but his body had too much meat. If he was on crank, it had not been for long. He dragged his left leg awkwardly behind him. He was filthy and disgusting, with strange white rubbery clumps strewn throughout his hair, but it all seemed too fresh somehow, as if it was a Halloween costume. Even though his clothes were filthy, they were almost brand new and fit him well. His noisy shoes looked expensive. As he clomped through the aisles, the odd little man engaged in a strange mumbling dialogue with himself. Zeb quietly fell in step behind him. Upon closer inspection, Zeb concluded he was either new to the streets, or an imposter. His fingernails were neatly trimmed and his complexion was flawless under all the gunk. *Why would he pretend to be homeless?* Zeb stood with his chin in his hand and considered this conundrum. He had heard about people who used drugs to control their mental illness only to go off the deep end when off their medication. This man was either legit or the best actor Zeb had ever seen. A few things were certain. With pale skin and dark circles under his eyes, the guy was obviously exhausted and a very real cloud of stench surrounded him.

Zeb decided to see if he could help. As the man browsed a rack of pants, Zeb came up behind and gently touched his shoulder. The little man flinched and spun toward Zeb, his left eye twitching. "Most delicious greetings to you, young squire." Zeb performed an over-the-top theatrical bow, bending at the waist as his hand swept just off the floor.

The man's eyes grew wide. He backed away. "You work here?"

"As surely as the Pope is Catholic. I am honored to be in your service this fine day."

The guy blinked a few times. "Need some new clothes, and some new shoes. Got about twenty bucks. That enough?"

"That's plenty." Zeb pulled a metal harmonica from his baggy pants, lifted it to his lips and blew softly through the instrument. Then with a sing-song voice, he launched into a poem. "A man needs shoes, shirt and pants. We won't leave him naked. For that we give thanks. Twenty dollars may not seem much. But for that we shall clothe thee and get you lunch." Upon completion of his rhyme, Zeb swung his arms in wide circles and stomped his feet, like some drunk 1920s flapper.

The man fixed Zeb with a blank stare. Then he looked around the store. "You serious? Am I being punk'd or something?"

"Not at all. I am a purveyor of peace, an administrator of cavorting, the prime minister of boogie. I proliferate my siren song of exuberance to the melancholy and defrocked. There's no need to be disconsolate and forlorn just because you're out on the streets."

The guy cocked his head sideways. "What's your deal, Bojangles? Couldn't decide whether you wanted to be a clown or a hobo? So you chose both?"

"I implore you, young squire." Zeb clasped his hands and shook them. "Do not take offense. I was merely inquiring how long you been homeless."

The little man's nostrils flared. "Homeless?! I'll have you know I'm the Chairman of the Student Senate Infractions Committee at NEIU. I'm going to Northwestern Law School next year. I drive a BMW for crying out loud!"

Zeb crossed his arms and smiled. *Definitely mental illness.* He had been around it enough to know it was best to simply play along with the guy's delusions. *He don't seem violent, but really don't wanna push him and find out he is. Have to keep him entertained.* "Good for you," Zeb warbled. "What fortune brings you to our little hamlet of Murfreesboro?"

"A guy stole twenty grand from my girlfriend. I'm here to help her get it back."

"The scalawag mongrel!" *Poor guy's completely out to lunch.* "That's most lamentable. Is this scoundrel also responsible for the unfortunate condition of your wardrobe?"

"All his fault. Almost got him yesterday, but he got away."

"How, pray tell, did this miscreant abscond from your custody?"

The man scrunched his face. "Tracked him down in my Beemer."

"Ah yes." Zeb forced a smile. "You drive a BMW." *If this guy has a driver's license, I'm Bill Gates.*

"Yeah." The man's eyes narrowed into angry slits. "When I grabbed him, he hit me over the head with... ah... with a brick. And then he kicked me with his steel-toed boots and ran away while I was on the ground."

"That's abominable. It seems the fates have dealt with you most harshly."

The guy stared curiously at Zeb for a long time. "They have. That rat Davis Sinclair's gonna pay for what he did to me. Got it all planned out."

Zeb raised an eyebrow and lifted his harmonica back to his mouth. As the distinctive music poured out, Zeb stomped his foot and snapped his fingers. When the tune stopped, Zeb slapped out a beat on his thigh and sang in a low bluesy voice.

"The rat stole the dough...

"But the squire's on his trail...

"That rat ain't got no chance...

"Gonna be grabbed by the tail...."

He blasted another harmonica riff to set up the big finish.

"That rat's got the dirty dog, trouble makin', stolen dough losin', cryin' for his momma Bahh Looos." Zeb played up and down the harmonica scale several times, then dropped to a knee with his head back and arms outstretched, as if he expected applause.

The little man was dumbfounded. Zeb stood and dropped the harmonica into the side pocket of his huge pants. He draped a brotherly arm around the guy's shoulders. *This dude really stinks.* "Young squire." He willed himself not to gag on the stench of old hot dogs and extreme body odor. "We shall outfit you with stylish habiliments and footwear, get you a decontamination rinse, and fill your belly with vittles. Then you can resume your quest for this nefarious reprobate."

"You got a big thesaurus tucked somewhere in those giant clown pants?" The guy pushed away Zeb's arm. "You talk like William F Buckley on speed."

Zeb looked him in the eye. "Can't tell me you don't want a hot shower."

The little man scratched his head and pulled a white clump from his hair. He flicked it disdainfully to the floor and looked at Zeb. His eyes softened. "Yeah, really could use one."

Zeb smiled and nodded. "True dat, young squire. True dat!"

FORTY-TWO

The Chairman wiped his mouth on his sleeve. The pizza had tasted so good, he did not care it had been in a restaurant dumpster ten minutes prior. The goofy dancing hobo had been right. A few doors down from the Goodwill, he had found several pies in takeout boxes perched on top of the trash, perfectly safe from contamination. The week-old rotting slop below the fresh boxes had a stomach-churning stench, but once the Chairman moved away, the smell was not bad at all. Behind the Goodwill, he had found an abandoned sofa where he now reclined as if at an ancient Roman feast. The stale pizza with rubbery cheese was a far cry from Chicago deep dish, but it still tasted awesome. He had not realized how long he had gone without a proper meal.

He thought about his tree-hugging friends back at NEIU. *If they could see me now. They pay lip service to sustainability, protecting the planet, and keeping waste out of the landfills. I bet they never ate out of a garbage can. They're just not as committed as me to reducing their carbon footprint. Hopefully there's not already dumpster diving club on campus.* He knew he could sell the idea to the green crowd and come off a hero.

Energized by the food in his belly, the Chairman rose from the sofa, grabbed the plastic bag of new clothes he had bought for twelve dollars, and limped along the back of the strip mall. Bojangles had said the crazy people at the health club next to the Goodwill came out the back door to run around the building. If the Chairman waited, someone would leave the door open and he could slip inside for a hot shower in the locker room.

He considered all he had been through. *Why'd I fall so hard for Madison? If she didn't bewitch me, never woulda come here.* He would have been in Illinois, living his monotonous life, hanging with pretentious friends he did not like, blissfully ignorant of the excitement the world offered when you broke free from your comfort zone. Despite the pain and setbacks, the past week had been the most exhilarating of his life. Within ten minutes, his thoughts were interrupted when two men and a woman, in workout gear and bright running shoes, strolled out the back door. They propped it open with a dumbbell and ran off around the corner.

The Chairman clapped his hands in excitement. "He was right." *Guess ol' twinkle toes knows what he's talking about.* The Chairman checked for rubberneckers, pulled open the door, and hobbled inside. Senses on edge, his whole body tingled with nervous anticipation. It was all just as the redheaded hobo had described. Careful not to make eye contact with anyone, the Chairman quickly headed to the locker rooms. His heart thumped as he tried to ignore the strange stares of those he passed. He quietly rejoiced when he saw the changing rooms. Without hesitation, he limped inside and found a shower stall.

The Chairman laid his plastic bag on a bench across from the shower, stripped off his disgusting clothes, and threw them into a trash can. Reflexively, he grabbed his car keys from the clothes bag and stepped into the stall. He pulled closed the thick plastic curtain, hooked the keys on the basket under the showerhead, and turned on the water. It was the most amazing shower he had ever experienced. The hot water reinvigorated him even more than the pizza. He took his time, nearly emptying the soap dispenser as he scrubbed off a week's worth of dirt, grime, and stink. His mood improved with each white glob that fell from his hair to the shower floor. Even his bad foot felt revived.

Twenty glorious minutes later, the Chairman emerged from the stall clutching his car keys. Dripping wet with nothing to dry himself, he walked to the sinks and pulled paper towels from the wall-mounted dispenser. The scratchy towels chaffed his skin, but ultimately did the job. He returned to the showers for his clothes bag. The Chairman scanned the benches. It was gone.

"Really?!" *Who'd steal a plastic sack full of crappy used clothes?* Then he remembered his last eight dollars had also been tucked inside the bag and his knees almost gave out. He grabbed the wall for support. *What am I supposed to do now?* Hundreds of miles from home, literally naked and penniless. He quickly dismissed any idea of pulling his soiled clothes from the trash. He would walk out to the Beemer stark naked before he would ever wear those disgusting rags again. *At least I pulled out the keys. How much more screwed would I be if those were gone too?*

Ok. Desperate times call for desperate measures. He peeked into the changing area, relieved to see it devoid of people. He carefully ambled into the rows of lockers and began to open unlocked doors. The Chairman moved as quickly as he could, glancing over his shoulder every few seconds, afraid a power lifter would show up any moment to pound him into next week. Finally in the second row he hit pay dirt, a full set of neatly folded, clean clothes. The Chairman grabbed them and moved to the next row where he hastily dressed.

Six minutes later, the Chairman sauntered out the health club's front door, his still wet hair slicked back in a Gordon Gecko 'do. The front of his blue and gray camouflage shirt featured the Democrat donkey under the words, "Shove gun control up your". The too-big green cargo shorts had no belt, so he was forced to grip them with one hand as he walked. He longed for a pair of suspenders, like Bojangles had worn to hold up his gigantic pants. On his feet were a pair of cheap rubber flip-flops which made a loud slapping noise with each step. He climbed into his BMW, ready for another run at Davis Sinclair.

FORTY-THREE
Saturday, May 21st

The day had been a blur, and now he was here.

Had he not been selling sporting goods at Jimmy Robinson's store just a minute ago? On top of the world, he knew in his heart he had this drinking thing licked. Now he was half in the bag, five empty shot glasses turned over on the bar in front of him, and four Bud longnecks in his rearview mirror. That was how fast the pendulum had swung against him.

Rooster's alcohol-addled brain fought to make sense of it. *How'd this happen?* That familiar fuzziness had already taken over his mind and senses. Everything slightly blurry, the sounds swirling around him just a bit muffled, his mind as sharp as an overripe melon. He was aware enough to feel the creeping guilt and shame of his poor decisions. *I'm such a loser.* His eyes teared up. *Got absolutely no control over myself. Got a good thing going at Jimmy's, and I'm gonna ruin it, like I ruin every good thing in my life.* Overcome with alcohol-soaked despair, Rooster laid his face in his arms on the bar and sobbed.

A big paw grabbed the neck of his shirt and jerked him backward. Already unsteady and light-headed, Rooster tumbled off the bar stool onto the wet, sticky floor, his shirt pulled over his head, the hand still gripping the collar.

"What the hell!" Surprise and anger replaced Rooster's self-loathing. He pulled at the shirt, desperate to get his head back up through the neck hole.

Buddy released Rooster's shirt. "What you doin' down there on the ground, boy?"

Rooster scrambled unsteadily to his feet and smiled at his friend. "Wouldn't of been down there if you didn't pull me off the stool, you big dumbass. Why you do that?"

"Thought you were sleepin' right up on the bar." Buddy's megawatt smile lit up the room. "It's only nine-thirty. No time for snoozin'."

Rooster swayed and closed his right eye to eliminate one of the two Buddys he saw. "Don't you worry about me. Still a lot of fuel left in this tank."

Buddy laughed and slapped his friend so hard on the back, Rooster would have been back on the floor, if the bar had not broken his fall. "Son. You're drunker than Cooter Brown."

Rooster gripped the counter. "Who's Cooter Brown?"

Buddy shook his head in disappointment. "Just don't know about you sometimes, son. Wheel's still turning, but I think the hamster's dead."

Rooster stared at him blankly. "What's that mean?"

Buddy grinned. "Tomorrow morning when your mind's workin' right again, you think about it. You'll understand." Before Rooster could respond, Buddy pointed across the bar. "Hey, I know that guy. Be right back."

An alcohol-fueled vertigo attack forced Rooster to drop onto the stool, grip the bar, and close his eyes.

"Hey, buddy?"

The voice had come from his right. Rooster slowly opened his eyes and silently prayed the dizziness would be gone. He saw a little guy with hair slicked back like Steve Buscemi in *Fargo*, and a pro-gun camouflage t-shirt.

Rooster blinked a few times, but his vision remained blurred. "I'm not Buddy." He pointed over his shoulder with his thumb. "He went that way."

"What?" The little guy asked.

Rooster clutched the bar and leaned toward the man. His hand slipped and Rooster sprawled out on the floor again.

"Shit." Rooster was about to pull himself up when he noticed the little guy's feet. The back ends of his cheap flip-flops were fastened to his heels with duct tape. Sure it was a hallucination, Rooster shook his head. But there they were, orangey-red slabs of rubber attached to his foot with standard gray duct tape. Rooster stood. "Dude, what's with the footwear?"

The man looked down as if he had forgotten what he had on. "They made too much noise. Don't like loud shoes."

Something about the little guy's tone made Rooster flashback to the crazed homeless man who had jumped him. *That dude had noisy shoes. Why's this guy talking about loud shoes?* He eyed the man suspiciously. "I know you from somewhere?"

"I don't know you. Why would I know you? I'm not even from around here?"

"Why were you looking for Buddy?" Rooster asked.

The man seemed genuinely confused. "Who's Buddy?"

"If you don't know him, why'd you ask me about him?"

"Got no clue what you're talking about. Hey, it's obvious I upset you somehow. Let me buy you a drink?"

Rooster sat on his stool and smiled. "Never turned down a free drink in my life."

"What you want?"

"Bud Light."

"Ok." The little guy moved down the counter with his arm raised to flag down the bartender.

"Hey," Rooster shouted.

The guy jumped. "What?"

"Where you goin'?"

"Just moving down here so they see me." He turned his back.

What an odd little character. Wonder why he's so jumpy. Another bout of dizziness forced Rooster to close his eyes and grip the bar. When his eyes opened, the man was back and a fresh Bud Light longneck sat in front of him. Rooster raised the beer toward his benefactor. "Thanks little dude."

Rooster drank a mouthful of the crisp golden liquid, but the flavor was off. He detected a slight acidic, almost metallic taste. He set down the bottle and waved for the bartender.

"What you doing?" The little guy asked.

"I'm calling the bartender over. Beer's skunked. Gonna have him get me a new one."

"No!" There was a hint of panic in the man's voice. "You can't do that. Just drink that one."

"Why? They got a cooler full of good beer. Not gonna drink this swill."

"What's wrong with it?"

"I don't know. Tastes like there's metal in it."

The little man smiled knowingly. "You sure it's not your fillings?"

"My what?"

"Your fillings. People with metal fillings sometimes taste them, especially when they drink alcohol. It can leech the metal off the fillings, and you taste the residue in your drink."

"That sounds like bullshit."

"You telling me you don't have any metal fillings in your mouth?" The man's left eye twitched.

Rooster stared at the bar top. *I do have metal fillings. Could this guy be right?* "How come this never happened before?"

"Those things are like little time bombs waiting to go off in your mouth. Once they start leeching metal you're gonna taste them every time you drink something until you get 'em replaced. It's not good for you. You can get heavy metal poisoning. You really need to get them looked at."

Rooster remained skeptical "How you know all this?"

"I'm studying oral medicine at Northwestern University," he said with authority. "Trust me. I know what I'm talking about."

"Sounds like a load of bunk to me."

"Ok." He rubbed his hands together. "Take another drink from that beer and if the taste's still there, I'll get you a new one. If I'm wrong you'll get a fresh drink. If I'm right, you can drink two free beers and go to the dentist on Monday."

"Fine." Rooster lifted the bottle to his lips. After swallowing the beer, he set it back on the bar. "Still there."

"Fine," the little guy sighed. "Be back in a minute."

Rooster stared at the half-empty Bud Light. *Drank half that thing in two gulps?* His amazement mixed with pride and self-loathing. *Definitely got a problem if I can drink that sucker so fast.* He wondered whether he could finish the bottle with one more gulp. *Of course I can.* He lifted the Bud Light and poured the remaining liquid down his throat.

By the time the little guy returned with the fresh beer, Rooster did not feel well. Dark spots crept into the edges of his blurred vision. His stuffed ears made every sound muffled and unintelligible. A massive headache had overcome him. He was chilled even though the hot air in the bar had been stifling a few minutes ago. His stomach grew queasy. He tried to recall what he had eaten for dinner. *Could I have food poisoning?*

The man set the beer down and peered into Rooster's eyes. Rooster focused on the guy's lips, but could not make out what he said. The man led him somewhere. Rooster felt the fresh air hit his face and wondered where this guy had taken him. His mind would not function properly. *Feels like I'm wading through oatmeal.* The little guy grabbed the sides of his head and forced Rooster to face him. "You don't look so good, Davis Sinclair," he said with an evil laugh.

Rooster fought with everything he had to focus. *Davis Sinclair? Davis Sinclair? Why'd that name sound so familiar?*

"Now you'll pay for what you did to Madison."

Wisconsin again? He was fading fast, his brain mushy and slow-moving. *That fruitcake homeless man? Didn't he ramble on about something I did in Wisconsin? Who is this guy?* "Who the hell are you?" Rooster finally managed to mumble.

"I'm the Chairman."

The Chairman? I hear that right? "You mean like Sinatra?"

Rooster never heard the response, as everything went black.

FORTY-FOUR
Sunday, May 22nd

The ocean felt warm as he paddled the surfboard. The hot sun had left behind a salty film as it dried his body. A soft breeze flowed through his wet hair and cooled his head. His feet in the sea on either side of the board, he rested his chin on the lacquered finish and took in sparkling aqua-marine ocean as far as he could see. Lazy waves rolled beneath him and lapped at the edges of the board as it gently rose and fell with the surf. He breathed in the warm salty air, perfectly relaxed and content, his mind filled with images of palm trees, salsa music, and dark-skinned island beauties.

Dragged back to reality by movement to his left, he snapped his head in time to glimpse something smooth and gray just as it disappeared into the water. *A dorsal fin?* His heart rate jumped. Adrenaline surged. *What'd I just see?* Muscles tense, he nearly rolled off the surfboard, but barely regained his balance. He glanced at the shore several hundred yards away. *That a shark?* Bile rose in his stomach. If a man-eater circled below, he was nothing more than a floating hors d' oeuvre. He pulled his legs onto the board, his feet just barely out of the water.

Something rubbery pressed against his toes, and he nearly jumped out of his skin. Frantically, he pulled his knee toward his chest, but it compromised his equilibrium. He tumbled into the water. Overwhelmed with panic, he splashed around, desperate to scramble back on top of the board. *Oh my God. I'm gonna die!*

A huge gray mass flew out of the water two feet away. By the time he realized it, the giant fish had already disappeared back into the blue-green waves. His mind whirled in a frenzy as he pieced together what he had seen. *Do sharks jump outta the water?* He expected his legs to be bitten off any second. He sensed a large mass beside him, the powerful creature roiling the water. He closed his eyes. *Is this the end?*

Something rubbery gently nudged his ribs. His eyes snapped open in confusion. *That shark taunting me?* Startled by loud high-pitched squeaks and squeals, he turned in time to see a dolphin poke its head from the water. Amazed at its sheer size, he scanned the area, shocked to discover dorsal fins and jumping porpoises all around him. At least twenty of them.

The bottlenose to his right broke into its distinctive chatter. *Looks like he's smiling. Dolphins like humans, don't they?* He recalled stories about how they saved people from sharks or pulled injured surfers to safety. *Is it possible I'm not gonna die?* The closest animal dipped its nose in the surf and flipped water at him, a sparkle in its eye. He laughed. *He's having fun with me.* Grinning, he playfully splashed at the dolphin. When the water hit the animal's eye, the porpoise let out a horrible shriek and backed away, its noises now lower and menacing, more a growl than a squeak.

An instant later, he flew through the air, propelled from the sea by the angry dolphin. After a belly flop, they surrounded him. They jabbed at him with their noses, and battered him with their powerful tails. The water foamed as they circled and hit him from all angles. Sharp teeth dug into his wrists, his arms yanked behind his back. By the time he comprehended his situation, the dolphins had already pulled him far below the surface, his arms wrenched awkwardly, as if they would be torn from their sockets. Startled at how fast they moved, the bright ocean surface drifted further and further away until he was engulfed in darkness.

Rooster's eyes fluttered. He saw nothing but pitch black. *What happened?* The dolphins still had his wrists pulled backward, but he was not sucking in ocean water. *Where am I?*

Groggy and disoriented, he struggled to pull out of his slumber. *Why can't I move my arms?* His brain was fuzzy and his body heavy, like the time he overdid it on sleeping pills and bourbon. Try as he might, he could not quite maintain consciousness. The moment his eyes closed, strange dreams overcame him. He was riding a powder blue dinosaur, in the parking lot of Jimmy's store, while Jimmy drank coffee and told dirty jokes. Then he and Buddy were in the jungle hunting for yeti with jumper cables, a laser pointer, and donuts. He flinched as an angry porpoise floated past his head. He grew confused, not quite sure where his crazy dreams ended and reality began. He rolled his head to encourage blood flow to his brain. Slowly, he regained his faculties.

Where am I? His skull ached like a wicked tequila hangover. *Don't remember drinking tequila.* The previous night was a total black hole, something he was used to, even if the situation he now found himself in was something new. Hands fastened behind his back, he lay on his side in a small space where he could not straighten his legs. He could not see anything in the darkness. He caught smells of carpet and rubber, and oil, or grease maybe.

Still groggy, he sat up and banged his head on a low metal ceiling. *That won't help the headache. Where am I?* His sluggish mind groped for an explanation. *Maybe I died and gone to hell. Would definitely be hell to spend the rest of eternity like this.* It was hot. His throat was dry. When he finally worked up enough spit to swallow, he noticed a slight metallic taste. Then it all flooded back.

The bar. The crazy homeless guy. "He drugged me. That little bastard." He closed his eyes and tried to replay the previous evening in his mind. *Called himself the Chairman. The Chairman of what?*

Even as he fought to concentrate, the drugs and alcohol still in his system caused Rooster to drift off. He saw the Chairman beside him wearing a cowboy hat and riding a goat. *Can't really be happening.*

The blackness confirmed his eyes were open. *That's odd. It's only when I see things that I know my eyes are closed. What was I just thinking about?*

That Chairman guy. He drugged my beer and then led me outside before I passed out. Did Buddy see us walking out? Rooster tried to be realistic. He and Buddy regularly hit the first bar together and then went their separate ways. There was no reason to believe Buddy knew anything happened.

His heart sank. *Maybe Buddy was dealing blackjack to those dogs.* The Saint Bernard nudged at his cards with his nose, but knocked over the bowl of Fritos. The Chihuahua jumped on the card table and began wolfing down the corn chips. Buddy asked Rooster if he wanted another beer.

Whoa, what's wrong with my head? Gotta stay focused. This is absurd. He was overcome with self-loathing and disgust. *Only I could end up like this. I'm such a loser. This has gotta be a new low. Locked in a casket or a trunk or something worse by a deranged homeless guy. This is what alcohol's created in my life. Chaos and destruction. Had the chance to quit and I blew it. If I would've just stayed on the straight and narrow, I wouldn't be in this ridiculous predicament.*

He tried to pull his arms apart, but something held tight. *What's that nibbling at my fingers?* His heart rate spiked. *Those damn dolphins attacking again. Wait a minute. I'm not in the water.* His brain mushy, he could not shake the effects of the mickey the Chairman had slipped him. He focused his mind on his hands. They tingled, because whatever held him tight, also restricted the blood flow. "There're no dolphins in here."

He felt the bindings with his fingers. It was rope. *What's this mental case have planned for me?*

Davis Sinclair. That crackpot had called him 'Davis Sinclair' and said something about Madison, Wisconsin.

Holy crap. Rooster mentally connected the dots. *He wasn't talking about a city, he was referring to a girl. Madison was one of the captains, on that women's rugby team, in Illinois. Did I call myself 'Davis Sinclair' in Illinois?* He smelled pizza, specifically a Chicago deep dish from Gino's East.

"No." He willed himself back to reality. "Can't drift off."

Mom's right. She wouldn't even recognize me if she knew what I been doing. I have so many aliases, can't keep 'em all straight. All because of alcohol. If I wasn't a drunk, I wouldn't have been stealing money from college sports teams, and wouldn't have a deranged lunatic with duct tape shoes stalking me. I destroyed my life because alcohol fuels all my decisions.

For the first time in his life, Rooster clearly understood the incredible trail of carnage his alcohol problem spawned everywhere he went. The heat seemed more stifling, his breathing more difficult. His head began to clear. He closed his eyes. *This how it's gonna end for me? What a waste of a life. God gave me a second chance when I jumped that car, and I squandered it.*

Rooster swallowed hard. "God," he croaked softly. "I been a screw-up my whole life. I'm probably an incredible disappointment to you..." He sucked in hot, stale air. Warm tears rolled down his cheek. "If you give me one more chance, I promise I won't mess it up. Please, just one more chance."

Rooster groped at the rope, his hands cramping. He found a loose end and ran his fingers along the cord to figure out what kind of knots secured him. *That isn't possible.* He refused to believe what his hands felt. Two big loops of rope came together near a pair of loose ends. *That moron Chairman didn't actually tie the rope in a big bow? Could anyone be that stupid?*

Rooster was about to yank on a loose end when a thought struck him. *Maybe it's a trick. What if pulling just makes the whole thing tighter?* He considered the Chairman. *Shoes held on with duct tape. Why would you bind wrists with rope when you got duct tape? Wrap that stuff a few times and I'd have no prayer of getting free. What an ignoramus. Even if he's smarter than I think, what've I got to lose?* His shoulders ached, his wrists were chafed, and his right calf twitched, about to seize up into a killer cramp. *Better do something soon.*

He gripped the loose end with his fingers, managed to work it between his hands, and pulled it away from the loops. The rope loosened significantly. *It worked!*

His adrenaline pumped. Moments later his hands were free. He massaged his wrists. As feeling returned, Rooster reached for his pocket. *If that bozo's dumb enough to tie my hands with a bow, maybe he's dumb enough to leave the phone in my pocket.*

"Yes!" His fingers gripped his most prized possession.

Rooster pulled out the device. It was seven forty-two a.m. *How long have I been in here?* The phone still had 30 percent battery life. Its dull glow allowed him to better make out his surroundings.

FORTY-FIVE

Definitely in a car trunk.

Rooster held his breath and listened. There was no motion, and no running motor. His mind was filled with images of cars piled three deep at the junkyard waiting to be crushed. He held his breath again and strained for the sound of heavy machinery, grinding gears, bending steel, or breaking glass. Nothing.

He remembered a movie where the hero was thrown in a trunk and the whole car was buried. *Gotta stop thinking like that.* He refused to let his brain derail his hopes for escape. Still, he now had a fresh sense of urgency.

Rooster used the phone's flashlight app to illuminate his cramped little tomb. His upper body was deep inside the trunk, near the back seats. He carefully lifted his head and shined the beam toward his feet. Before he could make out the end of the trunk, the flashlight turned off, the screen showed an incoming call, and a familiar ringtone sang out. "Not now." Rooster tapped the 'decline' button and the flashlight came back on. He wriggled his body toward the back of the car. It was slow going.

Just as Rooster had shifted into a position of which a contortionist would be proud, the flashlight turned off, interrupted by the same incoming number and ringtone. "Oh, come on." He declined the call. "Don't have time for this."

When the flashlight returned, he continued his slow crawl. On the other side of the trunk, a red cord with a black plastic handle dangled from the ceiling of the confined space. *Could that be a trunk release?* His heart leapt. He raised his hand to shine the beam toward it, but once again the light turned off, interrupted by the same incoming call. "For the love of God." If he did not answer, she would call back every ten seconds. He tapped the green 'answer' button and put the phone to his ear.

"What?!" He said in an angry whisper.

"Is that any way to answer a phone? I thought I raised you better than that, Sonny."

"I'm sorry, Mom, but I'm kinda in the middle of something."

"Then why'd you answer your phone?"

"Because you called me three times in thirty seconds."

"Sonny! Watch your tone. What could be so darned important that you can't take a minute to say hello to your mother?"

"Oh, I don't know. What if I'd been abducted by a crazy homeless man and was locked in the trunk of his car?"

"Quit being so cheeky. If that happened, your hands would be tied. How would you answer? You're still the same as when you were a little boy. Always coming up with outrageous stories. You should've become a writer or a puppeteer."

"A what?"

"A puppeteer. Like that Tina Gellman from down the street?"

"Who?"

"You remember. Little Tina Gellman. Her mother watched you for me when you were a baby."

"How am I supposed to remember that?" Unwillingly, he was being pulled into his mother's vortex like a cow sucked into a tornado. There was no telling where he would land when his body was finally thrown free.

She ignored his question. "Anyway, she's a puppeteer now. She works with marionettes on public television in Fargo, North Dakota. With your creativity, you easily could've been a marionette man."

Rooster stared out in the darkness. *Puppets? She's actually talking about puppets? This lunatic could be back any second to do God-knows-what. No way I'm really having this conversation.*

"Mom, can you please just get to the point of your call?"

"Why are you whispering for goodness sake? Speak up. I can barely hear you."

Rooster rolled onto his back and draped an arm over his eyes. "I can't talk any louder." *What does she want?* He screamed in his mind. *Get to the damn point! I don't have time for this!*

"Fine," she said, an edge to her voice. "I was watching Good Morning America this morning and they had a story about a man in California who sleepwalked right off a cliff."

Rooster sighed. *Gonna lose my mind. Where on earth is this going?* "Mom. This has nothing to do with me. Really gotta get back to what I was doing."

"Not so fast, Mister Smartypants. I called you because this could save your life."

"How? I don't sleepwalk."

"Don't you remember back when you were four years old? I woke up in the middle of the night and found you climbing up the stairs from the basement, fast asleep. We were so lucky you didn't hurt yourself. You could have fallen down the steps, or chopped off a limb with the hacksaw."

"A hacksaw? Really? First off, I don't remember some isolated incident from almost forty years ago. Second, I'm not aware of it happening again, before or since. And third, the first danger you can think of after falling down the stairs is lopping off a limb with a hacksaw?"

"I don't care what you say," she scolded. "I remember it like yesterday. I was so scared, I slept on the floor outside your bedroom for three weeks. Never happened again, thank God."

Rooster tensed his muscles. *When will this madness stop?* He had to speed up the call so he could turn on the flashlight and continue his escape. A smile crept across his face as he imagined hanging up and turning off the phone. *Could call later and say my phone dropped the call. She'd believe that. Right?*

She interrupted his thoughts. "Sonny, promise me you'll start tying a rope around your ankle when you go to bed."

"What? A rope? What you talking about?"

"The man in the news story. He knew he was a sleepwalker, and he lived in this big fancy house on the top of a huge hill. He was always afraid he'd walk off the edge of the cliff, and plummet to his death in the rocks below. So he always tied one end of a rope to his ankle and the other to the foot of his bed. That way the rope woke him up if he went too far."

"Wait a minute." Rooster was involuntarily drawn in despite his mind's desperate attempt to remain indifferent. "Thought you said he did walk off the cliff. His rope didn't work."

"No, Sonny. His wife secretly untied the rope, led him to the edge of the cliff while he was sleeping, and pushed him over. That way it looked like an accident and she collected twenty million in life insurance money."

"Are you kidding, Mom?" Rooster balled his fists and kicked his legs in exasperation. "This is what you called to tell me?"

"Of course I'm not kidding. I don't want you sleepwalking off a cliff."

He pressed his hand against his temple. He felt like his head would explode. *I'm really having a conversation with my mother about sleepwalking off a cliff. This crazy little dude followed me, attacked me, followed me again, drugged me, tied me up, and stashed me in a trunk. Don't know if I'm gonna escape or what I'll find outside if I do somehow manage to get out. And I'm talking to my mom about sleepwalking off a cliff.* Rooster laughed at the ridiculousness of it all. He was overcome by the tension and fear, his aching muscles, the heat, the lack of oxygen, the residue of the drugs, and his hangover. *What happens if I don't escape?* It was all too much for him. Something snapped. He burst into uncontrollable, maniacal laughter, as helpless as if he had been struck by a seizure. His whole body shook. His sides hurt. He could not breathe. Tears flowed. He prayed for it all to end.

"Sonny! What's wrong with you? You think this is some kinda comedy show? I don't like your attitude one bit, young man."

His mother's shrill words cut into his fit like a steak knife through Spam. The episode subsided. He caught his breath.

"Well?" She asked impatiently. "Are you ready to behave?"

"Seriously? Let me clue you in on a few things, Mom. I sleepwalked once forty years ago and haven't done it since. I live in a valley. No cliffs within fifty miles. There's no stairs in my current house, and I don't have any hacksaws laying around. Your fears on this one are a little farfetched."

"Well forgive me for wanting to protect my son." Her voice cracked. "I guess you know everything now and your mother is useless, something to be tossed aside like that stuffed gorilla you loved so much when you were eight."

Rooster closed his eyes, and tried to sort everything out. *Whatever happened to that gorilla?*

"Sonny! Just promise me you'll start sleeping with your ankle tied to the bed."

FORTY-SIX

A big grin filled the Chairman's face as he cruised through Murfreesboro. His revised plan for capturing Davis Sinclair had worked perfectly, and now he was on his way to show Madison the prize he had commandeered just for her.

Those girls are gonna be amazed when I open that trunk. Madison'll probably throw her arms around my neck and lay a big kiss on me just like she did at the Committee hearing. He remembered her perfume's pleasing aroma and envisioned her face close enough to smell her minty-fresh breath. His mind constructed a fantasy of how the scene would play out when he showed up with Sinclair. An angry horn snapped the Chairman back to reality. During his daydream he closed his eyes and his car had drifted into on-coming traffic.

"Oh crap." He yanked the steering wheel, but overcorrected. The car lurched onto the shoulder. The right tires jumped the curb. The Chairman's heart raced as he wrestled his Beemer back into his lane. He searched his mirrors and the road ahead for police. Relieved to see none, he exhaled a long breath and shuddered at what he would tell the cops if they pulled him over and found Sinclair in the trunk. *Not much I could say or do if that happened.* He slowed his speed from thirty-eight miles per hour to thirty-five.

Hope that pumpkin-headed bouncer dude isn't there. He recalled how the giant had pulled him down from the window and threatened to make his brains leak from his nose. He swallowed his fear. *Too close to winning Madison to let anything stop me now. I'll come up with something to deal with that Neanderthal.*

He checked the clock. 8:08 a.m.

Sinclair should've woken up by now. Especially when the car went up the curb. Wonder why he's not making any noise back there. What if I killed him? That could hurt my future political career. A dead guy in my trunk could turn out really bad for me. Even if he was a slimeball. He yelled over his shoulder, "Hey, Sinclair! You awake back there?" The Chairman tapped on the brakes. The car lurched. "That wake you up?"

The lack of a response worried him. He began to reconsider his plan, but he had already arrived at the rugby house. S*hould I pop the trunk and see how Sinclair's doing. What if Pumpkin-head sees me before I get Madison out of the house?*

The Chairman exited the car and was about to open the trunk when a young woman stepped out the front door of the rugby house. Her subdued make-up and modest flowered dress suggested she was headed to church. The Chairman dropped the key fob in his pocket to ensure he would not accidentally pop the trunk. *Gotta make my move before the bouncer shows up.* His heart raced as he headed up the walk toward her. *This is it. All my pain and suffering since I got to this backwater place is gonna be worth it when Madison melts into my arms with gratitude.* He pasted on his most charming smile as the distance between them disappeared. "Good morning," the Chairman said.

"Hi," she said tentatively as her gaze fell on his duct-taped flip-flops. "You looking for someone?" She inspected him more thoroughly, grimacing as she read the pro-second amendment slogan on his t-shirt.

"Yes. I'm a friend of the three girls from NEIU who've been staying here. I brought something for them. It's in the car. I really wanna show it to them."

The girl stepped onto the grass next to the walk. "Everyone's sleeping now," she said, a slight edge to her voice.

This isn't going well. Beads of sweat formed on the Chairman's brow. "I figured that," he said as pleasantly as he could muster. "But I really think they'll want to see this."

"Something in the car, huh? What is it?"

"Oh, it's a surprise." He forced a crooked smile. "If you'll go get Madison and her friends, I promise they'll like what I've brought them."

She moved further off the sidewalk and clutched her purse to her chest. "That's little unusual, don't you think?"

Her body language made the Chairman nervous. "How so?" *Gotta move fast. What if she goes and gets Pumpkin-head?*

She frowned. "Showing up at eight in the morning trying to lure girls to your car? You don't think that's kinda unusual?"

"I guess so." The Chairman tried to sound conciliatory. *This girl's becoming a problem. Time to take things into my own hands.* "Hey, don't worry about it." He walked past her toward the front door. "I'll just go knock and ask them to come out."

The young woman sprinted past him to the porch. "That's okay. I'll go in and get them for you. You wait here, and they'll be out in a few minutes." She stepped inside.

Before the Chairman could thank her, she had already slammed the door in his face. As he walked back toward the car, he pondered the best way to reveal Sinclair. *Has to be some drama and excitement.* He wanted to blow them away with what he had done. Actually he did not care a whit about the other two. He hoped Madison would be blown away.

He knocked on the trunk. "Sinclair, you awake yet? Time to rise and shine, dirtbag. You're about to get your comeuppance."

Sinclair's silence twisted a knot in his already jangled nerves. *That slimeball's either one cool customer or he's dead.* The Chairman envisioned his political future, shattered to pieces before it even got started. *Could I ever overcome a dead guy in the trunk? Ted Kennedy's career survived a woman dying in his car. Of course, she was in the passenger seat, not the trunk. And Teddy was long gone when they found her.*

His agitation growing, the Chairman ran his fingers through his hair. *Would Madison be horrified if she saw a dead Sinclair in the trunk?* The building tension made his head ache. He stared at the back of the car. *Of course, she'd be horrified. If that jerk died, it could ruin my whole plan. Should I take a peek? If he croaked, I could skedaddle before the girls come outside.*

He reached into his pocket for the key fob.

FORTY-SEVEN

The rugby house front door burst open and women poured out. The Chairman rubbed his chin as he watched them. *Looks like the clown car at the circus.* It could have been a slumber party fire drill with sleepy eyes, yawning, and a potpourri of pajamas and loungewear. They were led by the three NEIU rugby captains and the girl in the flowered dress who had gone inside to get them. She pointed at the Chairman and whispered to the others.

When he saw the glares and angry scowls on their faces as the gaggle approached, the Chairman dropped the key fob in his pocket and headed toward them. They met halfway up the walk, the Chairman and NEIU girls facing off like glowering boxers posing for publicity photos. Unnerved by their dirty looks, the Chairman glanced around nervously as the women formed a circle around the four of them. Some of the bigger ones were nearly as intimidating as old pumpkin-head. He smiled. *This is finally it.* The final pieces of his perfect plan were about to fall into place. *Unless...*

He sucked in a breath. *Please don't let Sinclair be dead.*

Crystal spoke first. "Peyton says you claim to know us, but I don't remember ever seeing you before."

Genuine shock filled the Chairman's face as he turned from her to Tiffany, and then to Madison, completely deflated. "I... ahh... I'm the Chairman. You know who I am!"

Tiffany finally put the pieces together. "Hey, it's that little guy from the Student Senate committee. The one who gave us three weeks to get the stolen money back."

"Oh yeah." Recognition flickered in Madison's face. "But what're you doing here? How'd you find us?"

"I followed..." His voice trailed off. *Probably not a good idea to share that.*

"You what?" Crystal spat. "You followed us?"

"That's not what I said."

"Then what'd you say?" Crystal demanded.

"Forget about that," Tiffany interrupted. "He told Peyton he's got something in the car for us. I wanna get a look at that and then go back to bed."

"Yeah." Madison eyed the Chairman's pro-gun shirt suspiciously. "What's in the car?"

No turning back now. "Go over and stand by the trunk." The Chairman imagined Madison in a red power suit standing next to him as he was sworn into the U.S. Senate. "I've got something exciting in there for you." *No doubt, she'll win me a few votes down the road.* He was thrilled this day had finally arrived.

The Chairman ignored their angry stares boring into the back of his head as he led all of them to the BMW. *This is gonna be awesome. Can't wait to see their faces when I open that trunk. All this negativity is gonna flip upside down.*

When Crystal, Tiffany, and Madison were lined up behind the car, the Chairman positioned himself so he could see all their faces clearly. "You ready?"

Madison stared at him and laughed. "Dude, I hope this is good. With all this buildup, anything less than Bradley Cooper or a pile of cash is gonna be pretty disappointing."

"Oh, I promise it's way better than that." The Chairman's confidence grew. He pulled out the key fob and raised his hand in the air. "Everyone ready?"

"Just open it already," Tiffany examined her nails. "I'm getting old over here."

The Chairman frowned. *What a Debbie Downer. She's sucking all the excitement outta this.* He held his breath, pushed the button, and focused on Madison's face. The trunk popped open, but Madison's expression did not change. Crystal's face was stoic. Tiffany actually yawned.

No, no, no! This is all wrong. They're supposed to squeal with delight. Madison's supposed to be throw herself at me. How can they not be impressed by what I brought them?

Tiffany interrupted his inner dialogue. "This some kinda joke?"

"Joke? What do you mean?"

Madison sounded bored. "Nothing in there except a rope."

"That can't be right." The Chairman moved to get a better look. Sure enough, the rope he had used to secure Davis Sinclair lay in a heap in the middle of the trunk. "I don't understand. He was there all night."

Crystal's eyes grew wide. "Who was there all night?"

One of the other girls chimed in with a horrified voice, "You had someone tied up in the trunk?"

The Chairman looked up to the sky. His plan had been so perfect. *How'd it all unravel so quickly?* "I had Davis Sinclair in there. I tracked him down and brought him to you, Madison."

"Ewww!" Madison's face puckered. "What made you think I'd want you to abduct someone? That's insane."

"It wasn't just anyone. It was Davis Sinclair."

"Who?" Madison asked.

The Chairman's voice rose in anger. "Davis Sinclair!"

This isn't happening. How do they not know Davis Sinclair? What have they been doing here? He could not bring himself to lay the blame on Madison, so his mind turned to the next most convenient target. *That jerkwad Sinclair has ruined everything. By escaping, he made me look like an idiot in front of Madison. Does he get off on torturing me?* Teeth clenched, eyes narrowed, the Chairman trembled. "Davis Sinclair. The guy who stole your money. The guy you came here to find. I found him for you."

Madison shook her head in wonder. "What kind of lunatic are you? You had some poor guy tied up in your trunk, and you claim you did it for me?! That's revolting."

"Wait!" the Chairman's eyes misted. *How'd it all go against me so quickly?* Madison's horrified stare tore his insides to pieces. If she turned on him now, how would he ever recover?

She's supposed to be mine. No, destined to be mine. She just doesn't know it yet. He went to another place in his brain and mumbled, "She's mine. It's destiny." He stared into Madison's face. "Destiny."

Madison twisted her lips in disgust. "Dude. You're creeping me out."

The Chairman moved toward her, gazing up at her with moist eyes. "Don't say that Madison." He reached for her. "You know that isn't true. Just give us a chance."

She backed away. "You're a few crayons short of the 64-pack."

"You're mine!" The Chairman wailed his banshee shriek as he lunged toward her and grabbed her arm.

Then it was bedlam. Everything was a blur as the women descended on him. It was like an out-of-body experience as what seemed to be hundreds of hands grabbed at his limbs and tossed him around like a rag doll. He felt the body heat of so many people huddled close together. He smelled flowery lotions, feminine deodorant, and hairspray, as they manhandled him. He heard himself scream. Then it was over.

By the time he regained his equilibrium, the Chairman was in the trunk of the Beemer, his arms and legs hogtied with his own rope. Dazed and confused, he stared at the women gathered around the back of his car. Their expressions ranged from anger, to bemusement, to satisfaction.

How'd this happen to me? Roughed up by a bunch of girls and unceremoniously dumped in his own trunk. It certainly was not an outcome he had considered when this whole misadventure had begun. This was more humiliating than the time in third grade when

Jumbo Jenny O'Brien wrestled him to the ground and sat on his chest until he admitted in front of all his friends that he was weaker than a girl. Afterward, everyone called him Nancy until he was thirteen.

Crystal reached up to close the trunk.

"Wait," he cried, totally defeated. "Please."

Crystal lowered her arm. They all scowled impatiently.

"What is it?" Madison asked.

"How can you do this to me? I was just trying to help you. You came here looking for Sinclair. What were you gonna do if you found him?"

Madison smiled sadly and shook her head. "We're not even looking for him anymore."

"How? Why? Don't you wanna get your money back?" *What's wrong with these girls? Don't they care about justice?*

"The girls here showed us how to make a fortune throwing keg parties." Madison's demeanor brightened. "They even have a bouncer friend who's coming to Chicago to help us out."

The Chairman stared at her wide eyed. "Pumpkin-head? You're taking Pumpkin-head back to NEIU?" *This is just too much. When did everyone turn against me?*

Madison looked at him with disdain. "Don't let him hear you calling him that."

"I'm all too well acquainted with your giant friend."

"Oh my God!" Crystal pointed an accusatory finger. "You're the pervert he caught peeking in the window."

The Chairman turned his head away. "I wouldn't know anything about that."

Madison frowned. "You're a creepy little dude. Come near me again, you'll be talking soprano the rest of your life."

"So that's it?" The Chairman asked. "Sinclair walks free?"

"We're heading home," she said. "You can do what you want."

Crystal again reached for the trunk lid.

"Wait," the Chairman cried. "How am I gonna get outta here?"

Tiffany laughed. "Don't be such a wuss. The rope's not even tied. We just wrapped it around you."

Without another word, Crystal slammed the trunk and plunged the Chairman into darkness.

He held his breath, straining to hear their conversation.

"I'm telling you," Madison said. "That guy's the banshee from the party last week."

"I don't know," Tiffany said. "You really think so?"

"He did scream like a little girl," Crystal said as the women broke into hysterical laughter.

FORTY-EIGHT

Rooster slowed his jog to a walk as he rounded the corner onto Main Street. He checked the time. 8:26 a.m. Sweat-soaked, filthy, and exhausted, somehow he had made it. When he escaped the Chairman's trunk, he had been forced to sprint all the way to the church. *Can't let that little weirdo cost me the second half of my rent money.*

He let out a long, relieved breath as he approached the Cumberland Baptist Church. He paused to stare at the site of his now-famous jump, and reflected on all that had happened since that Thursday morning. Those past ten days felt more like ten years. His dumb tendency to ruin everything positive in his life was as strong as ever, but he vaguely realized something fundamental had shifted since his Lamborghini leap. He was being refined. He was not quite sure what had changed, he just understood it had happened. It was still happening.

Realizing his battered club wear was totally inappropriate for church, Rooster tried to smooth his wrinkled shirt and jeans. It was an impossible task. He had laid on the bar's dirty floor and slept half the night in a car trunk. He reeked of beer and sweat and looked fresh off a bender. He ran his fingers through his hair and hoped for the best.

As he gripped the wrought iron handle of the big oak door, it occurred to him his mad sprint to the church had been fueled by more than simple greed. Something else bubbled up inside him. A strange curiosity about where all this would take him. He thought about Marcie and her small group. He wondered if it was in him to be more like them, to be a good man instead of the pathetic, selfish jerk he had become. *Guess this is a good place to find out.* He pulled the handle and stepped inside.

The lobby was emptying into the sanctuary, which made Rooster's arrival more obvious to the handful of people who milled around. Heads snapped in his direction with what he interpreted as judgmental stares. Highly self conscious, he glanced down to ensure his fly was not open. When he looked back up, Sallie Mae Johnston stood before him in a bold cobalt blue dress. Her big Texas hair crowned her head like fog draped over a mountain peak. Her friendly smile slowly dissolved as she gave him a visual once over. "Hi Rooster," she said, concern in her voice. "Everything all right?"

Rooster smiled painfully. "Hi Sallie Mae. I'm fine."

She grimaced. "You sure? You don't look so good."

"I had a bit of a rough night, but I'm ok now."

"What happened?"

"Ahh..." *She must think I been drunk in the gutter all night, especially after spilling my guts to the small group. Why'd I tell them all that?* He stared at the floor and considered how Sallie Mae and all of the others seemed to genuinely care about each other, how they all managed to find the good in one another. *That other stuff is what I'd be thinking if I saw me in this condition. She's probably concerned about me for real. I look like a big steaming pile of cow dung. Even if she did think those bad things about me, she'd be right.*

Rooster was pulled back to reality by the gentle touch of Sallie Mae's hand on his arm. She had a warm half smile and worry in her eyes. "Talk to me, Rooster. What happened?"

Rooster sighed. There was something comfortable and homey about her. Cartoonish hair aside, she was a real person, compassionate and caring. Rooster tried to remember why he had found Sallie Mae so repulsive when they first met, but he could not recall any of it. Instead, he was aware of his growing fondness for her. *Might as well tell her the truth.*

"I was drugged and kidnapped by a crazy homeless man who locked me in the trunk of his car all night," he blurted, acutely aware of how outrageous it all sounded.

Sallie Mae grinned. "No, really. Quit joking around."

"I'm not joking. After I escaped, I ran all the way here so I wouldn't be late to church." He saw conflict in Sallie Mae's face as she struggled to determine whether or not he told the truth. Rooster softened his tone. "Listen, I know it's hard to believe, but I promise you it's all true. You remember what I told you all about the other night?"

Sallie Mae nodded.

"Well, this whole mess is directly related to all that."

She raised her hands over her mouth in shock. "Oh my goodness, Rooster. How horrible."

Rooster waved his hands dismissively. "I can't talk about this right now. Have to get inside to see Sandy or I won't get..." He stopped himself, ashamed to admit he was being paid to go to church.

"You won't get what?"

"I, ahh... I won't get to see her before the service starts." Rooster headed for the sanctuary door before Sallie Mae could interrogate him further. As he pushed into the next room, Rooster fought the urge to search for the non-existent holy water bowl. His exhaustion level literally pulled him down. His upper body seemed to weigh a thousand pounds, as if he would topple over if he leaned too far forward. His legs felt embedded in concrete. To lift them became so difficult, he sort of shuffled along, dragging his feet to avoid a pratfall.

Rooster spotted Sandy in the back of the sanctuary. She wore yet another shapeless, curve-camouflaging outfit. *This woman's got a closet full of potato sacks. What's she trying to hide?* He lumbered toward her. His muscles ached. His eyes burned. His body screamed for sleep.

Sandy broke into a wide smile when she saw him. "Mr. Rooster. I'm so glad to see you here..." Her voice trailed off as she digested his condition.

Here it comes. Rooster braced for a scolding.

"Even if you are bit disheveled this morning."

"Yeah, I know I look like crap, but..."

Sandy raised her hand "Don't say anymore. You obviously had a rough time before you came here this morning, but the important thing is you're here, and we're happy to have you."

Rooster stared at his feet. *She must think I'm a total loser. I'm so pathetic, she won't even call me out for showing up to church looking and smelling like this.*

"Mr. Rooster?"

He turned toward her, unable to look her in the eye.

"Just like last week, I believe God has something for you today. I hope you'll pay close attention to Pastor's message."

Rooster smiled at her kindness. "I'll do my best."

"You better find your seat," she said as the choir began to file onto the stage. "They're getting ready to start."

"Thanks." Rooster turned.

"Mr. Rooster?"

He stopped and faced her.

Sandy smiled. "Don't forget to turn off your phone."

"I'll do it," he said with an embarrassed smile as he turned the phone to vibrate. The joyless, brush cut, announcement guy was already at the microphone. He droned on about missionaries, or the mission of the church, or some such thing as Rooster headed down the center aisle. He hoped his new friend Dottie Charles would be in her same place. *What if she's not here?* His stomach churned unexpectedly at the idea. *That's odd.* He barely knew this woman, yet his anxiety level rose at the mere prospect of not sitting next to her. He pondered the implications of that as he shuffled along.

Judgmental stares and whispers reminded Rooster of his less-than-stellar appearance. Out of the corner of his eye, he saw one man put a hand near his mouth to pantomime tipping back a drink, as he hit his wife's arm and pointed at Rooster. *Maybe coming to church wasn't such a good idea. These people can't have a loser like me walking among them.* Anger and resentment built up inside him. His mood brightened when he spotted Dottie's little white bun. It bounced up and down as she nodded her head in agreement with whatever the lifeless dude up on stage intoned. Although she was smack-dab in the middle of the row, there was an empty space next to her. Rooster stopped by the man in the end chair and tapped his shoulder.

When the man glared up at him, Rooster smiled and whispered, "I'm sorry, but I need to get in to that seat." He pointed at the empty space next to Dottie. The man sighed and rose. As he unfolded his long body, he was much taller than Rooster had expected. The man stepped out into the aisle. He towered over Rooster. As Rooster moved past, he laid a heavy hand on Rooster's shoulder. He moved close enough for Rooster to smell the stale coffee on his breath.

"You sure you're supposed to be here?" The man whispered, his voice dripping with condescension and self-righteousness.

As he stared up at him, Rooster felt like a total outsider without a friend in the world. He motioned for the man to lean closer. "The only thing I'm sure of," Rooster said in a tone only the man could hear, "is you're a damn jackass."

A self-satisfied grin filled Rooster face as he stepped in front of the man's chair and waited patiently for the rest of the row to notice him. The first woman smiled and pulled her knees to the side. Rooster turned his body to squeeze past eight people on the way to his seat next to Dottie. Most were indifferent to his interruption, but one angry-looking thirty-something woman eyed him like a suspect in a police lineup.

"Oh, I'm so sorry," Rooster said with a grin, almost before he 'accidentally' kicked her hard in the ankle as he passed.

"Ouch," she said in a hushed voice, staring daggers at him as she leaned down to rub her throbbing leg.

Rooster ignored her. Relief flooded over him when he finally got to his spot next to Dottie. He risked a peek back at the people he had passed. The jackass on the end was bent forward, glaring down the row at him. Rooster dropped heavily into his chair. Dottie turned toward him.

"Oh Rooster!" Her eyes sparkled with excitement. "I was worried you weren't coming."

Rooster smiled broadly, pleased she was pleased. He felt safe and welcomed next to her. "I almost didn't make it, but I sure am glad to see you, young lady."

"Lordy," Dottie said with a soft whistle. "You look like you were in the outhouse when lightning struck it."

Rooster shrugged. "I know. It was a rough night."

She reached over, and patted his knee. "Well, don't you worry one second about any of that. Whatever you been through, you're in the right place to get over it."

FORTY-NINE

Through sheer force of will and a few well-placed elbows from Dottie, Rooster managed to remain awake through the announcements and music. The choir finished with a rousing rendition of *I'll Fly Away* until the house was rocking. As the singers filed off the stage, the room filled with palpable anticipation. Rooster's adrenaline surged as he wondered what the crazy Colonel Sanders-looking minister might come up with.

As he ambled to the podium, the preacher's look was more traditional with a blue pinstripe suit, a crisp white shirt and a regal purple tie. He shuffled his notes and pulled a bottle of water from under the lectern, seemingly oblivious to the room of people impatient for him to get started. After a leisurely sip, he cleared his throat, and addressed the congregation. "Let's pray." He closed his eyes. The audience followed suit. Rooster reflexively clasped his hands and bowed his head.

"Heavenly Father," the pastor boomed. "This morning, there are people sitting among us who are at crossroads in their lives. Lord, send Your Holy Spirit to inhabit this place. My message is inadequate without You. But with You, all things are possible. Touch those who need You. Fill them with Your joy, Your peace, and Your hope. It is in the glorious name of Jesus Christ, our Lord and Savior, that we pray."

A loud "Amen" reverberated from the congregation. Rooster glanced at Dottie, who was captivated, a huge grin on her face. He wondered how long she had been listening to this minister. *Does she ever get tired of him? How can you sit through his sermons week after week, month after month, year after year, and not lose interest?* Rooster looked forward to what the man had to say today, but this was just his second visit. Would he still be full of anticipation after fifteen or twenty sermons?

The preacher's words pulled Rooster back. "This morning, I want to tell you about a friend of mine. Many of you know him, but few of you have heard his whole story."

The minister slowly walked to platform's edge and leaned forward. Rooster feared the old man would tumble off the stage.

"This man was dealt a very bad hand in life," the pastor said quietly, intensely. "He never knew his father. His mother was a prostitute and a junkie. He was born addicted to crack. Not a very promising start to his life. And unfortunately, it only went downhill from there." His words lingered as he made his way back to the podium. "At fourteen, his mother abandoned him to the streets." The preacher shook his head. "Fourteen! Can you imagine that? Forced to do unspeakable things just to survive. Lying, cheating, and stealing became a way of life."

He held his palms toward the audience. "But wait. It gets worse. So much worse." The preacher removed his glasses and produced a handkerchief from his coat pocket. "As he got older, he was targeted by the rival gangs who ruled his neighborhood." He breathed on the spectacles and wiped the lenses with his cloth. "He had to decide between joining a gang or getting beat up almost daily. Really not much of a choice, is it?" He put the glasses on and slipped the handkerchief inside his jacket.

"I bet you're not surprised to learn he joined the Southside Mafia street gang just to stop the harassment. Does this sound like a life of promise? I wonder how many of us would've been capable of making different choices if we'd been born under similar circumstances."

Rooster scratched his chin. *Would I have done better? Hell, I grew up middle class and still made a mess of my life. If I'd been dealt those cards, I'd probably be dead already.*

"By the time he was eighteen," the pastor continued, "this man was an alcoholic and addicted to heroin. He had participated in countless muggings and several home invasions. He fought in gang wars with knives, guns, and his fists." The preacher retrieved his water from under the podium. "Then things took a horrible turn." He removed the cap. "But he'd be the first to say, awful as it was, it saved his life." He took a long drink. "Hopped up on pills and alcohol, he got in a car with two of his gang brothers. It started out as a joy ride, but they got the bright idea to kill the leader of a rival gang. They drove by the guy's house and riddled it with bullets." He capped the water. "But there was just one problem."

The minister surveyed the room, which had grown deathly quiet. "They were so high," he bellowed, "they picked the wrong house. There was no one in that home except a sixteen-year-old honor student and the seven-year-old baby sister he was watching until his mom got home from work. They were both killed."

He stepped out from behind the podium to allow the crowd time to digest his words. "Fortunately," he continued softly. "They were so impaired, the police had no trouble catching them. All three young men were convicted of murder and sentenced to forty years in the Georgia State Prison." The pastor sighed. "Stop right there and it's just a sad story about a wasted life. It certainly looked bleak. But like Jesus said in chapter 18, verse 27, of Luke's gospel, 'What is impossible with men is possible with God.'

"Thankfully, the Lord had a plan for this man's life. What seemed an impossible situation was actually the beginning of a miracle. But before that miracle could take hold, my friend had to do his part and allow God to change his heart."

The congregation had become so silent, Rooster heard the clicking of the preacher's shoes as he ambled to the edge of the stage. "When he walked into that prison, he had choices to make. Would he simply put his head down and serve his sentence, a despicable life frozen in time? Or would he have the courage to take the lonely, narrow path toward redemption? Would he allow God to birth him again into a new life, a new purpose?"

The pastor crossed his arms, a pained expression on his face. "For the first few years in jail, everything seemed hopeless. He was just another number, literally prisoner number 17356. But God had mercy on him. A Christian ministry team came to the penitentiary for a special weekend-long event. My friend agreed to attend, but there was nothing noble about his purpose. He merely hoped to escape a couple days of kitchen duty."

The minister slapped his knee and hopped in excitement. "But you see how God works? All He needs is a tiny little opening, and He'll grab ahold of you. He'll give you the opportunity to change your life." The pastor strolled along the edge of the platform. He made eye contact with members of the congregation and allowed everyone time to reflect.

Rooster's mind spun as he stared at the preacher. *Has God given me a chance to change my life? Was my miracle leap an opening that allowed God to grab ahold of me?*

His mind turned to all he had experienced since that jump. *My coerced rent for church arrangement with Sandy. Marcie hooking me up with Jimmy Robinson. Spilling my guts to the small group. Fighting off the Chairman's first attack. Getting so blind drunk, the Chairman kidnapped me easily. My escape from the car trunk.* In the past ten days he had seen clearly the utter disaster that was his life. He had also caught a glimpse of the better him he could become. It was almost as if God had presented him a pair of alternate realities to consider. Like the preacher's friend, Rooster had to choose which way to go. For the first time he understood, to continue ignoring the decision would be a choice in itself.

The preacher continued in his booming voice. "My friend didn't realize until that moment how badly he needed something to believe in. There was a hole in his soul he had been trying to fill with drugs, alcohol, hate, violence, and every other awful, destructive influence he'd ever experienced. He was a broken man, primed for God to work on him. In those two days he went from ambivalent non believer to being sold out for Jesus."

A single person up front began to clap. Within seconds the applause spread through the sanctuary. A loud hoot came from the back. Someone shouted, "Praise Jesus." Wild cheers as raucous as any Saturday night SEC football game soon engulfed the room.

The pastor smiled broadly and held out his hands. Slowly the room fell silent. He looked around until sure he had everyone's attention. "Some would call it dumb luck my friend attended that weekend, but I don't believe in luck or coincidence." His volume rose as he bellowed, "I'd call that a God appointment!" Applause erupted again.

Rooster scanned the room. He had never seen anything like this before. *Are you even allowed to clap and cheer at church? Isn't that sacreligious somehow?* It all made him uncomfortable. He glanced at Dottie, as if a reassuring look from her would mean this was all normal, perfectly acceptable church behavior. Dottie grinned at him, her eyes red-rimmed with emotion. It reminded him of his mom's facial expressions during the climax of any *Little House on the Prarie* episode. Dottie winked and patted Rooster's knee before turning back toward the preacher.

"Wasn't easy being a Christian in that horrible place. He lost friends and endured emotional and physical abuse because of his faith. Yet for fourteen long years, he persevered, read his bible, and converted other prisoners. He lived out his faith and became a bright light in a very dark place. God was watching over him. He became a peace-maker and a model prisoner. When he came up for parole after eighteen years, twenty-seven people spoke on his behalf." The preacher shook his head. "They included fellow inmates, guards, other prison workers, and outsiders who had ministered beside him. Even the warden himself made a plea before the parole board for my friend's release.

"Imagine that." The minister smiled and slapped the podium. "He went from alcoholic, drug-addicted, misanthropic, murderer, gang-banger, to a gentle, kind, selfless, generous, lover of people, who inspires everyone he meets. I'm so very proud of my friend for who he has become, but I promise you don't just transform like that on your own. God did that!"

Another round of applause swept the room as the minister walked across the stage, absorbing the crowd's energy. "He was released from prison fourteen years ago. Since then he's become a successful business owner. He's ministered to countless young men in prison. I can't even fathom the lives he's had a hand in changing, because God first changed his. Anyone who's been around this place awhile knows I'm talking about Derek Simmons. Where's Derek? Stand up, Derek."

Heads turned to search for the man. More applause broke out as the crew cut guy who had droned through the announcements rose to his feet. Rooster was shocked. *Holy crap. That guy's done time for murder?* The man's red face featured an uncomfortable grin. Hoots and hollers filled the sanctuary as the din grew to its most ear-splitting level yet.

"Derek doesn't like the spotlight," the pastor shouted as the raucous clapping died down. "But he agreed to let me tell his story because he knows he is a living testament to the transformative power of God. When I think of Derek, it reminds me of Paul's first letter to Timothy."

The minister returned to the lectern and opened his bible. "Let's look at 1 Timothy 1:12. 'I thank Christ Jesus, our Lord, Who has given me strength, that He considered me trustworthy, appointing me to his service. Even though I was once a blasphemer and a persecutor and a violent man, I was shown mercy because I acted in ignorance and unbelief. The grace of our Lord was poured out on me abundantly, along with the faith and love that are in Christ Jesus. Here is a trustworthy saying that deserves full acceptance: Christ Jesus came into the world to save sinners, of whom I am the worst.

But for that very reason I was shown mercy so that in me, the worst of sinners, Christ Jesus might display His immense patience as an example for those who would believe in Him and receive eternal life.'"

The pastor carefully closed his bible and looked up. "Y'all remember the apostle Paul, right? Probably the most successful evangelist in the history of the world. He's credited with writing more of the New Testament than any other person. Yet he started out as a Pharisee. He existed to wipe out Christians. He tracked them down, persecuted them, and had them killed. Paul was the worst of all sinners." His tone strengthened. "He said it himself in the scripture." The pastor held up his bible, and tapped it. "If God can turn a man like Paul into one of the most influential people in history. If He can take a person like Derek, a murderer on the road to oblivion, and transform him into a pillar of the community, who is respected by everyone..."

The minister again retrieved his water bottle. As if his sole purpose was to hold the crowd in suspense, he slowly uncapped the bottle, took a long drink, recapped it, and put it away. He stepped to the side of the podium. His body language and serious facial expression conveyed the vital importance of what he was about to say. The audience leaned forward.

"If God can do that," he whispered, "don't you know anything is possible? Whatever you're facing. If you're on the wrong path. No matter how many bad decisions litter your past, God can help you change your future. Do you believe that?"

A chorus of yeses flowed across the room. Rooster found himself nodding in agreement, emotion flooding over him. Exhausted with his current way of life, he desperately wanted a new future. He knew in his heart, it was time to make changes.

"Whatever's holding you back from your potential," the pastor boomed. "Whatever's dragging you down. God can help you overcome it." His tone dropped to a whisper. "But He's not going to hit you with a lightning bolt, or change you against your will. Action is required on your part."

Rooster fidgeted, excited to discover what he could do to initiate these positive changes the preacher spoke about.

"You have to make the decision to change. Then you have to ask God to help you. God has a new and better future for you. The question is, will you embrace it? Or will you just continue down the road you've been traveling and miss the opportunity?"

Rooster stared at his hands. He had some huge decisions before him. Decisions that would determine whether he would pull his life back from the abyss and make something of himself, or spend the rest of his days as a pathetic loser. He seriously wondered if he was even capable of making wise choices.

The preacher seemed to read Rooster's thoughts. "Here's an idea to get the ball rolling. You know where you need to make changes in your life. Some of you have promised yourselves a million times you were charting a new course in those areas, only to fall back into your old ways. Instead of just thinking about it, take action when you get home today. Do something audacious to show God you're serious this time."

Rooster slammed his fist into his palm. *Yeah, I need to do something bold.* While the pastor wrapped up his sermon and led the congregation in a prayer, Rooster decided exactly what he wanted to do. *But do I have the guts to go through with it?* The service ended with Rooster still lost in thought. Vaguely aware of a nearby voice, Rooster returned to reality to find the sanctuary almost empty and Dottie next to him.

Her eyes sparkled with life. "Were you thinking about pastor's message?"

"Huh?" Rooster was still distracted by his thoughts. He focused on Dottie. "I'm sorry. You were asking me about the sermon, I think?"

Dottie smiled and nodded.

"Yeah. He gave me a lot to consider."

"You know," Dottie said. "Sometimes we know exactly what we have to do, but fear keeps us from doing it."

Rooster stared at her, confused. "Why'd you say that?"

Dottie smiled broadly. "You look pensive to me, like you're wrestling something in your head, and for some reason that business about fear just came to mind, so I shared it with you."

Rooster wondered if she had really read his thoughts. Uneasiness developed in the pit of his stomach. He glanced at Dottie. "You ever been afraid to make a big change in your life? Even though in your heart, you knew it was the right thing?"

Dottie carefully lowered herself into the seat next to him and laid a friendly hand on his knee. She stared him in the eye. "You know, fear is a funny thing. When it appears, it can get big and scary real quick. If you give in, it'll paralyze you into doing nothing. If you think about it, avoiding a decision is actually the same as making one. Usually the wrong one."

Rooster took in her words, nodded in agreement, and tried to mentally define exactly what he was afraid of.

"But I found in life," Dottie continued, "when I pull on my big girl britches and face my fears, I never regret the outcome, even when things turn out differently than I hoped. Most of the time, whatever had you scared, doesn't look nearly as big and bad as it did before you faced it."

Rooster climbed to his feet. "Thank you, young lady. You don't know how much I needed to hear that."

Dottie stared up at him. "I'm glad it was helpful."

Rooster grinned as he gave her arm a squeeze. "You're a wise woman. I got to go."

Dottie smiled. "Will I see you again next week?"

"I believe that's a distinct possibility." Rooster made his way through the row of chairs. He cracked the lobby door and peeked through, relieved to see Sallie Mae Johnston engaged in conversation. He ducked past her and out the front door. He felt guilty avoiding her, but there was no way he wanted to explain more about the previous night's events. He had to get home and take care of business quickly, before he lost his nerve.

With *I'll Fly Away* playing in his head, Rooster marched home with a purpose, psyching himself up to do it. As he approached the house, he saw Waylon standing guard in front of the doorway. As soon as he noticed Rooster, the animal yelped with delight and ran to his master. Rooster paused to pat the dog's head and rub behind his ears. "Good to see you too, Waylon, but there's something I have to take care of right now." He flipped aside the Mexican blanket and strode through the living room, dismayed by the still-lingering skunk aroma. He quickly pushed stray thoughts aside.

Just like a bandaid. Rip it off quickly. He headed straight for the kitchen cupboard, flung the door open, and grabbed the Eagle Rare. Before he could change his mind, Rooster pulled the cork and turned the bottle over in the sink, inserting the neck directly into the drain. He watched the brown liquid glug, glug, glug from the bottle with a strange mixture of excitement, awe, and horror. *It was half full.* He sighed with regret.

"Stop that," he ordered himself aloud.

Waylon wandered into the room. He sat down next to Rooster and stared up with sad brown eyes.

"I'm really doing it," he told the dog. "I'm doing something audacious, to prove this time is different."

Waylon's tail slapped back and forth on the linoleum. He nuzzled against Rooster's leg. Rooster reflexively stroked the animal's head, but stopped when he looked at the empty bottle in the sink. His stomach churned. Sweat formed on his brow. He longed for a glass of the bourbon he had just dumped.

"Have to finish."

Back at the cupboard, he snatched the Jack Daniels, unscrewed the cap, and turned it over in the sink. His chest hurt as he watched the bottle drain. He moved to the fridge with swirling emotions. His hands were shaking as he reached for the door. "I can do this."

He pulled out a longneck Bud, twisted off the cap, and breathed in the intoxicating, malty aroma. For a moment he stood paralyzed as an inner battle raged. He imagined sucking down the beer. He closed his eyes and dropped his hand to his side, his whole body tense.

The loud crash startled him. As he lifted an empty hand, he realized the beer was gone. It felt like a dream when he stared at the broken bottle surrounded by a golden puddle. He shook his head and tried to clear his mind. "Just do it," he ordered himself. After regaining control of his emotions, he returned to the fridge, snatched a pair of beers, popped the caps, and turned them over in the sink. A few trips later, it was done.

Everything was gone. He wrestled his emotions. *Am I happy? Sad?* He honestly did not know. He was just confused.

He staggered to the living room and collapsed on the sofa. Completely spent physically and emotionally, within minutes he was fast asleep. Waylon paced in front of the couch like a mama bear protecting her cubs.

FIFTY
Monday, May 23rd

As dusk approached, the temperature had fallen to a not-too-oppressive eighty-three degrees, although the humidity remained in the soupy range. It was surreal as Rooster stood in front of the historic courthouse and talked to the pretty auburn-haired Channel 3 reporter. Despite the moist air, she was cool as a cucumber. *Definitely better looking in person than on TV*. She wore a pair of tight cropped jeans, a form-fitting Tennessee Titans t-shirt, and sandals, instead of her normal on-camera clothes. Rooster had always preferred the relaxed weekend look to fancy dresses and high heels.

She pointed toward the courthouse. "When we go live at the top of the stairs at six oh two, I'll ask you a few questions about yourself and then we'll get right into that amazing jump over the Lamborghini."

Rooster nodded and pretended to listen. She was much smaller than he had expected, and younger-looking too. He had never thought specifically about it, but he had unconsciously assumed she was mid thirties and just slightly shorter than him, five foot nine or ten, maybe. In reality, he towered over her and she could not be a day over twenty-five.

"Rooster?" She had stopped talking and now stared at him, concern in her striking blue eyes. They were so vibrant he wondered whether the color was actually from contact lenses.

"You ok?"

He smiled. "Yeah." His underarms were slightly damp. "I'm sorry. Guess I drifted off for a minute there."

She laughed. "That's alright. Just please don't do that during our interview tomorrow."

Rooster projected exaggerated confidence, "Don't you worry 'bout that." He made sure his arms remained pressed against his torso to hide the growing dark spots on the pits of his royal blue polo. "How many people you think'll be here?"

Cassandra tilted her head, and gazed up at the sky. "Oh I don't know. The Tuesdays Around Town caravan usually draws at least five or six hundred." She flashed a big toothy grin. "But there's been a lot of interest and excitement for your appearance. Bet we have more than a thousand."

Rooster let out a low whistle and clasped his hands. "A thousand people. Imagine that."

"There'll be maybe a hundred thousand more watching on TV."

"Sounds like we'll have some fun." Rooster hoped she could not hear the anxiety in his voice. "Looking forward to it."

"Me too. I really appreciate you meeting me down here. I want this interview to go well."

"Hey, my pleasure."

An awkward silence developed as they stared at each other. Rooster unconsciously rocked from side to side and shoved his hands into the front pockets of his jeans. Cassandra broke the silence. "Well. Guess I'll see you tomorrow at five-thirty inside the courthouse."

"Yes," Rooster said just a bit to forcefully, glad to have the conversation lull broken. He reached out his hand, but quickly pulled it back to keep his wet armpits concealed.

She grabbed at his retreating hand, but was too slow and came up with only fingers. "Great to meet you." She pumped his fingertips as if that was perfectly normal to her.

Rooster grimaced. "Nice to meet you." His oafish handshake turned his uncomfortable meter up a few notches.

Cassandra released his fingers. "Goodbye," she said pleasantly as she quickly walked away.

"Bye," Rooster sputtered. *I'm such an idiot. She couldn't wait to get away from me.* He hoped their awkward farewell would not negatively impact the interview. Immediately, his mind constructed disaster scenarios where he proved himself a fool to all of metro Nashville. The tapes played on a loop in his head. He crossed the street and headed for the dry cleaner's drive-thru, which cut between two buildings on the public square. Eager to get home, he was glad to save steps with the shortcut.

As Rooster entered the alley, his first sales trainer, Diamond Dan Martin, popped into his head. "Visualize success," Diamond Dan had preached. "If you have an idea in your mind of what success looks like, it becomes much easier to achieve it."

Interview's going to be perfect. He tried to imagine in detail a successful TV interview, but he was too exhausted to focus. His emotions were still raw. Dumping all his alcohol had drained more out of him than he cared to admit. In a way, he mourned the demise of his old self. Sure, it had been a constant source of pain and destruction, but it was the only life he had known for decades. It was tough to see it disappear. His drinking had defined him. If he was not that guy anymore, who was he? What would now be the driving force in his life? He had so much to think about, it made his head swirl.

"Hey, it's twinkle toes, the jalopy jumper," called out the vaguely familiar voice.

Rooster stopped, afraid to move. *It isn't. It couldn't be.*

"Turn around, you dirty swamp weasel."

Rooster drew in a deep breath. *It's him. But how?* Rooster eyed the dry cleaner's door. Dark inside. Closed. They were alone together in the alley. He slowly pivoted until he faced Tony Ferrentino, resplendent as ever in his powder blue track suit. *Is it possible he's even fatter than when I was laying bets with him back in New York?* Rooster stood, mouth agape, as Tony slowly approached him. Sweat poured down the bookie's beet red face, like the juices of the Thanksgiving turkey when pierced with a fork. Rooster projected false confidence. "Tony, you keep forgetting dark colors are the slimming ones. Looks like you stole the warm-ups from the 1973 New York Nets."

"Watch your mouth, dummkopf." Tony mopped his forehead with a handkerchief. "They were ABA champs. Dr. J was on that team."

Rooster considered making a break for it. No way Tony could catch him. He glanced over his shoulder. A giant, younger version of Tony had entered the space between the buildings and made his way toward Rooster. *Oh shit.*

The new guy wore a strange baseball-style cap, which appeared to be made from silver snakeskin. Long gold fringe dangled from the bottom edge of the hat's entire circumference. Despite his fear, Rooster chuckled at the man's ridiculous getup. "Dude, that cap looks like it was made from the curtains at a Chinese brothel."

"For the love of Captain Morgan's wiener dog," Big Tony bellowed. "How many times I told you to lose that muto capello? You look like an extra-gay Liberace in that thing."

The big man reluctantly pulled the cap from his head. "You got no sense of style," he mumbled under his breath.

Rooster glanced between the two men, wondering what to make of them. Sweat trickled down the back of his neck. Both escape routes were blocked. Despite his gurgling stomach, Rooster could not resist throwing out one more zinger. "You need to upgrade your thugs, Tony. This ass clown looks like the love child of Captain Lou Albano and Janet Reno."

"Hey slimeball, watch your mouth," the goofy man exploded. "Make him show us some respect, Pop."

A wide grin creased Tony's sagging jowls. "I don't care about respect." His beady eyes zeroed in on Rooster. "All I care about is the hundred large you owe me. Just give me the money, and we'll be on our way."

Rooster swallowed hard and struck a more humble tone. "Listen Tony, I don't have that kind of money."

"Then we got a little problem, don't we?"

"No," Little Tony guffawed. "This schmuck has a big problem."

Big Tony glared at his son. "You little goat-licker. You're talking over my collections monologue. I'm on stage here. Would you interrupt Sinatra in the middle of *Fly Me to the Moon*?"

Little Tony was skeptical. "C'mon, get real Pop. You're hardly Frank Sinatra." He defiantly set his gaudy metallic hat back on his skull. "Frank Sinatra Junior. Maybe."

The old man shook his head. "For the love of all things holy, you're sucking all the joy outta this."

The elder Tony was now within two feet of Rooster, who braced himself for whatever might happen next. To his surprise, the bookie walked right past him to confront his son. "Gimme that!" The old man snatched the ball cap off Little Tony's head. He threw it on the ground and tried to jump on it. He managed to get up onto his toes, but his feet refused to take flight. Instead, he comically lifted one leg and mashed the hat with his toe, as if putting out a cigarette, all the while sucking air and wheezing.

"Hey," the son protested. "That's my *Street Pimp* cap. Cost me a hundred bucks."

As the pair erupted into a full-fledged screaming match, Rooster's heart leapt into his throat. The morons had given up their advantage. With nothing between Rooster and freedom, he edged away from the arguing men.

He felt the vibration first. His heart sank. There was no way to stop it. The sounds of Abba emanated loudly from Rooster's pocket. "*Well I can dance with you honey, if you think it's funny. Does your mother know that you're out? And I can chat with you baby. Flirt a little maybe. Does your mother know that you're out?*"

Both Tonys immediately fell silent, and stared at Rooster.

"That your phone?" Big Tony waddled over next to Rooster.

"No," Rooster quipped. "There's a concert in my pants."

"Stop being a lousy peanut-butter sniffing dingbat," Tony scowled. "Who's calling you?"

Rooster considered another smart remark, but thought better. "My mother."

"Answer it," the bookie demanded.

"Yeah right," Rooster said with an ironic laugh. "This is hardly the time to take a call from my mom."

"What kinda dirty scungilli are you? You would disrespect the woman who gave you birth? Not in front of me you won't. Answer that phone now."

He's serious. Rooster fumbled in his pocket for the device. He tapped the answer button and lifted the phone to his ear. "Hello?" He eyed the glaring men.

"Sonny? Is that you?"

Rooster sighed. "Of course it's me, Mom." He tried to remain calm, but his tone turned sarcastic. "Who else would answer my phone?"

Big Tony raised his hand menacingly and barked in a harsh whisper, "You be nice to her."

Rooster nodded. "Sorry Mom. What were you calling about."

"I'm so glad I caught you. You like to grill, right?"

"Grill?" He shrugged for the benefit of the Tonys, who had moved closer. "You mean like hamburgers?"

"Anything. Any meat or vegetables. Don't you have a grill outside that you cook things on?"

"Yes. Why?"

"I don't want you to grill anything anymore. It's too dangerous."

Rooster laughed nervously. The mobster thugs were close enough to overpower his nostrils with the Brut cologne one of them had apparently bathed in. "Don't worry, Mom. I'm not gonna blow myself up with the grill." He turned his back to the men, embarrassed by his side of the conversation.

"I'm not concerned about that, silly. I just finished reading an article in the newspaper. It said that grilling gets carcinogens on your meat and vegetables. So I don't want you to grill anything anymore."

"What on earth you talking about?" Rooster's wonder at her concerns caused him to nearly forget the menacing men behind him. "This is why you called me?"

"I don't want you to die of cancer. They did a study at a research center in Idaho and discovered that grilling causes cancer. That's how Mr. Donatello from down the street died."

"He got cancer from eating grilled food?"

"Don't you remember how the Donatellos were always grilling out? I'm sure that's what did him in."

Where does she get this stuff? "I thought Mr. Donatello died from driving his car into a bridge abutment." He snuck a peek at the Tonys, who seemed enthralled with his conversation. He wondered if they could hear his mom's side of things.

"I'm sure he only did that because his family couldn't afford the treatments for his grilling cancer."

Rooster's patience faded. "Mom, this is totally insane."

"Well forgive me for wanting to save you from cancer." Her voice was thick with emotion. "All I ever do is try to help my son, and he calls me crazy. Isn't that a fine how do you do?"

Rooster was suddenly exhausted. "Listen, Mom. I'm kinda in the middle of something right now. Gonna have to let you go."

"You're always in the middle of something. You never have time for me. What's so important that you can't take a few minutes to talk to your mother?"

"Oh, I don't know." Rooster wearily faced the Tonys. "What if two mobster thugs were waiting for me to finish this call so they can break my kneecaps because I owe them money?"

Big Tony frowned and wagged his finger in front of Rooster's nose. "Stop that," he mouthed.

"Now you're just being ridiculous," she said. "If you don't want to tell me what's going on in your life, just say so. You always had a fertile imagination. Always making up the most outrageous stories."

"Fine," Rooster said quietly. "I don't have anything to tell you right now, but I do have to go."

"What am I going to do with you, Sonny?"

"I don't know."

"Fine. Just promise me you won't grill anymore."

"Whatever you say, Mom."

They said their goodbyes, Rooster slipped the phone into his pocket and turned expectantly toward the Tonys.

The bookie asked, "What's that all about?"

It was more than a little weird how genuinely interested the big man seemed in his absurd phone call. "She doesn't want me to eat anything grilled anymore." Rooster felt ridiculous.

"Why not?" Little Tony asked.

"She said grilling causes cancer." *Am I really having this conversation with these guys?*

Little Tony laughed. "Your mom's loony tunes, man."

"Hey!" Big Tony slapped the back of his son's head. "You're disparaging this man's mother? I raised you better than that."

Little Tony winced and rubbed his noggin. "Sorry, Pop."

The father turned toward Rooster. "You listen to your mother. She knows what she's talking about."

Rooster slowly nodded. *I'm surrounded by insanity.*

"Now," Big Tony said. "Back to business. You owe me..."

His voice trailed off as a strange look came over him, a combination of disappointment, intense pain, and annoyance. Even more sweat poured down his face. The big man stepped from side to side, like a kindergartener waiting to go potty.

Concern filled Little Tony's eyes. "Pop? What's wrong?"

The bookie licked his lips and mopped his face with the handkerchief. "Home base. Gotta get to home base."

Rooster turned from one man to the other, as he tried to figure out what was happening. The old man's formerly red face was now pale white. Rooster thought Big Tony might keel over any second. *What the heck is home base?*

"You're kidding," Little Tony whined.

"No," the father said. "Now."

The son pointed at Rooster. "Can't we take him with us?"

Big Tony glared at Rooster. "We'll deal with you later." He began to waddle away.

Little Tony called after him, "Pop! We got him. We didn't come all this way just to let him go."

The bookie raised his right arm and, without a look back, pointed in the direction he was headed.

The son sighed. "Aww man." He scooped up his mangled hat.

Rooster asked in amazement, "What the hell's happening?"

"Damn Irritable Bowel Syndrome," Little Tony mumbled. He leaned close to Rooster's ear. "Don't think you're off the hook, loser. I promise you ain't seen the last of us."

Rooster stood there dumbfounded as the two men tottered away. He marveled at the absurdity of his life.

FIFTY-ONE
Tuesday, May 24th

Rooster was skittish as he hoofed it to Robinson Sporting Goods. After near death experiences, kidnappings, and physical attacks from seemingly every direction, he felt totally exposed just walking down the street. In constant paranoia, he visually scoured his surroundings. *Picked a helluva time to give up drinking.* He imagined how refreshing an ice cold beer would be on such a hot, humid morning. *That's the problem. Longing for alcohol at nine a.m. is exactly what created all this mess.*

A loud crack, as if a tree branch snapped, startled him. He spun, expecting to find the Chairman or the Tonys behind him.

Nothing. Breathing ragged, adrenaline pumping, his fight or flight instincts fully engaged. Then his right thigh was zapped by a bolt of electricity. Rooster leapt away from an unseen cattle prod-welding boogeyman, before he realized it was just a vibrating phone in his pocket. He shook his head, disturbed by how jumpy he had become. The worst part was he knew those mobster thugs and that unhinged lunatic Chairman were out there, on the lookout for him. Rooster forced himself to take long, deep breaths. He checked the caller's identity and answered.

"Hi Marcie," he said as pleasantly as he could muster. "What's goin' on?"

She was all business. "Hi Rooster. What're you doing?"

"Just walking to work." He wondered why she was not her normal, bubbly self. *Have I done something to upset her?*

"Oh. Over at Jimmy's place?"

"Yeah." *She fishing for another thank you for getting me the job? I already thanked her. She gonna dangle this over my head forever? Maybe that's why she got me the interview in the first place.* His mood soured.

"You have a few minutes to talk with me?"

He grew stand-offish. "Just walking. Knock yourself out."

"Uhh..." Marcie stumbled. "I heard you spoke to Sallie Mae Johnston at church on Sunday."

"And?" He wished she would just get to her point. He kicked at a stone and watched it bounce off the curb into the street.

"She told me what y'all talked about. Sallie Mae said you told her you been kidnapped, and then you ran off without saying anything else."

"Sounds about right," Rooster admitted, even though he did not like Marcie's accusatory tone.

"She also told me you looked and smelled like you'd been partying all night."

What right do they have to get all up in my business? "What concern is that of yours and Sallie Mae?"

"Guess it's none of our business," Marcie said coldly. "I'm just calling to make sure you're okay. To see how I can help."

"I'm fine." *What's she want from me?* He noticed a black BMW headed toward him. *The Chairman?* Panicked, he considered sprinting down a side street. Then he saw a blue-haired old lady inside. He let out a long breath.

Marcie softened. "Have to admit, your story sounds pretty outlandish. Sallie Mae's been worried sick about you for two days. She stayed home from work today, she was so upset."

"I'm not asking anyone to believe me," Rooster replied, his heart still racing. "But it's the truth. You can believe whatever you want. I didn't tell Sallie Mae to worry about me."

"That's the thing about allowing people to get close to you," she said quietly, compassion in her tone. "When they care, they sometimes worry about you whether you want them to or not. When you shared your story, all those people were honored you chose to trust them. We all want to see you make it."

"I didn't choose anyone." He did not want them to cheer him on, like some pathetic, mentally challenged puppy. "Just kinda happened. Once it started coming out, I couldn't stop it."

"Even better." Marcie had a smile in her voice. "God chose us for you to trust. I know you can overcome the stronghold alcohol has in your life, but you can't do it all by yourself."

"Why not?" He gave a wide berth to a blue pickup near the curb. The odds one of his pursuers hid behind it were pretty slim, but you could never be too careful.

"Because it doesn't work that way," she replied.

"I suppose you think you can help me."

"Yes, I do, but I can't help you if you're not honest with me. At least be honest with yourself."

Irritation bubbled up. "What am I lying to you about?" He bent down to search for feet underneath parked cars. He imagined gremlins lurked around every corner. He felt like one of the nameless, red-shirted members of a Star Trek landing party.

"This kidnapping business," she challenged. "C'mon Rooster. You can't fool me. I used to be a drunk. Your story sounds like a load of garbage. What're you trying to hide?"

"You think I don't know how ridiculous that sounds? If I was gonna make up something, do you think I'd actually come up with a crazy story like that?" He switched ears with the phone. "But hey, please believe whatever you want. I know the truth."

"You're saying you were actually kidnapped Saturday night?" A crack appeared in her shell of self-assurance.

"That's exactly what I'm saying."

"Where were you when they grabbed you?"

"That bar on the square that used to be the Blue Rooster."

Marcie paused to gather her thoughts. Then questions flew out in staccato bursts. "Who were you with?"

"Buddy."

"Why didn't he do something?"

"He didn't see anything."

"How'd they get you out without drawing attention to it?"

"One guy did it. Slipped something in my drink."

"Where'd he take you?"

"I passed out and woke up locked in his trunk."

"How'd you get away from him?"

"There was a trunk release inside there."

"How long were you in there?"

"I don't know." Rooster replayed the experience in his head. "All night, I guess. I got out a little before eight."

"You escaped from a kidnapper's trunk and then headed straight to church?"

"Yes."

"Why?" It was obvious Marcie was dubious. "If this all really happened, why wouldn't you go straight to the police? Surely you can understand why this all sounds so insane."

Rooster swallowed hard. The oppressive humidity made it difficult to breathe. Something inside of him ordered him to tell her everything. *Where'd that come from? Why should I confide anything to her?* The pressure was unbearable, as if he would burst if he tried to keep it inside one more minute. He believed she would not betray his confidence. *You'll be relieved to get it all out in the open.*

"Rooster? You still there?"

Rooster made sure no one could hear them. "Yeah, I'm here." He breathed deeply. "I... ah... didn't go to the police because the guy who grabbed me..." His voice trailed off.

Just spit it out, the voice ordered.

"He came after me because of something I did when I was in Illinois, before I moved to Murfreesboro."

"Something you did while you were drinking?" Her tone

suggested she already knew the answer.

"Yes." He braced himself for an interrogation about what he had done to the rugby team in Chicago. It never came.

"Why'd you go to church?" Marcie asked. "I woulda gone home, locked myself in the bedroom, and gone to sleep."

Amazed she had not pushed for more about his misdeeds, Rooster wondered whether he should spill the beans about his benevolence scheme.

Tell her, the voice commanded.

He so wanted to unload his burden. He needed to tell her.

"The church is paying my back rent," he said, unable to hide his embarrassment. "But only if I come to church and your group. If I didn't get to church, I coulda been evicted."

"They would've understood." She was suddenly fully onboard with his story.

"You didn't believe me. Why would they?"

"Oh, I see. What about your job?"

"I don't get my first check for two weeks."

"But didn't you..." She stopped mid-sentence.

Rooster shook the phone. Had he lost the connection? "Marcie, you there?"

"Yes."

"Didn't I what?"

She dismissed him. "Never mind."

"No really. Didn't I what? Tell me."

"Oh all right," she sighed. "Didn't you come into some money last week?"

The four hundred dollars on the TV stand. Anger flooded over him. *So it was Marcie who brought the cash. This is when she lords it over me? What she gonna demand in return?* "What about it?" He asked, an edge to his voice. "I owe you something now?"

"What's your problem?"

"My problem is I don't need your money. Especially if there's strings attached."

"Just calm down, you dumbass," she barked. "I didn't give you the money."

"You didn't?"

"Of course not," she said, as if talking to child. "I wouldn't give you any cash. I knew exactly what you'd do."

"You did?"

"Duh. Tell me where that money is now."

"I don't have it."

"And what'd you spend it on?"

Rooster considered lying, but he knew she would see right through him. "Drinking."

"Exactly. You weren't ready for a big pile of cash."

"If you didn't give it to me, who did?"

"George."

"George Jones?" George was the last person he would have expected to give him anything. "Why?"

"He was really touched by your story. He wanted to help." Her voice grew gentle. "But I gotta tell you, he was pretty hurt and disappointed you didn't say anything about it to the group."

"That's his problem." *What's with all these people expecting something from me? They barely know me.* "I didn't ask him for the money."

"Well, actually you did. Last week you basically asked everyone at my house for money. You told them all about your rent situation."

"Well. I. Ahh..."

"Don't worry. I'm not upset. I want to help you figure out how to put alcohol behind you once and for all. Surely you can see the destruction it's brought to your life."

"I guess." Rooster did not know how to take her directness. No one had ever approached him like Marcie, with total sincerity and no pretense. Everyone else pretended nothing was wrong because he always threw a tantrum when he did not want to admit the truth. Something told him Marcie could easily withstand his ire, and throw it all back in his face twice as hard.

"C'mon Rooster," she pressed. "You think normal people have

someone from their past chasing them down to kidnap them? You think normal people are missing the door to their house? You gotta see there's something seriously wrong with this picture."

Rooster wanted to remain stubborn, but she was right. "I agree," he finally said, not ready to be agreeable. He was happy to arrive at Jimmy's place. "I'm at work now. Gotta go."

"Ok."

He didn't know why, but she really cared about him. He believed she actually wanted to see him happy, healthy, and off the booze. The little voice told him to give her something positive, a reward for her steadfastness. "After church on Sunday," he said. "I went home and dumped out all the alcohol in the house. Haven't had a drink since." When he heard nothing but stunned silence, Rooster decided to get out while he was ahead. "I'll catch you later, ok?"

"Sure."

"Marcie?"

"What?"

"Thanks."

"Thanks for what?"

"Just, thanks," he said. "Bye."

Rooster disconnected before she could respond and headed through the front doors of the store.

FIFTY-TWO

The cool air inside Robinson Sporting Goods felt fantastic. "Hey Rosie," Rooster greeted the brunette behind the check-out.

She looked up from the weekly store advertisement. "Hey Rooster. Jimmy's been looking for you. He wanted you back in his office as soon as you got in today."

"Ok," Rooster said nervously. "I'm headed there right now." *Knew this was too good to be true.* A cloud of impending doom descended upon him. *What've I done now to screw things up.* His mind raced as he trudged along. By the time he reached the closed door - *Jimmy's door is never closed. That can't be good* - his thoughts were out of control. He half expected to find that wacko, the Chairman, and the rugby team girls telling Jimmy what a horrible person Rooster was. He pulled in a deep breath and made sure his shirt was fully tucked in. *I'll just tell him where to shove his stupid job.* He gently rapped on the door.

"C'mon in," Jimmy's happy voice sang out.

Rooster pushed his way into the little office. Jimmy, his seersucker jumpsuit no longer seemed nearly as absurd as when Rooster first met him, was perched on the window ledge. He gripped his bucket which passed for a coffee mug. That thing never stopped looking outlandish. An unfamiliar man sat in Jimmy's desk chair. He looked like he had money, with perfect black hair, graying at the temples, a crisp navy checked sport shirt, polished onyx cufflinks, and an expensive gold watch. Both men stared at Rooster, big smiles on their faces.

Rooster was confused. Already convinced this was the end for him, the happy expressions did not compute. He had been fired many times and no boss ever smiled before doing the deed. Some smiled afterward, but never before. "You wanted to see me?"

"Rooster," Jimmy said. "There's someone I want you to meet." He gestured toward the man and continued. "This is Mark Staples. He owns Murfreesboro Motors."

Rooster opened his mouth to greet the man, but Jimmy talked right over him. Mark smiled, raised his eyebrows, and shrugged in acknowledgement of Rooster's attempted hello.

"Mark and I been friends for thirty years. We share breakfast every Monday at the Broad Street Grill. You know, at that restaurant they only use local bacon? They grow it at the MTSU hog farm over on Lebanon Pike. Now that makes a big difference in taste and quality. For every fifty miles you move the pork from the slaughter site, you lose twelve percent of the flavor. The bacon they use at the Broad Street Grill is slaughtered less than five miles away. That's about as flavorful as it gets. Ain't that right Mark?"

As Mark nodded in agreement, Jimmy took a quick drink from his giant mug and continued. "Now imagine the flavor loss on pork imported from, say, Japan. And the US imports six hundred million to 1.2 billion pounds every year. And that's carcass weight! You can see why I'll never eat Japanese hogs. Flavor's completely gone by the time it hits your plate." Jimmy stared knowingly at the two men. "Now Canadian pigs are a little different," he continued, as if this all enthralled his audience. "Most of them are imported alive, on the hoof. But I never cared for the taste of Canadian bacon."

Mark abruptly leapt from his seat. "Enough! I swear, I'm gonna beat you over the head with that ridiculous coffee mug."

Jimmy grinned as he moved close to his friend and held the mug up on his shoulder. "I dare you to knock this off," he said with a comical forced scowl.

Mark busted out in laughter. Jimmy's stone face cracked and both men howled in delight. Rooster stood at the door, an awkward intruder.

When their laughter died down, Mark moved toward Rooster with an outstretched hand. "It's really nice to meet you."

"Glad to know you." Rooster forced himself to maintain eye contact. He firmly gripped the older man's hand.

"Rooster..." Jimmy began.

"Shut up, Jimmy." Mark smiled as he released Rooster's hand. "I gotta talk to Rooster, and then get back to work. I don't have an extra hour to listen to you ramble on about the two-tongued hummingbird of Indonesia, or the defecation rituals of the pygmy cannibal gypsies from the island of Mali."

"Ok." Jimmy grinned. "Floor's all yours. I need a refill anyway." He held up his coffee cup and left the room.

Rooster stared at Mark expectantly.

"Rooster, I hope you're gonna like what I have to say."

Rooster nodded. *So far it sounds better than getting fired.*

"That jump you did over the Lamborghini was amazing. I sell and service imported cars at my store. If anyone in Murfreesboro wanted a Lamborghini, they'd likely come by my place to get it."

"Ok." Rooster fidgeted. *Where's this going?*

"I'll get right to the point. I have this idea for a series of TV commercials, and they only work if you're the spokesman."

Rooster shook his head in wonder. *Television ads? I hear that correctly?* "I don't understand. I'm not an actor."

"That's the best part. You're just you. A regular, real guy, who just happens to be an internet sensation for jumping over a foreign sports car."

Rooster laughed nervously. "I don't know." He pictured himself in some ridiculous getup acting the fool in front of all Middle Tennessee. "Sounds way outside my comfort zone."

"I promise, they're very tasteful, and you won't have to jump any cars."

"I appreciate the offer, but..."

"And I'll pay you fifteen thousand dollars to do the first three spots. In fact, I got five grand in cash I'll give you today if you agree to it."

Rooster's eyes grew wide. A huge smile slowly filled his face. "Done!"

FIFTY-THREE

Rooster practically skipped toward the square. He had five thousand bucks in his pocket, the promise of ten more after the Murfreesboro Motors commercials, and the chance to earn a bonus thousand if he managed to mention Robinson Sporting Goods during his TV interview. He had a job he loved and he would soon have his front door back. *No more sad Mexican blanket.*

Rooster pumped his fist. "I'm back, baby!" Drunk with the euphoria of his first genuine winning streak in years, all lingering thoughts of the Chairman, the Tonys, and any other potential danger had disappeared. As he turned onto East Castle Street, just ten minutes from the square, he slowed to check the time. 5:07 p.m. He would arrive with plenty of time to spare.

Thankful Jimmy had allowed him to leave early, Rooster slowed his fast walk to an easy stroll. He considered what he might say to Cassandra on camera. How would he work in a mention of Jimmy's store? *Don't want it to seem forced.* Operating on auto-pilot, he nearly plowed into a woman with mousy-brown hair who seemed to appear out of nowhere. Startled, he lurched off the sidewalk to avoid her. "Whoa..." Rooster forced a friendly grin. "Sorry. Didn't even see you standing there."

"It's you," the woman said.

For the first time, Rooster took her in. Full figured, but not fat, she was poured into skintight jeans and a size-too-small, low-cut red tee. *Musta been a cutie fifteen years ago.* She smiled, but it did not match the intense glare in her eyes. Her body language made him uneasy. She positioned herself like a cowboy preparing for an old west shoot out. Something about her face and the way she moved was vaguely familiar. Rooster strained his brain, but could not put his finger on it. It had become an all-too-common occurrence to run into people he did not recognize who seemed to know him. *Musta met her during a bender.* He reached for his go-to response and pretended he knew exactly who she was. "Great to see you again." He hoped she was nothing more than a casual acquaintance. "Haven't seen you in awhile. Where you been hiding?"

Confusion filled her face. She opened her mouth, but said nothing. With cheeks pulled in, she puckered her lips and pressed them together like a fish.

Rooster shook his head. *Another wacko. Best be moving on, and fast.* He had interacted with more crazed people than he could handle lately. "Hey." He gently touched her arm. "So glad I ran into you, but I gotta go. I'm gonna be late for an important interview. Don't be a stranger." He brushed past her, eager to put some distance between them. Her familiarness and odd behavior gave him the heebie jeebies. It took everything in him not to break into a sprint. He held his breath as he walked five, ten, fifteen yards.

"Wait a minute!" Her voice was much too loud to ignore.

Rooster slowly emptied the air from his lungs. Overcome by an unnatural sense of foreboding, with slumped shoulders he turned to face her. Her smile replaced by a deep scowl, she shook with rage, a big red purse clutched against her chest. "Do you think you can just walk past me like I'm nothing?"

Rooster shuffled backwards. *Who the hell is this nutty woman? What've I done to her?* "I'm sorry. Have I done something to offend you?"

"You piece of garbage," she spit. "Don't you recognize your own wife? Why don't you look at the tattoo on your stomach?"

Oh shit. It's her. Doesn't look anything like I expected. "Wow." He prayed for the right words to extricate himself from his situation. "It's been a long time, Sally."

Her blood-curdling shriek made his skin crawl. "Sue! My name is Sue!"

His anxiety rising, Rooster suddenly noticed the oppressive heat and humidity. He searched for nearby people, but found no one. *How'd nobody hear that horrible screech? Five o'clock on a Tuesday night. Where the hell is everyone?*

"Did you really think you could just waltz through the rest of your life without ever seeing me again? Without having to answer for the hell you put me through?"

Rooster stared at his shoes. *Never did figure out what happened to her after Vegas. Still don't remember anything from that wedding night.* But the next morning was seared into his memory. Everything except her name, it seemed. At least he could always find that by checking the permanent ink on his belly.

"Hey, ahh Sal... er Sue..."

"Shut your lying mouth." She pulled a gun from her purse. "You can't sweet talk your way out of this one."

Rooster's eyes grew wide. *That's definitely not good.* He took in his surroundings, desperate to formulate a plan for escape. He considered running. *How good a shot could she be?* He thought about George Jones' brother and the stray bullet that killed him. *Anything's possible. Can't risk it.* Sharp pains hit his chest. *Just what I need, a heart attack before she can shoot me. This is insane.* He looked into the sky. *What're you trying to show me, God? You saved me from the car, and the Chairman, and the Tonys, and helped me give up drinking, only to let this unhinged whack job kill me?* "C'mon God," he whispered. "You can't be serious."

Like an answer to prayer, a huge boat of a car turned the corner and slowly rolled down the street behind Sue. The mint green 1984 Lincoln Town Car moved at a snail's pace. *Is he slowing down to check out our crazy scene? Maybe five miles per hour's his normal cruising speed.*

Her shrill voice interrupted his thoughts. "I should just pull the trigger right now and put an end to it." She jabbed the gun at him, a smile on her face. Either Sue had not noticed the giant Lincoln behind her, or she did not care. "How many other women's lives have you destroyed?"

She kooky enough to point her gun at me with cars driving by? Sue did not budge as the Town Car eased on past her. Rooster stepped into the behemoth's path, and waved his arms wildly. All he could see through the windshield was a pair of ancient wrinkled hands gripping the big steering wheel, some serious coke-bottle-bottom glasses, and the huge foam panel of a 1980s baseball hat.

"Get away from there!" Sue came at him with a Hollywood gangsta thug sideways waggle of her gun. "I'm not done with you yet."

Amazed the driver did not see him, Rooster jumped up and down, like an over-stimulated ADD five-year-old after his seventh candy bar. *This guy ignoring me?*

The car inched closer. The driver was ninety-five if he was a day. Rooster could see the hat more clearly. Bubble letters spelled out 'Born To Be Mild.' The old man stared directly at Rooster, but his blank expression made it clear he saw nothing.

Need someone to help me and God sends a damn Mr. Magoo. The Lincoln was almost on top of him, but he stood there defiantly, almost daring the driver to run him over. Of course the car moved so slow, hitting Rooster likely would have brought it to a complete stop. Reluctantly he stepped aside and the huge automobile rolled past. Gouges and dents in the side panels suggested the old man ran into more things than he avoided. When the driver's door was even with him, Rooster impulsively balled his fist and rapped on the window. The man's head snapped toward him, his eyes huge, albeit unseeing, in the coke-bottle glasses.

Rooster waved his hands and yelled at the glass, "I need your help!" Sue screamed and cursed behind him. He expected the crack of a gunshot any second.

Rooster reached for the door handle, but the moment he pulled on it, the driver laid on the horn with an earsplitting blast, and slammed on the accelerator. Rooster jumped away, as the big Lincoln lurched toward the curb. The front bumper caught the edge of a garbage can and sent it flipping and spinning onto the sidewalk. The Town Car swerved violently and nearly sideswiped a brand new gold Nissan Cube. The car screeched around the corner, rumbled out of sight, and left Rooster once again alone with Sue. He slowly turned toward her, surprised at how close she now was.

Sue cocked her head to the side. She looked up and mumbled to herself as if trying to remember something. When she felt Rooster's stare, Sue frowned. "You made me lose my place, you jerk." She opened the big purse and rifled through it until she located a stained and crumpled piece of paper. She dropped the purse to the ground between her feet and smoothed the paper against her stomach. She glanced at Rooster. "It was so perfect, but you had to ruin it, just like you ruined everything else in my life."

Rooster put his hands to his head. *Oh my God. How've I attracted all these deranged lunatics into my life?*

Satisfied with her smoothing efforts, Sue held the paper in front of her face and mouthed words, as if practicing for a stage production. "Do you think you can just walk past me like I'm nothing?" She said quietly to herself. "You piece of garbage. Don't you recognize your own wife? Why don't you try looking at the tattoo on your stomach?" She eyed Rooster and shook her head before she continued to read softly. "Did you really think you could just waltz through the rest of your life without ever seeing me again? Without having to answer for the hell you put me through? Shut your lying mouth." She pantomimed pulling the gun from her purse and theatrically raised it toward Rooster. "You can't sweet talk your way out of this one. I should just pull the trigger right now and put an end to it. How many other women's lives have you destroyed?"

"You're a complete whack-a-doo," Rooster shouted. "You reading from a damn script?" *She's unraveling before my eyes.*

Sue glared and jabbed the gun at him. "You shut up. I just found my place. I been waiting thirteen years for this, and there's no way I'm gonna let you destroy this too." She stole another glance at her paper, cleared her throat, and picked up her performance. "I should just pull the trigger right now and put an end to it. How many other women's lives have you destroyed?"

"You just said that." Rooster sighed. *Maybe I can knock her off script long enough to get away.* "Please put away your paper and let's talk about this," he said softly. "What a crazy time back in Vegas. We were both a little out of control."

"Shut your mouth!" Her face twisted in rage. The gun bounced in her shaking hand. "Your silver tongue can't help you now, Michael."

"Michael?" *Oh yeah.* He remembered the name on his tattoo. *She thinks my name's Michael Something.*

"You can beg all you want."

Beg? "I'm not begging for anything." Rooster grew angry. "You're not even listening to me."

"But you can't give me back the three years I spent in prison." Her little play headed toward the big finish. "You can't give me back the career I shoulda had."

This how it all ends for me? Sensing they neared the climax of her lunatic morality play, Rooster took a final look around. *What's wrong with this stupid neighborhood? Does everyone except blind nonagenarians work second shift?*

"I tell you what, Michael." Sue's voice grew shrill and agitated. "I'll let you live on one condition."

"Oh yeah." He felt stupid for playing along. "What's that?"

Sue lowered the gun as a devilish grin slowly spread across her face. "All you have to do, is give me back everything you stole from me. The money, the years, the career, everything."

Rooster laughed. "Yeah. Like that's ever gonna happen."

She raised her shaking arm, and pointed the wavering pistol at his head. "Exactly."

Rooster's shoulders tensed until they were next to his ears. He held out his hands and turned his body sideways in anticipation of the blast.

It did not come. Sue lowered the gun, disgusted with him. "This is the part where you drop on your knees and beg for your life."

"You belong in a straight jacket!" Rooster's heart fluttered wildly. *This is all too much.* His shirt collar seemed to tighten and his breathing became strained. He wondered how much more his nerves could take.

"On your knees," she commanded. "So we can wrap this up."

Rooster thought his head would explode. Gun or no gun, he had finally had enough of this madness. "Hey! Your big premiere's being cancelled because I'm leaving."

"You can't do that," she shrieked. "You owe me. You stand there and take it."

Rooster considered how much her gun was shaking when she held it up. *Stupid thing's too heavy for her.* Rooster forced a condescending smile. "Don't think you can even hit me from there," he declared with more confidence than he felt. "And even if you can, at least it'll put me out of the misery of, of...." He waved his hands between them. "This!"

"Damn you!" She raised the gun and aimed it at his face.

Rooster was shocked to see her once-shaky hand now steady as the Rock of Gibraltar. Her previously ragged breathing now smooth and regular. "Holy crap." Internal alarm bells clanged. *She's gonna do it!* He turned to run, but before he managed a step, a balding man with wire-rimmed glasses and ridiculously big teeth, raced past him.

"Darling!" The man shouted desperately. "Please don't do it."

Rooster did not wait around to see what happened next. He took off in a full sprint, quickly skidding around the same corner where the big Lincoln had turned just a few minutes before.

FIFTY-FOUR

Sue was dumbfounded as Tyler galloped toward her.

"Darling!" He held up his hands. "Please don't do it."

With a burst of rage, she screeched, "Tyler, what are you doing here? You're ruining everything!" The pistol and paper shook in her hands.

Unaffected, Tyler stopped in front of her, slightly bent, huffing and puffing. "I was afraid of this." He grabbed Sue's wrists. His grip tightened when she tried to pull away. "You coulda been taken away from me for the rest of your life." Tears rolled down his cheeks and dripped into his enormous mouth. "Sweetie, I can't imagine anything more awful than that."

Sue wrenched her wrists free, her expression like that of someone straining to lift a heavy weight. Her eyes stared off, unfocused. Her gun hand dropped to her side. "How'd that go so wrong?" She mumbled.

Concern filled Tyler's eyes. "Darling? You still with me?" He gently patted her cheeks. "Stay with me."

Sue's body lurched with a violent spasm. The gun clattered on the sidewalk as the convulsion knocked it from her grip. The creased and stained script fluttered from her hand. Afraid she would fall to the ground, Tyler pulled Sue into an embrace, which shook her back to reality. She burst into tears. Her whole body quaked as she buried her head in his chest. Tyler stroked her hair. "It's all going to be ok, Sweetie."

She looked up with red, puffy eyes. "You promise?"

"Of course." Tyler brushed a tear from under her eye. "Can we go back to Arizona now, Sweetie? Have you finally got all this outta your system?"

She slowly nodded.

Tyler pulled back and looked into her eyes. "Hopefully they'll just extend your probation."

Sue cocked her head. "What?"

"For illegally possessing a firearm while on probation. I'll have to report it. I'm an officer of the court you know."

Sue stared at him in disbelief.

"I could lose my job. They could disbar me, Sweetie. Where would we be if that happened?"

She sighed heavily and turned away.

Tyler pulled her to him and Sue flopped into his arms. "Don't worry, honey," he whispered in her ear. "I think we can keep you from being sent back to the pen."

Panic filled Sue's eyes. "The pen?"

"I'm thinking an insanity defense is our best bet."

Sue stared at him through blinking eyes, her mouth agape. "Insanity?"

Tyler flashed a knowing smile. "Of course. There's no doubt you're a total crazy-pants, Honey. Won't have any trouble convincing the court of that. I just have to figure out how to keep them from putting you in a sanitarium."

FIFTY-FIVE

Rooster finally stopped running just off the square. Hunched over, hands on his knees, he sucked wind, his heart pounded, and his mind messed with him. He expected to see that crazy woman, or the Tonys, or the Chairman. *That all of them? Have I forgotten someone? How many lunatics after me anyway?* He attempted to catalog the incredibly long list of people he had wronged because of alcohol. *They all coming to get me?* He shuddered at the thought. He faintly heard the hoopla of a big crowd. He was in no mindset to face them or the TV cameras. *Gotta get my head straight.*

He recalled the words of Diamond Dan Martin. "When you walk into that meeting, or take that sales call, you're onstage. Anything happening in your personal life must be put aside. When Elizabeth Taylor's in front of the camera, you think anyone knows she's hooked on pills and booze, or she's about to get her seventeenth divorce? Of course not. She's a pro. If you're going to win, you have to be the same way. I don't care if your dog just died, or a horde of ancient ninja warriors has taken a blood oath against your life. You must forget all that and give total focus to your performance."

Rooster smiled at the irony of Diamond Dan's advice in light of Sue's psycho scripted attack, and Big Tony's "collections monologue". *They trained by Diamond Dan, too? Sally was certainly focused completely on her performance.* Rooster pictured Big Tony and Sue, seated alongside him, in Diamond Dan's six-hour "How to win at Selling" class. The ridiculousness of it made him laugh out loud, which eased his nerves and helped him focus on his upcoming interview. He grabbed his phone. *How much time my nutso Vegas wife cost me?*

5:35 p.m. *Supposed to meet Cassandra at 5:30.* "Damn it." He broke into a fast trot.

As the square came into view, Rooster took in the carnival atmosphere. The news van was parked on the sidewalk, in front of the courthouse. A long pole rose from its roof into the sky. Attached to the top of the building was a huge banner with the Channel 3 logo and the words, "Welcome to Tuesdays Around Town". There were hundreds, maybe thousands, of people everywhere. Most stood or lazily milled around. Some had set up lawn chairs and tables, and a few had even spread out picnic blankets on the ground. There had to be at least two kids for each adult. He was amazed at the sheer volume of them.

At the top of the courthouse's front steps stood loudspeakers with enormous bunches of balloons tied to them. Several Channel 3 personalities stood near the big doors. They held microphones and bantered with the crowd. Behind them was some poor soul, forced to wear a cartoonish mascot-style monkey outfit with a preposterously oversized head. Despite the fact it was ninety degrees without a cloud in the sky, the costume included a yellow rain slicker and a wide brimmed hat with "Stormy" written on the band. With an umbrella in hand, the weather monkey ran and jumped behind the other TV people. Something about Stormy was slightly off, Rooster thought. The movements were spastic, bordering on manic. *Maybe he's having a seizure from the humidity.* Rooster was amazed at the scene. *Whoever's in that getup is gonna pass out from heat exhaustion, or burst into flames. If he drops dead, at least the kids'll have something to remember.*

The time for rubbernecking over, Rooster hurried through the crowd to the side door of the courthouse. He fully expected Cassandra to be frantic with him ten minutes late.

A mousy little dude with over-processed brown hair, in a too-big blue suit, stood on the stairs and blocked the door. Even perched two steps above Rooster, they were eye-to-eye. "I'm sorry," he said in a squeaky voice. "The courthouse is closed until the remote broadcast's over."

Unaware how adrenaline hyped he still was, Rooster nearly shoved him aside. *This wimp ain't stopping anyone.* But something inside told him that was a bad idea. He reined in his aggressiveness. *I've had enough drama for one day.* "I'm Rooster Michaels." He tried to sound humble. "Cassandra Nolan's supposed to interview me."

The little guy's face lit up with a broad smile. "The Lamborghini Leaper! Fantastic. Everyone's waiting on you." He stepped aside. "Please go on in."

Once his eyes adjusted to the dark hallway, Rooster saw Cassandra at the end of the room in a tall director's chair. Portable lights on big tripod stands pointed at her as a woman applied makeup. She climbed out of the chair when Rooster approached. She looked amazing, the stylish kelly green suit brought out the red in her hair.

"Good, you're here," she said with an easy smile, her makeup perfect. "I was a little concerned you wouldn't have time for Janet to work on your face." She flipped her thumb toward the lights. "Better get in that chair. Otherwise you'll look like a ghost on TV."

Rooster obeyed, but he was disappointed. He analyzed his feelings. *Am I frustrated because she seemed totally unfazed about how late I am? Or was it that I wanted her to be more excited to see me?* Cassandra stood next to the chair and reviewed the schedule of events. The makeup artist slipped a noisy tissue paper bib into his collar and applied heavy powder over his face with a big fluffy brush.

Cassandra checked her watch. "Only have a few minutes left. We'll step outside and do the interview at the top of the steps. Brian Dawson, Bill Champion, and Stormy the Weather Monkey will be up there with us. You know all them, right?"

Rooster nodded, but did not really listen. As he peered out the front door windows, he thought he saw out in the crowd a big guy in a red track suit with white stripes. *Was that Tony and his goofball son?* Before he could focus in, either Brian Dawson or Bill Champion, they both looked the same to him, drifted past the window and blocked Rooster's view. Rooster pulled in a long breath and tried to calm himself. *Just being paranoid. Of course, there's good reason to be paranoid with all these crazy people chasing me. If someone's really after you, does that mean you're not actually paranoid?* He drifted off, his head slowly nodding down, but Janet's fingers reached under his chin and gently lifted his face up.

His eyes raised, Rooster had the distinct sensation he was being watched. He turned toward the big doors, shocked to see the front of Stormy's giant head in the window, the big creepy smile reminiscent of *Killer Klowns from Outer Space*. The movie, which Rooster saw in high school, kept him awake for weeks. *That monkey staring at me?* Closing his eyes, he refused to believe it was possible. When he opened them, the mascot was gone. *Did I actually see that? Or just imagine it? I'm really losing it. Already have enough real people after me without adding a ridiculous cartoon monkey.* He shook his head, but Janet grabbed his chin.

"Hold still," she ordered.

Rooster pushed aside thoughts of macabre clowns and goofy monkeys. He glanced sideways at Cassandra, who continued to prattle. *What would she do if she knew I have no clue what she's saying.* He thought about Tony and his stomach churned. *So what if Tony's out there? What's he gonna do in front of this crowd? Nothing. He's mean and surly, but he's not crazy. Now Sue's completely off her rocker. What if she shows up?* He pictured his unhinged future ex-wife, on the roof of a building raining bullets on the unwitting crowd with a sniper rifle.

As he slowly returned to reality, Rooster could almost hear the loud clack as Sue worked the bolt action to chamber the next shell. *Man, that sounded real.* The noise clattered again, this time right next to his ear. Panicked, Rooster forgot he was in the tall director's chair, his mind totally focused on getting away from the sound. He lurched to the side, tipped over, and crashed to the floor, the chair reduced to a heap of twisted wood and canvass.

As Rooster lay tangled in the debris, Cassandra and Janet the makeup artist gawked in wide-eyed, open-mouthed horror.

"What happened?" Rooster asked, somewhat dazed.

"Oh my God." Cassandra searched Janet's eyes for confirmation of what they had just witnessed. Janet said nothing, but raised her hand to cover her gaping mouth.

"I... I... ah..." Cassandra stammered. "You... ahh... You drifted off." Her composure slowly returned. "You drifted off, so I snapped my fingers next to your ear. When you didn't do anything, I snapped again. You made an awful little squeal, and dumped the whole chair on the floor."

"Oh." Rooster felt dimwitted for his lack of a more intelligent response. *These women think I'm a total whack job.* He wanted to slink away, but the remains of the chair were twisted around his body like a bear trap.

Concern creased Janet's brow. "You a veteran? Something bad happen to you, ahh, over there?"

"No." With difficulty, Rooster extricated himself from the wrecked chair. "I been under a lot of stress. Guess I'm a little jumpy." He climbed to his feet and brushed off his clothes.

They all stared at each other for a few awkward seconds. Rooster saw real fear in Cassandra's beautiful blue eyes. *She thinks I'm gonna flip out on live TV.* He tried to sound reassuring. "I'm ok now. Really."

The courthouse door swung open and a man stuck his head inside. "Hey Cassie. C'mon. We need to get ready. Your tease is on in less than two minutes."

Cassandra stared at Rooster for a long second, then acknowledged the man. "Thanks, Dennis. We're coming." She snatched the tissue paper bib from Rooster's collar and handed it to Janet. She grabbed his arm with much more force than he imagined such a small woman could muster and yanked him toward the exit. "Just relax. All of this'll be over before you know it." She added under her breath, "Hopefully before something else crazy happens."

Rooster began to protest, but before he could say anything, Cassandra had pulled him out onto the courthouse steps. The crowd roared in anticipation. He lifted his arm to shield his eyes from the bright sunlight and surveyed the crowd, worried Sue or the Tonys were among them. From the corner of his eye, he noticed Stormy the Weather Monkey shuffling around behind them.

With a reassuring hand on his shoulder, Cassandra moved her mouth close to his ear. Rooster breathed in deeply. Her perfume calmed him. She smelled awesome, a slight floral scent intermingled with vanilla and almond aromas.

"Just stand next to me and smile," she said in a hushed voice.

God, she has a sexy whisper.

"All I'm doing is leading off the newscast with a live shot, teasing the viewers about your interview later in the show. You good with that?"

Rooster nodded. *She thinks I'm about to come unglued. She's treating me like some fragile five-year-old.* Cassandra now held her microphone with the Channel 3 logo displayed. He wondered what material the big channel number display block was made from. *Wood? Plastic? Cardboard? Looks so crisp and perfect.* He wanted to reach out and touch it. Instead, he forced himself to face the camera. The man who operated it made hand signals for Cassandra's benefit.

She leaned toward Rooster and commanded, "Look at the camera and smile. We're on in three seconds."

Rooster locked his eyes on the camera lens and twisted his face into an uncomfortable, toothy grin.

Cassandra flipped her long Auburn hair over her shoulder just before the man pointed at her. A small light on top of the camera glowed red. "I'm Cassandra Nolan, standing here with the fabled Lamborghini Leaper," she said, her voice filled with excitement. "Today the Channel 3 Tuesdays Around Town Caravan stops in Murfreesboro. In just a few minutes, we're going to introduce him to you, and we'll find out what was going through his mind when he made the death-defying jump that has taken the Internet by storm."

The cameraman drew his hand across his throat. "And we're out."

Rooster began to ask Cassandra how much longer until the actual interview. Before he could turn his head, the world suddenly spun out of control. As he tumbled down the courthouse stairs, all he heard were his elbows and knees cracking against the hard steps and his own grunts and oofs each time some body part slammed on concrete. A loud whooshing noise developed in his ears, as if he were on a plane at high altitude.

Cassandra shrieked in horror at the same moment his ears unplugged with a loud pop. With a heavy thud, he landed flat on his back at the bottom of the stairs, all breath driven from his lungs. His hearing now unfettered, Rooster became aware of the shouts and screams. Confused, he began to lift his head, but something big and yellow slammed into his face and knocked his head hard into the pavement.

Somehow Cassandra's voice cut through the bedlam. "Dennis, you getting this?" Children screamed and cried. People ran and yelled.

Rooster's head ached. The yellow mass engulfed him. He was confused. His mind refused to work properly. Something rubbery pushed against his face. He could not breathe. A heavy weight pressed down on him. *Tony figure out a way to get to me?* Muffled mumbles emanated from inside the yellow mass. Everyone shouted at once. Arms pinned under his back, Rooster struggled against whatever had attacked him. His skin scraped against the ground. Something fluffy slapped at him. It reminded him of pillow fights at summer camp. *Why can't I focus?*

A woman screamed, "It's Stormy!" A man's deep southern drawl shouted, "The dad gum monkey's gone crazy." A child's voice wailed, "Someone help him! That man's gonna hurt Stormy!"

After a struggle, Rooster managed to pull his arms free and wrap the yellow load in a bear hug. He rotated onto his side and threw the mass off his body. He thought his eyes had lied to him when he saw the big mascot costume roll away. *No. It couldn't be.* His attacker was

Stormy the Weather Monkey? *Never trusted that damn monkey.*

The mascot scrambled to his feet and prepared for another attack. The ridiculously gigantic monkey head smiled gleefully. Already battered and bruised, Rooster doubted he could fight him off again. His brain, still a little mushy from its slam into the sidewalk, could not quite piece together what had made the Weather Monkey so enraged. *Maybe the chair I broke was his.* The mascot lunged. Rooster closed his eyes and braced for contact. It never came.

Rooster opened his eyes to see Buddy gripping Stormy by the scruff of the neck like a prize fish. *What's Buddy doing here?*

"Hey, boy," the unmistakable Foghorn Leghorn voice boomed from above him. "Pick yourself up off the ground."

"Boy, am I glad to see you!" Rooster exclaimed.

Buddy flashed his megawatt smile. "Looked like you could use a little help."

The little mousey side door guard in the too-big suit appeared behind Buddy. "Please put Stormy down."

"Sure thing." Buddy laughed and threw the mascot hard to the ground. The giant monkey head tumbled off and rolled away.

"They killed Stormy," shrieked a little girl, which prompted a fresh round of children's cries and wails.

Rooster's jaw dropped when he saw the headless monkey. He pointed in amazement. "It's him." *This guy's like Jason from Friday the 13th. No matter where I go, I can't escape him.*

"The girls went back to Chicago," the Chairman snarled from inside the costume. "But I'll never let you get away with..."

"Shut your stinkin' mouth!" The mousey guy pressed a black plastic box against the Chairman's neck. A loud crack of electric current pulsed from the taser. The Chairman stopped mid-sentence as his head snapped awkwardly. His eyes bugged out and rolled back in his head as he passed out.

"That'll teach you to hijack a beloved character like Stormy the Weather Monkey," the guy declared.

Rooster stared at Buddy. "That's the crazy homeless guy who

attacked and kidnapped me."

Buddy leaned over to inspect the unconscious man. "I declare. This here fella looks like the dogs been keepin' him under the porch."

Rooster climbed painfully to his feet. "Buddy, I don't know what that means."

Buddy grinned knowingly. "You just think on it a spell, son. It'll come to you."

Rooster sighed and straightened his clothes. The whole throng of people stared at him, which made him incredibly uncomfortable. He needed to escape. He turned to leave and nearly walked face-first into a camera. Not a big TV news camera, it was more like the one used by the college student who had filmed his Lamborghini leap. The recording device dropped down and Rooster was amazed to see the same kid from the jump.

"Dude," the young man exclaimed. "That was epic. Got the whole thing. You getting tackled by the monkey. The monkey getting tased. This one's better than the jumping video. I guarantee it's going viral."

"You're kidding," Rooster said.

"No I'm not. Dude, can I just start following you around all the time?"

FIFTY-SIX

Even as it quickly dwindled, the crowd remained abuzz with excitement from Stormy's crazed attack. Cassandra interviewed a group of children, the scene expertly framed in the camera viewfinder with the empty monkey costume artfully splayed in the background like a big game carcass. The police had long ago extracted the Chairman from the outfit and shipped him off to the Vanderbilt Medical Center for a psychological evaluation.

Rooster was scraped and bruised. His body ached and his head pounded. *What else could happen today? Are the fates testing my will?* He thought about bourbon, mostly thankful there was not a bottle within easy reach. Of course, everything he had experienced was the direct result of bourbon. And beer. And tequila. And every other kind of alcohol. From gambling debts, to his lunatic wife, to the ridiculous weather monkey attack, he had no one to blame but himself. He saw that clearly now.

In the rational corner of his brain, Rooster was determined to end the chaos and destruction once and for all. However, so complete was his physical and mental exhaustion, he doubted he could resist any temptation at that moment. Rooster dropped his chin to his chest and sighed. A heavy arm draped around his shoulder. He glanced over to see Buddy.

"Son," Buddy drawled, "you had quite the day." He pointed at a storefront across the square. "Whatcha say we mosey right on over there to Liquid Smoke? I'll buy you a bourbon and a cigar so you can clear your head?"

Rooster stared blankly. That offer sounded so enticing, it hurt. Even though he knew a single sip would surely send him spinning out of control, he desired it with all of his being. He longed for a drink down to the very depths of his soul. Rooster licked his lips. He could almost taste the sharp oaky flavor of the Eagle Rare he knew he would drink if he set foot in that bar. He closed his eyes. The emotional battle raged within.

"You alright, boy?" There was real concern in Buddy's voice. "You're looking a little green around the gills."

Rooster gulped at the air, a drowning man who had just broke the water's surface. He understood an important decision had been placed before him. He thought about the Colonel Sanders-looking pastor and his Sunday sermon. "You have to make the decision to change," the minister had said. "Then you have to ask God to help you." Rooster recalled how the preacher's words had made him wonder if he was even capable of wise choices. *This is it.* This was that defining moment, when standing strong might finally change his life. He knew all too well the high cost of diving back into the bottle, but the siren song of his inner demons seemed so attractive.

He considered that for a moment. *Why do I prefer impairment to sober reality? What am I hiding from? Am I really so afraid my life will seem pathetic without a drink in my hand? Hell, my life IS pathetic BECAUSE of the drink constantly in my hand.*

Buddy gripped Rooster's shoulders and gently shook him. "Son, how hard you hit your head? Getting worried about you."

Rooster blinked as he drifted back to reality. He appreciated Buddy more than he had ever realized. The man was in his corner no matter what, and without judgment, but it seemed as if booze and partying were the cornerstones of their friendship. *Can it survive without constant alcohol lubrication?* He had to find out. *Time to stand up and be a man. Time to take some responsibility for my life and my future.* "Uhh,

Buddy?" Rooster fixed his gaze on the big man's yellow t-shirt, which featured a cartoon duck wearing water wings and a snorkel, surrounded by the words, 'Amateur Scuba Instructor'. *Where does he get these shirts?* "I decided I can't drink anymore."

When there was no response, Rooster glanced up to witness something he had never experienced, something he had actually assumed was impossible. Buddy was slack-jawed and speechless. Feeling the need to break the uncomfortable silence, Rooster began to talk, even though he had no clue what to say. "It's just that..."

Halfway through Rooster's awkward explanation, Buddy regained his bearings. He slapped his friend hard on the back as his face lit up with a bright-white Cheshire Cat grin. "Well butter my butt and call me a biscuit," he roared with a hearty chuckle. "Good for you, son. Good for you."

Relief washed over Rooster. "You're not disappointed?"

"Disappointed? Hell no. Why in tarnation would I be disappointed?"

"I don't know. Because it seems like everything we do together revolves around alcohol."

Buddy slapped his shoulder. Rooster winced. After the tumble down the stairs and his battle with the monkey, intense soreness had begun to set into his muscles and bones.

"It don't have to be all about drinking," Buddy reassured. "We'll find something else. You play golf?"

Rooster smiled. "Sure."

"Then we'll tear up the links."

Rooster grinned. "Just be sure you don't lick your golf balls."

"What's that?"

"Nothing. Just something my mother says."

Buddy cocked an eyebrow. "What's that supposed to mean?"

Rooster slapped Buddy hard on the back. "You just think about it awhile, Buddy. It'll come to you."

FIFTY-SEVEN

Rooster was wiped when he finally headed for home. Despite aches and pains, he was in a good place mentally and emotionally following his conversation with Buddy. It reassured him to know his best friend had his back no matter what. If Buddy accepted him alcohol-free, there was no reason to believe everyone else would not as well. He started to believe he could do this.

His mind wandered as he walked. *Can't wait to get home and have an ice cold... Damn. No more ice cold beers for me.* He eyed the dry cleaner's drive-thru shortcut. The last thing he wanted to do was walk to the end of the block, if it was not necessary. *What if the Tonys are hanging around waiting for me to cut through?* He stopped before the alley and surveyed the area. The news van and a police car were still parked in front of the courthouse. *Are those New Jersey thugs brazen enough to jump me a few hundred yards from the cops?*

"Surely they wouldn't expect me to cut through there again." Ultimately, his physical exhaustion made the decision for him. He turned into the alley, his senses on high alert. *Why didn't I take Buddy's offer for a ride home? The walk'll clear my head, I told him. What a moronic move that was. Sure wasn't thinking about the Tonys when I said that, and who knows if that lunatic Sue's still searching for me? At least the Chairman's safely tucked away at the loony bin. If I never see that crazy buffoon again, it'll be too soon.*

His heart raced. Halfway through the drive-thru, he risked a glance back. His breathing calmed when he saw no one. *Almost there.* His lips curled into a cautious smile. When he turned back around, his heart sank and his stomach churned. A huge red figure appeared at the end of the alley. Dressed in a fire engine red track suit with white stripes, Big Tony laughed, his jowls bouncing and his big belly shaking like a bowl of Jello atop a paint mixer. *I'm such an idiot.* His stupid decision to save a few steps had boxed Rooster in an area he could not easily escape.

"What you got to say now, smart guy?" Tony asked.

Rooster made a show of looking Tony up and down before he cracked, "Hey Kool Aid!"

A scowl filled Tony's confused face. "What's that supposed to mean, you dirty anchovy-eating goat licker?"

Rooster opened his mouth to answer, but another voice from behind spoke up first.

"He was saying you look like that big red pitcher guy in the Kool Aid commercials," Little Tony snickered. "You know, he runs through the wall when someone yells, 'Hey Kool Aid'."

Big Tony jumped up and down. "Enough, dummkopf. For the love of Ernest Borgnine's fifth wife, you're not helping here."

"I'm sorry, Big Guy," Little Tony apologized.

The father ignored his son and faced Rooster. "So you think I look like some giant cartoon drink guy? That right?"

Rooster rolled his eyes. "That or Santa Claus," he blurted without thinking. "Red's just not a very slimming color, Tony."

"Oh, is that so? Guess that explains everything. You think I'm Santa Claus and the hundred large you owe me was some kinda Christmas present." He cackled and shifted his gaze to the man behind Rooster. "You think this guy's dumb enough to believe that money was some kinda Christmas present?"

Little Tony laughed as if it was the funniest thing he ever heard. "Yeah, Pop. He looks pretty dumb to me."

Rooster glanced at the younger Ferrentino. A small straw fedora was perched atop of his black curly hair. Two huge pimples, one on his nose and the other on his forehead, had developed since Rooster had last seen him.

He pointed at Little Tony's nose. "Who's your friend?"

"Shut the hell up," Little Tony exploded. "You think you're a big comedian now, but if you don't shut your pie hole, we'll shut it for you."

Rooster was amazed at how easy it was to push their buttons. *If I'm going down, I'm going down swinging. Keep them agitated and discombobulated and Big Tony's intestinal problems could save me. Or maybe I can goad them into a mistake that'll buy me time to escape. How far can I push before they snap? One way to find out.* He addressed Big Tony. "Hey, what happened to your boy? Looks like his face caught fire and someone put it out with a pitchfork."

"I've heard just about enough of this!" Little Tony moved within a foot of Rooster. "Don't have to take this crap from the likes of you."

Rooster could not suppress a smile. His plan was perfect so far. Little Tony had already lost his cool completely. Rooster stole a glance at Big Tony, his hands clapped against his cheeks in exasperation. Rooster faced the son and began to formulate his next verbal assault. As he sized up the young man, Rooster realized how big and physically intimidating he appeared up close. Rooster drew in a deep breath.

His face beet red with rage, Little Tony muttered an unintelligible diatribe to himself. Rooster strained to hear. He seemed to say something about a "drunk ass hoser and a hawk." *Hoser?* Rooster thought. *Isn't that Canadian? Thought these guys were from Jersey.* None of it made sense. As Rooster puzzled over his inane mumbling, Little Tony jammed his hand into the front pocket of his big shorts and pulled out a gun. Rooster's eyes widened and his blood ran cold. *Uh oh.* His heart skipped a couple beats. *Pushed him too far. The kid's within an arm's length. Even Stevie Wonder could nail the shot from that range.*

Big Tony shouted and jumped up and down, but Rooster did

not hear a word. *This big goofy kid gonna blow my brains out?* Images of all he had been through the past twelve days flew through Rooster's brain, a movie on fast forward. The cow pasture. The Lamborghini. Sandy Wilson. Dottie Charles. Marcie's party. Jimmy Robinson. Throwing all his booze away. The first encounter with the Tonys. His crazy wife and the dude with the ridiculously giant mouth who kept her from shooting him. The Chairman. Cassandra Nolan. Stormy the Weather Monkey's attack.

Little Tony jabbed the weapon at him. Rooster twisted away, desperate to keep the barrel from lining up with his body. *C'mon God. Don't tell me you brought me through everything just to let me get blown away in an alley. Would you really do me that way?*

Little Tony turned his attention to his father. He stabbed the gun at the old man and made an impassioned speech. Big Tony bobbed and weaved his big frame out of the line of fire.

Rooster looked up at the sky. Whether or not God had actually heard him, this was a very fortunate development. Rooster reconsidered the wisdom of his plan to fluster the Tonys. He was nearly out of time. He had certainly thrown them both into a tizzy, but if he did not make a move soon, he might meet his demise right here next to the dry cleaners. He glanced at the "Closed" sign on the door. *Why is this place never open?*

Rooster looked from father to son and made some quick distance calculations. Little Tony continued to wave the pistol like a conductor's baton as he pled his case to the old man. The moment he decided how to proceed, Rooster sprung into action. His haste robbed him of any chance to really consider how poorly constructed the whole desperate plan really was.

He lunged at Little Tony and caught him totally by surprise. Rooster shoved the big man hard in the chest. Little Tony tumbled backward in a Chevy Chase pratfall. Rooster's entire half-baked plan depended upon the young Ferrentino being too uncoordinated to stop his fall and too unathletic to recover fast enough to get off a clean shot. Fully aware he was on borrowed time, Rooster did not wait to see Little Tony hit the ground before he launched himself at the old man. A shot rang out behind him. Either his adrenaline pumped so hard he did not feel the bullet, or the kid had missed. Already committed to his attack on the big guy, Rooster raced forward and offered up a silent prayer the next gunshot would not kill him.

The bookie's eyes grew large. He defensively held out his hands as Rooster executed a classic tackle of the beefy man. Channeling his inner linebacker, Rooster drove his shoulder into Big Tony's pillow-soft midsection. Rooster could only hear the blood rush to his head and the furious beat of his own heart as Big Tony slammed into the ground with Rooster on top. Afraid he had run out of time, Rooster quickly rolled off Tony and jumped to his feet. Little Tony shouted something. Without a backwards glance, Rooster took off in a mad sprint.

When Big Tony called out, "No! Don't shoot," Rooster braced himself for the bullet that might kill him.

Another gunshot rang out, followed by an agonized scream.

FIFTY-EIGHT

Totally focused on the old man, Little Tony had completely lost track of Sinclair. He looked just in time to see Sinclair lunge at him with outstretched hands. Little Tony slipped his finger inside the trigger guard and lowered his shooting arm, but he was too late. Sinclair's hands slammed into his chest with surprising strength and he toppled backwards. His shoulders hit first. The impact whipsawed his gun hand hard into the blacktop. He heard the weapon fire loud near his head, but he never felt his finger pull the trigger. The wind knocked out of him, Little Tony struggled into a sitting position just in time to see Sinclair lay out the old man like a tackling dummy.

He's gonna kill my dad. A tsunami of rage and fear billowed up in him. He shouted through ragged breaths, "Pop!" *Time to put an end to Sinclair and his disrespectful nonsense.* No sooner had the pair of men smashed into the pavement, than Sinclair was back on his feet, prepared to take flight. Little Tony raised the gun. "I'll get him."

With much effort, Big Tony had rolled onto his side so he could see his son. His eyes were huge in his overtaxed purple face. He wheezed and tried to speak. Little Tony ignored the old man and pointed the pistol in the general direction of the fleeing man. He closed his eyes and jerked at the trigger with his finger. The force of the blast knocked him onto his back and made his ears ring.

Then the screams began.

FIFTY-NINE

Big Tony grimaced. His boy had totally lost his cool and now everything was more complicated than it had to be. *How'd I raise such a loose cannon? If that dummkopf would just stay calm for a couple minutes, we could wrap this up and head back to New Jersey.* Man, did he ever want to get home to his padded toilet seat. Hard plastic pressed against his oversized posterior for hours at a time had taken its toll. The horrible chafing was worse than the Irritable Bowel Syndrome itself.

Behind Sinclair, Little Tony stamped his feet and waved his arms like a big baboon and muttered something about "pink glass Hoosiers." *What's Stella's idiot son carrying on about? Sinclair from Indiana?* When Little Tony pulled the gun out of his big shorts, Big Tony saw everything he had ever worked for on the brink of oblivion. *That stupid kid's gonna whack someone and get us both sent up to the big house.*

"Put that thing away, you swamp-water drinking monkey lover!" *This moron's gonna ruin me. Why'd I let Stella talk me into bringing him here? For the love of Fatty Arbuckle's straw hat, the cops are right down the street.* "I told you to leave that thing locked in the glove compartment." Big Tony was careful not to mention the gun out loud. *Can't afford to draw extra attention.* "What you doing with that? Jumpin' Jehoshaphat on a popsicle stick, there's cops around the corner."

Little Tony jabbed the weapon at Davis Sinclair, who jerked and twisted like one of those light in the loafers dance stars, frantic to keep away from the gun's business end. *Sinclair's no threat. Look at the fear in his body language. This scungilli-muncher son of mine is gonna push him too far.* Big Tony knew the situation could get dangerous quickly. Desperate people do desperate things they normally would never dream of attempting. When someone was driven past their breaking point, anything was possible. Sadly it did not have to be this way. Big Tony shook his head. *This whole thing coulda been a nice walk in the park.*

As the son's voice grew more shrill, the old man only heard a string of angry sounds, like the boy spoke a foreign language. Big Tony snapped to attention when the kid stabbed the gun toward him. "Hey!" He bobbed and weaved his big frame out of the gun's firing line. *This kid really my own flesh and blood? I'm not the sharpest crayon in the box, but I never done anything this idiotic.* "Watch where you point that thing!"

Little Tony lifted the barrel straight up. *At least that got through his thick skull. How'm I ever gonna leave the business to a numbskull like this?* Big Tony rubbed his eyes and tried to ignore his son's rambling. *What about Stella's nephew Donnie? That kid's got a good head on his shoulders. Maybe I could bring him in.*

"This guy's a smalltime deadbeat," Little Tony barked. "He don't deserve the respect you're showing him."

Big Tony rolled his eyes. *This ostrich-licker's seen too many mobster movies. No one cares about respect. It's all about getting paid. People who worry more about respect than money, do stupid, emotional things. Those kind of people end up broke and in jail. Or dead.* He sighed and looked down at his big red belly. Not a single principle he had used to build his business had rubbed off on his son.

The crack of the gun startled him. When he looked up, Big Tony saw nothing but Sinclair lunging. He instinctively held out his hands just as Sinclair jammed his shoulder into his belly. A guttural "Oof," rushed out involuntarily as all the air was driven from Big Tony's lungs. They tumbled together to the pavement and Tony was filled with fear. He had heard a gunshot, yet Sinclair was on top of him. *Did he kill my son? Did Little Tony fire and miss? Oh God. Don't take my boy.* No sooner had they hit the ground than Sinclair rolled off and gathered himself to run.

"Pop!" The boy's fearful shout was music to Big Tony's ears. *My boy's alive. What about the gunshot?* With herculean effort, Big Tony managed to roll onto his side. He could see the kid on his butt pointing the gun in his general direction.

"I'll get him," Little Tony yelled.

In his awkward half laying, half sitting position, Big Tony could barely breathe. His idiot son was about to fire his weapon. He sucked in a frazzled breath. "No!" Big Tony sputtered. "Don't shoot." A gunshot rang out. There was a flash of white light. Big Tony flopped onto his back. Then he realized he was screaming.

My dingbat salad-eating son just shot me in the foot. He had never experienced such pain. His toes were on fire. He twisted his body to examine the damage, but he was as immobile as a turtle on its back. When he lifted his neck to peer at his foot, all he saw was his own oversized torso. He floundered like a fish on the shore until he ran out of breath and finally had to lay down. His giant chest heaved from the exertion and pain.

A moment later, Little Tony loomed over him, concern in his face. He said something, but it all sounded like gibberish. Big Tony did not even have enough strength to scold the idiot. He blinked and sucked in air. The boy grew fuzzy. By the time he heard the police siren close in, Big Tony had already begun to lose consciousness.

SIXTY

There was no way the Tonys could catch him, but Rooster still ran until he was several blocks removed from the confrontation. He stopped to catch his breath and finally risked a glance back.

Weren't there two gunshots and then screaming? Those two goons somehow manage to shoot each other? That even possible? He checked his body for blood or injuries. Amazingly, he had escaped without a scratch. *Maybe God IS looking out for me.*

A police cruiser with blaring lights and siren raced past. When it turned into the drive-thru, Rooster grinned.

He began to whistle *I'll Fly Away* as he turned the corner and strolled toward home.

SIXTY-ONE
Wednesday, May 25th

As he pulled the door closed, Rooster smiled, never so satisfied to hear the click of an engaged lock. No more wild animals invading at odd hours. No more sad Mexican blanket. It seemed like forever since he last had a door on his house. He thought about his Maserati and the wild lifestyle he had enjoyed decades ago. He could not suppress amazement at the joy a simple door could provide after a period of depravation. *Don't they say the simple things in life are the best?*

A canine head poked through the doggie entrance built into bottom of Rooster's door. Waylon had taken to his new point of access quickly, and now easily came and went as he pleased. Rooster patted his head. "You watch the place, Waylon. I'll be back in a few hours."

Waylon pulled his body through the opening and walked with Rooster to the curb. Rooster scratched Waylon behind the ears. "Keep the skunks out." Rooster headed up the street. Waylon watched him for a few seconds and then bounded through his door.

As Rooster walked toward the Cumberland Baptist Church, his mind spun. *Has it really been just thirteen days since I lost my front door?* It seemed a lifetime ago. So much had changed. Now his rent was current and his door back in place.

It had been infinitely more difficult than he could ever have imagined to turn his back on the alcohol. Not an hour had gone by when he did not long for bourbon or a cold beer. It was a mighty struggle. There had been instances when he white knuckled his way from one minute to the next, wondering how he could ever live without booze. However, he was in a good place today. He felt hopeful. He had money in his pocket, the Chairman and the Tonys were safely locked away, and he actually looked forward to the small group meeting with his new friends.

His phone chirped. Rooster retrieved the device. "Hello."

"Sonny, is that you?"

"No Mom, this is DB Cooper, and I'm finally ready to tell the world where I hid the money."

"Who knows?" She whined. "For all I know you could be him. It seems I don't know anything about you anymore."

"Whoa. Slow down, Mom. What's this all about?"

"First you were jumping cars on the computer like some circus tumbler, then you can't remember basic facts about your childhood, and now I find out you're wrestling monkeys."

"Wrestling monkeys?" He laughed. "Where'd you get that?"

"Gertrude Longfellow from my sewing club. Her grandson saw something on the computer about you wrestling a monkey. Of course, after the last time when you were hurtling yourself over speeding vehicles, I was afraid to dispute her."

Rooster looked to the sky. *This Gertrude Longfellow's grandkid is becoming a big pain.* Rooster grimaced. *Who knows what I've done while drunk that's been caught on tape?* "What's the deal?" Rooster was a afraid to hear more. "This kid stalking me? Why's he so interested in what I'm doing?"

"So it is true!"

"What's true?"

"The monkey wrestling. You're making me the laughing stock of the sewing club. I thought no one could ever top Bertha Everhart's daughter Colleen getting mixed up with those gypsy con artists who went around scamming old people into buying basement waterproofing."

"What? Waterproofing? Who's Bertha Everhart?"

"C'mon, Sonny. You know Mrs. Everhart. When you were a baby she used to bring Colleen over the house every Thursday."

"When I was a baby?"

"I remember it like yesterday. I'd put you in the Nip-n-Nap and Colleen would sleep in your crib..."

"Oh yeah," Rooster interrupted with mock enthusiasm. "It's all coming back to me now. I used to wait until you and Mrs. Everhart got engrossed in your conversation. That's when I'd sneak over to the crib so Colleen and I could get high on gin-spiked Similac and rub baby powder all over each other."

"Ok, Mr. Smarty Pants. That's enough."

"Fine," Rooster chuckled. "What is it you want, Mom?"

"Why you wrestling monkeys? What's next? Boxing kangaroos?"

Rooster suddenly remembered the incident on the square. "You talking about Stormy the Weather Monkey?" *Please let this be about that, instead of some embarrassing exhibition of drunken stupidity.*

"Stormy? What's a weather monkey?"

"He's the mascot for Channel 3 in Nashville. And I wasn't wrestling him. He attacked me."

"Oh my word. The TV stations down there have crazy monkeys they let run wild? What kind of backwards place you living in?"

"No, Mom," Rooster laughed. "It wasn't a real monkey. It was a guy in a monkey costume."

"Oh Sonny. You always had a fertile imagination. Who would put on a monkey outfit to attack you? That's just ridiculous."

Rooster considered her response and smiled to himself. The Stormy situation was nothing compared to some of the preposterous predicaments he had gotten into with his boozing.

She deserves to know, the little voice in his head told him. *It's time to come clean with her.*

Rooster stared straight ahead. His stomach churned.

Do it! The voice demanded.

Rooster swallowed hard. "Mom, I got something to tell you."

"Is this real, or more of your fantastic stories?"

He ignored her question. "I've given up drinking."

"You've got to drink! If you don't drink, you'll die. What kind of crazy diet have you gotten mixed up with now?"

Rooster shook his head. "Alcohol, Mom. I quit drinking alcohol."

"So what? Why would I care about that?"

"I'm an alcoholic. My life's a mess because of drinking."

"You're not an alcoholic."

He was taken aback by her response. "I'm not going to argue with you, Mom, but I am. Don't you remember when I was a teenager and got arrested for underage drinking?"

"You were just unlucky."

"Four times! I was arrested four times."

"But you promised me those were the only times you ever drank. You were just unlucky to get caught every single time you ever did it. That's how I knew it wasn't a problem. You had to be so afraid of getting caught, you'd never drink again."

Rooster laughed at her tortured logic. "Mom, I was out drinking every weekend because I had... I have a problem."

"You don't have a problem."

Rooster approached the front doors of the church. "Whatever you say, Mom. I just wanted you to know, but I gotta go now. I'm walking into a meeting."

"What kind of meeting could you have on a Wednesday night?"

"I'm seeing a guy about learning how to train the dancing bears at the circus."

"Stop it. Really. Tell me."

Rooster spoke, a smile in his voice. "No. I got to hang up now. My phone has to be off. Something about the radio frequency drives the bears into a rage. I don't wanna get their trainer mauled. Bye." Before she could respond, Rooster disconnected, turned off the ringer, and deposited the device in his pocket. With a huge grin, he opened the big doors and stepped into the lobby. He was filled with anticipation, and maybe a little fear, about what embarrassing personal revelations might spill out of his mouth this week.

SIXTY-TWO

As Rooster approached Marcie's group, he saw all the seats but one filled by Marcie, Sallie Mae Johnston, George Jones, Dave, and a man and woman whom he had not met. When Sallie Mae noticed him, a huge smile lit up her face. She leapt from her chair, and hurried to meet him.

"Hi Sallie Mae." Rooster smiled as she threw her arms around his neck and hugged him tightly. When she refused to let go, Rooster worried every eye in the room was fixed on them. While pleased by her happiness to see him, Rooster was always uneasy as the center of attention. His good mood drained away. *How long's she gonna cling to me?* Queasiness crept into his gut. *This even appropriate in church?* Just as he was ready to push her away, Sallie Mae released her grip and stepped back. She examined his face with searching eyes. "I been so worried about you. You told me at church you been kidnapped, and then I saw you get attacked on Channel 3."

Rooster tried to ignore the growing tension at the base of his neck and flashed an awkward smile. The group had left their chairs to gather around him, which only ratcheted up his anxiety level. "Yeah." He sheepishly stared down. "I had an eventful couple days."

George asked, "You get hurt?"

Dave added, "Who was that dad-blang lunatic in the monkey getup?"

Horrified at the prospect of everyone staring at him, Rooster sat in a chair before the whole sanctuary could discover he was a fraud who did not belong there. "Why don't we all sit? Then I'll tell you everything you want to know."

The rest of the group took their seats. Marcie indicated the two new people. "Rooster, This is Rhonda and Dorris Burlingame. They weren't here last week, but I think you met them during the party at my house." She was a handsome older woman in her late fifties or early sixties with stylish gray hair, an aristocratic nose, and an expensive trendy dress. The man was about the same age with thick curly salt and pepper hair and a serious moustache that would have made Magnum P.I. proud.

Rooster stared at them, confused. I hear that right? Rhonda and Doris? He jumped to his feet, stabbed his hand at the man and asked nervously, "Rhonda?"

The woman laughed. "No, I'm Rhonda. My husband is Dorris."

The man grinned and took Rooster's hand amid chuckles from the group. "Dorris is a family name," he said as if that explained everything.

"Uhh. Ok." Rooster nodded knowingly, as if the response had cleared up any lingering confusion. *Family name? What's that mean? What kinda family gives girl's names to the boys?* After the handshake he retreated to his chair and sat quietly. They all stared at him expectantly. He earnestly studied the carpet. *Could this be any more awkward?*

"Rooster," Rhonda said pleasantly. "I know you met a lot of people there, but Marcie's right, we did meet at her house."

Rooster looked up and examined the deep smile lines at the corners of Rhonda's eyes. Something about how she said that and the way she eyed him rubbed him wrong. *She implying I should remember her? She know I had a few drinks to ease my nerves? What the hell's her problem with me?* He could barely hide his irritation. "Yeah, don't really remember any of that. I was drunk." *Why am I saying this?* Yet it now flowed out of him and he was powerless to stop himself. "If I did talk to you, I probably embarrassed you and me."

Stop it! His face turned red. *Who turned up the heat in here?* "I'm really sorry about that," he added sarcastically.

Rhonda leaned back, bewildered at what to make of his outburst.

"Rooster," Marcie said with concern. "You ok?"

Rooster mopped his sweaty forehead with his hand and wiped it on his pant leg. His mouth watered as he imagined an ice-cold Budweiser in a frosted mug. "It comes and goes." He adjusted himself in his chair. "I'm sorry. I'm good now."

"What comes and goes?" Sallie Mae asked.

"Nothing," Rooster said brusquely. "I don't know. Don't worry about it."

"Rooster," Marcie said, her face and voice encouraging. "You're safe here. Tell us what's going on. Maybe we can help."

He stared at her and did not know what to think. It seemed like a trick. *They toying with me?* A few minutes earlier he had been in a good place. *How'd everything turn so quickly? This what my life'll be like without booze? My mood and emotions whipsawing from one extreme to another? Can alcohol withdrawal turn you into a raging schizophrenic?* "Fine." Rooster breathed deeply and tried to calm himself. "Sometimes I think I got it all under control, and then ten minutes later I think my head's about to explode."

"That's normal," Marcie said. "When you last have a drink?"

He considered her question. "Saturday night. Haven't had anything since I escaped from the Chairman."

"The Chairman?" George asked.

"Yeah. The crazy homeless guy who kidnapped me." He faced Sallie Mae. For the first time, he did not notice her over-sprayed giant Texas hair. Instead, even though she expertly masked it with a smile and upbeat attitude, he saw the pain in her eyes and the awkwardness in her mannerisms. He could tell how uncomfortable she was in her own skin. He remembered her confession to social clumsiness and feeling like an outsider. It all made sense. Just like him, she desperately wanted to love and be loved, but unlike Rooster, she continued to put herself out there. She made herself vulnerable, always at risk of further disappointment. At some point, Rooster had just given up on people. He allowed his past wounds to scab over until they became so calloused, he did not have to feel anything anymore.

Rooster realized he had treated Sallie Mae like a cartoon character. He had ignored her innate value as a human being and ultimately dismissed her as not worthy of his time or concern. She was not a cartoon character. In fact, she was an awful lot like him, except she refused to give into the cynicism and fatalism which had so infected his life. Rooster blinked as he saw Sallie Mae again for the first time. Her moist eyes filled with worry as she nervously bit her lower lip. For some crazy reason Rooster did not quite understand, she had decided to care about what happened to him. It hurt her when he left her in the dark about the kidnapping. The knowledge his cavalier attitude had caused her pain ate at his gut like acid. He thought he might cry. *Why am I so emotional?* He could barely control himself. Rooster held back tears and wringed his hands. "Sallie, I owe you an apology."

"What on earth for?"

"For Sunday." He averted his eyes in shame. "For telling you about the kidnapping and then letting you worry about it. For disappearing."

"Don't be ridiculous," she protested. You..."

Rooster waved her off. "I need to get all this out." His voice cracked. "I got something to say to George, too."

"Me?" George asked.

Rooster stared at George's face. It was gaunt and creased with worry lines. His eyes were bloodshot. He looked really tired. This was a man who hurt down to the core of his being, and it was so obvious. *Have I been blind? How'd I not notice this before? Have I really been so self-absorbed that I failed to recognize what was plainly visible to anyone who cared to look? Did the drinking keep me from seeing? Or is all this some sort of awakening?*

"Rooster?" George said softly. "What'd you want to say?"

"Don't think I'm supposed to know it was you." He stole a glance at Marcie. "But I know you're the one who left the money in my house for me."

George looked down, embarrassed. "Don't..."

"Wait. You're hurting about your brother, but you still had the compassion to help some dumb yahoo you barely knew. You deserve to know what happened to your money." Everyone fell quiet. Rooster's words hung in the air like a toxic cloud. Several people shifted uncomfortably.

George broke the silence. "Listen, Rooster. You don't owe me anything. I had my own selfish reasons for doing it, but I gave you that cash with no strings attached. There's something about you, man. You're just the kind of guy my kid brother woulda tried to help. He had a heart for people the rest of the world wanted to give up on. For people who were maybe thinking about giving up on themselves." George put his hands to his face as tears flowed down his cheeks and his voice grew thick. "I gave you the money as a way to honor my brother. A way to keep the best parts of him alive in the world."

Rooster felt his own eyes grow misty as remorse washed over him. "I'm so sorry George." The sight of George's breakdown stretched the limits of his ability to hold it together. "I defiled your brother's memory, because I used that money to get drunk. Please forgive me."

"It's ok," George whispered.

"It's not ok. I can't tell you the regret that's filling my heart right now. I wish I could go back and do it differently, but all I can do is beg you to forgive me."

"Of course, bro." George wiped his eyes with the back of his hand. "Don't you see? You haven't defiled anything. The fact you're here pouring your heart out proves you were worth helping. My brother woulda been downright giddy to see how all this has been playing out."

Rooster breathed deeply, unable to hold back his tears. "Appreciate that, George." He brushed his wet cheeks with his hand. *This emotional roller coaster's just too much. If I don't find an even keel soon, I'm gonna crack up.*

A small smile appeared on George's lips. "Hey Rooster, what'd you do to piss off that monkey yesterday?"

Every head snapped in Rooster's direction, but for once he did not feel uncomfortable at all. "He got mad 'cause I told him even though he was wearing pants he'd always be the lesser primate compared to homo sapiens," he said in a deadly serious tone. "Oh," he added with perfect comedic timing, as a big grin filled his face. "And then I threw poop at him."

The group fell silent. Everyone looked at each other and wondered how to react. Marcie snorted and immediately clapped her hand over her mouth, her eyes flaring with embarrassment. With the tension broken, the whole group devolved into snickers and chuckles. Tears rolled down Rooster's face, not because his dumb joke was funny, but because the laughter had provided a much-needed emotional release.

As the ruckus died down, Sallie Mae placed a friendly hand on Rooster's shoulder. "Seriously." Her smile faded. "What was the deal with that crazy guy in the monkey outfit?"

"That was the Chairman. He somehow got ahold of that mascot costume so he could lay in wait for a sneak attack. Dude's totally bonkers. Apparently they found the real Stormy locked in a broom closet in the courthouse."

"No way," Dave exclaimed. "What's with that guy?"

Rooster sighed. "He's whacked out for sure, but he's just the tip of the iceberg. You wouldn't believe what I been through in the last week." He smirked. "I sure picked the wrong week to give up drinking."

"But where'd this Chairman come from?" Sallie Mae asked.

"Don't even know the guy. Never seen him in my life before this past week. I did something to his friends because of my drinking.

That's why he was after me, but even if I told you the whole story, you'd never believe me."

Marcie smiled warmly. "Try us, Rooster."

Rooster stared at her. He had never thought to tell anyone about his sordid past. *They already know I'm irresponsible and a drunk. Haven't driven them away yet with what I've done or said. What've I got to lose?* "Ok, you asked for it." Rooster proceeded to share everything. The Chairman, the NEIU women's rugby team, and the money he stole. The Tonys and his gambling debts. The future ex-wife he picked up during his wild night in Vegas. And all the craziness he had experienced because of them all. He unloaded the whole treasure trove of insanity and dysfunction.

SIXTY-THREE

By the time the group wrapped up with a prayer and a few minutes of support and encouragement, Rooster was physically and emotionally drained. He sat quietly as the people filtered out of the sanctuary. He was about to drag himself to his feet and trudge home, when he heard a familiar voice behind him.

"Hello, Mr. Rooster."

He stood and faced Sandy Wilson, in yet another shapeless potato sack outfit. "Hi there, Ms. Wilson."

Her intelligent brown eyes sparkled and she smiled widely. "Looks like you made it. You completed your end of our little bargain and now I have something for you." Before Rooster respond, she handed him a white envelope.

"What's this?"

"That's the other half of your rent," she said as if surprised he did not know exactly what it was.

"Oh." Rooster stared at the item in his hands and immediately heard the voice of his old benevolence scamming advisor John Toes. *You did it!* John exclaimed. *The church paid your rent. Now you can use your own cash to party.*

Rooster stared at the floor, afraid if he made eye contact she would know he no longer needed the money. Without realizing it, Rooster had already begun to calculate how many cases of Bud he could buy with an extra four hundred fifty bucks.

"For what it's worth," Sandy offered. "I'm proud of you. You're a man of your word. I hope this won't be the last time we see you here."

"Uh, yeah," he mumbled, still distracted.

Sandy smiled warmly. "You have a nice night, Mr. Rooster."

"You too," he called as she walked away. He stuffed the envelope into his pocket and suddenly felt the need to get out of there quickly. *Escape the scene of the crime before someone discovers your scam*, John Toes said in Rooster's brain.

Rooster pulled out the envelope, tore it open, and stared at the check inside. He wrestled with his conscience. *I got the chance to be a better man. To be more like George and the other people in the group. Hell, even if I'm never as good as them, I can stop being a scumbag and return the check since I don't actually need it. That is a lot of money.* He slid the check back into the envelope. *The deal was I come to church and small group two times each, and then I get the cash. No one said anything about returning the check if I found the rent money somewhere else. I fulfilled my end of the bargain. I earned this money. There's absolutely no reason to give it back or feel guilty about keeping it.*

Rooster was still clutching the envelope when he hit the lobby. A few steps from the front door and freedom, he noticed Sandy and Marcie in conversation. Pangs of guilt churned his stomach. *What am I supposed to do?* He turned the envelope over in his hands. His mind vacillated between his own selfish desires and the right thing to do. With a deep sigh, he headed for the two women. He wondered if their discussion had been about him. "Sorry to interrupt."

Sandy seemed surprised. "Mr. Rooster, I thought you left."

"No. Still here." He thrust the now-rumpled envelope at her. "Won't be needing this." His nerves jangled and slightly queasy, Rooster nodded toward Marcie. "She helped me find a job, and I already been able to catch up my back rent."

"That's wonderful," Sandy gushed. Marcie smiled knowingly.

"Thanks," Rooster said. "Guess you can give it to someone who really needs it."

"We'll do that," Sandy said. "Thank you."

Rooster resisted the urge to snatch the check from her and stuffed his hands into his pockets. "Well, better get going." He turned to leave.

"Hey Rooster," Marcie said. "I'm so glad you were comfortable enough to share everything with us. That was huge."

Rooster seemed doubtful. "I really hope so." He did not look back as he reached for the door.

"Wait," Marcie called out.

Rooster paused in the doorway, and slowly turned.

"You been through a lot. You sure you're ok?"

Rooster considered Marcie's question before he truthfully answered, "Honestly don't know."

Concern filled Marcie's eyes. "You need me, I'm here. Just call. Anytime. Day or night."

He smiled sadly. "Appreciate that."

On the way home, Rooster reflected on the evening's events. What surprised him the most, was not how the group heard his story with compassion and sympathy. He already understood these were good people who wanted the best for everyone. The thing that absolutely floored him was how good, how cathartic, it felt to admit everything out loud. The more ridiculous and outlandish his tale became, the more clearly he realized how insane it would be to ever drink again. Still, Rooster genuinely feared he did not possess the strength and self-control necessary to stay off the sauce, and that scared him to death.

SIXTY-FOUR
Six Months Later

He was confused and in the dark. *What happened? Where am I?* Still groggy, he slowly regained his senses. He could not move his arms. *Why's it so pitch black? Not a hint of light anywhere.* He sucked in warm stale air. Heavy material pressed tight against his face. He struggled to understand what was happening. None of it added up.

Suddenly, coarse fabric slid and scratched against his head, followed by a blast of cool refreshing air and blinding lights. He squinted and twisted away from the brightness. *This can't be good.* He mentally cataloged the people from his past who would like to see him suffer. He thought about his vulnerable position and shuddered. He forced open his eyes and took in his surroundings. His head throbbed as if he had been cracked in the noggin. As his eyes grew used to the light, he saw he was tied to a cheap metal desk chair in a small room devoid of any other furniture. He observed two banks of bright fluorescent lamps embedded in the ceiling, but what horrified him was the plastic sheeting spread between his chair and the linoleum floor. *Isn't that what the movie bad guys do before torturing someone? To keep blood from going everywhere?* His heart fluttered. *How'd they get me here?* For the life of him, he could not remember anything.

"You little salad-eating goat licker," the familiar voice boomed behind his head. "What you have to say for yourself now?"

Uh oh. Don't like where this is going. Wasn't he arrested six months ago? Big Tony Ferrentino waddled into view, resplendent in his bright green track suit with orange stripes. *How does this man continue to get fatter every time I see him? Doesn't his weight have to level off at some point?*

Tony smiled. "You think I'd just disappear? That you could ignore me and I'd go away?"

He checked the rope wrapped around his torso and tested the bindings. His arms were held fast behind the chair. Everything was tight. He would not go anywhere anytime soon.

Tony's mouth was close enough to smell the garlic and onions from his last meal. "Not much of a wise guy now, huh?"

"Hey Tony." He was surprised at the unsteadiness of his voice. "I been doing pretty good since I last saw you. If you give me some time, I can pay back everything. How about we set up a payment plan?"

"A payment plan?" Tony roared as spittle flew from his lips. "You think I'm Bank of America or something? That I'm gonna issue you a credit card?"

"Listen, Tony. Think about this. I'm no good to you unless I'm able to earn the money I owe you."

"Don't you worry," Tony said with an evil grin. "You and me are all square now."

"What?" His hopes rose. "How? What's the catch?"

"I did some research, you dirty dog sewer rat. Turns out there's a whole bunch of people who don't like you very much. In fact, they're so unhappy with you, my little friend, that they lined up to pay good money for the opportunity to have a few minutes alone with you."

His blood pressure spiked. *Where's Tony going with this? Who could he possibly have found?* "What's that supposed to mean?" He dreaded Tony's answer.

Tony laughed. "It means you're about to get extremely uncomfortable. And I collected the hundred large you owe me, plus interest. Enjoy."

Tony waddled off behind him. He heard a squeaky door open

and slam shut. Then he was alone with his thoughts. *Gotta get the hell outta here.* Panic overwhelmed him. He strained at the ropes, but nothing budged. He craned his neck and searched for ideas to help him escape, but the room was completely empty. His mind filled with the many people he had wronged, each new one more terrible than the last. *This could get really bad.*

He violently shook his body and the chair, desperate to loosen something. He tried to lean forward and stand up. Even with his body still lashed to the chair, if he was on his feet he could at least try to ease the ropes by banging the chair against the wall. He moved his head and shoulders back and forth, hoping to rock with enough momentum to tip up onto his feet. He only managed to knock the chair over and spill himself sideways onto the floor, still firmly attached to the surprisingly sturdy piece of furniture. The plastic sheeting stuck to his cheek. All he could hear were his own ragged breaths. He pushed with his feet and managed to turn himself to face the substantial metal door. *What's taking so long? When's Tony unleashing this horde of people who want a piece of me?*

He lay there quietly for what seemed like an eternity, steeled for whatever unknown horrors the big bookie had planned for him. Just when he began to think maybe it was all a big bluff, the door burst open and people flooded into the small room. He blinked in amazement and refused to believe his eyes. *How'd Tony possibly pull together this group?*

His crazy wife and the Chairman led the charge. He was not at all surprised they would sign up for this. In the crowd behind them were the three NEIU rugby captains. *Guess they're entitled. I did steal a lot of money from them.* Next was a man from a bar fight in Kansas City. *Bought that guy a drink when it was over. Coulda sworn we'd smoothed things out.* Behind him was the woman who sold him the auto insurance for his Maserati. *She still upset I got her fired for refusing to sleep with me? That's twenty years ago, for crying out loud.* On her heels were seven or eight vaguely-familiar women decked out in skimpy club wear. He simply could not place them. Another one of the alcohol-soaked black holes dotting the landscape of his memory. Then came John Toes. That one cut to the bone. *What could John Toes possibly have against me?* Pointing and shouting, they flowed toward him like a single organism. "Oh my God," he whispered. *What am I gonna do?*

Sue brandished her gun and a stack of crumpled papers. He glanced at the door. They continued to pour in. *Diamond Dan Martin? What'd I ever do to him?* Confusion and terror overtook him. *Who else is out there waiting for a piece of me?* Then they were on top of him. When Sue aimed her gun at his chest, the Chairman and several others scrambled for cover.

Sue's shrieking voice cut through the cacophony. "Now you get yours!" Then she pulled the trigger.

All sound disappeared and everything began to move in slow motion. The tip of the gun's barrel seemed to explode with a billow of fire and smoke. He actually saw the bullet fly out of the red and black cloud, headed straight for him. Helpless to stop anything, he watched the slug from the point of the pistol until it slammed heavily into his chest. He closed his eyes and waited for blood, and pain, and death. *This is it.* He tensed his body. Then he was screaming.

A loud voice boomed from above, "Calm down, son!"

Slowly, cautiously, he opened his eyes. It was so bright he could not see. "Am I dead?"

"What you mumbling about, boy?" The Foghorn Leghorn voice replied.

"Huh?" He shielded his eyes until he could see Buddy next to his lounge chair. "Can't see."

"Then put your sunglasses on, you numskull. I declare, you're about as useful as a doorknob on a Texas steer."

Rooster fumbled for the glasses. "What happened?"

"I'm hoping you can tell me. You were moaning and saying, 'No, no,' and acting all squirrelly in your sleep. So I gave you a little slap on the chest and next thing I know you're screaming like a chainsaw juggler with vertigo. What in blue blazes you dreaming about?"

Rooster slid his sunglasses into place. His heart rate and

breathing slowed as he regained his equilibrium. "It was crazy. Everyone from my past was out to get me."

Buddy dropped into his lounge chair. "Just relax, Son. You can deal with all that when we get back to civilization. Right now you need to kick back and enjoy all this."

Rooster settled into his chaise, stared at the emerald green ocean, and breathed the warm salty air. The gentle rustle of palm fronds and seagull caws in the distance relaxed him.

Buddy asked, "It just me, or is that sun as scorching as a cast iron skillet in a bonfire?" A thin layer of sweat glistened on his hairy chest.

Rooster smiled. "It's so hot, you can pull a baked potato right outta the ground."

"Not bad, Son." Buddy slapped Rooster's shoulder. "Except that in order to use that one, you need to be somewhere's you might find taters in the ground. You know, like a farm."

Rooster laughed. "C'mon, I'm new at using clever homespun southernisms. Cut me some slack."

Buddy shook his head and frowned in mock disgust. "You just leave 'em to the professionals, or you'll embarrass yourself."

"Hey," Rooster said. "I'm totally parched. How about grabbing me a cold one from that cooler next to you?"

"You want regular or light?"

Rooster patted his stomach. "Need to watch my figure." He closed his eyes and soaked in the sun and tropical aromas, holding his hand until Buddy gave him the cold, wet can. Eyes still shut, he popped the top and anticipated guzzling it down. He placed the can to his lips and tipped it back. The crisp, carbonated liquid was ice cold, just how he liked it. As the refreshing flavor of Diet Coke filled his mouth, he reflected on how far he had come the past few months. And how far he still had to go.

Buddy's deep, folksy drawl cut through his thoughts. "Ain't this the life?"

Rooster smiled to himself. It had been a throwaway remark,

something you say just because you are enjoying yourself. Buddy had not intended to be deep or philosophical. In fact, he could not have been more surface and superficial. However, Rooster was in a metaphysical state of mind. Right now at least, the truth about who he was and the challenges ahead of him did not scare him one bit. For the first time since childhood, life seemed worth living. He had hopes for the future, a desire to try and be his best possible self. "Yeah, Buddy," he said. "More than you'll ever know."

THE END

EPILOGUE

Sandy Wilson continues her work at Cumberland Baptist Church. She has used benevolence money as a carrot to introduce many people to the church and its small groups. After her knitting group pitched in to buy her a full makeover, Sandy replaced all her shapeless potato-sack clothes with a stylish new wardrobe. She was recently named to the Top 10 Most Beautiful People list in *Murfreesboro Magazine*.

Cassandra Nolan gained national attention with an Emmy award in the 'Breaking News' category when NBC News picked up her coverage of the Stormy the Weather Monkey attack. After being featured on the *Tonight Show*, the video went viral and her fortunes took off when it was spoofed on *Saturday Night Live*. Currently fielding offers from the major cable and broadcast networks, she is leaning toward starring in her own reality show on the A&E network.

After several failed attempts to rehabilitate the image of **Stormy the Weather Monkey**, Channel 3 quietly retired the formerly beloved character. The station managed to recoup a small portion of the $20,000 cost of the custom-made costume, when they sold it to Kansas-based Pittsburg State University, whose mascot is the Gorillas. In the aftermath of the Stormy debacle, Channel 3 was hit with a class action lawsuit, filed by notorious Nashville ambulance chaser Dirk Barnham on behalf of several hundred children who witnessed the event. The suit claimed, by not keeping tighter control over the Weather Monkey outfit, the TV station unnecessarily subjected the metro area's unwitting children to extreme emotional anguish.

After returning to Chicago, the NEIU Women's Rugby team co-captains implemented their house party fundraising scheme. A runaway success, it allowed the team to not only replace the missing $20,000, but to also buy new uniforms and upgrade its locker room and training facilities. The whole operation came crashing down when the police, after an anonymous tip, busted the group for a laundry list of offenses, including selling alcohol without a permit and allowing underage drinking. **Crystal, Madison, and Tiffany** were expelled from NEIU and the women's rugby program was shut down. **The Bouncer**, who never did return to Murfreesboro, married Crystal and the pair joined Tiffany to start a successful party-planning business. Convinced she and her friends had been treated unjustly by the police and the university, Madison vowed to make a difference by entering the political arena. She is currently the Republican nominee for Alderman in Chicago's Thirty-ninth Ward. Local political commentators have called the contest one of the most expensive, and dirtiest in the history of the city, driven by the two candidates' intense personal dislike for each other.

Jimmy Robinson was horrified when he learned on the internet the Columbian coffee cartel had secretly spiked the coffee supply with genetically-altered beans which increased caffeine tolerance and created an insatiable craving for bananas. He completely swore off the so-called "Frankenbeans" for more than two months. Eventually, Jimmy returned to his three-pot per day habit when his cardiologist warned that the twelve cans of Red Bull he drank each day to replace his coffee fix would eventually cause his heart to explode.

Marcie Dexter continues to lead her small group every Wednesday night at the Cumberland Baptist Church. There is still nothing plugged into any electrical outlet at her house.

As an officer of the court, **Tyler Brock** was compelled to notify the parole board **Sue Schwartz** violated her parole when she possessed and transported an unregistered handgun across state lines. The court quickly rejected Tyler's "Crazy Pants" defense and through a seldom-used legal loophole, the judge actually ordered more jail time than the crime's sentencing guidelines allowed. Serving six to eight years in the Lumley Unit, Sue is crafting a new speech she plans to deliver to Rooster upon her release. Tyler is working on Sue's appeal.

Sallie Mae Johnston's confidence has been growing as she continues to work on her interpersonal skills. Her peers in the Toastmasters of Rutherford County recently voted her the club's best impromptu speaker of the year.

Rooster's mother quit her sewing club in disgust when Gertrude Longfellow bought the last bolt of Wonder Under at McNabb Fabrics and refused to give her a yard of it to finish the gingham appliqué on the denim western shirt she was making for her son's birthday. Despite the fact her Sonny now lived near Nashville and desperately needed appropriate cowboy clothing, the sewing club backed Gertrude and suggested Rooster's mom only wanted the fusible material to make her son a costume for his next outrageous internet exploit.

George Jones decided the best way to honor his brother was to set up a foundation to help people society deemed lost causes. The organization got up and running thanks to a $15,000 donation from Marcie Dexter and $5,000 cash from an anonymous donor, dropped in George's mailbox along with a note that said, "When I grow up, I hope to be more like you and your brother."

Little Tony Ferrentino shot off his father's right pinky toe, but finally gained the old man's respect when he took full responsibility with the police. Convicted of reckless endangerment and illegal discharge of a firearm, he was sentenced to three years at Roan Mountain state prison. Originally given just eighteen months, the judge doubled the sentence for "showing up in my courtroom dressed like a dad blang clown."

Big Tony Ferrentino escaped any punishment in the dry cleaners shooting, but was laid up for almost a year due to complications from his toe injury. Unable to walk or care for himself, he lost more than a hundred pounds when his wife **Stella** left him stranded and helpless on the sofa, while she took a month-long Caribbean cruise to escape his constant complaining.

To avoid jail time, **the Chairman**'s parents had him committed for eight months to the Gary Busey Method Acting Clinic and Sanitarium in Santa Claus, Indiana. Currently the Democratic nominee for Alderman in Chicago's Thirty-ninth Ward, he has been dogged by negative publicity after several embarrassing videos surfaced on YouTube. His campaign has vehemently denied claims the Chairman is the person seen in grainy black and white security camera footage of a wild-eyed man sprinting from a Murfreesboro, TN, minimart wearing nothing but tighty-whitey underwear and expensive-looking loafers. Despite spending several hundred thousand dollars on his campaign, the Chairman still trails his Republican opponent by ten points in the heavily left-leaning district.

Rooster Michaels lost his potentially lucrative gig with Murfreesboro Motors when, during a brief relapse, he showed up drunk for his third commercial shoot. Buddy locked Rooster in his spare room for sobering up, followed by several days of intense discussions about Rooster's future. Rooster has not had a drink since he emerged from that room, two years and ninety-nine days ago. He now has a standing appointment every Sunday morning next to Dottie Charles in the seventh row at the Cumberland Baptist Church.

Several months ago as he held court with friends, **Buddy Junior Hollandsworth III**, answered a call from an unknown number. After a fifteen minute hushed conversation, he told his companions, "I got the call," and immediately left the gathering without explanation. He was last seen leaving his house dressed in full desert camo, carrying a large duffle bag and several rifle cases. His truck has been parked at the Arnold Air Force base near Tullahoma, TN, for the past four months.

Made in the USA
Lexington, KY
30 October 2017